LOVE'S CAPTIVE

Myra Nour

Futuristic Romance

New Concepts   Georgia

Be sure to check out our website for the very best in fiction at fantastic prices!

When you visit our webpage, you can:

* Read excerpts of currently available books
* View cover art of upcoming books and current releases
* Find out more about the talented artists who capture the magic of the writer's imagination on the covers
* Order books from our backlist
* Find out the latest NCP and author news--including any upcoming book signings by your favorite NCP author
* Read author bios and reviews of our books
* Get NCP submission guidelines
* And so much more!

We offer a 20% discount on all new Trade Paperback releases ordered from our website!

We also have contests and sales regularly, so be sure to visit our webpage to find the best deals in ebooks and paperbacks! To find out about our new releases as soon as they are available, please be sure to sign up for our newsletter
(http://www.newconceptspublishing.com/newsletter.htm) or join our reader group
(http://groups.yahoo.com/group/new_concepts_pub/join) !

The newsletter is available by double opt in only and our customer information is *never* shared!

Visit our webpage at:
www.newconceptspublishing.com

New Concepts Publishing
5202 Humphreys Rd.
Lake Park, GA 31636

ISBN 1-58608-689-8
© copyright Myra Nour
Cover art by Eliza Black, © copyright

NCP books are available at special quantity discounts for bulk purchases for sales promotions, premiums, fund raising, or educational use. For details, write, email, or phone New Concepts Publishing, 5202Humphreys Rd., Lake Park, GA 31636, ncp@newconceptspublishing.com, Ph. 229-257-0367, Fax 229-219-1097.

First NCP Trade Paperback Printing: 2005

Printed in the United States of America

ACKNOWLEDGEMENTS

I'd like to thank Mary Ann, who edited my book and became a good friend; Tracy for her astute read/critique, and Jamie, who fell in love with the characters so much, she almost thought they were real. To my daughter, Christina, thanks for your encouragement.

Most of all, a huge hug and kisses to my husband, Simon, who read, edited and critiqued the book, and provided loving support throughout the writing process. Thanks for being my handsome prince and giving me boundless inspiration for the hero.

Other Titles from NCP by Myra Nour:

Demon Killer (Shifters Anthology, now in Trade Paperback)
A Vampire's Kiss
Heart of the Dragon (now in Trade Paperback)

Prologue

"Get out of the way." Olga jabbed her elbow into Serena's ribs as she muscled her way out the heavy door.

Serena spun around once outside. "Do you want to go at it again?" she hissed.

"Ja, ja, another day," the large woman sneered as she walked briskly away. "No time right now. I have a hot date." She paused and flippantly threw her barb, "I just beat you ... you forget already?"

Serena stood fuming, frustrated for losing to her arch rival Olga, too tired to really pursue her anger further. Besides, the 'Viking Princess' was almost to her car, the fog swallowing the sound of her heavy footsteps, just as it enveloped her figure.

She sighed, shifted her feet impatiently. Roger. He was late again. Borrowed her car for his own business and didn't even have the courtesy to bother getting here on time. She was exhausted after her match, wanted to soak in a hot tub, steam away her anger and painful bruises.

Why do I bother with him? Because, she laughed inwardly at herself, he is one of the few tall-enough men who wanted to date her. Not every man found a six foot two female wrestler appealing either, even if many had told her that she was gorgeous.

Serena stared at the black night, its dense atmosphere sending a chill down her back. The clouds overhead obscured her vision even further. She frowned at the only light pole nearby, the one with a shattered bulb. She'd told the maintenance people several times about it ... like they care, she thought. So, she stood in an inky pool of darkness next to the Coliseum's employee exit, her gloomy mood reflecting the thick night air.

Suddenly, a flash of bright light cut through the darkness. Gazing intently in the direction of Olga's car, but seeing nothing out of the ordinary, Serena again took up her contemplation of thoughtless Roger.

Thudding footsteps drew her attention to the mist, now crawling toward the steps where she stood. Must be Roger--no--there were two sets of footsteps. Serena quit slouching against the step rail, became alert and wary. After all, she was alone in the dark.

She squinted, just making out two solid figures amongst the

tendrils of slowly drifting cloud vapor. Two men. Funny looking though. Both couldn't have been over four feet tall, their girth as round as their height. They wore raincoats and felt hats, as if trying to hide their features from observant eyes.

The pair approached a few slow steps closer and Serena tensed. They were up to something. She didn't like this one little bit.

"Who are you looking for," she said loudly, making her voice deep, commanding.

"For you," a polite, foreign-sounding voice replied.

A sickly yellowish light shot from the dark and enveloped her body. Serena fell slowly to her knees as an icy blackness filled her mind.

Chapter One

She woke with a headache throbbing in her temples. A cheerful female voice encouraged Serena to open her eyes. She almost wished she hadn't when she cracked them to peer warily around. The gamin face which swam into focus was as full of good spirits as the voice had been. Both were equally annoying. Serena took her eyes from the petite woman talking to her and gave her surroundings a thorough once-over.

Bright pink walls and diffused lighting gave the room a soft, feminine appeal. She hated it. She sat up. A long, thin bed was beneath her. The only other furniture was an identical bed across the small square room, and the woman who was enthusiastically trying to hold her attention sat on the other bed.

"Hi, I see you've finally rejoined the living. My name is Nicole."

Serena's eyes refused to focus properly. Feeling very unsure of her surroundings, she fixed the woman with a hostile, mute expression.

"Oh, I see, still got that godawful headache from that weird gun. And you're probably wondering where you are and how you got here and who I am and where is this room?" The verbose woman spread her arms to encompass their environment.

She held up one hand, hoping to slow the flow of words.

"I'm sorry, I always ramble on when I meet new people or when I'm in an unfamiliar situation," she apologized.

Suspicious, she asked. "Where are we and what's going on here?"

The woman shrugged. "I don't know anymore than you do. I woke up probably an hour before you did."

"Do you have any idea where we are, or who kidnapped us?"

Nicole shook her head, a confused look on her face. "I guess it must have been those two fat men who shot me."

"Sure," she agreed as she examined the other woman. She seemed awfully composed for someone in their situation. Suddenly, her fear of a seemingly uncontrollable predicament turned to anger. "What do you take me for, an idiot? All right, sister, who are you and who else is involved in this kidnapping?" Serena demanded as she grabbed the small woman's dress by the front. "Well?" Her voice rose in volume with her frustration, and she shook the smaller woman to elicit an answer.

The frightened look on the other woman's face sapped all of her anger as quickly as it had overcome her. She let go of Nicole and strode the few steps it took to reach the door. The woman watched her with a sad, knowing expression.

She couldn't find anything that resembled a doorknob and tried to pry her fingers between the crack of the doorjamb, to no avail. She pounded on the barrier for a few seconds and yelled out her frustration, then finally kicked the door. Serena walked slowly back to the bed, plopped down, put her head between her hands, and rubbed her hands agitatedly through her hair.

"It's OK," Nicole said soothingly. "I was really upset when I realized there was no way out. I've tried that door lots of times. No dice. I just hate being cooped up," she continued when she received no answer.

Serena looked thoughtfully at her, the short space between them leaving little room for misjudgment. Kindness was reflected in those deep brown eyes and something else, something she'd missed through her emotional outbursts. Nicole's lip trembled slightly and her eyes had a telltale shimmer of unshed tears. The much smaller woman sitting across from her was very frightened, but she had tried to be kind. She wondered briefly if the woman's chatter was a sort of defense against her fear or an attempt to distract her during her first shocked awareness.

They jumped as screeching static resounded abruptly through the small room.

"What the devil was that?" Serena exclaimed as she looked around cautiously.

"It sounded like a very poor quality intercom system."

The scratching message cleared, so the words were clearly understood. A female voice told them to go to the doors, which would now open for them and, once in the hall, follow a red light. The woman/machine warned them not to go anywhere but where the light directed, otherwise they would be punished.

It continued, "Look upon the bracelet on your left wrist. If you do anything other than what you are instructed, this ornament will send out an electric shock. It's only a mild shock, not enough to truly hurt you, but enough to convince you to follow directions."

Unexpectedly, the door slid back into the wall with noiseless ease. Serena went through first and glanced up and down a long, metallic gray hall. Nicole's head bumped her arm. She moved aside. They saw doors all along the corridor opening silently and tall, attractive young women peering or walking cautiously from the rooms. When a red beam appeared over their heads and started slowly down the hall, she became irritated when not one woman made a move.

She motioned to Nicole and strode briskly after the light. The others followed more slowly. Serena hated the unknown more than she feared a scary, known fact. So she continued to lead the little expedition, which soon turned into a tide of nubile young females as they passed more doors and frightened women waiting at the entrances.

Her patience was at an end when a door up ahead opened and a hostile Olga jumped defensively into the corridor. Before Olga could open her mouth and start a confrontation, Serena stated, "I'm not the enemy, at least not this time."

"Who are all these women and why are they all following you?" Olga stared suspiciously at her. "You all look like a bunch of old cows at feeding time," she sneered to the grouped girls behind the red-head.

"I don't have the patience to argue with you. We're all in the dark here as much as you."

"I'm going to find a way to escape. Anyone else coming?" Olga strode off angrily when she received no recruits.

Serena realized that she couldn't meekly accept her fate either. She glanced down at her companion. She didn't really know her new friend well. Would she come along?

Nicole seemed surprised when Serena raised her hand and yelled down the hall after Olga, "Wait up, I'm coming with you."

The Viking Princess paused and waited for her to catch up. "Better someone with guts than one of those limp wrists," she indicated the cowering women.

"You can't blame them for being scared," Serena commented as they started down the seemingly endless gray corridor. They came across a door set within the wide expanse of wall. It opened automatically when they approached and they had just managed to peer inside, before they heard a voice boom near their heads. It was male this time.

"You were warned."

Serena gripped her bracelet as the promised electric shock zapped her nerve endings. She fell to her knees, nausea crawling for purchase in her belly, as the pain continued to lance through her system. It seemed to last for hours, but she knew it couldn't have been more than a few seconds. Breathing heavily, she looked at Olga, who was on her knees as well, sweat beading on her forehead.

"Do I look as bad as you?"

"Worse." Olga's lips were stiff, squeezing that one word out with difficulty. They both got slowly to their feet as if by mutual agreement.

"Did we see what we thought we saw?" She asked in disbelief as they walked back the way they'd come.

Serena nodded. "I think we can forget about our plans for escape." They stayed silent the rest of the short journey, each remembering the room they had abruptly entered. It was filled with odd flashing machinery and a mechanical humanoid, which turned at their entrance. It had been working knobs over a console and regarded them with flat red eyes for a few seconds before it turned back to its work, paying them as much attention as it would flies on a wall, Serena thought.

The young women grouped in the corridor immediately started in with anxious questions when the two tall women returned. For once, Nicole saw the discretion of silence as she saw their strained features.

One pretty girl questioned nervously. "What's going to happen to us?"

Serena shrugged and turned away from the panicky expression on the girl's face. She realized that soon enough they would know more than they wished about their future.

She had been convinced by both her painful lesson with the bracelet and her blunder into the robot-inhabited room, that there was no simple explanation for their situation. But nothing in her life had prepared her for what followed.

The red beam reappeared and they were guided into the lounge area, where the truth about their kidnapping was unveiled. Their kidnappers weren't men at all, but strange piggy-looking aliens, pink-skinned with large ears. They were called *Moyds*--Pulack the captain and Rolan' his assistant, to be specific. And they weren't even the true abductors, but simply flesh merchants for the planet *Volarn*.

The women were shown an "interstellar transmission" from the King of Volarn, information that was shocking and unbelievable, and took many hours to fully sink in. They were being taken to Volarn as mates--"baby factories" in Serena's eyes. *That's their problem. I want no part of it*! It didn't matter that the Volarnians fertility problem was so severe, they had little choice left.

The fact was they had been abducted by aliens and were traveling aboard a space ship. The journey took a month, one that seemed to drag on endlessly. Serena wondered how they'd all made it through, without somebody getting seriously hurt. She and Olga had many confrontations, but had not come to blows. Their mutual experience with the bracelets kept them at arm's length. The Moyd made it plain that any fighting would result in getting zapped again.

She didn't feel any real antagonism toward her former rival anymore, but she had plenty for their kidnappers. She received the same impression from Olga, but felt the tall blonde woman snapped every once in a while simply out of boredom.

The games in the lounge became boring, the video library exhausted. Their true captors, the Volarnians, had supplied numerous tools for learning their language. Serena was determined to learn the alien tongue, convinced that knowing as much as one could about your opponent could be useful.

She picked it up quickly with the aid of the marvelous language and speech instruments. Her every mistake and mis-pronouncement was exaggerated and dissected, making it easier to correct. She could even carry on a decent conversation in the alien tongue. But, even she got tired of studying the Volarnian language.

Then there'd been the exhausting task of keeping her friend out of trouble. If she wasn't teasing Olga, who easily rose to Nicole's verbal baiting, her intense interest in Dr. Melat, the ship's doctor, kept Serena's warning instinct on alert.

She worried about Nicole's crush on the blue-skinned alien doctor. The self-same doctor who had examined them all, making sure they were all healthy and fertile. Nicole seemed fascinated with his pointy-eared similarity to Spock, her favorite alien character, and the fact that his personality reminded her of a doctor she'd worked for and loved in the past. Their mutual interests in medical treatments and technological instruments from both cultures only fueled their relationship.

She'd just beaten Nicole at a game of checkers when the irritating, static-filled intercom popped to life. Their boredom was at an end. Tomorrow they would land on Volarn. Animation seeped throughout the large room, which had often served as their respite from the tedious monotony. Pulack appeared and announced procedures for the landing. He talked at length about how they were to conduct themselves once off the ship.

"Like we're a bunch of uncouth barbarians," Nicole huffed.

"Perhaps we are to them," Serena said thoughtfully.

* * * *

It couldn't have been more than two hours since she and the other women had been sequestered in the awe-inspiring bedrooms within the huge castle. Time for them to get refreshed from their long journey and dressed up for tonight's ceremonies. Her "hostess", the older woman assigned to oversee her care, was kind and under other circumstances Serena may have liked her.

Yet, it pleased her on some primitive level to shock the woman, Surad, by choosing a simple black dress from those offered. Perhaps black's not a favored color, she thought. The woman handed her a matched set of accessories, consisting of necklace, earrings, bracelet and belt. Surad exclaimed over the value of the *lais* metal encrusted with red jewels set in dragon settings.

Serena could have cared less, getting costumed in the Volarnian apparel mechanically. She admitted though, once examining herself in the full-length mirror, that she was pleased with the results. She looked and felt barbaric, a state which somehow made her feel more ready to meet her kidnappers with confidence.

It seemed but a short time later a knock on the door signaled the return of one of the male guards. His stern features didn't change a bit, but she could feel his curious sidelong glances as he urged her into the hall again.

Nicole almost skipped from across the hall when she spied Serena's entry into the corridor. She was taken with her friend's changed appearance. Much different than the plain garments they'd been made to wear on the ship, she wore a dress of hunter green with jewelry of gold and brown intertwined metal. Interspersed every few inches in the metal were large amber cut stones. Nicole looked pagan.

"What do you think?" She questioned anxiously as they moved down the hall in response to a guard's request, joining the gathering group of young women.

"You look beautiful, Nicole, like a fairy about to escape to the depths of the forest," Serena laughed. "But I think the previous owner was a tad bigger than you."

"Tell me about it," Nicole giggled as she looked down. Whereas the other girls' dresses hit their legs about mid-thigh, Nicole's costume flirted with the top of her knees. Her saving grace was the slits on either side which parted to show glimpses of her slim legs. "I guess I'm lucky these dresses are made in such a simple fashion. This one was easy to pin and tuck, otherwise it would have swallowed me up." Nicole plucked at the volume of material over her tiny waist.

"You look fabulous." Nicole examined her tall companion. She glanced to their rear and then to the front several times. "You know, I think you're the only one wearing black though," she noted.

"I know. I don't have to look around to see that. My hostess had a fit when I wanted to wear this," Serena indicated her dress.

"Hmm, who can tell about aliens?" She dismissed the subject with a nonchalant shrug.

She was surprised Nicole's natural curiosity didn't lead her to further questions, something she'd experienced in-depth during their month long exposure as roommates. But then she quickly realized the reason--the group of women had been halted by the guards in front of an immense open doorway.

She examined the *basami*, Volarn's version of a dragon, detailing the arched entrance. They were the same as the ones she wore on her jewelry but larger, fiercer looking creatures. They snarled in frozen vicious grimaces, as if guarding the portal.

Someone was speaking Volarnian inside, but with the crush of bodies surrounding her, Serena couldn't make out the words. Several guards urged the girls forward. Prodded was more like it, she thought, for they all seemed hesitant to step through the doorway. She felt dry-mouthed herself and her heart seemed to be racing entirely too fast. Nicole squeezed her hand and then kept a light contact by touching their wrists together as they started forward. She was sure this was Nicole's way of bringing courage to her tiny frame but it gave her a calming sense of comfort also.

They entered a room large enough to hold several hundred people, and that was probably the size of the crowd Serena saw awaiting them. A mixture of male and female Volarnians awaited them, but a large portion of the assemblage was made up of handsome men. The sights were too many to absorb all at once, but she tried, for it was like stepping back into the pageantry of the past. Her eyes widened in wonder.

All the males were huge and muscular, with their distinctive black locks brushing the tops of their massive shoulders, held back from broad foreheads by metal head bands. Their clothing ranged the full spectrum of colors, just as the dresses brought for the captives. Serena was glad to see that many of the males, as well as several female Volarnians, wore the same distinctive black material as she'd chosen to wear.

The men's costumes were similar to the simple lines of the women's dresses, but appeared to be two separate pieces. The tightly fitting shirt was tucked into the kilt skirt, with both sides split to show off their muscular thighs. The males' skirts hit their brawny legs at mid thigh also and appeared to be made of a rough-textured suede.

The lovely females were only slightly shorter versions of the males, with more delicately proportioned features. They were as feminine as the males were overwhelming in their masculinity. Most of the women's ebony hair was waist-length and intricately coifed for the occasion. The few women Serena noticed who wore black outfits like hers, had hair that only reached to their shoulders. Being dressed in similar fashion to the men gave them the appearance of being cut from the same mold. These women wore their hair as the men, straight, with a metal headband holding the heavy length back from their fine features.

As the guards organized the Earth women into a line stretching across the width of the room, she continued to observe her surroundings. All the women were heavily laden with jewelry. She noticed that some of the men wore necklaces, but all Volarnians, male and female, wore bracelets. Every one of the planet's inhabitants wore a bracelet on their right wrist and many also wore matching armbands, particularly the men.

The row of beautiful Earth women, in their elegant garb, was breathtaking. The only common note was the incongruous bracelet they still wore, a reminder of their passage here. Serena rubbed the ugly thing idly.

Her attention zoomed back abruptly to the throne room as her eyes found the alien who must be King Rhamus. Her breath was sucked in, and she realized she'd held it for several seconds when it came rushing out. He was the most handsome man, alien or human, she'd ever seen. The transmission aboard ship, when the king had welcomed the women and explained their upcoming role, certainly hadn't done him justice.

Her thoughts wandered further as she speculated that he probably had a gorgeous wife already. She squashed those thoughts as it sunk in just how traitorous they seemed to herself.

As some pompous older Volarnian male began to pace back and forth in front of the captives giving some kind of speech, Serena examined her feelings. She was disturbed at herself, but on closer examination, understood this alien King represented the ideal man to her. It was as though someone had gone deep into her psyche and drawn out her ideal of the perfect man and thrown him together here on Volarn. How ironic that an alien and not an Earth man drew such a reaction from her.

Serena knew that the physical aspect was only one part of the concept of the "ideal mate", but it wasn't just his looks. Something indefinable about this man drew her like a magnet. She was puzzled by her continued reaction to his presence and her breathlessness when gazing in his direction. If her romantically inclined mother had been here, she would have told Serena that maybe, for the first time in her life, she had found a man who was capable of causing a "toe-tingling" reaction in her.

* * * *

Rhamus was impressed by the Earth women as he slowly looked them over. He was disappointed there were no more tall ones than the handful he saw, but Pulack had warned him that the females were much smaller on Earth. And even though his instructions were for at least six *kriegers* tall females, he knew that getting a sufficient number of tall, healthy, attractive, fertile women wouldn't be an easy task. He couldn't help the feeling of excitement as he noticed the endless variety in the female's hair, eyes and even shadings in skin color.

Volarnian women were very beautiful, but natural selection in their ancestry had created a population of black-haired beauties with differing shades of their violet eyes only. Many Volarnians, including Hartoos, his royal advisor who was putting on quite a show right now for the assembled Volarnians, were opposed to changing the long established gene coding of their planet by mixing with the many varieties from Earth.

The King smiled wryly to himself. Hartoos and all other opposition had finally shut up when faced with the reality of their situation. Only the race with an extra eye had come close in coloring to their own, and even Hartoos wasn't willing to change their gene pool that much to sustain the black hair, pale beige skin and violet eyes of the Volarnian race.

A full-figured blonde caught his eye. She was short by Volarnian standards but tall for an Earth woman. Rhamus continued his review of the women, stopping to examine the taller females longer. It was important for his people's genes to continue, and imperative that the royal line be propagated since there were only he and his sister Kasha left.

Rhamus smiled at the thought of his beloved sister. She was a member of the smaller warrior group made up of only women. He saw no hope of children coming from her loins to help sustain the throne anytime soon. Kasha had found no mate to her liking, so continued her dedication to warriorhood.

The old tradition of choosing the ruler of Volarn by a contest of strength and leadership was no longer utilized, but a King or Queen was still expected to be a wise ruler and strong adversary. He needed to pick from the largest and strongest females to ensure these traits. Rhamus couldn't allow small, weak children to be born for the throne. He just hoped the *Tarthra* choosing would cooperate.

Rhamus had the responsibility of seeing that the royal blood established by his ancestors over two thousand years before continued. It was not just a matter of manly pride or even royal continuance. In his mind it meant the salvation of their world as they knew it.

Hartoos' sudden appearance in front of him shook Rhamus out of his thoughts. He smiled in response to his councilor's words. Hartoos brought fresh enthusiasm to his speech, encouraged by the King's attentiveness. Rhamus again took up his pleasurable duty of previewing the women. A tall girl with long, black hair and skin of a lovely golden brown shade caught his attention for a brief time before he continued. He glanced at several more of the taller females and became a little worried; they were all very attractive and, if not for the Tarthra, he would find himself in deep trouble.

Of course the "choosing" always worked, but it had never found a match for Rhamus in all his adult life. He hoped for the sake of the throne that he could find one. Then there was the concern put forth by Hartoos, that the "choosing" wouldn't work with an alien species. If it did work, but he still couldn't find a match with this group of females, he'd have to wait for the next shipment of captives. It frustrated him to think that his quest for a Tarthra match might still elude him. And, he wondered, what kind of female was right for him, if he had been unable to find a life-union among an entire race of Volarnian women?

Chapter Two

He gripped the arms of his chair and felt a physical reaction rising in his loins when his eyes lit upon one of the tallest women. A voluptuous figure with large breasts and a tiny waist, coupled with a face as exquisite as any aristocrat's gave him pause. Rhamus ran his eyes down the long, slender legs. He loved beautiful legs on women and was not disappointed by the curves of the female.

A muscularity could be seen beneath her skin which he found surprising in an Earth woman. Usually such sleekness, like the feline beauty of the *alati,* was seen only in their warrior women. Rhamus' eyes jerked quickly back to the female's body. She wore the *Getra's* ceremonial uniform.

The King thumped his right fingers several times on the throne's arm and tried to reason out why the Earth woman wore a warrior woman's garb. He glanced around the throne room as if for an answer, and his eyes lit upon Kasha. She seemed to wear a secret smirk.

Rhamus laughed aloud. His sister turned to look and seemed surprised by his humor. She apparently realized his source of amusement, for her lovely features twisted in aggravation that he would find her little trick so amusing.

He could understand her irritation. And he was pretty sure who had donated the black outfit. Kasha probably didn't think any Earth woman would choose the Getra costume when they had so many wonderful dresses to choose from. Then there was the Earth woman herself, who looked as if she had been born to the Getra. This must infuriate Kasha.

It took years of hard work and dedication to be a warrior, and even further sacrifice to become a Getra. To top it all off, the woman had put her hair up in a high pony-tail as the Getra did before going into battle.

In trying to understand Kasha's reaction, Rhamus found himself staring more intensely at the Earth woman. He couldn't seem to take his eyes off her. Glancing back to Kasha, he noted with curiosity his sister staring intently at the woman as well then quelling a giggle, a most un-Kasha reaction. She stared at the woman's hair as a secretive grin played across her features. He couldn't fathom her humor. The woman's hair looked fine to him at this distance, neatly fixed, the color a dark brown.

Rhamus wondered at the grin Kasha sported after the fuming looks earlier. He shook his head. His sister was ever one to change moods as fast as a *wootaz* changed its colors. Hartoos had finally finished his eloquent speech and it was time for Rhamus to start the Tarthra.

Rising, he turned toward the women. "Most respected guests," he began, and his words encompassed both the Volarnian audience and the group of nervous women, "long have we waited on Volarn for this day. You are our hope for the future, our promise of a life beyond the present generation."

He paused for a moment, his glance running quickly, seriously over each one of them. "Believe me when I say we owe everything to you. You will always have our respect, thanks, devotion, friendship and, we believe, love. As we begin the sacred Tarthra ceremony, you shall come to know about your love and new life on Volarn." He walked slowly down the steps of the dais and approached the women cautiously, as if he thought a fast approach would spook them like a flock of *elag*.

* * * *

Serena watched closely as the King descended his dais and approached the women nearest him. He barely glanced at some of the women, but paused several times at a few of the taller ones. Serena ate up his appearance with her eyes. He was a little above average height for a Volarnian male, slightly over seven feet tall, his muscles hard and defined.

The King stopped in front of Olga for what seemed an inordinately long time to Serena. Not her rival in the ring, she moaned inwardly. Anybody but Olga! Rhamus frowned and began again moving at a steady pace down the line of women. Serena was distressed to see him spend the longest period of time yet, observing the attractive girl with black hair and golden skin. She was very beautiful. Finally, he moved on and Serena felt breathless, for he was only a few women away from her. She had surmised that the King was choosing a partner for the banquet tonight and she wouldn't mind in the least dining with such a man.

* * * *

King Rhamus was very impressed with the variety of beauties as he walked slowly down the line, stopping at females he found especially attractive. The blonde with the wonderful green eyes held his attention for a minute, but a deeper look into those orbs told a different story. He didn't need the choosing to know this one was not for him. Her eyes were hard. She would make living in the same household a constant challenge and Rhamus wanted someone softer, more agreeable. He wanted a peaceful home, for he fought enough battles when away from it.

He was taken with the black-haired beauty and spent a few minutes getting his visual fill of her before moving on. He wanted to give every one of these fine women a chance, but he felt restless, forcing himself to observe each one in turn, as he approached the Earth woman in warrior black.

Rhamus sucked in his breath when he stopped in front of her. His eyes roamed the soft, creamy complexion and lush lips made for kissing. They paused in their upward journey and widened in shock at the strand of hair that curled next to a high cheekbone. He backed away without giving her further consideration and marched angrily down the line of women.

* * * *

Serena's heart felt like it was beating heavier in her chest when the virile, handsome King stopped in front of her. She noted that his thick blue-black hair was coarse like a lion's mane and framed a face, which could only be called extremely masculine. His lips were thicker than many Earth males, but not feminine looking. As with all Volarnians, his lips were wider than a human's. Set upon a squared jaw, his lower face was exciting. Serena's eyes started upward and shyness seemed to overcome her.

The next instant, she was shocked to see the King's startled expression and his abrupt departure. As he strode quickly away, Serena heard a very unlady-like snicker from one of the women wearing black who stood near the dais. Serena's only reasonable and somehow depressing conclusion was that he must have found her unattractive.

He stopped at a few more women then moved on quickly. She could swear he was angry. His body language certainly appeared to uphold this conclusion. But she wasn't sure, since Volarnians might have a different body language than humans. She started to feel uneasy. Had she done something to offend the King of Volarn?

"Pulack!" The King bellowed when he reached the end of the line. After the fat merchant came panting up to him, Rhamus angrily demanded, "What is that red-headed creature doing here?"

"Your Majesty?" Pulack answered in confusion.

"Don't act dumb with me, little man." He poked a finger into the Moyd's meaty chest. "You know I hate red hair."

"But your majesty, it's ... it's a different red than your enemies. And besides," he added bravely. "You didn't say not to bring back redheads from Earth."

The King folded his arms and stared angrily at the Moyd.

Pulack cleared his throat and humbly said, "Who can know the mind of royalty?" When the King continued with his stony silence, he asked, "Your Highness, did you take a good look at the girl? Believe me, she is without equal."

"Of course I looked at her, you idiot! How else would I have seen that despicable hair?"

"But, Your Majesty, did you see her wonderful figure? And her face would be the envy of any court beauty."

"Yes." The King mumbled in a perturbed manner.

Keenly, Pulack continued, "Did you look into her eyes, Your Highness?"

"Her eyes?"

"Yes, she has extraordinary ones," he said mysteriously.

"Is there anything else you didn't tell me?"

"No, Your Highness." His sweaty hands were thrust quickly behind his back.

Glancing back in the direction of Serena, the King asked, "Since we're discussing that female, why is she wearing the Getra ceremonial uniform?"

"I had nothing to do with that," the piggy alien responded in alarm.

"Mmm." Rhamus surveyed the room and noticed the grin on his sister's face again. "Kasha," he said in a low, firm voice, "would you join me over here please?"

The princess strolled over nonchalantly and inquired sweetly, "Are none of these Earth women pleasing to you, brother?"

"There is much that doesn't please me just now, but the Earth women are not included, except maybe one ... what do you know about the redheaded woman wearing the Getra uniform?"

"What would I know about it? I am only your sister. I'm not privy to the details of the royal court."

"That's only because you choose to have it that way."

"Now quit playing the innocent with me." Rhamus looked sternly at his sibling.

"Oh, all right," Kasha relented sheepishly. She stared off over the heads of the crowd. "I simply contributed a dress like everyone else was asked to."

She jumped in before her brother could reply. "But it was only a joke. I didn't think for a minute anyone would choose it." She admonished as she stared accusingly at the woman wearing her uniform.

"Well it looks like your little prank backfired this time." The King smiled and felt in a better humor.

"But she doesn't have any right to wear it," she said petulantly.

"Then you should not have placed it with the other dresses."

Pulack cleared his throat to gain their attention. "She and one other female may have more of a right than any of the other Earth women to wear the Getra uniform."

"What do you mean?" Rhamus asked curiously.

"The redhead is a warrior woman of sorts back on Earth." Pulack went on to explain about Serena and Olga being wrestlers.

"You mean they're entertainers," Kasha stated derisively.

"Since when have you started sneering at entertainers?" Rhamus turned a questioning brow to his sister.

"You know I respect entertainers." She pointed an arm at the redhead. "But few female entertainers have earned the right to wear a warrior's uniform, and the puny Earthlings even less so," she finished angrily.

"Your Majesty," Hartoos interrupted the trio. "Is there a problem? Everyone's waiting for your Tarthra choosing." The advisor dared to push the King a little further. "Your people insisted you be first in the choosing, and no one else can proceed until you do so."

Rhamus eyed his councilor for a few seconds and then clapped him on the shoulder. "You're right as usual, my friend." The King walked briskly down the line and seemed to pause near the redhead and then sped up and went past her to the beautiful black haired girl.

Serena couldn't hear what the small group of people was saying, but she noted nervously that the Volarnian woman pointed to her and knew she was the topic of their conversation. Apprehension and a strange joy hit her at the same time as the King started back in her direction. He paused just before reaching her and then kept going swiftly until he stopped again in front of the woman with black hair.

She watched in distress as he appeared to spend a long time contemplating the girl. Then he did something that she found very perturbing, he placed his right hand up to the girl's cheek. A very tender gesture it seemed, and it looked like he was going to kiss her, but suddenly he backed off as he had done to her. The King turned slowly and started back down the line again and didn't pause until he reached her.

* * * *

Rhamus was angrier than ever as he turned from the lovely dark-haired girl. He was definitely attracted to her and felt the Tarthra might work, and had been on the verge of using its power. He had even positioned his hand on her cheek and then changed his mind abruptly.

The pull was too strong. He decided to look over the red haired female thoroughly, so that he could prove to himself that the choosing wouldn't work with her, then he would be able to continue with the Tarthra. He was sure the feelings that distinctive hair drew from him would nullify any vibrations of the Tarthra.

What's wrong with me? I'm laughing at Kasha one minute and hate's sluicing through me the next? Rhamus glanced down the line of Earth women, his eyes stopping on the redhead as if drawn by a force outside himself. *Goreth*, that bright head of hair shone like a beacon.

A beacon of hate, drawing forth those buried feelings he'd striven so hard to submerge beneath duty and honor. Rhamus frowned. He'd disliked the enemy no more than the average south Volarnian--that is, until that fateful day his father was killed--by the prince of west Volam.

Rhamus had met Xarath only once, on that day which was forever burned into his memory. The ambush had been swift, and they were outnumbered, the patrol saved only by the skill of his father and Uleka, famed swordsman of south Volam. He'd turned when he heard a shout and saw his father in a furious confrontation. A teenaged warrior, slim to the point of scrawniness, had snuck up behind his father, stabbing him in the back while two warriors engaged him in a fierce frontal attack.

Rhamus had shouted and started forward but could not reach his father in time. As he'd held his dying father's head in his lap, his gaze had been drawn briefly to the fleeing figure of the young warrior who had murdered the King. He would never forget that face, evil already stamped across its youthful features. The coward had given his soldiers a hard chase but got away on swift runner's legs. Now Xarath was the King of west Volarn.

His features softened for a moment as his father's strong, intelligent face floated before him. It'd been his father who'd personally overseen his training as a warrior, and passed on an understanding of the enemy, their motivations, lusts and taste for treachery. Many were the times they'd managed to escape the confines of the castle, the servants and warriors, spending precious hours in personal discussions that didn't involve the kingdom--times Rhamus still treasured as his most priceless memories. The wisdom and love of his father had been taken from him at an early age, the weighty responsibilities of the kingdom riding his shoulders ever since.

Rhamus found that his slow walk had taken him unerringly back to the Earth woman even as his thoughts occupied his attention. He stopped directly in front of the redhead and then his eyes flicked briefly back to the area next to her. He puzzled over the gap between this woman and the next, and then he glanced down to a tousled head of hair.

"Pulack!" The King's voice boomed in the large room. After the Moyd hurriedly joined him, Rhamus asked with tension evident in the volume of his question, "What is this child doing here?"

"Oh, she's not a child, Your Majesty, but a full-grown woman."

"Why is she here? I think I was explicit in my instructions."

"Well," Pulack pulled uncomfortably at the neck of his shirt, "it was a mistake."

"A mistake! How could you make that kind of mistake!" The king lowered his hand to waist level.

"You see, Your Highness, she was wearing a long dress with very high shoes." He measured out a hand span. "And of course there will be no crystal charged for this one." He tried to soothe his irate, royal customer.

"What did you plan to do with her, put her on a platform and pass her off as taller?" Rhamus asked suspiciously.

"Your Majesty can see that she is wearing flat heeled slippers," The Moyd stated, feeling panicky. King Rhamus hit so near the truth of his and Rolan's mistake with the female, he didn't want the King to think they were careless merchants, else they might be cut out of any future payments of valuable crystal.

"What am I going to do with a half-grown Earth girl?" Rhamus asked sarcastically.

"Now wait just a cotton picking minute!" Nicole took a step closer to the King to gain his attention.

"I may be small to you, but on Earth I'm an average height. And I don't like to be talked about as if I were a speck on the wall. I have ears and a brain too." Her stubborn chin went up mutinously.

Everyone in the court stood transfixed by the exchange. Although many of them knew no English, they could tell the woman was being impertinent.

Serena's whole body tightened up as she got ready to join in the gathering vortex, with her tiny friend at its center, as usual.

The King's previously angry features went through several stages of expression including further anger, a calming down as he realized the ridiculousness of the situation, and finally humor. "Pulack, what have you brought me, a *sooeul*?" The King laughed.

Unbeknownst to Nicole, the sooeul was a tiny flying lizard with a fierce defensive nature, which often took on creatures of a much larger size and just as often lost. It was an extremely pretty animal, without much common sense, but it still earned the respect of the Volarnians because of its willingness to tangle with odds larger than safety dictated.

Pulack sighed in relief and many giggles and laughter could be heard from the surrounding court. Nicole decided to take advantage of the humor that seemed to follow the exchange between her and the King, even though she was sure it was at her expense. "Since everyone seems to be in a good mood now, I'd like to take this opportunity to request that Pulack drop me back on Earth the next time he goes to pick you up some more women."

"What's this Pulack, are you telling our business throughout the galaxy?"

"No, no, Your Majesty. I did tell the female that you might give us permission to take her back, since she can't be of any use to you here." He hurriedly added, "Of course, we'd use the memory eraser so that she would never know she'd been here."

"You're making sense for the first time tonight. But what am I supposed to do with her in the meantime?" Rhamus seemed to puzzle over his question, then asked, "When are you scheduled to select the next group?"

"Six months."

"It won't work, make it three," he stated flatly.

"But, Your Highness, we already promised to do a job for the *Biluganus*," the Moyd protested.

"What's worth more, the Biluganus steel alloy, or Volarnian crystal?"

"All right, all right," he surrendered. "If Your Highness ever gets tired of being a King, you can always come work the trader's route with me," he grumbled.

"Agreed," Rhamus chuckled. "Now, who is going to be responsible for this woman for three months?"

"I think I'm big enough to be responsible for myself," Nicole piped up, hands propped on each hip, as she confronted them.

The King glanced down kindly and shook his head in wonder at the petite woman. "You do not understand the ramifications of an attractive woman who is without the protection of her family. And you are not under the protection of a designated Volarnian warrior, as any woman would be, who was without family."

When she was about to argue the point, he explained, "Little one, we have a planet populated by a majority of males and many of those are not married. It would be asking for a death sentence for you to be unprotected."

"A death sentence." She paled.

Seeing her distress, he said. "Not your death sentence, although you may be injured due to your size. But any man who would dare force himself on a woman would be sentenced to death." At her shocked look, he expounded, "We have many laws which I'm sure would seem harsh to you humans, but believe me when I say you need a temporary protector during your stay here."

"I guess I could keep her locked up in the ship," Pulack volunteered.

"No, please don't do that to me," she pleaded. "Your Kingship," Nicole appealed. "I know you don't know me, but I'm a very social person and I have to be around people." Her pretty eyes filled with tears. "Why I'd just die if you shut me up in that smelly old ship for three months by myself."

"Smelly." Pulack almost shouted.

"Now, now," Rhamus waved his hands soothingly. "We'll think of something, won't we, Pulack?" The King looked sternly at the merchant. "It wasn't your fault you were brought here 'by mistake'." He spoke softly to her.

Serena was on the verge of stepping forward to intercede when she noticed Dr. Melat making his way hurriedly toward them. He had an apprehensive look on his face and placed himself next to Nicole when he arrived at the group.

"Your Highness, I will accept the responsibility of looking after Nicole during her time here," he said.

"You, Doctor?" The King asked in surprise.

"Yes, me. Is there something wrong with my acting as a guardian?" He grated out.

"It's not you personally, but you are not a warrior."

"I may only be doctor and I may not be a Volarnian warrior, but on *Cromotrie* I was trained in the ancient art of *laytor*. Therefore, I am quite capable of seeing after the young lady," Dr. Melat said proudly.

"Laytor!" The King and Pulack chimed in at the same time.

"We are truly honored to have such a skillful fighter amongst us," Rhamus complimented. "Maybe one of these days you can show my warriors some of your techniques, that is, when you're not too busy in your laboratory."

The doctor nodded his head and he asked, "Will she be in your way while you're working? I can only guess how exacting such work must be, and I'm sure you will not want your mind distracted by worrying about other 'small' matters?"

Dr. Melat chuckled at King Rhamus' pun and the way Nicole drew herself up in reaction. "No, she won't be a distraction. As a matter of fact, she may be of some assistance. Nicole's job back on Earth was as a helper to doctors."

"I resent that remark," she mumbled aside to Dr. Melat.

"We are honored then, little one." At her questioning look, Rhamus continued. "We do not have assistants to our healers, the *vassi*, but they are highly respected here. Therefore, if you assist healers on your world, you are in a highly respected occupation in our eyes."

Serena was thrilled by the developments of the last few minutes. Nicole would be looked after and be near the doctor, which is just what her heart desired.

She became nervous again when the King turned from Nicole and the doctor, who strolled off to join the crowd of onlookers. He stopped in front of her just as he'd done before.

Her stomach fluttered when the King slowly looked her up and down. This time she could tell he liked what he saw by the heat in his eyes. And when his hand came up to rest lightly on her right cheek, she was overcome with a sudden urge to touch him. Unconsciously, she turned her face into his palm and rubbed against it ever so slightly. The King gently turned her face back toward him and stared deeply into her eyes. Serena saw that he was as stunned as she was by her reaction to him.

Finally, she was close enough to inspect those wondrous Volarnian eyes. She discovered that the King's were somewhat different from the other natives she'd met so far. Most had ranged from pale lavender to a deeper violet. His were darker, almost a purplish-blue, and there was a distinctive dark blue ring outlining the iris of his eyes.

An intense heat seemed to radiate from the King's hand and eyes. Serena felt as if he were drawing her closer to him by a magnetic force. At first she struggled and her mind reacted with fear but, as if sensing her fear, the King forced her to look deeper into his eyes. Somehow Serena knew that he would not hurt her. She felt herself opening up, becoming pliant to his will.

As Serena accepted the strange wash of feelings that passed over her, she noticed a reflection of the same in the King's expression. He appeared surprised. An acceptance came over his handsome features as he drew Serena further away from herself and into his power.

The attraction Serena felt earlier seemed mild now compared to that which he stirred this time. There was an electrical feeling to the charged atmosphere surrounding them. Her lower lips were swollen and her sensitive clit hidden between them throbbed. She suddenly wanted his hand there, his fingers sliding between her moist flesh. She moaned softly as her nipples pebbled painfully. Her whole body screamed "take me".

Inhaling a deep breath, she sought to control the desire galloping through her nerves. Staring at Rhamus' handsomely expressive face helped her connect with him emotionally and push her passion back slightly.

Somehow, it seemed as though she knew the King better than anyone else in the room, but could put no words to describe it. She only knew that she liked what she "read" about the King from their personal contact.

As the magnetic force that flooded her body earlier suddenly became stronger, it was if she was invisibly pulled toward him, and then they were only a hand span from each other. She knew instinctively that he wanted to kiss her, but waited for her to make the first move, and when Serena moved within a breath away from his lips, the King moved into her space and their lips met. Wet, warmth, and an aching need filled her mind.

She'd been kissed by other men before, but never had she been in the hands of such an expert. Heat curled in her belly and seemed determined to move lower as their kiss continued.

The lust that had sprung to life but seconds ago ravaged her body once again. Pushing her breasts against him, she groaned into his mouth when her aching nipples met the muscular barrier of his chest. She clutched at his biceps to keep from grabbing his hands and shoving them between her thighs. There was a madness in her blood--one that disregarded the many eyes upon them. If he had ravaged her at that moment, on the cold floor, she would have been ecstatic.

Trying mightily to ignore her demanding body, she concentrated on their kiss.

Rhamus' lips were soft, firm, demanding. A thrumming sensation shot between her and the King. Out of the corner of her partially closed eyes, a soft bluish light materialized. It surrounded them like a cloud and appeared to be the source of the thrumming sensation.

The King seemed to sense her distraction and pulled back just a short space, again giving her a searching look. He concentrated on her face as if memorizing its details. A shout went up from the crowd and he turned to nod and smile at them.

Chapter Three

When Rhamus stopped in front of the red-haired woman again, he had wanted to hurry through his inspection to dispel the illusion of attraction he felt. He purposely started slowly from her slim feet, going up those elegant legs, coming to a halt at the high, rounded breasts which thrust against the soft material of her dress. By the sacred crystal, her figure was everything he could ever have desired.

Rhamus tightened his self-control, ignoring his pulsating *cini*, and viewed her face. His eyes were drawn first to the tendrils of hair lying against those exquisite cheeks, a curl of distaste twisted his handsome lips and helped cool his ardor.

Next, he gazed into the female's eyes and it was his undoing. Pulack was wrong, they were past extraordinary. The lovely eyes staring back at him were the truest pale blue of the priceless *arj'ak* crystal, the most powerful and sought after Volarnian crystal. Only the most influential or richest Volarnians owned any quantity of arj'ak, it was far too scarce, and the present problems with the western Volarnians made mining for it even more difficult.

The King stared into those wondrous orbs for a long time. He noted much that he did not need the Tarthra to help him see--a strong woman, a fighter, but at the same time there was a sensitivity she tried to keep hidden. Her eyes mirrored his confusion at the strong attraction between them.

His hand seemed to go up of its own volition and Rhamus accepted the inevitable--he could not deny his attraction, but maybe the Tarthra would prove futile. He stared at his right hand as he placed it gently along her cheek, it bore the symbol of his kingdom, a ring set with a large arj'ak crystal. His heart seemed to skip a beat when he glanced between the ring and her eyes. They could have been made from arj'akian crystal, they were such a perfect match.

When he set his hand ready for the Tarthra, he was momentarily taken aback by the woman's reaction. She almost nuzzled his hand! The fiery response he sensed in her was being reciprocated within himself. His cini throbbed and demanded he sink its length into her soft flesh. For a few heart beats, he lost control of his tightly reined feelings and his breathing became labored. He was on the verge of losing complete control. That thought was astonishing. Using the meditation he practiced when connecting to the crystal's power in his sword, he calmed his senses with a mammoth effort.

Rhamus knew as any young man trained in the Tarthra, that his next step was to let the choosing take over. The fear that came into the woman's eyes--this helped him let go of his continuing resistance to the choosing. A passion such as he'd never experienced before vibrated through his body. Clearly, she was feeling the same way.

Stifling his rutting urges, he accepted the Tarthra's power. He was pleased by her response to him, but was unprepared for the electrifying jolt, which coursed through his veins when their lips met. Only his years of strict training allowed him to tap into the crystal's power, disregarding those lush lips and the throbbing sensation they induced.

As Rhamus loosed the power from the crystal, it entwined his fate with that of the woman. His mind control coupled with the crystal's power left no doubts of the Tarthra's outcome. A Volarnian male's chosen one was matched in heart and soul by the Tarthra.

For the brief span of time when the power surged through them both, Rhamus knew much of the chosen one. He found a liking and respect for the strong, yet fragile woman. He noticed her distraction due to the blue power enveloping them and broke the contact, nodding to his people as they shouted their approval and acceptance of the Tarthra choosing.

* * * *

The King introduced himself, which seemed anticlimactic to Serena after the emotional intensity she'd just experienced with him. He asked her name and rolled it on his tongue, giving it a charming accent. She was impressed with his ability to speak English.

She was as awkward as a school girl when Rhamus took her hand and guided her to the dais. A glow shimmered along her nerve endings from their earlier encounter. It made her feel lulled in some sense, almost as if all emotion had temporarily deserted her. This strange calm helped carry her past the crowd of people, for she and the King certainly were the center of attention.

He escorted her to the smaller throne next to his. She was fascinated by the ornate chair he directed her to, running her hands along the intricate detail of the carvings depicting more of the fierce dragon creatures. On the back of the King's throne was a heavy carving of one of the vicious dragons, its head rising above Rhamus in an open-mouthed snarl, as if guarding the chair's occupant. The rather small wings spread out above the King's shoulders, and the armrests were representations of the beast's sharp-clawed limbs.

She liked the dull copper color of the chairs, but almost jumped out of hers when the coolness of the metal suddenly turned warm. Somehow, the rigidity of that structure took on a softer texture and the whole piece of furniture conformed to the curves of her body. The only thing that kept her from bolting was a gently restraining hand that Rhamus laid upon her arm nearest him.

"Don't be alarmed. The *kalyx* metal takes a little getting used to."

"I'll say," she shifted her weight in the chair. "How does it do that?" At his questioning look, she finished, "I mean, the temperature change and especially the way it seems to move whenever I do."

"I can't explain the properties to you. But this substance is imported from a drab little planet, which would go unnoticed if not for this spectacular product. The kalyx," Rhamus patted his chair arm, "makes its home planet almost rival Volarnian crystal in importance and trading value. This wonderful metal warms to the body temperature, whether a human, Volarnian, or even one of the cold-blooded species inhabiting this galaxy. Somehow this hard metal becomes softer, like the finest *rezel* leather, and then it conforms itself to the individual's body proportions, making a most comfortable piece of furniture."

Serena got her fill of looking the King over as he explained kalyx to her. Not that she didn't find the information very interesting, but he was so much more a visual treat. Gazing upon him as if intent upon his explanation, she let her eyes run casually over the ridged muscles in his powerful biceps, and then to the wide chest, which strained the seams of his sleeveless shirt.

She noticed the dragon motif carried out again in an armband that encircled the King's left upper arm. The headband the King wore appeared to be of the lais metal, carved in the popular dragon pattern with inset crystal eyes of sky blue. His shirt and skirt were a pale sky blue. In fact, he seemed to be the only person whose complete outfit was made from this particular color, although Serena noted quite a few Volarnians who wore the color as trim on their costumes. She wondered if it had the same significance as the wearing of purple did to the ancient kings of Earth.

The shirt seemed to be made of the same material as her dress and laced up the front. But the kilt was made from a leathery material, which closely resembled suede. This led her eyes downward for a closer inspection of those marvelously muscular thighs. The slits on each side of the kilt went up about six inches and gave her plenty of iron-hewed thighs to contemplate. And yet, there was something about his brawny thighs and arms that bothered her. Something didn't look right, but she couldn't quite put her finger on what it was that puzzled her.

Serena's inspection was interrupted when she noticed a Volarnian male using the same strange process on the other women that Rhamus had used earlier on her. He was a much younger man and appeared excited. Instead of going up and down the line of women as the King had, he went straight to one girl. She watched in fascination as the couple went through the attraction phase and then kissed. Her eyes widened when a blue glow surrounded the couple. So that's what we looked like, Serena mused. A shiver ran up her spine as she thought of the thrilling sensations this process had evoked.

The young man led the enraptured girl off to join the others watching on the sidelines. One after another, the handsome Volarnian males went through the process of choosing an attractive partner. She was surprised when a few of the males didn't appear to find a woman to their liking and would walk off unhappily. They would nod their head at another male who, as if by pre-arrangement, would immediately take the unlucky one's place. She became more attentive when a very tall, heavily muscled Volarnian male stopped in front of Olga. He made the voluptuously built blonde look small and feminine.

Serena watched closely. Olga seemed to become softer and almost submissive in her reaction to the tall male. If anyone looked like they could just melt right on through the floor, it was the flinty-natured Norsewoman. She was amazed and hoped that the Volarnian man knew what he was doing, then shook her head silently at herself. Why was she worrying about some Volarnian male she didn't even know?

She should be cursing him and any other Volarnian, except, Serena glanced sideways at the King, for him. Maybe later, when I can shake loose from this spell that he seems to have put on me, I'll be ready to curse him for his royal directive, which brought us here. The large man chose Olga and paraded her by the King's chair. He seated them both in the chairs near them.

"You gentlemen seem to be going through a lot of trouble just to choose a dinner partner," she commented dryly. The King looked at her with an inscrutable expression. When he didn't answer, she asked, "That is what this is all about, isn't it?" Serena waved a hand to encompass the Earth women remaining unchosen and the one man going through the procedure.

"One could say we were choosing a dinner partner ... for life."

"What do you mean?" Alarm flashed through her.

Rhamus leaned toward her and placed his hand over her hand, as it gripped the chair arm. "The Tarthra is the Volarnian's way of choosing a life mate."

"You mean a wife?"

"Yes."

"But you can't just choose someone like that! We don't even understand what's going on." She stared in dawning horror at the other women who had already been chosen and seemed absorbed in their partners' attentions. Even Olga was looking at her tall Volarnian with starry-eyed wonder.

"It is done," The King murmured in an uncompromising tone.

"You mean we're already married?" Serena asked in disbelief.

"No, we have not been joined by the traditions of our Volarnian marriage ceremony, yet."

"Then it is not done," she said in relief.

"It will be so, as soon as all the allotted males have gone through the Tarthra."

"You can't force a perfect stranger to marry you!"

"Whether you are perfect remains to be seen." Rhamus said with levity as he picked up her hand and rubbed the palm lightly with one finger.

Serena jerked her hand away as if she'd been scalded. How dare he flirt with her and try to make jokes! And how could his mere caressing of her hand cause such a weakness in her limbs?

He propped one hand under his chin and contemplated her boyishly. "There will be no force used against you or any of the others."

Her lips were rigid with her displeasure. "How can you hope to have us all married off then? You think your good looks will sway anyone?" Serena kept on even though the King was left with his mouth hanging open with his ready reply. "It takes more than a handsome face...."

"And a god-like physique." He interjected with a grin that left her speechless for a few heartbeats.

Her eyes couldn't help but play over his powerful body.

Rhamus' grin became huge at her response and a flush of embarrassment washed over her at being caught ogling him. "You interrupted me," she said petulantly, speaking rudely because she was upset.

"Pray, continue." He waved his hand graciously.

Serena got a grip on herself mentally and continued calmly, "On Earth, we do not have this 'choosing'. We get to know someone, slowly. We date, hopefully become friends first." She explained reasonably. "Then, if both partners feel they love each other, usually the man will ask the woman to become his wife."

The King clapped his hands in glee. "It is the same, without the long wait." He held up his hand when she looked ready to bite his nearest hand. "Now it's my turn to explain. You may have heard of our blue crystal, how it is priceless in trading value." At Serena's reluctant nod he asked. "Did you wonder why it is so valuable?"

"Of course," she answered in annoyance at his straying from the subject. "I thought it must be like our diamond--its value is in its beauty. But what does that have to do with this choosing thing?"

"Only the arj'ak, used by one trained in its use, can produce the effects of the Tarthra. All Volarnian males must go through years of rigorous training as warriors in order to control the power in the crystal. This power can be used in a deadly manner as a weapon, or something as pleasant as the Tarthra."

"You mean you kill with it?"

"I don't wish to discuss unpleasant topics right now. Let's just say that in Volarn's past, the arj'ak was used for killing. Now it is highly discouraged to kill with the power. Anyway, as I said before, one of the more pleasant uses of the crystal is the choosing of one's mate."

"Did you choose me because of my eyes? They are the same color as your precious crystal, I notice," Serena asked sarcastically.

"That might have had something to do with the physical attraction involved, other than your more obvious assets." Rhamus gave her body a warm perusal that set her pulse up a few beats. "But the attraction is just the first step and is not the most important element which the crystal seeks out."

"Seeks out? Does the crystal have radar?" She continued in her sarcastic vein, agitated at herself for her reaction to the King.

"I don't understand what this 'radar' is, but I think I understand your continued resistance to me."

"What resistance? I'm sitting here trying to have an informative conversation with you. If I were *resisting* you, you'd know it, believe me!" She finished angrily.

"I'm sure you mean that, my warrior woman," Rhamus teased.

"I am not one of your warrior women," she snapped.

"No, but were you not a fighter back on Earth?"

"Yes. And that's why you will find out how well I fight, if you think to force me into something I don't wish to do."

"Force will not be necessary. You will choose that which you desire," he said smugly.

Springing to her feet in anger, she declared, "I *desire* to leave this planet and your presence!"

Holding up the bracelet arm, Serena fisted her hand and

exclaimed. "Is this how you plan on getting our acceptance?"

Rhamus placed a gentle but strongly restraining hand on the agitated woman's arm and pulled her firmly back to the chair. "The control bracelet will not be used on any of you. I will remove it once we are wed. You may consider it part of our marriage ceremony, a symbolic gesture of your release from your mother Earth's bosom, to your new family here."

Seeing her clenched jaw, Rhamus lowered his tone and added, "You may wish to leave Volam. I grant I would feel the same in your place. But, before this night is out, you will learn that your desire will be--to be by my side."

"Why you jerk!" Serena hissed, turning to glare anew at her tormentor.

He grinned at his partner's steamy expression. "I take it from your tone, that jerk is something with an unsavory reputation." He raised his eyebrows as if receiving her next revelation was the dearest thing to him.

How could one continue holding onto resentment when the object of your anger turned your very insults into a joke and his very presence made one breathless?

"May I continue?" Rhamus asked politely, turning a smile upon her that was warm and confident. At Serena's tight-lipped nod, the King said, "Going back to our previous discussion of the Tarthra. The arj'ak crystal intertwines with the user's psychic energy, which he directs in the choosing. The power helps the man to see much about his intended and to feel if his attraction will go further than an initial magnetism. Then, when the couple joins in a kiss, the man can sense the seed of love that lies between them and will continue to grow."

"Love." She scoffed.

"Yes, love," he said quietly. "I know it will take time for you to understand and believe in our Tarthra, but you will. All our marriages are chosen with the Tarthra and there are no ... I don't know the word Earth people use for when couples split apart."

"You mean divorce." Serena looked sharply at him. "Oh, really? You don't have divorces?" Skepticism edged her retort.

Rhamus again shook his head patiently, ignoring her sarcasm.

She resisted the urge to stare at his wide shoulders. "So all your 'choosings' are ideal and there are no unhappy marriages?"

"I am not saying all marriages are perfect. Every couple has problems to work through and arguments arise. After all, our women are almost physically as strong as our men. Unlike your Earth, women are regarded as equals."

"I'm not sure I like your tone in reference to Earth," she worked to control the agitation in her voice.

Seeing Rhamus' quiet, accepting countenance, she changed the direction of their conversation. "So, you are equal. Tell me then, when do the women get to do the 'choosing'?"

"They don't."

"Then you're not completely equal," she stated in triumph.

"Maybe not in your eyes, but in ours we are. It is simply that it takes years of training. It made sense in the beginning to train the male warriors." Rhamus stared off in the distance. "We once were entangled in continuous, violent wars, so all our young males became warriors. It was an easier process to also train them in the way of the Tarthra."

"What about your warrior women? Are they trained?"

"The Getra are not trained. It is unnecessary. All males are trained and a Getra may be chosen by a male if the Tarthra so chooses. Also, our warrior women cannot choose to go into the Getra until after their first *ventyl*. It is then too late to start the training."

"What is a ventyl?"

"The cycle of fertility."

"Why must the Getra wait until the ventyl? Why can't they start training as early as other warriors?"

Rhamus seemed to withdraw into himself, as if by doing so he could withdraw from the subject. "Long ago, when the power of the crystal was discovered and the vassi came up with the Tarthra, the warrior women of Volarn could choose this honorable profession as readily as any male. Legend has it that these Getra were trained in use of the Tarthra also. Then the power hungry amongst our people abused the tremendous power of our arj'ak crystals. The horrible price was the world war and, eventually infertility for many of our women."

The King paused as if in mental pain. "When we realized the result, all fertile Getra chose to become civilian, marry and bear children. With the high percentages of infertility among our people, it didn't take long before we were forced to create a law mandating that young women had to wait until their first ventyl before choosing the Getra. Those who tested fertile were forbidden to follow the warrior's path. Thus evolved the Tarthra and warrior's training of males only."

Serena didn't know what to say. She sensed that she'd opened up an old wound. Maybe she didn't love this man, but she felt no need to cause him pain. She decided to distract Rhamus with a more pleasant train of thought. "You were saying earlier that this Tarthra can sense love between a man and woman who don't even know each other?" She leaned forward to gain his attention, but changed positions when his eyes flicked to the gaping neckline of her dress.

"Yes, the crystal picks up on each individual's thoughts, feelings and personality. If there is an attraction, all these elements are pulled together by the warrior's control of the power. If there is a successful match, the arj'ak crystal projects its power around the couple."

"That all sounds very mysterious, but it doesn't prove the couple is in love," Serena replied quietly.

"No, there is not full-blown love in the beginning. But all couples who have been matched through the Tarthra's power soon find love and have strong marriages."

"It's a lot to ask us Earthlings to believe in something we don't have on our world. Besides, how do you know it will work on us?" She asked.

"We don't know if the end results will be the same, a good marriage, but already you see that the actual choosing does work with your people." Rhamus waved a hand toward the remaining couple.

Serena felt a pulse of fear and alarm pass through her when the last couple was surrounded by the blue aura of the crystal. Oblivious to all, they were caught up in an intense kiss. What was going to happen next? Things were already happening far too quickly.

After the entwined couple finished the Tarthra and left the floor to join the others, a lone young man came slowly forward to stand before Rhamus. He was tall and slim and could almost be a younger version of the King, maybe a brother.

"Are you sure there's not one left for me, maybe one they forgot on board the ship?" The young warrior joked, forlornly addressing the King in a familiar manner.

"I'm afraid not." He shook his head and grinned back. He motioned toward Nicole and Dr. Melat. "Pulack's mistake left us short by one female."

Rhamus seemed to sense her curious eyes, and turning to her, said, "Serena, may I introduce my cousin Jarvic?" Turning back to his relative, he finished his introductions.

"Very pleased to meet you." The charming young man straightened and inclined his head slightly in a courtly bow.

Influenced by his infectious smile and handsome face, she returned his smile.

Rhamus cleared his throat when he noticed Jarvic's avid attention to Serena. "You may have first choice of the next group that Pulack brings."

Jarvic dragged his eyes from Serena. "I guess I can wait a few months, if it means I may be as lucky as you."

"Maybe so." He glanced thoughtfully at his future queen. His look seemed to declare his doubt.

"The shortage of women was bad luck for you, but I'm glad it was you, cousin. Some of the other warriors wouldn't have been so generous in their waiting." Rhamus commented.

Jarvic smiled good-naturedly and said, "I'm not too sure I am ready to be tied to one woman yet, anyway." His conversation with the King was interrupted by the appearance of Hartoos. As his cousin strolled nonchalantly off, Rhamus appeared amused to hear him say under his breath, "I wonder if Pulack could find another beautiful woman with hair the color of fire."

Hartoos bowed, then stood formally, focused on the importance of his announcement. "Your Highness, the Tarthra has been concluded for all the women, as you can see. It is time for the marriage ceremony."

Serena glanced worriedly at Rhamus, who had a most serious expression on his face. When he gallantly held out his hand, she placed her much smaller one in his and let him lead her to stand beside him on the dais.

They faced the crowd of Volarnians and Earth women. Hartoos stood with his back to the onlookers and solemnly faced them. Serena chose not to make a scene--she would simply refuse to say the words that would bind her to the King. She hoped that he would not try to use force on her in front of all his people.

As Hartoos started eloquently through some sort of speech and supposedly the marriage ceremony, she couldn't help but notice that Rhamus continued to keep his strong hand clasped completely around hers. She marveled at the sensations contained within those two small portions of their joined bodies, at the tingly feelings radiating within the sphere of their contact. Serena jerked back in alarm, but could not pull her hand from the strength of his grip.

Hartoos had paused in the proceedings. In horror, she heard Rhamus repeating vows of protection and fidelity that, although phrased in an antiquated fashion, sounded all too familiar. The advisor then turned to her, repeating the words and then pausing for her answer. Serena's brows knitted together in anger as she stared at Hartoos and refused to look at the man waiting in silence beside her. Her hand had fisted in response to her temper, but a spreading warmth began radiating from their contact, and a weak feeling seeped through her.

Time seemed to slow when she finally turned to look at Rhamus.

He had a saddened expression in his eyes as he again exerted the arj'ak's power, this time there was a sense of control coming from him. The thrumming sensation she'd felt during the Tarthra again overtook her senses and the blue light surrounded their joined hands. Serena's fledgling resistance flowed from her and peace replaced it.

A short time later, she wondered why she had even thought to resist in the first place. Serena felt the paradox of her situation. Her reactions were slowed down while her feelings escalated.

As she stared into Rhamus' wondrous eyes and repeated soon forgotten words with Hartoos' prompting, all her being ached to be in her love's arms and share this feeling.

Chapter Four

Rhamus took her right wrist in his other hand. Unclasping the ugly bracelet, he replaced it with a delicately made one crafted of the valuable lais metal, with a raised carving of the dragon. Between each clawed foot, the creature clutched a large crystal. Her eyes were drawn to Rhamus' thick right wrist where he wore a matching, wider band. The basami on both of their wristbands held an arj'ak crystal in one claw and an aquamarine in the other.

She examined the wristband Rhamus wore on his left wrist with curiosity as well. It was exactly the same as his other, except the dragon's claws were closed around one large arj'ak crystal about four carats in size.

Through her haze, Serena felt Rhamus seat her again in the strange chair. Hartoos then gathered all the men and women who had been matched in the Tarthra together, facing the two thrones and their occupants. The King's advisor again went through the marriage ceremony. The men answered in unison and the women were "persuaded" by the arj'ak's power to succumb to the ceremony, as she had been.

When the ceremony finished, Rhamus stood up. He gently grasped Serena by the upper arm, then escorted her into an adjoining room. The Tarthra participants followed the royal couple into the banquet room, taking seats along both sides of a long dining table, which took up much of the central portion of the room. The King and new Queen were seated at the head of the table, side by side.

Later, Serena had trouble recalling the wedding feast. The details were blurred as if she'd drunk too much strong wine. She remembered numerous toasts by the male Volarnians, the anticipatory expressions on the warriors' faces, and the confused expressions of the newly wed women. She vaguely recalled a sumptuous feast of exotic foods that she barely picked at, and a fruity tasting liquor that she sipped hesitantly.

She did remember that every time she shook her head trying to clear the fuzziness and she'd turn to Rhamus with dawning suspicion, her new husband would stroke her hand and stare into her eyes. Soon, she'd feel her awakening resistance dissolving beneath his hypnotic influence.

It seemed but a short time later that Hartoos was announcing the end of the wedding feast and the warriors were escorting their new wives to their rooms at a much faster pace than when they entered the banquet hall. Rhamus walked with Serena in the same dignified manner he'd exhibited so far. It took quite a few minutes to arrive at the door of the King's chamber, having been stopped and greeted all along their passage by the nobility.

He led Serena across the large chamber to a comfortably stuffed chair and then took up a stance across the room. While he waited for Serena to shake off the effects of the arj'ak's influence, he poured a drink from a cut crystal decanter and sipped on the dark blue wine.

Serena closed her eyes for a few moments. She felt so drained and tired. She opened her eyes again and slowly turned her head to assess her surroundings. At first her glance passed over the King standing nonchalantly against the wall. Her eyes were filled with images of the elaborately decorated chamber.

It made Surad's room seem poor by comparison. And the King's room was a suite, with a complete set of furniture for the sitting area. The pale blue of the arj'ak crystal dominated the color scheme. Touches of dark blue and the golden brown of the stone walls were used in trimmings on the bed covers and pillows. It kept the room from being overwhelmed by the rich, sky blue shade. Her wondering eyes came to rest on Rhamus.

"Where am I?"

"In the royal chamber. It's a bit overdone for my taste, too." He seemed to astutely guess her thoughts. He shifted away from the wall and stood seemingly relaxed, arms folded, an enchanting smile playing across his features. At Serena's continued silence, he said, "My great aunt Surad surprised me by redecorating this room for me after my father's death. I think she felt that sleeping in my father's bed chamber with all his things around me would make me feel sad."

Rhamus got a faraway look in his eyes. "Perhaps it would have made me sad, but I would have preferred keeping it the way it was." Very softly, he added, "I loved my father."

Serena had been examining the furniture as he spoke, noting the intricate detailing of the dragon creature she had seen earlier carved on many of the furnishings. "So Surad is your great aunt," she stated. "Why let her redecorate if you didn't want it done? Aren't you the King?" She asked sarcastically.

"Because it pleased her to do so. Besides, I often sleep in the barracks with my warriors."

"A King in a barracks?"

"Yes. A Volarnian King is more a warrior than a simple figurehead. And I've had no reason to be drawn back to this chamber, until now."

"You may be wishing to rejoin your soldiers sooner than you think, if you take one step closer," Serena jumped up and warned Rhamus as he started slowly toward her. He stopped and contemplated her and she sought to change the subject. "So you like to please your aunt?"

"Yes, as a matter of fact I do." His look encompassed her from her slim ankles to the top of her fiery head. "Do you not like to please those you love?"

Serena sensed a verbal trap but couldn't stop her quick temper from flaring. "I have no one that I love, therefore, I don't need to worry about pleasing anyone." She gritted her teeth in a parody of a pleasant smile.

Rhamus laughed and her faux smile turned to a grim frown. He strolled over to her. It took every effort of will for her to not retreat from him, and hold her ground. She felt like a frightened little girl. Not because he was intimidating in his height or strength, but because of the way his presence made her feel. She wanted to fight that weak feeling of surrender, to literally fight him if necessary.

"Do you not love anyone, my little Serena?" He asked playfully.

"I am not your Serena and I'm not little," she ground out. "And I already said I don't love anybody."

"I am glad to hear there is no one else in your heart, for whether you will admit it or not, you love me, Serena. There is no room for anyone else," Rhamus said with confidence.

Serena was speechless with rage. He took another step closer and her anger weakened when the attraction she felt for him blossomed anew. The pulse in her neck beat faster, stronger, and she was frantic when he took another step forward. He was an arm's length away--too close. She took a step back to secure her comfort zone. She might as well be a gazelle being stalked by a lion. When she took another step back, he kept pace. As the back of her knees bumped into a piece of furniture, she lashed out in verbal defense, "You play unfair! You are using that Tarthra spell on me again."

"Serena, stop fighting me."

"Fighting you?" She shrilled, then calmed down when she remembered that she really could put up a good fight if necessary.

Rhamus sighed. "Contrary to what you believe, I am not using the power on you right now." He looked at her closely. "If you're feeling sensations that apparently you find disturbing, it's only because you find me attractive and deep in your heart know that you love me."

"You Volarnians are crazy!" She took a step closer to him and jabbed a finger into his hard chest. "It's not possible to know that you love somebody when you first meet." When Rhamus opened his mouth to protest, Serena held up her hand in a halting motion. "You might as well save your breath. I don't believe in this Tarthra choosing, like I said. You Volarnians are using spells or maybe it was something you put in our drinks."

Rhamus reached out, grasped her hand, then pulled it back to lay flat against his chest on the right side. "Do you feel my heart beating?"

She was distracted by two things--the rigid masculine chest beneath her fingers and the confusing fact that she did feel Rhamus' heart beating on the wrong side. Then she recalled Volarnian physiology was different from Earth people.

"My heart beats with love for you, Serena, even though I fought hard against it at first." His eyes went unconsciously to her hair. "It may take time for you to accept the truth of the Tarthra, but I wish you to know that I accept." His voice became warmer as he added, "And I approve."

Serena wanted to react to his outrageous statement and not his hand and strongly beating heart. But his words helped her piece together the puzzlement she'd felt at his behavior when he kept going back and forth during the Tarthra. He was fighting his attraction to her because he hated her hair color! "Let go of my hand," she almost pleaded.

He did let go, but placed the hand he had gripped hers with alongside her cheek, as he'd done in the Tarthra. Serena again felt a churning sensation in her gut and reacted. "You are going to use the power over me again, to make me do what you want!"

"No, I will not make you do anything against the desires of your heart. But that doesn't mean I won't try to show you where your heart lies."

Rhamus brought his lips crashing to hers so suddenly, she didn't have time to react or think. Again, she was caught up in the intense whirlpool of desires that he seemed capable of stirring in her. She didn't know when he placed his other hand on her back, but was only too aware of the sensations he created when that arm gripped her tighter.

Her breasts were crushed against his unyielding chest and she keenly felt the difference in their two forms. As her softness met the rigid hardness of his frame, her breasts suddenly felt highly sensitized, and she ached to push them more firmly against his strong male body.

Rhamus moved his hands and began caressing her arms, pushing her back slightly so he could gain access to her breasts. When his large callused hands covered her sensitive mounds, their rough texture sliding against the silky material of her bodice created a sensual friction. Her nipples reacted by beading into tight buds. An excitement was building within as their kiss became more intense, intimate. She groaned as his tongue played with her lips and then her tongue. Serena responded in kind and felt Rhamus' moan in her mouth. For the first time since she'd been brought to Volarn, she was infused with a sense of power and control. She could make him feel the same uncontrollable desires as she felt herself.

Rhamus was creating wild, wonderful sensations with his experienced kissing. She was bereft for a moment when his lips left hers, but when he brought his mouth to her ear and his tongue swirled around the sensitive lobe, she ceased to feel deprived. She moaned and her head flopped bonelessly as fire lanced through her blood.

His lips nipped and kissed their way from her ear to her neck and Serena went limp with desire. She groaned and turned her head to give him better access and Rhamus, realizing that he'd stumbled on one of her erogenous zones, made full use of her surrender.

Unexpectedly, he swept Serena up in his arms and carried her to the huge royal bed. She wondered at his strength, that he could so easily carry a woman as large as herself. After he laid her down and stretched out beside her, they hungrily began kissing again.

Rhamus kissed and tongued her neck until she was almost senseless with the hot flashes of desire he stirred in her. Serena's breasts felt swollen as he rubbed them, and she pushed her aching nipples into his palms. A soft sigh of satisfaction escaped her as his fingers smoothed her burning flesh with caresses. She was so hot with desire, she barely noticed when he efficiently deprived them both of clothing. She was past being embarrassed about her state of undress with a virtual stranger and welcomed the feel of all his male hardness pressed to the length of her. She was shocked at how hot his body felt, as if he had a furnace lit inside.

Her husband's caresses became firmer, more demanding as his hands pressed and kneaded her soft flesh as no one else had ever dared. Serena reveled in the sensations. When he trailed kisses from her neck down to her breasts, a lance of pleasure coursed from her breasts to the juncture of her thighs. Her pussy was swollen and needy, crying out its need for his touch by the moistness gathering between the folds. His nuzzling of her nipples set up a throbbing in her clit. She felt ready to explode.

Serena's hands seemed as restless as Rhamus'. She stroked his back, tentatively touched his muscularly shaped buttocks, then boldly when she discovered how he responded to her caresses. Her back arched as she sought even deeper contact, and her hands gripped his buttocks boldly, pulling him toward her. Grinding her groin against him, she received the more burning contact she wanted. She received new, different sensations as his strokes worked down to rub her bottom and thighs.

"Yes," she moaned, unaware she had spoken. She flinched beneath his invasive fingers and then cried out in pleasure. Then his hands began to caress her clit and she knew she couldn't take it. She had to stop him, for to go on was to lose complete control of herself.

Serena tried to push Rhamus' hand away, but it had insinuated itself between her thighs. The next minute she was pushing herself against that hand, urging it on. Her hips rocked as she fucked his fingers with her slick folds, groaning wildly as desire pulsed through her.

He brought one of her hands to his lower belly. She was astounded by the combined sensation of the heat and hardness of his male organ. Her breath hitched as she slid her hand up and down his magnificent cock. Something stirred between her lower lips, a fiery response apart from her own passion. Due to her maidenly state, Serena had no idea of the impact it would have on her senses. Somehow, the contact of her hand with his organ called to her like some heady drug. Suddenly an urge to have Rhamus inside her flooded her senses, although she didn't understand fully what that meant.

When he positioned himself between her thighs, she guessed what came next and wanted it as much as she sensed he did, yet she was scared. If Rhamus was a typical Volarnian male, their male organs were much larger than the average human.

Serena's thoughts surfaced and she said a little uncertainly, "You're so big."

He soothed her and gently whispered, "Don't fear, my love, it will not hurt."

When his cock pushed into her, it felt like a hot poker stabbed her sensitive flesh. Her whole body went rigid. She desperately tried to sit up and throw him off her as tears trickled down her face. "Get off me, you beast, you promised it wouldn't hurt!" She accused.

Rhamus still lay on her and refused to budge, although he withdrew the contact between their lower bodies. He had a puzzled look on his face. "I don't understand. Dr. Melat assured us that we could make love with human females." His eyes lit up with dawning. "Is it because I am so much larger than human males?" Concern flashed across his face as he inquired. "I did not hurt you, did I?"

"That's what I've been trying to tell you," she fumed. "Yes," she almost screamed, "You hurt me a lot."

Her husband wiped Serena's tears away with his hand and shook his head in confusion. "Truly, I don't understand. You are the same body size as a small Volarnian female. We don't have any problem when we make love to our females." He watched her face intently and seemed relieved when the pained expression left her eyes and her tears stopped. "Are you still hurt?"

"Not much, now," she acknowledged. "It might not be exclusively your size."

"What do you mean?" He questioned in concern.

A pink hue rose in Serena's cheeks and she asked, "Can't we talk about this in a different position?"

"No, I am quite comfortable and I am not pressing my weight down on you, so I know you're not uncomfortable either. Tell me, why did your face turn a pink color?"

Her embarrassment forgotten, she looked with annoyance at her new husband. "I guess Dr. Melat didn't inform you about all aspects of human behavior. And as a matter of fact, I am uncomfortable. That is why I turned pink."

"Earthlings turn pink when they are in discomfort?" Rhamus looked puzzled. He raised himself another inch off her.

"No, we turn pink when we're embarrassed," she said impatiently.

"I see." He looked relieved. "We Volarnians turn a paler color when we feel embarrassed. So," he charged ahead. "By your own admittance, you are in no physical discomfort. Then why did you feel embarrassed?" His eyes took on a wicked glimmer as he inquired. "Tell me, wife, was it not my size that you are too embarrassed to discuss?"

"Are all men the same throughout the galaxy?" Serena asked in disgust. "Thinking only with the thing between their legs."

"Oh, wife," Rhamus rested his chin in his fisted hands on top of her chest and searched her face with his warm gaze. "You are good at changing the subject."

He kept staring at her intently. Serena decided the only way to shut him up was to just get it over with and explain matters to him. "OK," she conceded, then asked in frustration, "But if I tell you, will you please get up off me?"

"A Queen ordering a King," he teased and shook his head in

mock wonder.

"Fine. If that's how you're going to be, then I won't tell you anything."

He laughed softly. "I give up, my Queen. Never let it be said that a wise King doesn't know when to retreat." He waited in patient silence while his wife seemed to compose herself, as though she was a general readying herself for battle.

"I said it might not be just your size, because I am still a virgin." Serena admitted quietly, waiting for his disbelief.

Rhamus' features didn't change a bit as he asked, "What is a virgin?"

"Don't play the idiot with me," she again tried to push ineffectively against his heavy body. "Even though Pulack told us how liberated and equal your women are supposed to be, surely you must have a few virgins on Volarn."

"You don't seem to believe me when I tell you I don't know what this 'virgin' means." Now Rhamus appeared frustrated. "Perhaps if you would take a minute to quit acting like a Getra and throwing verbal barbs, you could explain this word to me."

"Oh," Serena realized her mistake and felt doubly embarrassed. She was annoyed when the tell-tale blush crept up her face again. She cleared her throat. "I didn't realize that you might not understand the meaning of the word. You speak English so well, I forget that you may not know every nuance."

She stared at her husband's chin while she spoke. "A virgin is a woman who has not been with a man."

Rhamus' eyebrows went up in astonishment. "Is that all?"

"What do you mean, 'is that all'?" She asked angrily.

"I meant no insult, it's just that many of our young women who don't find a Tarthra match after reaching their ventyl, have relations with Volarnian males of their mutual liking. And besides, Pulack told me that it is much the same on Earth," he added reasonably.

"Just wait until I get my hands on that little piggy alien," she spit out.

Rhamus sighed. "I do not understand your continued anger."

"I'm angry because Pulack insulted the women of my planet. And I'm mad at you, because in spite of the fact that I told you my deepest secret, you don't even seem to care about the gift I've given you and the pain that you caused me."

"I do not understand how Pulack insulted you and a planet full of women, but I concede there may be cultural differences in question. And I do appreciate the fact that I am your first man," Rhamus gave her an almost boyish smile. "But I still do not understand your anger at this 'pain' you speak of. Did you not tell me a few minutes ago that the pain was gone?"

When Serena's eyes appeared to tear up again as if in some mental anguish, he asked, "Is there pain connected with the act of sex, that humans suffer? We

Volarnians certainly do not." He looked alarmed as he added. "This will be a problem if you suffer so each time."

She peered into his eyes searchingly and saw no deceit. "You mean that your women don't have pain when they are with their first man?"

"Of course not," Rhamus dismissed the notion with a wave of one hand. "There should only be pleasure in sex." He glanced quickly at his wife in sudden dawning. "Do Earth women have pain during their first encounter?"

"Yes," Serena said wearily. "That's what I've been trying to tell you."

Rhamus placed his hands on either side of her face. "I am truly sorry if I hurt you." He gave her a gentle kiss on the lips.

Her husband's sincere expression did much to salve her hurt feelings. "Now that I've explained, can you please get up?"

"But you haven't finished explaining my wife. You did not tell me why there is pain. And, will there be pain if we continue?" He asked quietly.

Serena clenched her jaw, then she relented. "You are going to have to ask Dr. Melat why there is pain, for I cannot explain it to you."

At Rhamus' look of disbelief, she said. "There are just some things that humans, especially women, find too personal to discuss with a stranger. And as far as your other question, there is no pain after the first time."

"All right, I will accept that Earth women seem reluctant to talk about such matters, for Pulack did inform me that humans are often secretive about their bodies."

Rhamus cocked his head in contemplation, then laughed and sprang to his feet beside the bed as Serena's eyes sparkled with temper. "Your Majesty, I await your pleasure," he teased as his look hungrily took in her unclad state.

Her face flamed crimson as his invasive visual probing seemed to sear her with heat. She saw in a glance that she wouldn't be able to quickly grab the covers for concealment. They had been tucked into the foot of the bed by a thoughtful servant. Making an instantaneous decision, Serena leapt out of the bed and ran across the room to retrieve her dress. She turned quickly when she heard Rhamus approach and held the little scrap of cloth in front of her torso as she turned to face him.

* * * *

Much of his lovely wife was revealed while she reposed for an instant of time upon his bed, and then he glimpsed her back parts as she fled across the room. He wanted to get his fill of viewing her beautiful body, but knew now was not the time to press her. Instead, he mentally stored away the picture of those luscious round breasts, tiny curving waist and rounded bottom for future consideration until his wish could be fulfilled.

Rhamus was immensely satisfied that the promise of her clothed beauty was far surpassed by the reality of her nude body. In spite of his distaste for her red locks, the brief glimpse of those bright red curls at the juncture of her thighs caused him to wonder at his own prejudice, for he discovered a fascination at the sight.

Chapter Five

Serena sensed Rhamus' inventory of her, but felt somewhat safe behind the small piece of material she held to her chest and spread out to hold in front of her lower body. Now that they faced each other across the room, she was too inhibited to slip the dress quickly over her head. It would put her in too vulnerable a position, exposed completely to his view.

When Rhamus seemed to pause for a moment in thought, she could not control her wayward eyes. She was shocked at the full view of her husband's hard male body and annoyed with him for the easy manner in which he stood, as if fully clothed in front of all his subjects. Serena's eyes swept the steely length of him, noting the ridges of muscles in his arms and legs, and the steely abdominals that showed the hard won separation of muscle.

Her traitorous eyes traveled down to look in wonder at his large cock that now lay flaccid and non-threatening. She became disconcerted when it suddenly seemed to be filling out even as she watched, and glanced up in alarm at her husband's wide grin.

"Can you please turn your back while I put on my dress?" She almost pleaded, feeling jittery as he approached her slowly.

"It would be useless to put on clothing that would be coming right off again," Rhamus noted with determination.

As she backed away cautiously, looking behind her for pieces of furniture, Serena said in alarm, "You promised."

Shaking his head, he answered. "I promised to get off of you, if you remember."

"You tricked me!"

"No, not tricked, my Queen," he smiled wickedly. "I told you a King knows when to retreat, but he also knows when to advance."

Serena ran for the door and was too surprised to let go of the dress when it was jerked hard. She was pulled back in a half circle and slammed against her husband's immovable chest, knocking the breath from her for a second. Before she had time to think, or draw a deep breath, Rhamus' brawny arms were clamped around her, trapping her arms between their bodies. He loosed one arm while containing both hers and used the other to grip the back of her head in one huge hand, then invaded her mouth with hot, fierce kisses.

A shiver of fear ran down her back but finally melted into quivers

Myra Nour

of excitement as he stormed past her crumbling defenses. The dress slithered out of her hands and lay forgotten in a gossamer pool at their feet.

A sense of deja'vu struck Serena as Rhamus first muddled her senses with desire from his kissing and then again carried her to the bed. She struggled briefly to control the white hot needles of desire which consumed her very thoughts. It took only a few strokes of his deft hands and demanding kisses for her to melt. In spite of her fear, she ached for his cock to fill her once again. Her pussy was moist with need. As if sensing her capitulation, Rhamus loosened his iron hold from around his wife's arms and casually draped her arms around his neck.

Serena ran her hands up through his thick hair. Escalating feelings of pleasure tingled through her body in prickly currents that traced a path between the sensitive areas of her body where he caressed, and through her throbbing clit. Rhamus' hard cock bumped against her upper thigh, seeking entrance, and Serena tensed for a heartbeat, but relaxed in the next when she felt the ease of his silken passage.

Once he started the rite of actually making love, she was thrilled that the sensations created in their foreplay were but precursors to the true event. She sighed heavily. This felt right. Pleasure so intense it felt unreal ran throughout her whole body. Her skin was hot and sensitive to each little stroke. Serena's breasts were swollen and her nipples beaded into tight buds which quivered at every caress.

Rhamus slid slowly inside, filling her completely. He captured her mouth in a deep, hot kiss. Her mouth went lax when his tongue slipped in and out of her mouth, while at the same time his cock slid back and forth in a matching rhythm.

Her hands scraped gently up and down her husband's back and then alternated with wild rakings of his muscular torso, as the heat between them ran the gamut from slow and tender to savage and erotic.

Serena felt as though she were on a roller coaster ride, approaching the hills with rising anticipation and a release of tension as they plunged down the other side. Rhamus' expert love making kept her reacting in waves of throbbing feeling, finally enthusiastically hurtling toward the steepest hill.

His body suddenly stiffened. Serena looked into his handsome face and watched as he threw his head back in a parody of both pain and pleasure. She guessed that she'd just witnessed her husband's release, for she could also feel his seed spurting in bursts of hot fluid that hurt her sensitive tissues. She wondered at the strength of her new husband, so physically majestic that even his seed held immense power of its own. Yet, Serena felt an odd sense of frustration.

"I am sorry you didn't reach your pleasure," Rhamus smoothed the hair by one of her temples. "I am afraid it's been too long since I've enjoyed the company of a female as lovely and responsive as you."

He moved off her body and stretched out beside her, pulling her to lie against his length, placing one of her arms across his chest. Serena did not feel as exposed in this position, for he could only see her hip if he glanced downward. She found his gentle stroking of her arm as it lay on his chest soothing after the steamy session they'd just finished.

A feeling of shyness kept Serena from asking Rhamus what he meant by his statement, so she pursued the safer subject. "How can someone who looks like you, and is the King besides, not have plenty of women to keep you company?"

Kissing the top of her head, he said. "The King has many responsibilities. I lead my warriors in border patrols quite often, or I am in council with my staff about affairs of state. Besides, it wouldn't look good for the King to have a string of mistresses."

"I thought you implied that Volarnians are very liberated in their thinking concerning sex?"

"That's true, but the royal family must be above the people in their actions. Not that having a lover is frowned upon--even a King must have his pleasures sometime." Rhamus quirked a crooked smile at her. "Now, I think it's time we got some sleep. It's been quite a day for both of us."

Long after his breathing indicated he was deep asleep, Serena lay wide-awake, thinking over the events that had brought her here. She'd been leading a fairly normal life ... well, not really. Being a female wrestler was not considered to be "normal" by most women. But, she'd been paying her own expenses and had managed to put away a little cash for the day when she could hopefully quit the business and go back to college.

Now those hopes were dashed, unless she could find a way to escape and return to Earth. Was it fate that had put the two strange aliens in her path, or merely bad luck? Fate? Serena mulled over that, wondering if her present circumstances were enough self-punishment to fulfill her own sense of guilt and justice.

She'd gotten into wrestling due to quirky fate, attending a match with college friends on a lark and drawing an agent's attention by her stature and figure. He'd slipped her his card, which she quickly dropped in her purse and forgot. That is, until her aunt died and hard luck stepped in.

With no place to live and no means to continue college, Serena had discovered the wresting agent's card while scrounging for change in her purse. She'd phoned him on a whim and, well ... the rest was history, as they say.

It was strange, but as much as she hated the "business", it did fulfill her need for punishment. Working in a profession looked-down-on by most women, putting up with the crude comments and rough crowd who attended, and even wearing an ultra short costume which she found uncomfortable in front of all those eyes were all part of it, and therefore perhaps gave her some sense of absolution.

But, not enough, never enough to cleanse her mind of the belief that she'd caused her family's death. Maybe this is my fit punishment, Serena thought, then quickly discarded it as unacceptable. Even if she deserved her abduction, being taken to another world and forcibly married off, none of the other women did.

Herself ... maybe she didn't deserve saving, but that wouldn't stop her from getting involved in trying in every way possible to secure the other ninety nine women's return to Earth.

Her last thought that night was how odd that she could feel so comfortable laying next to a stranger, and how easily her breathing became synchronized with his after her thoughts had calmed.

* * * *

Rhamus felt a contentment he had not experienced in a long time, since before his father was killed. The rise and fall of his new wife's slow breathing lulled him toward a sleep as deep as hers.

Waking early, as was his habit, Rhamus started to stretch, then stopped swiftly as he looked down and remembered the previous night. The new Queen slept on undisturbed, looking totally peaceful and somehow ethereal in the pale sunlight that bathed her with its rising warmth. She lay draped across his body, one thigh crossing his nearest limb. Rhamus examined the little he could see of his lovely wife at his leisure. It was enough to peak his interest.

He looked closely at her pale skin, so different from his own, and ran one finger lightly down the red-gold hairs on her arm. He couldn't see her exquisite face, and found himself looking at her red hair, almost as if all other choices had been eliminated. It wasn't just one shade of red but, as the sun touched it golden red highlights glimmered among deep shades of mahogany.

Rhamus had never spent so much time contemplating a woman's

hair color before. All Volarnian women had the same lustrous midnight black hair. He found it disturbing that he seemed drawn to a shade of hair he found so detestable. He stroked one hand slightly across the velvety skin on Serena's thigh. Maybe, he thought ruefully, it's because that hair sits atop such a delectable body.

As the daylight that seeped into the room from the large windows turned brighter, Rhamus carefully untangled Serena from around him and went to the bathroom to shower. When he started to step into the cleaning chamber he was surprised by the blood he saw smeared on one thigh. He examined his leg carefully. A warrior must always be watchful of injury and the resulting infection that could overtake him, if not cared for properly.

He didn't remember receiving any blows from the previous day's excursions. Against Hartoos' strident harpings, Rhamus had worked out early in the morning with his closest friends. Nervous about that night's important ceremony, he sought to distract his thoughts.

Finding not even a scratch, Rhamus decided that the blood must have come from his wife. He was concerned that he had hurt her more than he had imagined, and concluded that humans certainly had a different physiology than the Volarnians. Stepping into the bedroom as he dried off, he was glad to see Serena had awakened. He couldn't hide the smile that crept to his face at seeing that she had pulled the sheet from the foot of the bed and covered up. The warm night had precluded any need for covers, but his modest wife found need for them now. "How are you feeling this morning?"

"Fine," Serena answered politely, as if they were exchanging pleasantries across a crowded room, and Rhamus wasn't standing uninhibited and splendidly displayed for her curious eyes. He strolled closer as he vigorously rubbed the dampness from his hair.

"No pain this morning?" He asked casually.

Just as casually, she replied in a dry tone, "No pain."

He gave her an intense questioning look, then walked over to the closet and selected clothes. Feeling safe, Serena propped up against the headboard and watched her husband get dressed. She sat up straighter and squinted her eyes across the short distance.

No wonder I couldn't figure it out, she thought, as she finally identified the difference in Volarnian bodies. Rhamus had not one strand of curling hair upon his chest or legs. She didn't know if this was due to some odd Volarnian custom or genetics.

The King was soon clothed in an outfit that Serena found to be very unusual, but attractive. Gone were the embellished clothes he had worn for the marriage ceremony. Now he was clothed completely in black, just like the other warriors, except the hem and edgings of his costume were trimmed in pale blue.

His crown of lais had been exchanged for a plain headband of dull gold, and he pulled his hair into a loose pony tail at his neck. He wore a wide band on his left wrist of the same golden metal, but again with the basami holding a large arj'ak crystal.

Although the King wore the same basic tunic as yesterday, the skirt was replaced by soft baggy pants. They were made of the identical suede as the skirt. She thought Rhamus looked very primitive, and very handsome.

"I'm curious," she stated as he finished adjusting the fittings of his armband. "Why are you wearing pants instead of the skirt?"

"Skirt?"

"The lower garment you wore last night."

"Simple. We will be riding the yasmir when we go on border patrol, and if you don't wear 'pants' made of rezel leather, your legs will suffer much irritation. And this 'skirt' you speak of, is called a *daco*."

"What is a yasmir?" Serena asked curiously and asked another question before he could respond. "Is it like our horse?"

"I'm not sure what a 'horse' is, but it is our riding beast."

"Are they the animal which has long, shaggy hair--the ones that pulled our carriages here from the ship?"

At his nod, she changed the subject again. "I know the band on your right wrist is the marriage band, but what purpose does the wristband on your left arm serve?"

"Remember, I mentioned the power of the arj'ak crystal is used by warriors." He held out his left wrist toward her. "We channel the power through this band into our bodies, giving us more energy and strength when we fight our enemy." Striding to the bed, he gave her a quick peck on the mouth before she could draw back. "As much as I enjoy your lovely company, I must be going."

As Rhamus reached for the door handle, she asked, "About this border patrol, will you be gone all day?"

"I could almost think you asked because you will miss me, but, in reality, I am sure you will be glad to see me gone for a while. That is why I've decided to go with my warriors on this border patrol, which may take us two to three days, depending on circumstances."

"Circumstances?"

"Uh huh. Dependent on Xarath, the King of west Volarn and whether he decides to engage us in skirmishes or not." At her worried look, which pleased him enormously, Rhamus added, "Don't worry, these confrontations seldom lead to bloodshed."

Serena got to her knees, not noticing that the sheet had slipped and much of her breasts showed, the pink of her aureoles peeking tantalizingly above the blue of the sheet.

Rhamus paused before closing the door, caught by the aching beauty of her disheveled state.

"What am I supposed to do while you are gone?"

Laughing, he shook his head. "I can see you are not worried about me, but about whether you will be bored. Don't worry, my Queen, Hartoos will keep you very occupied with learning about Volarn and the responsibilities that go along with your new position." He left without further comment.

Serena was very agitated by his last remark. How dare he make her sound like some mindless ninny whose only concern was whether she would be entertained while he was gone!

Waiting for a minute to make sure Rhamus was not returning, she sprang to her feet and went into the bathroom. She forgot her distress at his remark, for the bathroom was like stepping into a bathroom fantasy.

As with the one in Surad's suite, the fixtures were made from the same shimmering, pearly substance, but this theme was carried further in the King's bathroom. The large expanse of flooring, which was one-half the size of the King's chambers, was also made of the iridescent material. The rainbow hued substance in Rhamus' bathroom was a little different in that its predominant color was a glow of blue throughout the tiled floor and fixtures.

The walls were tinted the sky blue of the arj'ak crystal, with artful frescos of the native landscape. Serena was impressed by the natural beauty captured by the artist. Carved trim of the lais metal, encompassed the circumference of the room near the ceiling. The valuable silver metal coordinated with the blue colors in the room, for hints of blue light glimmered off its shiny surface.

The bathroom was very ornate, overwhelming her by the sheer richness. She just couldn't picture Rhamus ordering such an elaborate room and wondered if his aunt Surad had a hand in its creation, too.

On the way to the shower, Serena was astounded by a large sunken tub and stopped at the edge to stare in wonder. The tub was large enough to hold several people. Instead of being made of the same material as the other fixtures, it appeared to be crafted entirely from dark blue crystal. Its smooth surface suggested it had been carved from one very large stone.

The spigot was the now familiar dragon in complete form, his mouth open, pointing downward. She guessed that the water poured through the mouth of the beast, but she didn't see a way to turn it on and off. She would love to soak in the tub, but didn't want to wait the length of time it would take for it to fill up.

Serena figured out how the faucets worked when she went into the shower and found the same dragon, but on a larger scale. She had to fiddle with the creature until she discovered that pushing one wing turned on cold water and the other wing hot water.

Very clever, she thought, but a lot could be done to improve the quality of the shower--the water poured down in one big gushing stream of water. Haven't they ever heard of a shower massager, Serena wondered. She took a long, hot shower, feeling her muscles relax. It left her feeling surprisingly refreshed and ready to take on the challenges of her unwillingly adopted world.

Wrapping a fluffy towel around her, she walked over to the discarded black dress, which lay in an inky pool where she had dropped it last night. She turned her nose up at the thought of wearing it again. There were too many fresh memories attached to it that she didn't want to deal with at this moment.

Opening the closet curiously, wondering if she dared borrow some piece of Rhamus' clothing, Serena was surprised to find several of the toga dresses hanging inside. She chose a lovely lavender dress and the accompanying gold belt and jewelry attached to the strange hanger. She'd been intrigued before by the hangers and wondered how they worked. The dress straps lay against a strip of metal, but there were no attachments holding it that she could see. It must be some kind of magnetic system that worked on clothes as well as metal, she thought.

The dress came to just above her knees, which Serena liked much better than the more scantily made black dress. But from the fashions she noticed on the native women, the previous owner of the lavender dress must be quite tall. A light tap sounded at the door. "Come in," she called out.

A young attractive Volarnian entered. "I've brought your breakfast, Your Majesty," she said shyly.

Smiling to reassure her, Serena looked around and saw a small, charming table near the fireplace and motioned for the girl to set the tray on the glass top. Interestingly, the base of the table was made from the same mahogany-colored wood as the floor and fashioned in a strange six-legged structure. Ugh, she thought, as she studied the design. The legs reminded her of insect legs the way they were set straight out and then slanted down sharply at mid-juncture.

"What's your name?" Serena inquired as she addressed the girl and inspected the overflowing platter.

"Lalme. I have had the honor of being assigned as your maid

servant."

"I don't need a servant," she answered, but at the girl's stricken look tried to explain. "I've always seen to my own needs."

"But you are the Queen," Lalme hung her head and whispered. "I am sorry, Your Majesty, I am sure you can find someone who will satisfy your needs, since I seem to displease you."

"Lalme," Serena relented, "of course, I would love for you to be my maid servant." She smiled gently back at the girl who raised her head hesitantly.

"You will have to forgive me, for I have only been a Queen less than a day. You may go while I try to tackle this huge breakfast."

The girl giggled, bowed her head and left. Serena picked up a utensil that looked like a combination fork and spoon and poked at the mounds of food. The cook must think Earthlings are voracious eaters, she thought humorously. A large plate contained two eggs whose size took up the whole dish. She took a tentative bite and found them delicious. Several plates contained sliced and whole samplings of exotic fruit. Serena tried several, found some that were inedible to her taste buds, but a few that she relished.

As she nibbled her way through the substantial meal, Serena examined the elaborate china. The plates, drinking goblet, and pitcher were made of delicate blue china with hand painted flowers of various shades covering them. The pitcher held a violet colored fruit drink, which she found tasty and poured into the exquisitely designed goblet. Beside the flowers painted around it, there were sparkling crystal solitaire gems set inside the heart of each flower.

Turning the goblet in her hand, she noted blue, gold, green and purple gemstones. The stones seemed to serve a utilitarian purpose as well, for they made the slippery cup easy to grasp. When her fingers slid under a jewel, the goblet rested firmly in her grip. Lais also lined the lip of the drinking cup, pitcher and plates.

Serena could almost think that Lalme had been peeking through the key-hole, for no sooner had she finished with a sated sigh then the girl tapped on the door and entered. Lalme smiled happily as she looked at the quantity of food eaten, as if she herself were responsible for its preparation.

"There's a lot of food left," Serena waved at the tray, "but I ate all I could manage. Tell me," she asked. "Is this a normal serving for Volarnians?"

This time Lalme put a hand over her mouth to hide the giggles. "No, Your Majesty, it's just that the royal cook didn't know what you liked, so I guess he included a little of everything."

Chapter Six

"Lalme, can you do me a favor?" She cajoled. At her maid's eager look, Serena asked, "Will you call me Serena instead of Your Majesty?"

"But I can't." The girl exclaimed in horror. "You are the Queen!"

"But if that's what I wish?" She pressed.

"It wouldn't be right." The young Volarnian stood her ground on the etiquette of the royals.

"What if I gave you an order to do so?"

"Hartoos would have my head, Your Majesty."

"All right," she looked thoughtful, then asked, "Since it looks as though we may be spending a lot of time together, what about calling me Serena when we are alone?"

With a pleased tone, Lalme answered, "I guess there'd be no harm."

Seeing the Queen get up and distractingly pat the hairs that flowed from her disordered braid, Lalme said, "If Your Majesty ... I mean, Serena, if you would sit in front of the dresser, I will fix your hair."

"Never mind, I can do it."

Daring to be impertinent, she said, "If you insist on being so self-reliant, my Queen, I won't have many duties to fulfill as your maid. And I really am quite good at fixing hair."

Walking over to the dresser, Serena looked with distress at her messy hair and unconsciously mimicked Lalme's earlier remark, "I guess there'd be no harm in letting an expert work on this." She ran her fingers down a strand of hair hanging annoyingly in front of her face.

She was glad that she allowed Lalme to untangle her long tresses, and she almost nodded off to sleep as the young Volarnian slowly combed it out. But she had to put her foot down with her enthusiastic maid after her hair was put in order. She wanted no hairdo with curled embellishments or intricate weavings, as Lalme suggested.

"You have beautiful hair," her new maid complimented as she ran the brush down the waist length locks. "The color is so wonderful."

Serena returned the girl's compliment. A short time later, she looked in the mirror with satisfaction. They had compromised with pulling her hair into a simple pony tail at the nape of her neck. She had to admit that Lalme's addition of a ribbon to match the dress looked good.

The girl stepped back to admire her handiwork. The red tresses curled in soft waves to Serena's belt. They were chatting amiably for several minutes, starting the process of getting to know one another, when an enchanting bird song drew her toward the balcony.

"That's a sooeul," Lalme informed her.

"Oh, I remember studying about those ... small flying lizards on the language tapes." She frowned. "Are they dangerous?"

"No," Lalme laughed. "They're only aggressive toward each other." She cocked her head at Serena and asked, "Have you seen any of our landscape yet?"

She shook her head. "They didn't give us much of a chance--it was a short ride here in those strange carriages.

"Come on", Lalme waved her arm toward the balcony. "Let me show you some of our gardens, at least from the balcony."

Serena strolled with enthusiasm outside. The temperature was a very comfortable eighty degrees, just as the Moyd's had informed them, even though it was Volarn's summer season.

Rubbing her hands along the large block-shaped stones the balcony and most of the castle were composed of, Serena admired their natural beauty. The smoothly polished stones looked like huge tiger-eyed jewels with their golden hues, creating the illusion further by their indiscriminate streaks of brown slashes strewn across their surface. She let the coolness of the marbleized stones soak into her palms.

Turning her face up to the bright sunlight, she was delighted the two suns were described as in the videos. One sun was only slightly smaller than Earth's, while the other was but a small speck of light. Each sun's distant orbit kept the temperature from being too extreme.

She gazed with pleasure at the gardens below. Strange, exotic plants and flowers of every color radiated away from the castle, growing to the very base of forests giants, at least on this side of the palace.

The lush growth of gigantic trees sprouted thick limbs twisted into interesting gnarly shapes. High up on the branches, a heavy dark canopy of leaves, each as large as her hand, crowned each tree. Serena was fascinated with the deep navy blue of the leathery leaves.

The grass made a soft pale blue carpet with its densely packed growth. Her gaze turned upward to Volarn's sky, which held its own enchantment. Its pale lavender was strange, surreal, and lovely.

Its rich color was softened by wispy golden clouds. Serena began to relax as she soaked in the majestic beauty, forgetting for the moment the uncertainty of her future and simmering anger.

Lalme was pointing out different flora and naming them, when a sharp rapping on the door caused them both to turn in unison toward the door.

The girl opened the door and admitted a sudden rush of people. A lanky older Volarnian male and three women of various ages came swooping down upon Serena. Bowing and acting entirely too excitable, the male introduced himself as Jidroon, the royal tailor. She couldn't remember all the other strange names he rattled off when waving toward his staff members.

The tailor took matters into his hands very swiftly. Feeling as though she were caught in a whirlwind, Serena found her body being measured from all angles, while one of the women jotted notations on a tablet. Jidroon clapped his hands and said, "What a marvelous figure, Your Majesty!"

She didn't know quite how to take his character. The next instant he was fingering a curl down her back and remarking on her lovely hair. She felt like a show horse on display. Yet his attitude was not offensive, but like that of an artist appreciating a beautiful sculpture or painting. Serena felt like she was outside the proceedings, watching as Jidroon ordered his assistants about and brought strips of cloth to hold up against her skin and hair for observation.

Seeing her bemused expression, the tailor remarked, "You will have to forgive me, Your Majesty, it is not everyday one receives the opportunity to outfit the Queen." Holding up a long-fingered hand as if expecting her to protest, he continued. "Do you like this particular shade?" One of his assistants held up a deep mauve sample of silky cloth.

"Yes, I do like it. But before we go further in choosing colors for dresses, can you tell me more about the previous Queen?"

"Previous Queen?" Jidroon seemed distracted by the question as his hand flitted through an offering of rainbow hued swatches draped over one of the women's arms.

"The lady who was the Queen before me? I don't even know if Rhamus has been married before."

"No, the King has never been through the Tarthra with anyone else. The last Queen was his mother," Jidroon informed the present Queen.

"Oh. Is his mother still living?"

"No. She died giving birth to the King's sister, Kasha, some twenty years ago."

"Um."

"I know what you mean, you'd think someone of her age and stature would know better than to pull the pranks--" Stopping in mid sentence, Jidroon looked a little uncomfortable. "I am sorry, I rattle on so, Your Majesty. Of course you would know nothing of Kasha's little jokes."

"No, I don't, but I understand she's the one behind the black uniform I wore for the marriage ceremony," Serena commented dryly.

Jidroon shook his head in agreement. "Now, Your Majesty," he held up a breathtaking sample of iridescent white, "how do you like this fabric?"

"It's wonderful." She touched the lovely piece. The tailor and his assistants spent some time showing her the samples they had brought with them and discussing different designs. Although all the dresses were of the toga type, some had slip straps, while others had a strap across one shoulder only. Some styles were straight cut with slits on one or both sides, while other styles were gathered at the waist.

The Queen and royal tailor disagreed in one area of creating the costumes for a royal personage. Jidroon wanted the classic toga styles with many trimmings, designs and ornamentation, while Serena favored some of the more distinctive styles of Earth, with less adornment. They finally compromised when Jidroon agreed to produce some of Serena's homeland stylings for special occasions, and the Queen agreed to let Jidroon add more detailing to the ceremonial dresses.

They would be gorgeous creations, and Jidroon expressed both anxiety and anticipation to see his people's reaction to his new work. As they conferred about several more ceremonial dresses, Serena began to realize just how much she was enjoying herself. She had buried longings for princess dresses and Cinderella dreams along with her childhood and her family. A bittersweet smile formed on her lips as she thought of the little Serena of long ago and how beautiful she had felt as she paraded in front of her parents in some full-skirted confection made by her mother.

Smoothing her hand down a short length of unbelievably soft material that Jidroon held for her approval, Serena asked, "How is this cloth made, by weaving?"

"Weaving?" Jidroon's brows drew together a moment, then cleared in understanding. "Oh, weaving. You mean like the looms make for the farmer's wearing apparel?" The tailor became distracted by a pale yellow scrap he held up excitedly next to the

Queen's deep red hair color. He'd never experienced so much fun in creating costumes before, with the interesting coloration differences offered by Earthlings hair and eyes. He mumbled distractingly, "The *konkol* weaves it for us, of course."

"The konkol? Is it like our silk worm?"

"Worm! No, the konkol is no such creature as a lowly worm."

Jidroon went on to explain about the weaver of cloth and Serena took a step back in horror. He had just described an animal that sounded too much like a spider. Except, if Jidroon was to be believed, the konkol was a monstrous size compared to Earth's varieties.

"We have whole factories of those industrious creatures. Why, we even do a pretty good export business of their silk to other planets."

A wave of her hand and the stricken look on her face convinced Jidroon to change the subject, but he couldn't figure out what he had said to upset the Queen. He took on a professional air and efficiently finished his task of helping Serena select a wardrobe fit for the King's consort. He departed with his staff members, informing Serena that they would have her daily wearing apparel ready and delivered in three days.

Serena had really enjoyed the time spent with the royal tailor and his assistants, until he mentioned the spider-like konkol. She walked briskly out through the large double doors leading to the roomy semicircular balcony. Serena took several deep breaths of fresh air to clear her head of the disturbing image of lunging spiders, and gazed at the beautifully landscaped gardens. She hoped that soon she would be able to explore the gardens at her leisure, their sweet perfume held the promise of beauty. The pleasure of nature was always relaxing to her.

A trilling, warbling sound drew her attention away from the scenery and back to the doors she'd just passed through. Looking around curiously, it took Serena a minute to locate the direction of the wondrous chirping. Her eyes opened in shock and she shuddered as she spied the largest spider web she'd ever seen stretching from one corner of a door cornice upward to the stones nearby.

Not waiting to try and find the bird that was responsible for the singing, Serena ran back inside, stopping only to slam the doors shut tight. She continued on hurriedly until she reached the middle of the room. Her heart raced as she stared in disbelief and trepidation at the closed balcony doors. Serena was happy for the third interruption of her morning, when a knock rapped lightly at the door. Surad entered cheerfully.

"What's wrong, my dear?" She inquired, concern edging her voice when she noted Serena's pale face and enlarged pupils.

"Nothing," Serena responded automatically. She waved off Surad's attempts to find the source of her fright. She didn't want to even think about what she'd just seen, much less discuss it.

"Well then, we better be on our way." Surad took her nearest elbow companionably and strolled with her to the door.

"Where are we going?"

Surad screwed up her face comically. "I'm afraid you are scheduled to attend training under Hartoos."

"Oh," she glanced worriedly at her escort. "You make it sound as fun as a day of basic training."

As they walked slowly down one of the castle's long hallways, Serena found herself answering Surad's curious inquiries concerning her remark. She enjoyed the older woman's company, deciding her first impression of Surad had been right. She was a kind, gentile lady, and her demeanor only added to her noble persona.

Her appearance was as unique as the lady. No streak of the Volarnians' fabulous black hair showed in the thick gray braid Surad wore over one shoulder. And though she had many wrinkles around her eyes, she was still very attractive. Surad was as tall as Serena, her thin frame straight with pride, portrayed through her fine bearing.

She, and other elderly Volarnian women did dress differently though. Their typical apparel was the now familiar toga style dress, but were floor length instead of above the knees.

Serena could easily answer the elderly lady's questions while examining the wonderful and elaborate hangings on the stone walls. She didn't know how she'd missed these fantastic pictures painted with painstaking detail when she'd traversed these halls yesterday.

They entered a room to find all the other women from the ship. Accompanied by the loud buzz of conversation and awed, jealous glances shifting her way, Serena was led to a front row seat that apparently had been reserved for her. It stood out from the other chairs with its elaborate carvings of the basami dragon. She craned her neck looking for Nicole but couldn't spot her curly head anywhere.

A Volarnian male strode to the front of the room. "Good morning, ladies. I am Yarra, one of the royal tutors. Today we will begin your introduction to Volarnian history and culture." She found it fascinating, but after several hours passed she was glad when lunch was announced.

Two young girls came in and escorted them to a dining area. A deliciously fresh salad of their native crunchy lettuce was served along with several choices of some type of light colored meat. Serena stuck to the salad and the tangy dressing--she'd eaten far too much breakfast and was not very hungry.

She tried to question as many women as she could during their lunch break to see how they were managing. Many of the women were still confused and angry, reflecting Serena's own feelings. Others seemed to be in bliss.

Serena noticed Olga several seats away and was surprised by her quiet manner. Maybe marriage agrees with her, she thought. All too soon, the group was directed back to the instruction room.

She was stopped by one of the girls and directed to another door just down the hall. Hartoos respectfully greeted her, saw that she was seated in a comfortable chair, then began immediately to lecture on the etiquette of the nobility. Serena found Hartoos's teachings much more tedious than Yarra's. His monotone, self-important attitude and dry subject combined to make her feel like a young school girl.

It didn't take long before she began stifling yawns behind her hand. The afternoon wore away slowly. When Surad finally appeared to guide her back to the royal suite, Serena was never so happy to see another person. She was very glad when Surad informed her that she could spend the rest of the evening in the bedroom, dining there if she wished. At first it was a peaceful time as she relaxed in the big, comfortable chair and thought about all the interesting people she'd met since coming to Volarn.

Serena sat up sharply when her wondering mind suddenly crystallized on one hard truth. She'd been floating through her experiences since yesterday, as if the arj'ak's power still affected her. *What's wrong with me? Wasn't it just last night I was thinking of escape?* Serena sat for a long time sunk in the chair's softness, no longer concerned with relaxation, her mind a stew of thoughts and plans.

The next morning when Surad came for her, Serena was ready. "Surad, I am really concerned about the other women. As Queen, it is my duty to see to their welfare, even before my own. Isn't that right?" Serena hoped that playing to Surad's sense of duty as a royal would get her what she wanted.

Surad shook her head in pleased surprise. "Yes, Your Highness. It's good that you are worried about others' welfare. What are your thoughts?"

"I think it'd be nice to convene a meeting with the other women before we go for our daily instruction. I want to speak to them, see how they are doing, and see if they have any problems they need help with."

The older woman patted her arm. "That's a wonderful idea, Your Highness. I will tell Hartoos as soon as we arrive at the tutoring room. Of course, he will have a fit," she shrugged her shoulders, "but a Queen's wish comes before an advisor's, even if he is instructing the Queen."

"Two more things," Serena stopped her before they left the room. "Can Nicole be sent for, to attend the meeting? She is my best friend and I really need to see that she's doing OK."

"Of course, Your Highness. I'll send a guard to fetch her. And the other request?"

Serena asked the older woman to call her by name instead of "Your Highness". She was surprised by Surad's quick acceptance.

True to her word, Surad stopped a warrior outside the royal chambers and sent him after Nicole.

When Surad informed Hartoos of Serena's wish, he fumed for a minute, but then graciously gave up the room for the meeting. The women were starting to filter in slowly, apparently not overly concerned with Hartoos' insistence on punctuality. Serena began questioning them one by one. She had spoken to quite a few by the time Nicole arrived, excited and out of breath from running down the corridor.

"Serena, the guard told me you called a meeting of all Earth women."

"It's good to see you too," she laughed as they hugged. It didn't take long to surmise that Nicole was one human who was content with her stay. She was fascinated with all the new medical information she was learning from the alien doctor, and still found him interesting, too. Beside, Nicole knew that she was to be allowed to go home during the next "shipment".

"How's everybody else here doing?" She asked Serena after they strolled apart from the other women for a few minutes of private conversation.

"I haven't had a chance to speak to each one yet, but a few have me worried. There are some women who seem relatively satisfied with the turn of their lives, but one is very depressed. I'm not sure who I feel more worried about."

"I guess I can understand how those 'satisfied' women feel, but what's happened to the sad one you mentioned?"

"She has a fiancé back home and has crying spells." Serena paused for a moment and looked toward a slim black haired girl who could have been no more than eighteen.

"Can you go to Rhamus about her problem?"

She was glad her friend lumped them together in the solving of a difficult problem. She was going to need Nicole's assistance the most. "I could go to Rhamus, but I've thought of a more permanent solution for all of us."

"What?" Nicole's eyes grew even larger with excitement.

"Escape."

Serena's hand on her shoulder kept Nicole from repeating the word in a screech. Instead, she whispered, "Escape? How?"

"With the ship," she ignored Nicole's look of disbelief. "You're the only one who has maintained contact with Pulack, Rolan', and the ship. Do you think you can find out how the ship is run? For example, does it take both Pulack and Rolan', or can just one of them pilot the ship to Earth?"

"I already know the answer to that."

"How?" Two voices asked the question, and Serena turned to see that Olga had slipped in close to them. She repeated her question, ignoring Olga's interruption and Nicole's bristly response to her.

"Rolan' and I both had some free time on our hands this morning. Pulack is off on a trading trip for several days, traveling by carriage, and Doc went to take care of a sick expectant mother. Rolan' started telling me about space travel and I happened to ask him about piloting the ship."

"Unbelievable," Serena said quietly.

"Oh no, it's true, he told me all about it. He can run the whole ship with the help of the robot, even though Rolan' is just a beginner pilot."

"I didn't mean I did not believe you, Nicole ... just that it's unbelievable timing. And that Pulack left at such an opportune moment. By the way, why didn't Rolan' go with Pulack?"

Nicole giggled. "He's allergic to yasmirs. What did you mean by everything being timed so well?"

"What better opportunity would we have to escape?" Serena eyed Olga meaningfully and got a responding nod of understanding. "Many of the husbands are gone on patrol, this is only the second day Hartoos is instructing us, thus no one has a clear picture of how he will be conducting his classes."

"What do you mean?" Nicole asked. Olga looked on curiously.

"I've got a plan, one I thought we could put into effect in a few days but I think the sooner, the better."

"You're right," Olga said. "I've spoken to some of the other women and I suspect several of them might turn us in if they found out about any escape plans."

Nicole sucked in her breath in horror. "You're kidding?"

Olga's serious expression and vigorous head shaking convinced them that she was on target in her assumption.

"Why would they betray us?" Serena asked in a low voice.

"Who knows for sure?" The blonde shrugged. "Maybe the magic from that Tarthra thing still has them in a spell, or maybe they led such pitiful lives back on Earth, they'd grasp at anything that seemed better. All I know for certain is that some of them talked of 'love at first sight' with their husbands, and they already think their men walk on water." Olga's lip curled up in the familiar distaste she liked to display at any person or subject she found objectionable.

Serena was astounded at Olga's depth of emotional understanding of the women in question, an assumption she might have made too, if she'd spoken to those same women.

"What about you, Olga? You seemed pretty chummy with your husband?"

Serena had the same thought as Nicole, but would have worded it more diplomatically. They didn't need any squabbling amongst themselves now; it was imperative they be united in their cause. Serena watched the expressions flitting across Olga's face and was pleased that when she responded to the impertinent Nicole, she chose to address her as a parent speaks to a wayward child.

"It's true I like Zares very much," she looked off in the distance for a moment, as if puzzled by her reaction. "I can't say if it's love I feel, since I have never been in love before. But I do know one thing. I want very badly to get back to Earth."

"Why?" Nicole asked.

"You are determined to know all my business, aren't you, brat?" Her eyebrows drew together threateningly.

Serena placed her hand in a calming gesture on Olga's forearm and gave Nicole a stern "shut up" look. "We mustn't fight amongst ourselves now."

"You're right," Nicole said guiltily. "I'm sorry for being such a pain." She addressed the larger woman directly.

Olga looked at both of them briefly. "I say we call a truce, at least until this is all over." Serena and Nicole nodded their agreement. "I guess I will answer your question now. Maybe I would be suspicious of my behavior with Zares, if I were you. You want to make sure I'm not one of those others." Olga's derisive tone made it clear she meant the women she suspected would betray them.

Again Olga looked off in the distance, as if searching for something. "I *must* get back to Earth. You see, my brother Eric is missing, and I have to find out if he's still alive or ... dead."

"But no one was supposed to be brought here if they had relatives," Serena said in puzzlement.

"That's right," Nicole confirmed. "Rolan' said they used a truth ray on us, and asked all of us if we had any relatives living. It would have brought unwanted attention on their mission to kidnap women with relatives. Too much risk that they'd eventually be found out."

Olga frowned in concentration. "I was so depressed for several days when I heard Eric was missing and presumed dead, that my mind only concentrated on the 'dead'. I guess when the Moyds questioned me, that's the answer I gave them."

"What happened to Eric?" Nicole asked gently.

"He was a Green Beret and was deployed to some country, I don't know where. You see, we had a falling out several years before, about a boyfriend Eric didn't think would be good for me. He was right, but that didn't change all the arguments and bad feelings. We'd stopped talking the last year and Eric's best friend, Tom, took it on himself to tell me what went on in Eric's life. Then he'd tell Tom how I was doing."

"A go-between for brother and sister?" Serena said sadly.

A distressed expression came over Olga's face. "We're fraternal twins and we've always been close, until our big argument. We're both very stubborn, I'm afraid." She stopped for a second at the "humph" sound Nicole made at her last statement.

"What happened?" Serena asked.

"Eric and Tom were deployed to the same country. Tom was killed, so my connection was broken. The military tried to track me down, but I'd moved several times, and Tom was the only one who knew my current address. Apparently Eric hadn't given his superiors my address."

"How did you find out Eric was missing?" Nicole asked softly.

"When Tom didn't contact me for a few weeks, I finally called his post. It seemed like it took a zillion phone calls before they got me in touch with Eric's commander.

When they confirmed that I was Eric's sister, they gave me the bad news." Olga gave Serena an odd smile. "That's why I was so ... angry the night of our match. It'd only been a few days since I heard about Eric and Tom."

"I'm sorry, Olga." Serena's eyes shimmered with unshed tears. "I lost all my family when I was young."

"And I lost my mother two years ago," Nicole added, then, "When are we going to kick alien butt?"

Chapter Seven

Serena and Olga laughed at her remark and Nicole joined in after a few seconds.

"We're not going to kick anybody's butt," Serena said. "But I think we ought to seize the opportunity that's been handed to us."

"I agree," Olga said. A silent communication seemed to spring between them. "You were perhaps thinking today would be a good day for an outing?"

"My thoughts exactly." She glanced around the room. "We need to get organized and move out *now!*"

"Now?" Nicole whispered in shock as she jumped to her feet and followed the larger women as they approached the others.

* * * *

How could things have gone so wrong? Serena and the other women were surrounded by warriors, probably a whole patrol. She looked up at the nearest one and then down at herself, sprawled on the cold metal floor. Sitting up carefully, she found her strength returning quickly. She got to her feet and the others followed suit.

The warriors, very kindly she thought, directed them out of the ship using a small door on the far side. I guess that answers my question about another door, Serena thought glumly. They were directed back into the carriages in which they'd come. Nicole sat next to her, still groggy and silent. She thought back over the last hour and how close they'd come to escaping this planet.

After making the decision to try for a break, she had carried out her plans with Olga and Nicole's help. First, Serena had hidden a dagger under her dress, one of many that decorated the walls around the castle. She pulled it out and briefly looked at the ornate handle with the large arj'ak crystal in its center. It must have belonged to someone important, Serena smiled grimly to herself. Now the dagger had more important services to render than decorating a wall.

It had been fairly simple at first and everything went surprisingly smooth. They'd waited until Hartoos made his appearance. Serena threw her arm around his throat in a choking grip and stuck the knife to his side, just enough for him to feel it there. When she told him her plans, he blustered and tried to talk them out of it, but finally quieted and went along with them.

Hartoos had gone to the door and called to a guard, giving him instructions while Serena stood behind him out of view, the dagger keeping contact with his flesh through his shirt. The guard gave the advisor an odd look when he requested carriages to carry all the women, but soon the vehicles had pulled up near the back entrance.

The warriors driving them looked annoyed to be detailed to such duty, but none of them appeared suspicious. Apparently, Serena thought, Hartoos was known for his eccentricities in teaching. Everything went off without a hitch. The warriors dropped them off in front of the ship and, as instructed by Hartoos, drove off to return the carriages and yasmirs back to the stables.

"You won't escape, Your Majesty," Hartoos said again, one of many times he'd tried to negotiate with the group.

"Looks like we're doing a pretty good job so far," Serena said in a pleased voice. "Those warriors didn't even question your orders to take the carriages back." Serena still pressed the dagger into the man's side.

Hartoos sighed heavily and shook his head sadly. "Did you fail to notice, my Queen, that not all your numbers are even here?"

"What do you mean?" She pressed the dagger slightly as alarm flashed through her.

"First, can you please put the dagger away?" He requested. "I know your skills in fighting and I think I am outnumbered enough that I cannot escape." At Serena's withdrawal of the knife, Hartoos took a deep grateful breath.

"OK, the dagger's gone, so what did you mean?"

"Look around, count if you wish, but you will find that not all one hundred of your Earth women are here."

Serena's quickly glanced around the milling women. "We suspected as much. It doesn't matter, even if those women are squealing on us right now, we'll be gone in no time." She prodded Hartoos and directed the women to follow her.

Once everyone was inside, she asked the computer to shut the door, which it did obediently. She looked around and located what looked like the control panel for the outer door, then with Olga's help, she ripped the panel cover off, exposing the wires beneath.

Gritting her teeth in anticipation of a shock, Serena cut the wires, but no sparks erupted. She requested the computer to open the doors, but nothing happened.

"That takes care of any interference from the outside," Serena grabbed Hartoos by one elbow. "Computer, where is Rolan'?"

The familiar red beam appeared, and the women followed, Serena dragging a protesting Hartoos along. When the beam stopped and the door slid open, Rolan' stood transfixed by their sudden appearance. He was inside a small galley, his hand stuck inside a jar.

"Your Majesty," Rolan' said, as he extracted his hand from the container. He could only see her, Hartoos, and Nicole in the open doorway. "What brings you here?"

Serena smiled. "We're here to get you to pilot us back home."

"Back home?" He looked shocked, then shook his head vigorously. "I'm sorry, but that's impossible."

"Don't mess with me, little man," she threatened, taking a step closer. "Did you know I could easily break your arm or do all kinds of damage to that soft body of yours?"

Sweat broke out across his forehead. "Yes. I imagine you could, but it still wouldn't help."

"Oh? You think you're tough enough to withstand a beating?" Olga said as she slid past the group at the door and stood next to Serena. Both women's angry countenances said they meant it.

Droplets of sweat ran down his face. "Beating me up won't help. I can't get this ship off the ground!"

"Wait a minute," Nicole said. "You told me this morning that you could pilot this ship."

"Yes, I did," he admitted. "But what you ladies don't understand is that our fuel is depleted right now."

"That can't be true," Serena growled angrily.

"It's true!" Rolan' took a step forward, hands held out pleadingly. "We use arj'ak crystals, but they only last a few years before they have to be re-powered. Why, this very minute, our crystals are being powered up by Volarnian technicians."

She took a threatening step forward and Rolan' stepped back. Serena's face showed she did not believe a word of what the alien said. Nicole put a restraining hand on her upraised arm, the hand fisted and ready to strike.

"I know a way to see if he's telling the truth or not. We could use the truth ray on him."

"Do you know how to use it?"

"Sure do. Yesterday I was asking Doc about it and he showed me how it works. And he said it was safe to use on any species."

Serena looked at Rolan' who didn't seem worried a bit about Nicole's proposal, and that worried her more. Gathering the women, she nudged Rolan' and Hartoos to a faster pace, as Nicole led the way to the medical area. The lab was packed when they all crowded into it a few minutes later.

Nicole went over to a bookcase and withdrew a small oblong

object. She directed Rolan' to sit in the only chair in the room. His large eyes looked sorrowful as Nicole approached with the truth-seeking instrument, fiddled with some buttons on the machine, then pointed it at Rolan'. A thin blue beam of light shot out and struck him between the eyes.

"Tell us everything about the fuel needed to run this ship," she said matter-of-factly.

Rolan' started talking, his sentences ran together, reminding Serena of the way Nicole talked when she became excited. A great sinking sensation hit her stomach as he repeated the same information he'd given earlier, adding details of how the Volarnians processed the crystal.

"Anything else you want to ask him," Nicole turned to Serena, unable to keep the disappointment from her voice.

"How long before the technicians get the crystals finished and bring them back to the ship?"

"Probably two more days."

Nicole switched off the ray hitting Rolan's head. "Do you think we can stay here for two more days?"

Serena shrugged. "I just don't know. I think I've sealed off the port door effectively, but there may be another." She looked at the instrument Nicole held. "Ask him if there are any more doors, and how we can defend ourselves from outside attempts to get in."

As Nicole started to turn back to Rolan', he quickly said. "Computer, execute order 7-0."

Everyone looked around in confusion as a hissing noise erupted into the room. A sharp-smelling mist came pouring from the ventilation shafts. Desperately, Serena grabbed a sheet off the examining table and dashed over to the nearest vent, attempting to stop the vapor. She had half of it covered, when the odorless smoke insinuated itself into her lungs and her body began going limp. She crumbled slowly to the floor, losing her sense of sight before she passed out completely. She could not see that all the others were falling to the floor as well, including Hartoos and Rolan'.

Now, here they were in the carriages again, headed back to the castle. As the huge palace came into view, Serena felt a great sadness well up. Flashes of memories from home nudged at her mind. A bitter anger at her own failure to aid herself and the others depending on her, overcame the sadness.

"Serena, no one could have done better. How could we know Rolan' had some secret code to knock intruders out?"

She laughed derisively. "We might have if I hadn't jumped the gun and let a few days pass while you ferreted out information."

"Don't be ridiculous," Olga snorted. "In a few days, our husbands will be back."

"She's right." Nicole urged her friend to listen to reason.

Serena looked at them both, united for the second time today in a common cause. She smiled wearily at them, tears brimming in her eyes.

"At least you--we tried," Olga said. She stared at the women in the nearest carriage. "If not for you, or me, none of those mice would have tried anything." She turned back to Serena, gaining her eye with an intense look. "Now our husbands know we are women to be reckoned with. Ja?"

Taking a deep breath, she released some of the tension she'd been holding in, feeling better immediately. "Yes, you're right. We should never be willing to go down without a good fight."

"Bravo!" Nicole agreed. "You might not have kicked alien butt, but you certainly showed them not to take you for granted."

They smiled at their much smaller companion. "Include yourself in that statement. We couldn't have gotten as far as we did without your help," Serena said and Olga nodded in agreement.

Nicole smiled happily back at them, basking in their approval. The carriages stopped suddenly. They all turned and looked at each other. A deep quietness overcame the three as they were led back to the tutoring room.

"I think we've have enough excitement for one day," Hartoos said, taking control of the situation. "You ladies may retire to your rooms."

Surad appeared immediately and walked with her back to the royal suite. She waited for the older woman to make some remark about their attempted escape, but she didn't. Surely she knew what had happened?

Her companion informed her there was an hour break before she would return and take Serena to the banquet hall for dinner. Serena tried to protest; she only wanted to spend some quiet time alone, not be bombarded by new people and more conversation.

"I can understand how you feel, my dear. Once you have been Queen for a while, you will not be expected to attend every dinner in the banquet hall. But at this time it would be wise to give the nobility of Volarn a chance to become acquainted with their new Queen."

She looked wearily at Surad. Serena plopped down in the comfy chair after Rhamus' aunt left and closed her eyes. She opened them in surprise when Surad tapped on the door to gain entrance later. Had it been an hour already?

Surad made a tsk, tsk sound when Serena stood up. She began to straighten the Queen's clothes, then combed her fingers through the young woman's mussed curls. Finally, she stepped back and shook her head at her polishing efforts. Not the appearance one wanted in the King's consort, without the proper clothes and jewelry, but presentable.

Surad reassessed her own opinion when she examined Serena's statuesque figure, lovely features and unusual hair. Her nephew's wife would look beautiful in any outfit she chose to wear, even the more rugged clothing worn by the garden workers would appear majestic on such a figure.

The two women, one older, dignified and of Volarnian descent, the other a young, fair Earthling, made an interesting pair as they strolled into the dining hall. Serena felt uncomfortable when Surad showed her to a large chair at one end of the long table. She looked down the polished length of the table at the many strange faces staring back at her.

Her examination stopped at the other end of the table, which was occupied by the King's pretty sister. The princess was chatting to the nobles on either side of her. Serena could swear the girl's lip curled in disdain while staring rudely in her direction. Kasha whispered to the young people grouped around her.

That's all I need, she thought, another sour grape like Olga messing up my life--not that it wasn't in a jam already, she thought glumly.

A kindly male voice interrupted her thoughts. "I wouldn't let her attitude bother you."

Serena looked at the elderly gentleman who had spoken to her with a charming clipped English accent. He sat next to her, on the right side, so she guessed that meant he was a noble of some importance. He appeared to be even older than Surad, for many lines creased his face and his long fine hair was pure white. His eyes shone with dignity and gentleness, qualities she found appealing.

"You mean the King's sister?"

"Yes." He pointed toward the other end of the table. "Kasha has ruled too long as the only love in her brother's life. I would venture to guess that she is resentful of you."

"If she only knew how much I don't want the King's attention." Serena was embarrassed when she realized the Volarnian man had overheard her mumbling to herself. "I'm sure she's heard about the failed escape today."

"No, it's not that at all. True, Kasha and everyone else here know about what happened. But, our people would expect no less from themselves if they were in your place. The Volarnians respect your attempt, but that doesn't change Kasha's jealous attitude."

"How do you know so much about the princess?"

The old man smiled fondly at the subject of their discussion. "Because I was her tutor during her youth and I know that willful spirit thoroughly." Dipping his head in a bow the old man said, "My name, Your Majesty, is Nuad."

Smiling pleasantly back at him, she inquired with little hope in her voice, "I guess there's no use asking you to call me Serena instead of Your Majesty?"

"Actually, it is considered proper etiquette in Volarnian society for the nobility to call the King and Queen by their given names in private, if the royal consorts so desire, Serena." Nuad leaned near and whispered the last statement. She smiled at his reply.

She was soon enjoying their conversation of mundane happenings of the court, and gathering more useful information about the people of Volarn than she'd learned all day from Hartoos.

On her left side was a younger woman who seemed to interrupt constantly. Serena found this annoying since the lady in question was quite boring with her gossipy talk, and irritating with her snobby attitude.

A stream of servants appeared, bearing large platters of food, which they distributed along the table and offered to guests. But first they set an astounding selection around her end of the table. Thank goodness the talkative lady seemed to love eating and spent the rest of the evening paying attention to the delectable dishes being offered, Serena observed.

Nuad kept a running commentary on the dishes being offered so that Serena would become familiar with them. She smiled, seeing the teacher coming out in her dinner companion.

Glancing down the table, she noticed a servant paused several chairs away as an attractive young woman delicately selected a shelled creature from the platter.

The talkative woman picked up two of the creatures and began tearing into them with vigor. The delicacy was a shelled beetle about the size of her hand, with a small head and many legs sticking out from the edges.

The deep purplish gleam of its shell made her queasy. Clapping one hand over her mouth, Serena fought to hold back the bitter taste rising in her throat.

"Is something the matter?" Nuad questioned, concerned.

Pointing at the creature, she asked. "What is that?"

"It's called an *auk*."

Finally seeming to notice her queasy look, he asked, "Is something wrong, my dear?"

"No. You see, on my planet, we have an insect called a beetle and the auk looks just like one. But we don't eat beetles on Earth." Not wanting to insult him, Serena didn't add that the Volarnians' eating of giant beetles would be seen as disgusting back home.

"I see," Nuad shook his head understandingly. "It's a cultural difference, but one I'm sure you will overcome."

"Do you have any other kind of meat besides these beetle creatures?" She asked hopefully.

"Yes, we have elag meat."

"What is an elag?" Serena asked cautiously.

"It's a ...what is the English word?" Nuad looked thoughtful, and then said with sudden remembrance, "Similar to your bird." He described the exotic peacock-ostrich birds she had seen when approaching the castle.

"Great. Do you think I could try some of it?"

"Of course, my dear, but you may not like it." He paused and then with a grin and a shrug, added, "It's an acquired taste."

It took a while, but eventually a servant set a tray of dark, stringy meat before her. A sharp, acrid odor rose from it.

"Your elag."

Serena took a small slice. She knew immediately that she definitely did not like the taste. It was very tough and sour. She finished that piece and valiantly reached for another one.

"Please, don't eat it if you don't like it," Nuad urged.

Serena let the slice drop back on the plate. "You were right, it's pretty awful. I just hate that I requested it and now I can't stomach it."

"You are the Queen of Volarn. You do not have to make excuses for your behavior," he lectured.

"And even if you were not the Queen, we can't expect you to love everything about Volarn."

She wished the Volarnians had such a tolerant attitude toward marriage. They certainly expected all the women to be head over heels in love with their handsome mates.

Staring down at the food, Serena thought out loud, "I wonder what Rhamus is eating tonight?"

"Probably wild auk."

"I hope not elag," she laughed.

"Not unless they had extremely bad luck in the hunt for their dinner," Nuad remarked with a smile.

* * * *

Rhamus got wearily off his yasmir and stretched to get the kinks out of his back. He and the patrol had ridden hard all day. He'd urged them on until his youngest warriors sagged in their saddles, and even his most experienced warriors shot questioning glances at their leader.

Making their usual rounds, they stopped to check with farmers and remote fortresses for activity from the western Volarnians. They found that Xarath and his troops had been causing minor problems and some patrols from the most remote fortresses had engaged in a few skirmishes.

Fortunately, there had been only one serious injury to his troops. The deep laceration one young man had sustained in a sword battle had festered and infected the warrior's body with a deadly bacteria. The *naci* germ was responsible for the missing limbs of many retired warriors. If a healer was not near enough to help, the only choice to save a warrior's life was to cut off the infected leg or arm.

Dr. Melat had shots, which could save a warrior's life, but only if given very shortly after the wound was sustained. With Rhamus' support, Doc had trained one warrior in each patrol and equipped them with the necessary medical supplies. Rhamus became frustrated as he thought of the many Volarnians who refused the doctor's modern medicine, choosing to seek out the vassi's aid instead.

The young warrior's friends had become separated from the patrol during the fighting. Unable to locate the medic for the preventative shot, they tried to reach a healer. By the time they had managed to get him to a vassi, he was suffering the high fever and convulsions that signaled his impending death.

Stripping off his shirt, Rhamus splashed cool water from a pan over his shoulders and chest. He felt more refreshed as trickles of the water cleansed the dusty road dirt from his upper torso. He thought with anticipation of the hot bath awaiting his return. He wished he could as easily wash away his sad thoughts of the young man's death. He turned in surprise at a loud chuckling from behind him. Jarvic was slapping his thigh in merriment.

"Cousin, I don't remember running into an alati while we were on patrol."

Jarvic's idiotic grin irritated Rhamus and he growled, "What foolishness is this? You know we did not see even one of those dangerous felines during this whole patrol."

"Well, your back certainly looks like it did, Your Majesty," he pointed out cheerfully.

Rhamus twisted and tried to see his back but to no avail. He rubbed one hand across his lower back and encountered the faint tracing of a scratch. Puzzling as to whether he'd run into the thorny bushes of the *inlo* tree without realizing it, he continued to rub the scratch as if that would revive his memory. And, in fact, it did as he remembered the heated exchange with his new wife and her clutching at his back during the heightened moments of their lovemaking.

Grinning at Jarvic, he remarked, "It seems I did run into a female alati, the kind that you want to leave marks upon your body. Maybe you'll be so lucky next time in the Tarthra."

Rhamus had the last laugh as his remark hit home, and Jarvic gave him a droll look. He strode over and gave his cousin a slap on the back.

Several of the younger warriors, including Jarvic, went out to hunt for dinner. As he relaxed and talked over the day's events with Zares, the group of young men returned. Each of them had speared a wild auk on the end of their sword. One of the younger recruits had made a sloppy job of his kill by spearing the auk through the body instead of the heavy muscles joining the head and body. His kill gaped open; entrails and liquids dripped along the route he took to the cook's pot. The young man's face was pale with embarrassment from the ribbing piled on top of his head.

Rhamus lounged back and watched the good-natured teasing. As the auk began to sizzle and cook within their own shells and send out an enticing aroma, he nodded off to sleep. Zares shook him awake a short time later. Even though the auk's smell was tantalizing and his stomach rumbled with hunger, he wished his friend had let him nap a little longer.

Rhamus was having the most sensual dream about a fiery-haired maiden with skin like silk and wild, wonderful hands that sent bolts of pleasure shooting through his body.

As his straight white teeth tore through the tasty auk meat, he wondered what his wife was doing and if she was surviving her first day as Queen.

Chapter Eight

The meal was sumptuous and really quite good, excluding the beetles, which Serena was trying very hard to put out of her mind. On the ship she'd learned from the video tapes that any food the Volarnians ate, humans could digest as well. Only they failed to mention the nasty tasting elag.

Thanks to Hartoos' teachings, she knew to keep eating slowly until most of the guests had gotten their fill, for when she finished, all guests had to stop eating too. Feeling as though she couldn't take another bite if her life depended on it, Serena finally put down her napkin, signaling the end of dinner.

Nuad took her elbow in a gentlemanly fashion to escort her to the throne room, where he informed her there would be entertainment. She had studied ballet as a child. Her natural curiosity forced her to admit that she was looking forward to her first glimpse of music and dance from this strange planet. Maybe it would take her mind off her great sense of failure from the foiled escape.

When Kasha rose and started toward them, Nuad slowed his pace and politely waited for her to reach them. The princess smiled and complimented Serena's attire. She was a little suspicious of her pleasant attitude, so different from her rude glances earlier in the evening, but began to relax somewhat when Kasha's conversation was filled with humor and polite questions concerning Earth.

Maybe I've misjudged her, Serena thought. She couldn't help but notice how changed Kasha's appearance was from the day before. Yesterday she'd worn the Getra uniform, tonight she wore a softly feminine mauve toga that set off her black tresses beautifully. They were the same height, some few inches shorter than the norm for female Volarnians. Kasha's curves were slimmer, her muscles toned, her features exotic, sultry.

Serena shuddered when she saw one part of her new relative's costume, an extremely large brooch perched on her left shoulder. She remembered the royal tailor's description of the konkol and guessed that the ornament was fashioned after the spider creature.

The brooch must be a real life representation of the creature, for the size and color were exactly as Jidroon had told her. It was only a few inches in diameter, but its long spidery thin legs made it appear larger. The black body hair, shining with dark blue highlights, looked surprisingly soft and stuck out two inches from the creature's body and legs. Its large red eyes seemed to twinkle with lively interest.

Kasha kept making polite conversation, then she casually reached up and stroked the back of the konkol. Serena's eyes widened in shock and her breathing froze as the brooch came to life and stretched its back to receive the caress. One of its long hairy legs reached out and stroked Kasha's hand in mutual affection, and a humming sound came from its nightmarish body. She heard someone screaming shrilly. When Nuad anxiously shook her, she realized she was the source.

Looking around in a daze, Serena saw that some of the guests were staring at her in open-mouthed wonder. Kasha's mouth, however, was stretched in a jubilant smirk. Nuad took her arm and quickly and efficiently escorted her out the door. Before Serena even knew it, she was at the door of the King's suite.

Once inside, Nuad still maintained a grip on her elbow in a reassuring manner and guided her to sit in her favorite stuffed chair. He walked briskly to the wine decanter and, pouring a large goblet full, brought it to her.

Serena took the glass mechanically and gulped the fruity wine down like water, not even noticing its rich flavor. After it hit her stomach, a relaxed feeling began to seep into her bones and she could unclench the fists in her lap. Nuad sat across from her and leaned forward to pat one of her hands kindly.

"You don't have to tell me what that was all about, unless you want to ... but I'm a good listener."

She looked at Nuad closely and saw nothing but gentle sincerity. "I don't like to talk about it, but I guess I wouldn't mind telling you."

He smiled encouragingly. "Sometimes it helps to talk about those things that we fear."

"I don't know if you are aware that many of my people are afraid of spiders."

At Nuad's confused look, she explained, "Our spider and your konkol could be cousins, except your spider is huge compared to ours back on Earth."

"My dear, I had no idea." Nuad looked surprised. "But I have a feeling there is more to the story."

"Yes," she shook her head in agreement and paused in reflection. "When I was a little girl, I was bitten by a spider."

"Bitten?" He repeated in astonishment. Seeing Serena's annoyed look, he said, "It's not that I don't believe you. It's just that the konkol are very gentle, even the wild ones will only bite in defense of their young. Konkols are kept by many of our people as pets."

"Pets!" Serena shuddered at the image. "Our spiders *will* bite, and even though they're very small, many of them have poisonous venom."

"How old were you when this happened?"

"Five."

"That must have been a terrible experience for such a young child," Nuad said emphatically.

"And that wasn't the worst of it," she disclosed, feeling more comfortable with Nuad's sympathetic behavior. "The venom from the spider that bit me caused the skin around the bite to...." Serena paused a moment, looking ill. Taking a deep breath she continued, "It can cause flesh to be eaten away." She pointed to the side of her right calf where a large scar was discernible. "It took a long time to heal and was very painful." Nuad was staring at her strangely and she couldn't decipher the train of his thoughts.

"I am truly sorry you had to experience this encounter with our konkol during your first public appearance as Queen." He stared off in the distance and mumbled to himself, "I wonder if Kasha knew about spiders?"

"She certainly did!" Surad came swishing suddenly into the room and went to stand behind Nuad's chair, placing one hand on the back.

"Woman, how could you hear me clear across the room?" He sounded irritated.

"How could I not hear you," she replied saucily. "You forget your age, and the fact that I've warned you more than once that your voice comes booming out at the most inappropriate times."

Serena bit her bottom lip to keep back the smile that threatened to break out. She had a feeling there was more than met the eye when it came to Surad and Nuad's relationship.

"What do you mean Kasha knew about spiders?" Nuad questioned. "I happen to know personally she doesn't like to sit down and learn new information that she doesn't find useful. She has flatly refused to attend any of the lessons Hartoos and his assistants have given on Earth culture."

"Ah, but Rhamus specifically told her to leave her pet in her room until we could get the Earthlings used to the idea of having the konkol around. He knows about this natural fear many humans have of ... their konkol."

"This is very distressing and embarrassing." Nuad stood up and paced.

"Yes. I want to apologize for not being at the dinner tonight my dear, so I could oversee matters properly. I was sitting with a pregnant mother who has been sick." Then turning to Nuad, she said, "Don't worry, I will take care of this problem."

"You know Kasha will not listen to you."

"I don't intend to deal with her weird quirks of ill humor," Surad answered smoothly. "I will simply inform Rhamus of her behavior upon his return."

"Please," Serena interjected. "I don't want to be the cause of a scene between brother and sister."

"That's very generous of you," Surad replied. "But you will find that there are times when Rhamus has to pull Kasha's reins in. Don't worry any further," she smiled kindly.

The older Volarnians stayed for a few minutes more, exchanging veiled comments toward one another, which had her in a better frame of mind in no time. After they left, Serena reflected on their conversation. She'd never been called "my dear" so many times since becoming acquainted with the two older people. It was another quirk of the Volarnian language, the elderly used endearments for the young people, especially "my dear". On further reflection, Serena decided it was kind of nice and did make one feel cared about.

Her dreams that night were filled alternately with huge spiders who tickled her skin with their long hairs as they tried to crawl up her legs, and a dark-haired lover who caressed her thighs and sent an urgent longing pulsing through Serena's sleep. She woke suddenly and completely from the last dream and looked down in surprise at the fine sheen of sweat clinging to her skin. Her right hand lay upon her thigh in a caressing posture. Still in the grip of slumber's twilight edges, Serena wondered if she'd stroked herself in her sleep, as her imaginary lover had done.

It took a long time for her to regain sleep's embrace. She almost wished for the return of the terrifying spider-filled dreams, rather then the ones filled with her handsome husband and his far more disturbing presence.

The next morning, bleary-eyed and tired, she found it hard to concentrate on Hartoos' lectures, and yawned in an obvious manner, hoping it would shorten the advisor's lessons. Her efforts were to no avail, for she had to spend the whole afternoon being instructed in the duties of royalty. *Why do I have to be subjected to all this?* These are not my people, she fumed.

Serena was very grateful when she was finally escorted back to her room. She was happy to hear the servant announce a two hour break before dinner, but distressed that she would be required to go through another ordeal with Kasha at the dinner table. She napped on the large bed and woke befuddled when a knock came on the ponderous door. She'd slept almost all the time away. Surad entered carrying feminine attire in her arms, followed by the enthusiastic Lalme.

"That rascal Jidroon spent all of today sewing you a dress fit for a Queen," Surad said enthusiastically, holding up the iridescent material Serena had admired yesterday. The cloth had been made into a dress, which shimmered in Surad's hands, the light catching the varicolored hues reflected in each soft fold. It was a simple toga style with two slip straps and slightly gathered skirt.

"Can't I just have my dinner in my room?" She questioned wearily.

"Serena, I know how you must feel." Surad paused at her young charge's dismissive look and explained, "I may not have your fear of spiders, but I do have an embarrassing fear of the sooeul. And every time I see one of those creatures, I just want to run the other way."

Apparently Nuad had filled her in on the details of their conversation. "Those tiny lizards?" Then Serena added in the next breath, "Why is it embarrassing?" She found her interest piqued in spite of her worry.

"It's a harmless little flying animal. But when I was small one flew in my long hair and became entangled. I hit at it trying to dislodge it, and the poor thing was chirping shrilly in my ear."

Surad paused, but continued on, as if determined to finish her tale. "When my mother finally came to help, it was dead." Surad shuddered. "So, you see, every time I see one of those little things, I shriek and run for cover."

Serena could almost laugh at the picture of the dignified Surad screaming and running to hide from a small harmless creature. But the older Volarnian's irrational fear was too closely allied to her own to dismiss lightly.

Feeling closer to the older woman, she asked, "Surad, why haven't you asked me about the escape?"

Smiling gently, she answered, "I already know all I need to about it. No one blames you or the others for trying."

Then, clearing her throat to draw Serena's far away look back to her, Surad switched subjects completely. "You must show up for dinner tonight, if only to dispel the talk concerning the incident last night, and show Kasha a thing or two about the proper behavior of royalty."

"Will she have her pet with her?" She questioned anxiously.

"No. I have instructed the guards to not allow her into the banquet hall if she tries to pull that stunt again," Surad confided with calm assurance. She held up the wondrous dress. "Now, let's dress you as befits a true Queen." It didn't take long for Surad to help gird her in the regal costume.

Serena did feel more confident when she looked in the tall mirror at her changed appearance. The dress fit perfectly, which by Volarnian standards meant its length touched her mid-thigh. The silky material clung to her body, showing off its curves beautifully. She was slightly uneasy with the amount of cleavage the low neckline revealed, but knew letting one half of the bosom peek above the neckline was normal for evening wear.

Sliding one hand down the sides of the dress, Serena noted the way the undergarment fit and made the look of smoothness outside appear natural. It did away with the necessity of wearing bra and panties. The Volarnian undergarment wasn't tight or uncomfortable, and was made from the same silky material as the dress.

A delicate, lacy belt of lais with matching headband, earrings, and armband, set off the gown's color perfectly. The lais was so lightly made that it appeared to be a heavy thread with a metallic appearance. It picked up the multicolored hues of the dress, and the rainbow shades shimmered off the accessories as she moved.

The intricate laciness of the pieces were set with many small arj'ak crystals. The slipper shoes complimented the dress with their reflective iridescence and edging of lais and tiny crystals. Between the lais metal and the arj'ak crystals, she knew the whole outfit was priceless.

Serena started to pull her hair back into a pony-tail after brushing it out to shiny waves, but Surad stopped her hand and requested that she allow Lalme to fix it for her. Her maid pulled her hair from her temples into a high pony-tail, leaving the rest to cascade in flowing waves and ringlets. When Lalme finished her coiffure, Serena had to admit it had the element of simplicity that she liked, yet gave her an elegant appearance.

The headband held one large crystal in the center of her forehead, as if proclaiming her Queenly state. Lalme wrapped a matching piece of crystal decorated lais around the pony tail. Surad clapped her hands together once in appreciation.

Lalme exclaimed, "You're the most beautiful Queen ever." Never mind that she had been too young to remember Rhamus' mother, the last Queen.

She couldn't help the shiver of apprehension that ran through her as she and Surad approached the doors to the banquet hall. Nuad was waiting nearby and escorted both of them to their seats. Serena was thankful that the old gentleman again sat on one side of her and Surad took up the seat on her other side. She looked around for Kasha, but the wayward princess was nowhere to be seen.

Feeling freer without the presence of the disapproving Kasha, or maybe coaxed by her guardians on either side, the other guests began to chat in a friendly fashion to her. Surad related in a quiet voice to the nobles nearest to her a shortened version of why Serena feared konkols. Serena soon saw how quickly gossip could spread, as jewel-bedecked ears were bent in the retelling of her story. At first she was slightly miffed at Surad for sharing her dark secret, but then saw the wisdom of the older woman's actions as she noticed a difference almost immediately in the assembled nobles' expressions.

No timing could have been more perfect than the entrance of the princess at this point. Kasha strolled in nonchalantly and plopped down tomboyishly in the chair at the end of the table. She gave Serena a smug look, then finally seemed to notice the disapproving glances directed at her from many of the guests. Serena hid a smile as she noted the quietness at the other end of the table, contrary to the raucous behavior that Kasha and her friends had displayed last night. The friendly banter at her own end of the table made Serena feel more comfortable with the nobility.

The food was as rich and abundant as it had been the night before. This time she had a good appetite and did justice to the overflowing platters set before her. Not wanting to be taken for a coward she ate several large pieces of auk. To her happy surprise, she enjoyed it. Nuad shook his head, pleased with her acceptance of the Volarnians' favorite meat.

Serena stared at Kasha across the length of the table and plastered a huge smile on her face at the princess's sour expression and dark petulant eyes.

Nuad leaned over and whispered, "Best not to make an enemy of her."

Picking up a piece of fruit and nibbling at it delicately, she remarked, "Who's making an enemy? I hope she and I can eventually be on friendly terms if nothing else. But, I won't be intimidated by her ferocious stares."

"It seems the rumors are true," a woman sitting next to Nuad commented.

"What rumors?" Serena asked suspiciously.

"That you're a fighter." Surad commented with a wicked air. "And it's quite true," she nodded conspiratorially to Nuad.

"A fighter?" He questioned in surprise.

"Yes." She smiled. "Does it surprise you that an Earth woman is capable of being a fighter like your Getra?"

Nuad patted Serena's hand. "Don't get me wrong, my dear. It's just that I wasn't aware that you had female warriors on your planet."

"That just proves what I've been saying all along," Surad interjected dryly.

"What?" He questioned cautiously.

"That in spite of your reputation as a widely knowledgeable teacher, you don't know everything."

"You're a wicked old woman with the tongue of a basami!"

Serena worried that the two elderly people were on the verge of a verbal battle, but soon saw that it was a verbal game they probably played often, and enjoyed immensely. She listened to their amusing remarks fly back and forth across the space of the table and found her mind drifting. Serena wondered what Rhamus was doing and when he was coming back. More importantly, what was he going to say about her attempted escape?

As if her very thoughts had magically conjured him, her husband came striding through the door surrounded by his warriors of noble rank. They paused upon the threshold and greeted various friends and family. Rhamus waved a hand downward to the guests who started to jump up at his presence. The warriors were covered in dust and looked extremely tired, but apparently in good spirits to be back home again.

Jarvic immediately planted himself next to a very attractive young woman and started teasing her, to the annoyance of her husband sitting next to her. The other warriors took up empty chairs scattered along the table, apparently left vacant in case of their early return.

When Rhamus started toward her, Serena couldn't help but admire the way his muscular thighs flexed and bulged to the rhythm of his ground-eating stride. She had been startled at first that the King and his warriors would put in an appearance at the elegant evening meal covered in grime. But then, the King of Volarn was not a figurehead--he was a soldier. Serena could also smell the wafting odor of male sweat mixed with the strong scent of the yasmir.

None of the other guests seemed to pay the slightest attention to the warriors' state of dress or their earthy, manly odors. Serena did not find the musk odor coming from the men offensive either. The yasmir's odor at the dinner table might take some getting used to, but she'd never been finicky.

A servant brought the King's chair forward and placed it beside

Serena at the head of the table. Rhamus greeted his aunt and old friend cheerfully before turning his attention to his wife. "How are you faring?" he asked pleasantly.

"Fine," she answered, feeling ill at ease with his overpowering presence so close now.

"What have you been up to?"

"Just ... you know, learning a lot of new stuff." She glanced nervously at Rhamus and saw laughter twinkling in his eyes. "You know?" Serena asked accusingly.

He grinned. "Of course, as does everyone else," and waved a hand toward the nobles.

"And I guess you think it's very funny--"

Rhamus interrupted, "No. I don't think it's amusing. In fact, I salute your effort. I was just surprised you got as far as you did."

"Why, do you think I am incompetent?"

He laughed as he nonchalantly picked up her hand and kissed it in a gentlemanly fashion. "On the contrary, I think you're capable of much, it's just that I would have expected such a brazen act from a Volarnian." He ignored her attempt to pull her hand from his grasp.

His expression turned serious. "That's why I ordered a guard just for you, and Rolan' is working on more security measures for the ship."

"Great," Serena couldn't keep the distress from her voice.

"I missed you, my wife." He grinned wickedly as if they shared some secret longing. His light, playful kiss caused a strange reaction. She felt warm and needy, as if she wanted to reach up and stroke that wondrous hair and feel the masculine outlines of his rugged face. Serena's eyes were glued to Rhamus' lips as he spoke and a little warm spot in the center of her stomach lit up with the teasing caress of his voice and remembrance of his passionate kisses. The charming way he turned her defeat into a brave attempt made her feel mollified somewhat.

"Did you not miss me, even a little?" He held up two fingers and measured a tiny space between them, his eyes taking on a sorrowful expression.

Serena couldn't stop her warm smile in reaction to Rhamus' silliness. "As a matter of fact, I did miss you." At his confident grin that sprang immediately to life, she added, "It's been hard being a new Queen all by myself. It would have helped to get some guidance from an old pro like you," she finished sweetly.

"I can see I will have to work harder to burn the memory of our time together in your mind, before next I leave on patrol."

At his words, Serena's mind jumped back to the memory of their last night together and her cheeks flushed hotly.

"Ah-ha!" Rhamus said gleefully. "Maybe I won't have to work quite as hard as I thought." At Serena's sour expression, he changed tactics. "Now, my Queen, I have a fierce hunger. One will have to wait a bit to be satisfied, but the other can be taken care of immediately."

He reached across Serena to take a large handful of auk. His arm brushed against her breast, causing a tingling sensation. The King seemed to have abandoned all the finer points of etiquette as he tore into his meal with gusto.

"So, Nuad, tell me what my sister has been up to?" Rhamus questioned suddenly after he began to slow down his eating pace.

"What do you mean, Your Highness?" Nuad asked cautiously.

"I know my sister. She acted nervous when I greeted her at the door." Rhamus stared at the three of them, each in turn. "I know she's pulled something. The question is, when are you going to tell me about it?"

Surad cleared her throat. "I have every intention of filling you in on Kasha's latest escapades, but I don't think now is the time." The King's aunt inclined her head toward Serena. "You have only just returned to your new wife. I don't think you want to disturb your first reunion with your sister's misbehaviors."

Rhamus folded his arms and relaxed back in the large chair. "This all sounds very mysterious, but I guess it can wait."

She sat quietly as the three Volarnians discussed several small incidents that occurred while Rhamus was gone, and he was questioned about the patrol. Serena learned much by listening attentively to the natural flow of conversation, much more than she could absorb from Hartoos's dry teachings. She learned of the hard, disciplined life of the Volarnian warrior and the dedication of those soldiers to preserving their way of life.

She was upset when Rhamus told of the young man who had died, as if she knew him personally. Serena's quiescence didn't last long, she was too curious. "Why doesn't the United Federation step in and stop the fighting between you and the west Volarnians?" Serena interjected rationally, glad that she'd listened closer than she realized to Hartoos' lectures.

All three stared at her as if she had sprouted wings like the basami. Rhamus chose to answer his Queen. "If we let the Federation 'step in', they would place a governor to rule and eventually take control of our planet. They are not the benevolent benefactors many of my people believe them to be."

"Oh, I didn't realize." Serena looked thoughtful.

"Then how do you keep the Federation from taking over the planet, anyway?"

"That's a good question, Serena." Rhamus smiled at her astuteness. "The Federation knows we could easily use the power of the sacred crystal again, if we choose to, and only their most powerful weapons could possibly defeat it."

"And by doing so, they would destroy the environment on the planet, making it useless to them," Nuad finished. "Of course, we can't expect Serena to understand the implications involved. She is used to a different governing system and has never been exposed to a galaxy-wide one."

Rhamus looked at her thoughtfully. "The next time you have lessons with Hartoos, get him to go into the dynamics of the interplanetary systems."

Right, Serena thought, I'll be sure to do that.

Rhamus slapped both his hands lightly on the table. "My friends, I take my leave of you." He stood and patted his stomach. "I've had my fill of good food and pleasant company, now I can't think of anything I'd enjoy more than a good hot soak in my tub. And the delightful company of my Queen." Rhamus extended one hand to draw her up beside him.

Chapter Nine

How could she refuse to go with him in front of all these people, Serena thought to herself. They made a leisurely exit, stopping to exchange pleasantries with his people along the way.

Rhamus paused near his sister's chair and remarked, "I understand you and I are due a discussion." Kasha's pale face told him that Nuad was right on target as usual.

After arriving at the royal suite, he began to immediately undress and Serena nervously puttered with objects on the dresser as she watched him covertly. Even with her anxiety as to his next move toward her, once he was nude, she couldn't help but admire his hard physique. He surprised Serena when he walked into the bathroom instead of approaching her, but then feeling silly in her forgetfulness, she remembered just how badly her husband needed a bath. He had even expressed that desire out loud.

"Serena," he called after several minutes passed and she heard the tub filling with water. "Can you come scrub my back, please?"

She was torn with indecision. She wanted nothing more than to stay as far away from a naked Rhamus in a tub as she could, and she wanted to answer his reasonable request so that she could have a legitimate excuse to gaze upon that perfect male body.

Giving in to her curious, lustful side, Serena approached Rhamus slowly. His head was laid back against the wide rim of the tub, eyes closed in complete relaxation. She could almost see the tension and weariness seeping from him.

Opening his eyes, he smiled gently at her, then raised one hand and pointed to the edge of the tub. "Why not sit and talk for a few minutes, tell me about your time as the new Queen."

Finding this unthreatening, Serena gladly sat on the edge and stuck her feet in the tub after removing her slippers. The water was quite warm and gently effervescent. She filled Rhamus in on the events of the past two days, highlighting the more interesting and leaving out those incidents she'd just as soon forget. Serena giggled when she told about Jidroon's visit and his consternation at her wanting a different kind of dress.

* * * *

He lay with half closed eyes listening to Serena talk, watching her unobtrusively so she wouldn't feel uneasy. She appeared younger, more carefree as she absently splashed water with her toes. He noted the transformation of her features as she smiled when telling him of the enjoyment she received from Jidroon's dry wit, her trials with Hartoos, and her problems with the auk.

He wondered idly what it would take for him to bring such warm smiles to her face. Rhamus slowly examined the lines of her face through hooded eyes, noting the high cheekbones and slender nose.

His eyes were drawn to the mass of red curls that tumbled about her shoulders and he had a sudden urge to run his hands through their weight. He curiously noted the odd way Serena's hair came to a slight point at the center of her forehead. His people didn't share this human divergence, but he found it interesting and saw that it gave her face an enticing heart shape. He wondered how she felt about her failed escape attempt, and was determined to change her mind about wanting to leave, both Volarn and him.

After Serena stopped talking, she trailed her feet through the water slowly and stared dreamily at the ripples, almost as if she had forgotten his presence. "Would you mind scrubbing the dirt off my back?" Rhamus held a sponge out to her.

Looking askance at him, she said. "But I'll ruin this gorgeous dress if I get in the water." She held out the delicate skirt for emphasis. She felt as though it had brought her luck tonight in dealing with the dinner and Kasha.

He grinned hugely. "I guess it's too early in our marriage to request that you strip down and join me," he said with a fake sigh at Serena's mutinous look. "You may join me in your dress. Don't worry," he added at her disturbed look, "the material made from the konkol's silk is extremely durable and water won't hurt it a bit."

At her hesitation, he remarked, "Just slip off the jewelry and the dress will be fine." Leaning back wearily, he said, "I really can't do justice to washing my back." Stretching his arms in a careful manner, he added, "My shoulders ache from wielding my sword so much."

It didn't take Serena but a minute to unclasp her jewelry and belt then, quickly undoing her hair, she twisted it in a high bun. She eased carefully into the slippery tub. Standing but an arm's length away from him, she inquired. "Do you always fight battles with the west Volarnians when you go on patrol?"

Rhamus kept his eyes slitted so as not to alarm his charming wife, who was still as skittish as a young yasmir. If she could see his eyes fully, she would be unnerved by the scalding heat they contained. He had been momentarily disappointed when she put her long tresses up, for he wouldn't be able to run his hands through it as he longed to do. Her efforts at slipping slowly into the tub worked, but failed to leave her dress unscathed, for water had sloshed upwards and coated the front with wetness.

The dress plastered itself to her like a second skin and he noted with rising pleasure the dark pink nubs, which showed clearly through the now transparent cloth. His cini reacted, becoming stiff with the need for her. Lazily, feeling anything but such emotion, Rhamus answered, "Most of the time we don't run into our enemies. Usually we only find the damage they've left behind. The infrequent periods when we do run into each other always end in a skirmish." He threw the sponge the short distance into his wife's hands and watched as she approached thoughtfully and fully unaware of the danger zone she entered. Rhamus turned slightly and presented his broad back for her ministrations. Serena scrubbed his back thoroughly, knowing how good that must feel to tired and aching flesh. She couldn't resist writing her name on his back and giggled at her own childishness.

"What are you doing back there?" He tried to peer over one shoulder, then turned around to face her completely. "Since I can't see what you were up to and you don't seem inclined to tell me, I insist you do the same for my chest."

"You insist!" Serena tried to sound appalled, but fell far short when his playful tone and boyish grin pulled a responding smile from her.

"Yes, I think I am still King and as such, I can order my subjects to do as I wish." He looked down his nose at her in a thoroughly haughty manner.

Rhamus' attempt to stare her down went against everything that she had learned of this man so far. She covered up another giggle that threatened to escape. "But I am the Queen." Serena threw her nose up in imitation of his haughty pose.

"Ah," he reached and grasped her nearer hand, "but even the Queen must be subject to the King's ... desires."

Suddenly their game took on a more serious quality and Serena found that she wanted the play to continue, no matter what direction it took. She stepped close to Rhamus and sponged water over his wide chest, and then traced her name on his front. She found that breathing seemed harder standing within the circle of his arms, that she'd dropped the sponge, but her hands continued to rub his firm chest in large circular strokes.

"Is this how Earth women mark their mates?" He asked archly.

"Hmm," she almost purred. "No, but maybe it's not such a bad idea."

He ran one callused hand up and down her left arm, as if washing her in return. Shivers of pure pleasure ran up Serena's arm at his caressing. She extended her strokes to include his large biceps and felt them bunch in reaction to her touch. She looked in Rhamus' eyes and saw the unveiled heat of his gaze and knew that a similar longing was reflected in her own eyes. He ran his hands up both her arms, pressing and kneading gently. Then his hands slid down her back and began a circular massage to the small of her back. Serena felt herself relaxing completely.

It seemed only natural that both their arms went up in synchrony and encircled one another's necks, both rubbing each other's napes in a continued assault on their sense of touch. Their kiss was slow and befitted the languorous feeling that seemed to surround their coming together. Rhamus slowly slipped Serena's dress down, exposing her lush breasts to the strong rhythmic pressure of his hands.

Her senses were invaded with the soft swish of the warm water as they moved, the feel of his steely body beneath her exploring fingers, the wonderful taste of the soft flesh of his mouth, and the texture of his tongue as it played havoc with her own. And then there were the hot stabs of pleasure he caused to shoot throughout her body, wherever his experienced hands rubbed and stroked.

A few deft caresses of his hands around her hips and her dress slid down. Serena kicked the last barrier between their bodies off in one quick movement. Rhamus' hands regained their purchase on her slick body and began a further stroking of her hips and upper thighs. She sucked in her breath at the heated contact of their lower bodies, her soft mound against his hard male member making her feel utterly feminine.

Her body was flushed with heat, especially the joining of her thighs. The delicate flesh felt swollen and achy. Serena had come to recognize her response as sexual desire and welcomed it. She wanted Rhamus. Wanted him to bury his hard cock in her.

When he raised one of her legs, it took Serena a moment to realize what he intended. Before she could protest that this feat seemed impossible, he'd raised her up and wrapped both her legs about his waist and entered her slightly. She stared with wonder, realizing that the strength needed for this position did indeed reside in his bulky arms. She guessed that the buoyancy of the water didn't hurt either. Her channel gripped him firmly and she sighed as he stroked in and out. His large staff seemed to soothe the aching inside her.

Watching her face closely, Rhamus slid slowly inside the innermost part of her body, stopping only when he filled her

Myra Nour

completely. Her languid expression gave him all the signal he needed, that she suffered no more pain, unless pleasure could be called a pain of sorts. He began an unhurried rhythm as old as time itself, and his wife responded with little shuddering quakes of her soft body that told him he had picked out the right keys to their mutual enjoyment.

At Serena's lustful response, his cini became even harder. She whimpered when he plunged into her with one thrust. But her face told him it was a pleasurable response. His balls were tight, as if a band choked them. His wife's seductive movements almost sent him over the edge, but he maintained control by using his powers of concentration.

Serena's head whirled with erotic images and her body quaked with wavelike sensations as Rhamus continued his invasion on her senses. She felt as a creature apart from herself because until today she had not been aware of this person who resided inside her. This person who groaned and stretched her breasts up so her partner could reach them with his strong hands and soft tongue. This woman who wiggled and undulated upon her husband's staff, making him groan loudly in response.

The frothy bubbles natural to the water, plus those stirred in their movements, created an erotic feeling against Serena's highly sensitized skin. It was if those bubbles were invading her body somehow, running through her veins in tickly, sensual rivulets. Fire ran through her veins and she moaned. She gripped his neck tighter, shoving her hips forcefully upon his cock. Her slick inner flesh slid easily against his hard length, eliciting a need for relief.

Her breath came in short gasps and Serena noticed that Rhamus' breathing seemed more labored, too. She knew the minute he reached his orgasm by the clenched muscles and his loud moan, just as she felt her inner body clutch at his member and catapult her into her own release. Her head flopped weakly on his neck and she savored each slow stroke of his engorged staff. She shuddered and panted against his skin as tiny orgasms quaked through her.

After a minute, he eased Serena down his body and she reveled in the sensation this created. He stretched back down in the tub, truly relaxed now, and pulled her down to sit beside him. Serena found herself relaxing too and almost drifted off to sleep. But Rhamus' voice kept her somewhat alert as he told her funny little quips concerning his patrol, thankfully leaving out any details of the bad things that had occurred. He played gently with her fingers and Serena somehow felt very cherished by that simple act.

Serena's head jerked up from a nodding doze when Rhamus

stood up abruptly and drew her up to stand beside him. Looking at him questioningly and sleepy-eyed, she was caught off guard when he placed his arms under her knees and picked her up like a little child.

He stood her up after he reached the bed and, taking the towel he'd laid out earlier, quickly dried himself. He spent longer toweling her dry. Her nipples were hard from contact with the air, but as he ran the towel over them, they became painfully tight. When he reached her legs and asked her to spread them wider, she sucked in her breath. Her lower lips throbbed as he dried her inner thighs and moisture gathered between them.

Feeling a little like she was caught in a dream, Serena watched as he reached up and undid her hair. He smoothed the tangled curls with his fingers slowly, and she thought the sensation of her husband gently combing out her hair as sensual as if he were caressing her in more intimate places.

Next, he gently guided her to lie down and stretched out beside her. Rhamus whispered huskily to her words of love. She couldn't understand every word, since he spoke in Volarnian, but it still had the sizzling effect she had pictured in her dreams, of an imaginary lover courting her with a sexy foreign language. Her lover spoke an alien tongue, but one which still had sensual sounds. Shivers ran down her neck all the way to her hips as he continued his verbal assault on her senses while driving her crazy with his probing of her ear lobe with his tongue.

He was giving too much, she thought, so grabbed his head, turned it and began to give Rhamus back the same treatment he had accorded her. The skin on his ear was warm and somehow licking it caused a lance of pleasure to shoot through her pussy. It didn't take but a few strokes of her tongue and he was groaning and whispering her name. Her own response increased as she found the power that she held within her grasp to turn him on. She was squirming and her clit beat erratically.

A short time later, he was again making love to her, but fast and furious this time. She grasped his buttocks hard between her hands and pushed him back and forth, helping him, urging him on to an even more furious pace. He placed her legs over his shoulders, giving him deeper penetration. Serena panted and closed her eyes. Ecstasy swirled around and around through her body. Groaning, she pulled him down for a kiss. He sucked her panting breaths into his mouth, and that excited her even more.

Rhamus pulled back and then got off her. "Ride me."

His words were an order, not a request. He stretched out, his large cock rigid and filled with blood. Serena didn't care if he was being bossy, she wanted to do as he commanded.

Licking her lower lip, she gazed at the purplish head. Deciding to take back a bit of control, she bent down and placed a kiss to the tip. Rhamus' breath hissed and his cock jerked. She had never performed fellatio on a man. The thought made her insides liquid fire, but shyness at such an act and fear kept her from sliding her lips upon his flesh. What if she bit him?

He watched her as she positioned her body over him, his eyes molten pools of purple flame.

"Yes," he groaned as she slid oh so slowly down onto his staff.

Rhamus' hands circled her breasts and she leaned down so they hung over him. His eyes turned darker as he gently squeezed her mounds. Pulling her toward him, he sucked one nipple while she undulated on his cock. The harder she plunged upon his flesh, the more forcefully he pulled on her nipple.

"Oh." She panted and pushed his head tighter to her breast. Her vagina clamped around his rigid length, her inner muscles tightening, then releasing.

Giving her nub a last lick, Rhamus pushed her body up into a straight position. Getting the hint, Serena rotated her hips, grinding her lips against him. Placing one hand behind her, she rubbed his thigh while the other hand played with one of his nipples.

Her clit was being pulled back and forth by her movements, and her channel was gloriously filled with his hard flesh. She moaned, and then shuddered as several orgasms gripped her. She felt Rhamus' cock swelling inside her.

"Come for me," she demanded, feeling the one in control now.

"Argh," he growled, spilling his seed in forceful bursts.

Flopping forward, she caught her breath while atop his body. Then giving him a quick peck, she rolled off and snuggled by his side. Rhamus gathered her in his arms, her back to his chest, his arms encircling hers. Serena's breathing finally slowed to a normal rate and she stared off into space, wondering about the wild lustful woman she seemed to have become. She had spent years disciplining herself, leading a rational, calm life (other than being a woman wrestler some nights).

She did not recognize the sensually responsive woman of a few moments ago, and never knew she existed. Serena did not mind that her body and mind seemed so keyed into sexuality, she was just surprised and felt slightly embarrassed. *What did Rhamus think of this wild woman he held?*

Serena found out in the next few minutes when he spoke with

enthusiasm of their coupling. He seemed surprised only that Earth women were as capable of being responsive, as apparently Volarnian women were, in the sensual realm. She relaxed deeper in his arms as she realized he thought nothing strange about her behavior, but seemed to welcome it wholeheartedly.

Stroking his shoulder, she stopped in puzzlement and looked closely at his arm, stretched across her waist. Her eyes opening wide, she realized that he truly did not have one hair upon his skin. "Rhamus," Serena inquired, "are Volarnians hairless, or is it perhaps a custom for your people to shave their body hair?"

"Hairless?" He responded with his own puzzled tone. "We have much hair growing upon our heads, as you can see, and quite a bit in our nether regions too." He chuckled. "And what do you mean by *shaving*?"

"You know…." She waved one hand uncertainly. "When you scrape off the hair on a certain part of the body, using a sharp instrument to do so."

"Sounds quite tedious," Rhamus stifled a yawn and then tweaked Serena's nose playfully. "But to answer your question, my curious wife, we don't grow hair on any parts of our body except those I already mentioned." He rubbed one hand up and down Serena's arm. "Unlike you hairy Earthlings."

"Hairy!" Serena sat up and twisted to look with annoyance at her husband's laughing face.

His eyes moved lazily down to his wife's breasts, which jutted out impudently. Still keeping his eyes glued to her chest, he said, "If you wish to continue our discussion, I'd suggest you lay back down." Glancing wickedly into her eyes now, he added, "Or are you interested in less talking and more action?" He stroked one breast for emphasis.

Serena's quickly reddening face told him that it hadn't occurred to her, to his relief. He knew he wouldn't do justice to his lovely bride if they had another active bout of lovemaking. Their two heated sessions were too much even for a strong man such as him after two hard-ridden days on patrol.

Laying back down and wiggling to get into a comfortable position, Serena finally found a good spot, like a kitten cuddling down in a warm blanket.

"Thank the sacred crystal you finally got comfortable," Rhamus said dryly. "Your wiggling was about to start something up again."

She turned her face up and caught his mischievous expression but, glancing down, she could see the rigidity, which had risen up under the sheets and knew he wasn't just teasing.

"By the way, I'm glad you were still here when I got back."

She gazed into his eyes for a few seconds and then closed hers, feigning sleep. She had to admit to herself, there was a small part of her that was glad too.

Rhamus awoke early and looked down at the beautiful young woman sharing his bed. They had moved during the night. Serena lay stretched alongside his body, one leg casually draped over one of his. He noted her long, thickly lashed eyes were still closed in slumber. He wanted to see them open so he could gaze into their breathtakingly blue depths, as luminous as the arj'ak crystal. But her sleeping state gave him an opportunity to examine her beauty without threat of her withdrawing from him.

Her full lips tempted him, but he still did not wish to awaken her, so resisted kissing her to wakefulness. Her long tresses were fanned out behind her and draped over parts of himself and her. He breathed in the fresh herbal scent coming from her red curls and brushed his free hand through the silken mass. Rhamus picked up one long tendril and watched in fascination as it curled around one of his fingers, almost as if it had a life of its own.

"I thought you didn't like my hair?" Serena said, catching him in the act of playing with it.

He jumped guiltily and a sheepish look came over his features. "Let's just say I might have been hasty in my judgment," he said diplomatically. "It certainly has qualities I find very attractive." He brushed his hand down her hair again.

Serena tugged the curl out of his hand and asked, "Certain qualities?"

"The length--I love long hair." He tapped one finger on his chin as if in deep contemplation. "And it's extremely soft to touch, I like that, and ... the curls are fun to play with."

Pushing hair out of her face, she struggled to a sitting position with as much grace as she could muster. Seeing that her husband's lustful eyes went immediately to her bare bosom, she drew the sheet up to cover her as she sat cross-legged next to him.

Serena pushed him to the edge of the bed. "Get going. I'm sure kings always have busy days." With a reluctant sign, Rhamus jumped to his feet and started to dress.

Catching his wife admiring his backside, he grinned and asked. "Aren't you going to get dressed as well?"

"I'll get dressed as soon as you leave."

"Ah, but I thought you might enjoy going with me this morning," he remarked mysteriously. Then he spoiled it by adding, "Since you were so restless while I was gone."

So much for his laying the escape topic to rest. Serena sat forward and said, "You want me to go train with you? I think I've had enough training lately."

Throwing a pair of rezel pants at her, he watched with amusement as they landed with a whack on Serena's head and one leg wrapped around her neck. Snatching the clinging pants from around her head, his wife looked fit to kill him.

"You might try those on for size. I got them from one of the Getra--not Kasha."

"I'm not going anywhere with you," she said testily. "Throw a pair of pants at my head and then expect me to come to heel! You are a barbarian!" She shook the pants in one clenched fist for emphasis.

"And you're beautiful even when you're angry." Rhamus strolled close to the bed and stared back unruffled into his wife's glaring eyes. "Suit yourself. I just thought you might enjoy a morning ride on one of my yasmirs."

Staring at him for several seconds, Serena blinked and said, "Oh." Her contrite tone vanished the next instant as she grumbled, "You might have just told me instead of playing your little game."

Rhamus grinned and grabbing her hand gave it a loud, smacking kiss. "But, my *jicha*, I am beginning to warm to this game of teasing you."

She wanted to resent his remark, but couldn't, not when he called her the same endearment that he had used the night before, when whispering huskily in her ear. "Can you please turn your back while I get dressed?"

His wife seemed eager now, so he complied and faced the other direction, but she hadn't said anything about not watching her in the mirror. Walking quickly to the closet, he withdrew a simple dress and threw it to her, then again took up his observation of the mirror.

Serena wished he would stop grinning at her like an idiot. She grabbed the dress he threw at her, while maintaining the sheet across her bosom with the other hand. When she finally stood and was adjusting her dress, she flashed Rhamus a suspicious look, for he had turned immediately when she finished dressing as if he had eyes in the back of his head. Her eyes widened as she spied the mirror and remembered her own peeping behavior.

She examined at herself in the mirror. The purple dress he'd chosen went well enough with the black rezel pants, and she really loved the comfortable, soft material.

"It's a shame," Rhamus said suddenly.

"What?" She eyed him cautiously.

"To cover up such lovely legs." He ogled her in an overdone

fashion, eliciting a grin.

Strolling over slowly to him, she remarked, "You wouldn't want these legs to gather scratches. With wounds and scratchy Earthling's hair, it would put your unprotected skin in jeopardy." Serena ran one finger down her husband's arm.

"That's not the kind of jeopardy you will find yourself in, if you don't quit teasing me." He grabbed her errant finger and held it so she couldn't back away.

Serena was responding to his play on words, her breath caught in anticipation as she imagined that he was on the point of kissing her passionately. A loud knock pounded on the door. Jarvic entered to Rhamus' growled response.

Jarvic stopped on the threshold and, grinning, said, "Maybe I came at a bad time?"

He casually dropped Serena's finger and chose to ignore his cousin's glib remark. "What is it?"

Before answering, Jarvic strode quickly to her side and said good morning cheerfully, complete with a courtly kiss to her hand. Seeing the threatening look on his cousin's face, Jarvic relented temporarily with his teasing. Sighing he said, "I came to let you know the yasmirs are saddled and ready for the morning ride you had mentioned last night."

Rhamus' sarcastic "Thank you" went unnoticed by the handsome rascal as he took her arm and proceeded to escort her down the hall to the accompaniment of his amusing stories. "Did the King tell you about the time we dated sisters?" He grinned at his cousin's groan, ignoring Rhamus' annoyance with him, and kept a firm grip on Serena's arm.

Jarvic seemed to get a big kick out of his cousin's possessive behavior, the way Rhamus attempted several times to casually reclaim his wife's arm and remove his. Serena, although clearly entertained by Jarvic, kept giving her husband little glances of interest.

The warrior kept a fast pace and soon delivered them all to the paddock where the yasmirs waited. He was replaced at her side when Rhamus, irritated, managed to jostle him aside as he opened the gate. He stepped back cheerfully and started whistling a favorite love tune as his cousin guided his wife to a beautiful mount.

Chapter Ten

She was in a wonderful mood by the time they all arrived at the yasmir's corral. She was again struck by the similarity of the yasmir to the legendary unicorn, except the Volarnian mount was a very hairy version. And their colors were astounding, a bright mixture of blue, golden brown, dark red, and yellow yasmirs. Rhamus went up to a magnificent blue yasmir and held out his hand for her to approach.

"It's beautiful," Serena whispered as she put out her hand tentatively. Gaining courage from the animal's quietness, she stroked its velvety nose. Intrigued with the three foot horn, she ran her hand along its rough spiral. Smoothing her hand down the yasmir's neck, she was surprised by the softness of its long hair. The yasmir's four-inch long hair was crimped, like a woman who had styled it carefully.

The yasmir nuzzled her hand, and then blew gently against her arm.

"Arri's being awfully friendly toward a stranger," Rhamus looked puzzled.

"I guess he likes Earthlings." She grinned. "But then, I've always been good with horses."

"Horses?"

After Serena explained horses to him and revealed her love of riding to him, they talked for several minutes about the fine points of riding animal flesh. Rhamus seemed really pleased with her interest in the subject and she enjoyed immensely their companionable time together.

Taking her hand, he led her over to a dark red yasmir. She eyed the creature briefly, then turned to Rhamus with a confused expression. It was a very old yasmir, its coat dull and lifeless, its ancient back swayed.

Looking uncomfortable, he said, "I know she doesn't look like much, but old Daras will still give you a decent ride." He patted the aged yasmir who nickered softly in response.

Turning to view the large selection of riding stock in the corral, Serena inquired, "Why can't I have one of those?" She pointed hopefully toward several fine looking mounts and added, "I assure you, I know how to ride quite well."

"It's not a matter of your riding ability, but the temperament of our yasmirs. They are wild natured and feisty, basically untamable unless you get them as a colt and raise them. Not only that, but a yasmir will only allow the one who raised them to ride them."

Waving in the direction of the mounts Serena had shown interest in, he said, "So you see, none of those yasmirs would allow you to ride them."

"Then, what about old Daras?" She inclined her head toward the sway-backed animal.

Rhamus patted the old nag and answered, "When the yasmir reaches a great age for them, they lose the wildness in their nature. So the old ones are used for children's mounts, or for someone who hasn't hand raised a colt. Also, they are used for pack animals and to pull the carriages."

"Well, I guess it won't be exciting, but at least it will be a ride."

After they all mounted and wound their way out to a meadow area, heading for the forest edge, Serena regretted her last comment. It took every bit of equestrian skills she had to stay seated upon her ancient nag. If Daras was an example of the Volarnians well-mannered horse flesh, she didn't know if she'd ever be able to manage a younger mount.

She noted the friskiness of Rhamus and Jarvic's yasmirs, but also the tight control they kept on them. She couldn't help but admire the connection between rider and mount. The riders possessed splendid riding abilities, the yasmirs, a natural wildness and beauty.

"Can you hold old Daras at a slow walk while we exercise our mounts? They always like a good run in the morning and I'm afraid your yasmir may try to run too, and it wouldn't be good for her," he said.

"Sure," Serena acceded readily. She didn't even want to think what the end result would be if Daras was to go rushing off madly after the other two yasmirs. With a loud whoop, Rhamus and Jarvic set their steeds off at a breathtaking pace across the meadow, racing each other like two young boys instead of grown men. Serena had a hard time restraining Daras. She had to clamp down hard with her knees and rein to keep the ancient mare from dashing off. The old yasmir trembled with the urge to run.

She watched with fascination as they performed several daring stunts, picking up a dropped scarf while riding full speed, and turning around and riding their mounts backwards. She shook her head at their antics. The two warrior's riding tricks seemed expressly to show off for her, but she couldn't keep the thrill of their performance from pervading her spirits. It made her almost wish she could be as daring. After the two warriors finished their run and their yasmirs were blowing from being winded, Serena rode sedately up to them.

The yasmirs and their riders seemed ready to travel at a much slower pace. Even old Daras plodded along in a more manageable manner, as if just watching the younger yasmirs had worn her out too. This freed Serena to transfer her concentration from her mount and view the forest they were entering. She had always loved the forests back home and found herself as fascinated with the Volarnian trees as she'd been when first seeing them from a distance during her ride to the castle.

Again, she was struck with the beauty of the huge blue leafed trees. The forest was shady, cool, and full of bird songs, or whatever passed for birds here.

Many rustlings of busy creatures rose into the crisp air as they passed through the carpets of dense leaves. Luckily, they traveled along a wide trail, apparently heavily used and thus kept free from limbs and other forest debris.

Several hours later, the small group returned to the castle. Serena felt a little sore. But they'd stopped several times for leisurely breaks and spent a lovely time eating lunch by a sparkling clear stream. In spite of her stiff legs, she was exhilarated and ready to continue exploring. She conveyed this wish to Rhamus and he asked Jarvic to familiarize her with the castle. It would take several days to complete a tour of the whole interior, and then there were the grounds to be seen too.

"Can't *you* take me on a tour?" She asked wistfully. "Not that I don't want to go with you," she explained to Jarvic, and saw them both giving her an all-knowing look that shut her up instantly.

Rhamus took her hand and squeezed it gently. "I would love to be the first to show you our home, Serena. But I've got some business that just can't wait any longer. If you wish to wait until tomorrow, I can go around with you for a little while."

"No, no." Serena waved her hands in dismissal. "I know you've got more on your mind than attending to my every wish." She finished with an understanding smile.

Rhamus stared at his wife's warm smile. "I can't deny that," he placed a hard, callused hand upon her arm and rubbed lightly. "But neither can I deny that serving your every *desire* is my wish." He accompanied the last statement with a roguish grin that set Serena's lips in a firm line of disapproval.

"I think Jarvic and I can manage just fine." She wound her arm through the warrior's and started toward the entrance. She waited for Rhamus to catch up to them, but when she turned to look, he was smiling sweetly at her, then turned and headed off in another direction. She was annoyed at her quickly lit temper, when he had only been teasing her again.

"Is Rhamus going to talk with Kasha?" Serena inquired curiously. She had not felt comfortable asking Rhamus that question but felt no qualms about asking her escort.

"Yes, I suspect he is." He smiled slightly and started whistling a lively tune.

As with the other previous occasions when Jarvic had been her companion for a short period of time, he proved to be an amusing and charming host. Serena enjoyed her tour. She examined each tapestry, painting, or weapon to her heart's content.

Admittedly, her valiant escort appeared impatient more than once, but never complained. She really became excited over the numerous rooms they traversed, losing count of the variety of uses the rooms were put to, whether it be a guest bedroom or a storage room for food goods. Soon, even the excitement of yet undiscovered rooms and antiquities, began to pall as Serena felt her feet begin to lag with tiredness.

Jarvic sighed in relief when she asked if they could continue their tour another day. He left her at the door of her suite with a promise to return the next day. Serena rinsed the smell of old Daras off with a quick shower, then settled down in the stuffed chair and daydreamed.

She jerked awake when a soft kiss landed on her mouth and, looking up, she thought her daydream most vivid. Feeling silly, she realized it was Rhamus who stood in front of her, not the romantic, imaginary husband of her daydream.

He pulled up a low stool and sat, his head level with hers. "Looks like you had a tiring afternoon."

"Yes, but it was very exciting." She went on to comment about different rooms and items she'd seen during her tour.

"I can see that I need to be your escort next time."

"Why?" Serena cocked her head to the side slightly.

"Because if anything brings you that much pleasure, I'd like to be involved." Rhamus looked most serious.

"Oh," she looked flustered. "You are simply incorrigible!"

Ignoring her remark, he switched to the subject, which had brought him to her. Giving Serena an intense look, he said, "You need not worry about my sister's antics anymore." Smiling slightly, he added, "But you may have trouble getting acquainted with Kasha now--I made her pretty angry. But I know she's feeling guilty about her behavior."

"Only time will tell," Serena commented, at a loss for any words that would not sound vindictive. She wasn't too sure she wanted to know Kasha any better.

"Why does she hate me so?"

"I'm not sure it's hate … I don't think Kasha would accept any woman. She may feel they would take her place in my affections."

"Nonsense!"

Rhamus nodded, then shrugged. "I practically raised Kasha after our father was murdered--she followed me everywhere." He stared off into the distance. "She even talked me into allowing her to join the Getra, because she wanted to be a warrior like her brother."

A knock on the door signaled Lalme's entrance with a large tray. She placed it on the table where Serena had eaten breakfast the day before. As she looked at Rhamus in surprise, he pulled her up and waved her toward the laden tray.

"I thought you might enjoy eating in tonight, since you've had such a busy day." Her pleased expression told him he had made the right choice.

Serena was as ravenous as Rhamus had appeared yesterday at the dinner table, even though they had stopped and eaten a light lunch while out riding. Jarvic had proved an efficient companion by making sure a servant had provided them with curious but delicious bundles of meat and pastry, and fresh fruit for a quick breakfast.

Rhamus made her flush more than once during the meal. Hoping to turn his mind from the physical side of their relationship, Serena asked him about the duties of his kingship. She was pleased to learn more about this side of her husband. He was intelligent, insightful, and sensitive to his people's needs. She sat spellbound as he recounted judgments made and laws created.

She examined her husband as if for the first time. She looked past the warrior's bearing and handsome features to the sensitive soul behind the successful ruler. She liked this man very much. He could be strong and a good leader, and yet had a generous nature. Serena found herself wanting to get to know the person beneath the sinewy body. He was the kind of man that she could call a friend.

The awakening of revealing self-knowledge startled her. She shifted in her seat as if shaking off this unfamiliar "warm fuzzy" feeling she was experiencing within herself. I cannot allow myself to fall in love with this man, she thought firmly. This was immediately followed by a devilish inner question, "Why not?" To distract herself, she asked another question.

"Tell me about your warring with west Volarn. Can't you

negotiate peace?"

"Xarath is the present leader of west Volarn. He seems determined to win back the ruling of all Volarn."

Serena was surprised by the revelation that west Volarn once ruled the whole planet. "When did your enemies rule all of Volarn?"

"A long time ago. One of my ancestors used the basami to bring about peace and return rulership back to each side."

"The basami?"

He smiled. "The story is old, really a legend. My great grandfather found and raised a baby dragon. They were reportedly very close and the basami would allow my ancestor to ride on his back. My ancestor flew over our enemy's castle on the back of his dragon as all his troops surrounded it below. The appearance of a fierce warrior flying overhead upon the back of a huge basami, made the people fear my ancestor's mystical powers. They laid down their weapons and pledged fidelity to south Volarn."

"How did west Volarn come to rule your people in the first place?"

"Xarath's great great grandfather enlisted the aid of a powerful sorcerer, Cark, a vassi who tapped into the dark powers of the arj'ak crystal. The king arranged for the sacred crystal to be stolen from its keepers, then Cark used his powers along with other vassi, to turn the sacred crystal into a destructive weapon."

"I thought all vassi were good? And what is this 'sacred crystal'?"

"Most are, but a few throughout our history have turned to using their powers for evil purposes. The sacred crystal is the largest and most powerful of its kind."

"What did they do with the sacred crystal?"

"Cark apparently persuaded other vassi to use their skills to overthrow our government. At least they tried, and nearly won. There was much destruction from the crystal's power and many people killed, from both sides. The vassi barely seemed able to keep the crystal under control. Sometimes its power would escape and kill many of their own people. It also caused the rampant infertility for Volarnian women, especially ours. And the wastelands to the north are the result of the sacred crystal's destructive power in the wrong hands."

"Is that how they took over?"

Rhamus shook his head no. "The king's metal workers and vassi also discovered a way to use the arj'ak in a hand weapon similar to the Moyd's stun gun. These weapons were able to send out a killing ray of power when directed by the user, somewhat like the method our warriors use when tapping into the power for sword fighting. They invaded our cities after we had been effectively disabled by the sacred crystal. By the time our vassi developed weapons, it was too late for my ancestors. West Volarn ruled over us until my great grandfather's time."

"What happened to the sacred crystal?"

"A group of our most powerful vassi went to get the sacred crystal back from our enemies. There was a fierce battle of magic and wizardry that day. Legend says that streams of power spewed from the vassi's mouths and fingertips as they fought with the powers from within themselves. Cark finally brought forth the sacred crystal and tried to turn its power on our vassi."

"Well?" Serena urged.

Rhamus paused, "Nothing happened. Either the power of both sides canceled out the sacred crystal's power, or it refused to cooperate. From then on, it was a battle between the two vassi groups. Philosophically, you could say that good won over evil, since the southern vassi won the day. Or, maybe they were simply more powerful sorcerers."

"I would like to think good won over evil," Serena said thoughtfully. "And your ancestor didn't take over rule of west Volarn?"

"No. It would have been too big of a job. We were still outnumbered by their warriors, so he left them to self rule." His jaw clenched in agitation. "But, after my great grandfather's time, our enemy started harassing our borders and both sides engaged in many small battles, just as we do today."

"Do you still use, or even have the weapons?"

"No. We asked the Federal Republic of the Galaxy to mediate our peace settlements, and it was decided by both sides to have them destroyed. The Republic now serves as our protectors against more technologically advanced races, which might be interested in such a crystal rich planet. Of course, they are well compensated by payments in Volarnian crystal."

"Rhamus, have you ever thought that the arj'ak crystal may cause your people's sterility? The warriors use it a lot, don't they?"

"A good observation. But we had the Republic's scientist come here and check out our crystal. It was found that only the sacred crystal caused the sterility. And only when its dark powers were used."

"Where is the sacred crystal now, and is it safe?"

Rhamus eyes were serious, but he smiled at her attentiveness to his story. "It is in the Zanzai mountains, watched over by its chosen guardians, the elders. It is unfortunate that it has to be so."

"Why?"

"When it was stolen long ago, it was in a holy place the vassi established in a city central to both sides. West and south Volarnians could make pilgrimages to get help and advice from the vassi."

"Who are these elders?"

"The three most powerful vassi in all Volarn. Only people with fierce determination and a great desire to gain knowledge or healing from the sacred crystal attempt the journey." At Serena's puzzled look, he added, "It is dangerous."

"It is a shame it's so far out of reach for your people now. I was wondering how are the elders chosen?"

"It is a process shrouded in mysticism and magic. I can't tell you much about it, since an elder has not been chosen since before my father's time. But it is said that the sacred crystal chooses those it wishes to serve as its guardians, those pure of heart and intent. Our legends say the sacred crystal has no favorites, that it may choose a vassi from south or west Volarn."

"Enough about old tales, I need to talk about present day, right now." He waved a hand as if dismissing the subject. "Serena, I said I talked with Kasha after I left you earlier. Would you tell me about your fear of konkols?"

She was surprised by the quickness with which Rhamus changed subjects. Looking into his eyes and seeing the sincerity of those expressive orbs, she said, "Apparently Surad already told you what happened? Didn't she tell you about my phobia?"

Shaking his head, he said, "No. She felt that it was something that should come straight from you, to my ear." He leaned over and placed his head next to her mouth.

The brush of his lion's mane against her lips was more than Serena could stand. "How can I tell you anything, when you make every topic between us a teasing contest?"

"Come now, my Queen," Rhamus grasped one of her hands gently within the warm covering of his larger one. "I may tease you," he paused at her derogatory "hmmph", "but you know I can be perfectly serious." Seeing her pursed lips and arched eyebrows, he continued, "We just had a most serious conversation a few minutes ago."

Serena sighed and surrendered, at least this once. She explained her fear of spiders to him, just as she'd done earlier with Nuad. He stayed silent through the telling, an inscrutable expression on his face, so that Serena could not read his reaction to her story.

"I am truly sorry for Kasha's behavior," Rhamus stated

vehemently, as soon as she finished.

His strong response helped soothed Serena's earlier irritation with him. She dreamily contemplated the way his hair brushed the tops of his brawny shoulders, almost like a lover's caress.

"Hey, daydreaming again," he said dangerously close to her, his wonderfully molded lips but a head span away from her own. She held her breath and then let it out slowly in disappointment as Rhamus backed away slightly. She looked down in puzzlement as her husband unclasped her hand as it still lay within his, and placed something soft and tickly against her palm.

"Rolan' swears that the only way to apologize properly on Earth, is by the giving of flowers."

Serena held up her hand and stared at the many tiny petals that lay within. She looked up in amusement at her husband, waving her hand slightly in front of his face. "This is the Volarnian's idea of giving flowers?"

Rhamus clasped her hand and pressed her fingers around the petals gently, then uncurled her hand. Serena gasped in surprise at the wonderfully fragrant odor that arose from the crushed petals.

"They smell like roses!" Looking like a little girl that had just been given the biggest lollipop in the candy store, she added, "Roses are my favorite flower."

"Good," he said, jumping quickly to his feet. "Then, if you will come with me, I will show you the rest of the flowers I wish to give you."

His look was both secretive and mischievous. Serena could not resist his charming invitation. She was infected by his boyish mood and let Rhamus hold hands with her without protest, enjoying the companionably safe feeling of their play. As they strolled down the endless corridors, she didn't have a clue where they were headed and didn't particularly care. As the walk became more than a short stroll, she was glad of his hand pulling her along. Her legs were beginning to feel like jelly as her muscles protested their ill use today.

"Was there anything that you wished for while I was gone?"

He asked innocently enough, although Serena suspected he had an ulterior motive, like wishing she would express she'd missed him. That she would never do, although if she were honest with herself, she had thought about him from time to time. His question gave her an opportunity to express a concern she did have. "Yes, as a matter of fact, I really missed--Nicole."

Rhamus looked disappointed. "Well then, we will remedy that. I will arrange for Nicole to visit with you once a day," he finished thoughtfully. They had traveled through a long stretch of the castle's halls and now approached an entrance to the outside. "Wait here a minute," he instructed, then walked quickly to a guard nearby. The soldier was startled by the King's presence, but pleased that he made a personal request known to him.

The young warrior shook his head, then turned and entered the castle. "What was that all about?" She questioned as Rhamus rejoined her.

"I asked him to go and tell Surad to make arrangements for Nicole to visit you."

She stared at her husband. He was so kind. Immediately after her request, he sought to fulfill her wish. *No, he's just trying to get in my good graces.* This inner conflict was followed with "why"?

"Come on, over here." He grabbed her hand again and quickened his pace as he walked quickly toward a tall stone wall, almost dragging her in his haste.

They went through an arched entrance into a garden area that went on as far as Serena could see. Rhamus dropped her hand and let her stroll slowly forward in wonder. It was enchantment come to life! Tall bushes higher than her shoulders were covered in the soft-petaled flowers he'd laid in her palm and appeared to fill the whole garden.

The flowers were grapefruit-sized, in every conceivable color. Each flower was made up of hundreds of the delicate petals. The air was saturated with rose-scented perfume that permeated every sense and plastered itself to the skin like a fine mist.

"They are called the *crespassno* flower," Rhamus interjected into Serena's stunned silence. "I hoped that this would be enough of an apology," he waved an arm to encompass all the flowering bushes that surrounded them.

Chapter Eleven

"Yes, apology accepted," her smile lit up her eyes with its brightness. "But I don't think you should be the one apologizing. Although," Serena added as she picked up his hand in fervent appreciation of his gesture, "I am glad you did."

Rhamus walked slowly with her now and led Serena to a bench within a complete circle of the crespassno bushes. She had been so mesmerized by the scent that she had been blind to another astounding event. Serena looked around in bemusement at the hundreds, no thousands, of colorful flying objects flitting among the blossoms and the air all around them.

At first she thought they were some kind of small butterfly but, upon capturing one, gazed with astonishment at a crespassno petal. She caught another and again felt just as surprised when a petal was revealed. Looking around, Serena saw that piles of the tiny petals had blown in drifts that had to consist of hundreds of thousands of the flower parts.

"Having fun?" He teased in a relaxed manner as he lounged back on the bench and watched her.

"I don't believe these are flower petals. I thought they were some kind of flying insect." Serena puzzled over the frail object in her palm.

"Hmm, believe it." Pointing to her hand, Rhamus said, "Those little flowers are a curse, the way they fly about when the wind blows a little, getting into one's hair and making you smell like a woman."

"Does everyone think them a curse, and if so, why have a whole garden full?"

Shrugging his shoulders, Rhamus pointed out, "The gardeners have to spend a lot of time trying to keep those pests from the other garden areas, their seeds blow all over. So, we learn to live with them. It's easier to devote large sections to just the crespassno instead of fighting to weed them from the other flowers."

"If they're that prolific, I'm surprised they haven't taken over the whole planet."

He shook his head. "A good point." He leaned over and reached beneath a nearby bush. Bringing his hand up in front of her face, he showed her a tiny brown beetle which clung to his little finger.

"This is a wootaz. It has a voracious appetite and, fortunately for us, its natural food source is the root of the crespassno bush." Even as he spoke the beetle changed colors so that it faded into the lighter beige of Rhamus' skin.

"A chameleon bug," Serena laughed. She watched intently as Rhamus placed the beetle on a pink crespassno flower, and it changed colors again.

"Well, now I've seen everything." At his raised eyebrow, she said, "A pink beetle." The bug in question flew the short distance to the bushes' bottom and began to dig industriously into the dirt.

"If you dislike these flowers so much, why show them to me?"

"I don't know," Rhamus shrugged. "I thought you might like them since my mother favored them so much." Glancing sideways at her, he continued, "Besides, I think they're pretty." Looking off at a far point, he said, "I often come here when I want a peaceful setting to do some thinking."

Serena stared at her husband. First he tells her what a pestilence the flowers were, then how much they meant to him. Almost everything she knew of this man had opposing sides, two sides of one very intriguing coin. He was a leader, yet gentle natured and thoughtful. He was a warrior, a killer, and often made her feel as though she were being stalked by a great cat. Yet he could be patient and kind with her. And now he hated the inconvenience of an intrusive flower, yet loved its beauty and the fact that someone close to him had loved it as well. He was an enigma.

Serena reached to a nearby bush and plucked a flower. "You know, back home, we have a weed called the dandelion and we play a game with its 'petals'."

"What game is that?" Rhamus leaned closer.

"Well, you make a wish and then blow the dandelion, and if you blow all the petals off, then your wish will come true," Serena finished lamely, feeling awkward at explaining a child's game to a huge warrior who gazed at her with an amused expression.

"Then we must try it." He grabbed a flower for himself. "You go first, since it's your game."

Feeling obligated to see this silliness through now, Serena took a deep breath and blew hard. She was pleasantly surprised when the petals erupted into the air and blew away.

"Now, what was your wish?"

"Oh, you can't tell your wish, or it won't come true." Serena giggled at Rhamus' frown.

"That doesn't sound like much fun. What good is a wish, unless it's shared?" At Serena's noncommittal shrug, he took a breath and scattered his petals in an explosion of overdone male force. "Good, now my wish will come true." Turning to Serena, he said, "My wish is…."

Serena covered Rhamus' mouth playfully with one hand, "You must not tell, remember?"

He gripped her hand and placed it on one of his shoulders. "Maybe I'm making up my own rules for this game. Maybe they're rules that only apply on Volarn." Serena's eyes dipped down coyly as he continued, "My wish is for my Queen to kiss me."

Forgetting that it didn't fit the rules of the game played back on Earth, Serena wanted nothing more than to join Rhamus in the spirit of his game. She leaned forward slightly and that was all the invitation he needed. Wrapping his arms snugly around her, Rhamus kissed her gently on the mouth, as soft as the petals floating by them.

She could taste the perfume that invaded their skin with its exotic, flowery persistence. His kiss deepening, Serena answered in kind with an increased pressure of their joined lips and playful involvement of their tongues. His hands were restless and roamed her back, reaching to stroke her thighs as well.

Serena ran her hands through her husband's thick hair, creating a sensual delight for herself and Rhamus. Not realizing their impassioned movements created a precarious position for them on the small bench, both lovers felt their joined bodies shift too late to stop the short fall toward the ground.

He landed on the bottom, a large pile of petals cushioning his fall. Serena giggled at the petals that puffed up all around as their bodies landed hard. Tiny bits of flowers clung to their skin wherever bare flesh was exposed. She raised herself up, her position of sitting astride her grinning husband was both embarrassing and of a sensual nature.

Gripping the back of her head gently but firmly, Rhamus brought Serena back down to stretch out atop him and began their kiss anew. Inside her head, she thought of all kinds of reasons why they shouldn't be engaging in such behavior in a very public place, but her body refused to listen.

It didn't take long before her body burned with the need for more of her husband's caresses, ones that couldn't be satisfied within the confines of a public garden. Her hands gripped Rhamus' hair in a tight clench as he continued his oral assault on her senses while his large hands played havoc with her bottom.

Pulling her closer so she could feel his hard cock, Serena needed no further urging to stroke herself up and down his length. Her vagina grew wet and if not for the undergarment, she would have easily slid onto his staff. She was on the verge of throwing caution to the wind, but a small sound interrupted their heated foreplay.

"Uhum." A throat clearing sound jolted through the sensual cloud that surrounded their intense petting. Serena slid quickly off Rhamus and turned a beet red face to Nicole who watched them with a quirky smile lurking in the corners of her mouth.

Serena saw the direction of Nicole's stare and wished she'd not rushed to jump off her husband's body, his large cock still plainly in view even beneath his doca. His expression was cool, but Serena had the feeling he was as angry at the interruption as he had been burning with desire a minute ago. He stared at Nicole, not the least concerned about his body's display.

"What are you doing here?" Serena inquired uncomfortably, breaking the awkward silence.

Examining her nails, Nicole gave the couple a reprieve to compose themselves, "Well, somebody sent a royal order that I be brought to visit you."

Rhamus and Serena managed to arrange themselves in a sitting position, side by side, before Nicole's intent eyes swung back to look at them with lively interest. Hearing her response, they turned instantaneously and looked at each other, then turned back to the intruder of their tryst. "Who told you to come here now?" He asked in a less than agreeable tone.

"Your aunt." At his groan, Nicole continued, "She said there was no sense wasting time, since Serena's missed me so much, and you did give permission for the visit."

Looking at the disappointed glances the two of them shot each other, Nicole commented, "Of course, I can see I wasn't missed as much as Surad supposed." She gave them both a brilliant smile to convey there were no hard feelings, at least from her end.

"It's true I gave the order," he sighed.

"Sometimes my dear aunt puts too much of her own interpretation to my orders. And besides, didn't you two spend some 'quality' time together very recently?" Ignoring his implication, Serena got up to greet her friend. "One never can see your friends too much."

"Oh, I think I could win an argument against that one," Rhamus growled.

Nicole had a fit of giggling as Serena walked the few feet toward her. Flower petals stuck to just about every part of her anatomy, especially where any skin showed. Gone was the beautiful, dignified woman. In her place was a comical figure that looked like a cross between a human flower and a harpy. Serena hugged her friend, who sneezed when they parted.

"Nicole, are you allergic to flowers?"

"No, but when you hugged me, one of those petals went up my nose."

Both women succumbed to the giggles, irritating Rhamus. He sprang to his feet and started toward the castle. Over his shoulder he said, "I'll leave you two to your visit." Eyeing Serena meaningfully, he added, "And, my Queen, I expect to see you shortly in our bedroom."

"My, my, he doesn't leave much to the imagination," Nicole said merrily as she watched him leave. He stopped several times to try and brush petals off his clothes and skin with little success, one time shaking a leg fiercely.

"He certainly is a handsome specimen, flower petals and all," Nicole's impish tone set Serena off in gales of laughter that she tried to contain behind one hand. Her friend joined in, their peals of gaiety only made Rhamus stomp more vigorously as he fought to shake the clinging petals off. They saw him bark an order to the guard at the entrance, when the young warrior gasped at the King's appearance. The guard's shocked eyes never left his ruler, even as he straightened in attention at his post.

"Now," Nicole grabbed one of Serena's hands and pulled her down beside her on the bench. "Tell me all about you and that handsome husband. Looks like you and he are getting along pretty good. Was he very angry about our escape attempt? Did you ever stop blaming yourself, Serena?"

Serena looked away for a moment, her gaze faraway, then swung her eyes back to Nicole. "Rhamus and everyone else have been almost nonchalant about our escape." She went on to fill Nicole in.

She shook her head in wonder. "I guess we're lucky they have such an outlook." She giggled. "Of course, Rolan's been giving me these suspicious looks, like I instigated the whole thing!" She grabbed Serena's hand excitedly, "But the best thing is, Doc wants to keep me by his side all the time."

"Do you think he figures you are going to try something else?"

"No," Nicole shook her head vigorously, setting her curls bouncing. "He acts like he's scared to let me out of his sight. I think maybe he realizes he almost lost me. What about you? Are you ... we, going to try another escape?"

Serena shook her head slowly. "I don't think that's possible unless something comes to our attention. Keep your eyes and ears open, Nicole. As for me, I've decided to make the best of it. If they insist I be Queen, then I'm going to be the best one I can. That includes looking after the other women's best interest." She went on to share some of her ideas with her friend.

They both paused in their conversation to admire the gorgeous sunset that streaked across the sky. The purple and lavender shadings were intermixed with streaks of golden clouds, and pink, blue, and coral hues.

"Wow."

"That means it's getting late."

"Right." Nicole's expression reflected her friend's disappointed look. "But, we wouldn't want your husband to come stomping back out here looking for you," she smiled.

The guard who had escorted Nicole to the garden walked a few paces toward them, anxious to get rid of this duty. Nicole eyed the guard grumpily. "I guess that means it's time to go." The two walked together until their ways parted, Nicole waved a forlorn goodbye as she disappeared down another corridor.

"I was getting worried about you," Rhamus said as Serena entered their suite. He laughed hard and, glancing in the mirror, she joined him. Even though she'd tried as valiantly as her husband to knock flower petals off her body, there were still many sticking to her. Rhamus had showered and Serena followed suit, scrubbing at the clinging petals.

She was startled when Rhamus pulled the shower door back. He was nude, his cock hard, and a wide grin was plastered on his face.

"You already took a shower." She couldn't hold back a nervous quiver from her statement. She felt so vulnerable standing naked in front of him like this.

"There are more reasons to shower than simply cleansing one's body." With those words, he stepped in. "Let me do your back." He took the sponge from her and started running it along the small of her back.

In seconds his hands replaced the sponge and she closed her eyes to better soak in the sensations. Rhamus' strong hands kneaded her flesh and relaxed the muscles, while his mere touch set tingles racing along her nerve endings.

The scent of roses surrounded them as he stroked her back with the crespassno soap. Streams of hot water gushed over her front side from the spout, caressing her skin as well. She could feel Rhamus' presence behind her, although only his hands had stroked her body so far. It was like standing in the presence of an impending storm. Every nerve ending felt him there. Every fiber of her being wanted to shove backwards into his body. Only curiosity as to what he had in mind kept her from doing so.

Her whole back had been massaged before her husband made his next move. Rhamus' body pressed against her backside, his cock wedged between her slippery cheeks. She sighed and arched toward him as his hands slid around and caressed her breasts. Palming a breast in each hand, he kneaded them until they plumped up in reaction. Then his fingers lightly pulled and rolled her nipples. She held her breath as his playful caresses caused rippling waves of pleasure to lance through her nubs.

Unconsciously Serena slid her slick bottom back and forth across his hard staff. It was a delicious feeling.

"Yes, I like that," he whispered huskily.

His words seemed to sink into her, making her insides grow hotter. Already she ached for him to take her.

Her breath hitched again when one hand sleeked down her body and his fingers splayed over her mons. It was as if he were marking her as his. Yes, she wanted to be his. His love slave if he wished-- anything to soothe the raging torrent running through her. The urge to push against him could not be denied this time. Serena arched, seeking his touch. Chuckling in her ear, he obliged by sliding one finger into her folds.

A soft whimper was pulled from her as his finger slipped back and forth slowly. Her hips moved in a rhythm matching his sliding motions.

"Tell me how that feels." He whispered against her ear, then licked the lobe.

"Good," she groaned. She felt incapable of saying more.

That finger slid inside her channel and Serena shuddered. Her vagina clamped down on his finger, begging for more.

"Tell me what you want." Rhamus sucked her earlobe into his mouth, working magic with his tongue.

Serena moaned. Her body was boneless, a greedy creature eager for his every touch.

His finger slipped out and circled her clit. "Tell me?"

Beyond self-conscious control, she whimpered, "For you to fuck me." She had never used that word before, but her body burned and screamed its dark need aloud.

Unexpectedly, he pushed her upper body forward, and then replaced his finger with his cock. It penetrated her channel easily, filling her completely. She gripped the bar on the shower door and spread her legs a bit wider. She wanted more. Wanted to be filled until she couldn't take anymore.

"Yes, jicha," he moaned. "Let me know how much you want it."

Answering his words with her body, she shoved backward onto

his staff, moaning at the sensation it evoked. It was as if he filled her every fiber, even reaching into her limbs. This is what she had desired. Electric sparks shot from her pussy and lanced through her veins.

"Oh," she moaned as he plunged into her with one long forceful stroke.

His power pushed her upper body into the glass and she whimpered loudly. Her breasts were squashed against the hard door while Rhamus rammed into her soft channel. It was a wicked sensation and she reveled in it.

"Yes," she screamed, losing the tight control she always kept over herself.

"What do you want?" Rhamus' husky voice was edged with a raw excitement.

"This." She rammed back onto his cock. Her fingers scraped along the glass as waves of ecstasy washed through her.

Rhamus released one hand gripping her hip and slid his hand to her lower lips. A finger dipped into her hot, slick flesh, finding her clit. It was too much. Serena screamed and her body bucked. She shuddered as an orgasm flushed through her.

Whimpering, she rotated her hips as she rode out several more orgasms.

His loud groan pleased her as she felt his seed gush into her sensitive flesh.

After catching her breath, she turned and gave him a soft kiss. Not satisfied, Rhamus pulled her closer for a burning kiss that demanded her surrender. It did not surprise her that their foreplay soon turned into another hot bout of sex, only that it happened so quickly. Serena hadn't gotten used to her husband's astounding virility yet.

Her true shower didn't get completed until much later. After stepping from the shower, she felt refreshed but also drained. But such a nice tiredness.

Settling into a chair across from Rhamus, she broached a subject that had been on her mind. Maybe he would be more receptive after their steamy session.

"Can I talk to you about some concerns that have been bothering me?" she asked.

"You may talk to me anytime you are worried about something."

Serena plunged right in, telling Rhamus about Deborah, the woman with the fiancé.

He strolled over to the window, his head down, deep in thought. Turning, he said, "Perhaps she can be sent back."

"Yes," Serena smiled sweetly. "She can go back with Nicole."

He stretched out one arm and she snuggled up next to him, happy that Rhamus had conceded so readily to helping Deborah.

"Have you been outside at nightfall and seen our moonlight yet?" He held out his hand in an open invitation.

A moonlight stroll on the balcony appealed to her, but Serena hesitated, remembering the spider web outside. She didn't feel like answering his questioning look, so let him continue hand in hand with her through the doors. Momentarily forgetting the web when they stepped outside, Serena sucked in her breath at the beauty of the night. The two suns had set after she left Nicole, and three moons of various sizes lit up the night with a radiant glow.

One moon was huge, about twice as big as Earth's and seemed so near, Serena felt like she could reach up and touch its bright surface. The second moon was one-half the size of the familiar moon of home, while the last moon was apparently far away, and barely visible as a pinpoint of brightness.

"It's so beautiful," Serena spoke softly, feeling as though a louder tone would break the wondrous spell.

"Hmm. Wait until all seven moons are in the same orbit." Rhamus pulled her into the circle of his arms as they both gazed upon the tranquil scenery. They stayed that way but a short time, yet it could have been an eternity.

Serena didn't know how long they could have stayed thus, wrapped in each other's arms. The spell was broken by the sudden intrusion of a bird song. It sounded like the same one Serena had heard on the balcony during the day. Its vocal range was astonishing, from low pitched to high, with a lovely melody entwining in the notes of its own musical creation.

"What kind of bird is that?" Curiosity pulled at her, urging Serena out of her dreamy state.

"What is a bird?"

After Serena explained birds to Rhamus, he chuckled and told her they didn't have any creatures on Volarn that came close to Earth's singing ones. "The elag is feathered, but it squawks. And then there is the sooeul, which chirps and sings, but it is a flying ... what you would call a lizard. But the song which enchants you tonight, is the night call of the konkol."

* * * *

Rhamus felt Serena stiffen in his arms and then remembered her fear. He sighed inaudibly. "Do you wish to go back inside?" His wife's quick response and clinging hands convinced him that they had a long road ahead to overcome this fear of hers.

He went to the wine decanter and poured them both a small drink. Serena took the cup gratefully and sipped it down quickly. He distracted her with funny little incidents from his past. It seemed that Kasha was always at the center of the plot when they were children. He soon had his wife laughing and relaxed. Rhamus enjoyed being able to pull her away from her intense fear and lead her to happier thoughts. Her soft smiling face led his thoughts in other directions. Taking Serena's hand, he drew her up and into his arms. She didn't put up a defense, but came to him willingly. In spite of the fact they had shared two sizzling encounters in the shower, he hungered for her as a starving man longed for food.

Rhamus started a slow assault on Serena's senses, wishing to wipe away any other thoughts. She eagerly embraced him and returned his ardor, kiss for kiss, stroke for stroke. He was pleasantly surprised at her immediate response. Usually, Serena appeared to be trying to fight something inside herself, to resist him and her own urges before her sensitive body took over and succumbed. Earlier in the shower, she had reacted with passion to his advances, but only after he had stirred her senses with erotic foreplay. As they sank into the soft mattress, he knew that his lovely wife was using sex to try and take her mind off her dark fear.

He admittedly didn't mind being used by his wife, what man wouldn't mind in such a manner. Rhamus broke the contact between their lips and stared briefly into her unique, clear blue eyes. They had lost all fear and now were lit with fires of lust for him, pleasing his male ego immensely. But as Serena pulled his head down for another joining of their mouths, he determined to find a way to help her overcome this demon. To have those jewel-like orbs filled only with the normal emotions, love, joy, need, sadness, but never fear, was a worthy goal.

Sliding one hand down her side, he skirted her breast and stroked her ribcage. Serena's slight sigh gave him satisfaction. He had discovered that by teasing her first, her response was greater when he finally caressed some sensitive spot on her body.

Using his thumb, he rubbed the underside of her breast and watched her eyes close. Slowly, he ran his thumb upward, barely touching her hardened nipple. Her breathing increased and her body arched toward him.

Bending down, he captured her mouth in a deep kiss, then drawing back, he whispered, "Open your eyes."

When she complied, he asked, "Would you like something wet and soft on this?" Rhamus' thumb rolled her nipple.

Her eyes were sultry, but still she blushed at his question. "Yes."

Her voice was husky with desire, matching her expression.

Surprising him, she placed a hand behind his neck and pulled him down.

"Oh, yes," she sighed when his mouth closed over her beaded nub.

His guts tightened and his cock got harder as he drew on the succulent flesh. Every vein in his body screamed "take her", but he thrust that urge aside. Part of his pleasure came from turning Serena into a passionate fireball.

Using just his tongue, he flicked her nipple while watching her lovely face. Her eyes were closed again, her creamy skin flushed with desire. Pushing her breast up, he took the nub into his mouth, sucking like an infant. Serena moaned and her hand stirred restlessly in his hair.

Popping her nipple from his mouth and adjusting her legs, he held his engorged length in one hand, nudging the entrance to her *raslus*. Her arms came around his back and he took it as a signal that she was ready. He decided to tease her a bit first. Slowly, he slid the head up and down her slick flesh. Her breathing increased as he worked it over her sensitive inner lips.

Only when she opened her eyes did he ease his cini into her opening, sliding inch by inch inside. Her blue eyes had darkened with lust. His staff throbbed with the need to bury itself in her, while his heart seemed to do a flip flop by gazing at her.

Pushing into Serena with one stroke, Rhamus enjoyed the way her breath expelled in one soft sigh. While caressing her breast he leaned down and kissed her deeply. She returned his kiss with a searing passion.

Groaning, he drew back. He was close to climaxing. Easing his staff out, he slid it gently in and out, with just the tip entering her.

Serena moaned as her nails raked his back. After a few more thrusts, she was panting. Her insides spasmed around him and he could not hold back any longer. The orgasm pulled at his muscles and blood, zinging through his body with a savage joy.

Afterward, he rolled to the side, pulling her body with him. As he stroked her arm, he thought about their sessions today. Sex had been amazing. He had thought his mistress of the past had been satisfying, but she paled in comparison.

Much later, Rhamus continued caressing Serena's arm as she lay on his chest, sleeping soundly now. His hands combed through her hair as it draped across one shoulder, feeling the silky texture. Holding a strand up to examine the red color, he frowned. He had been a fool to make such a big thing out of nothing. Truly Serena's hair was different from the west Volarnians. He'd just been too blinded by hatred to see the difference at first.

He appreciated many attributes of his new wife. He could not have thought up a lovelier face or figure to fulfill his own dreams. Even her hair he found to be fascinating. Going beyond the physical, Rhamus realized there was much he admired about Serena. Things he had observed and reports of her past he had received from Pulack.

He admired her warrior spirit, the way she was easily embarrassed by his teasing, the sexual magic that existed between them. He liked her loyalty to friends, her willingness to defend her people, and even her attempt to lead them to freedom. And he respected her taking on the huge load of learning experiences as she was prepared by others to be his Queen.

He felt empathy for her fears, for he had a short-lived phobia of yasmirs at a young age after being thrown on his first solo ride. A sprained ankle and willful nature had kept him from attempting to ride again for several weeks, until his father's usually patient face wore an irritated and disappointed expression. Rhamus would do anything to please his father, so he had reluctantly gotten back up on his yasmir. And once he learned to control his mount, it was love of a youngster for his yasmir that developed, not fear.

Rhamus knew there was much more lurking beneath the surface that he had not surmised yet about Serena. He was determined that he would use his time wisely with her, to discover more of her history and traits to be admired. The Tarthra had sealed their fates together, now he had to work at opening the gates to the Serena who still sought to hide so much from him. He had not fought against the choosing from the first, knowing it was always right, but he couldn't expect Serena to know of the Tarthra's power and its unerring ability to seek out those capable of loving one another.

The Tarthra had many powers and one was the ability of prediction, at least in areas of the heart. Only the vassi were trained to use the sacred crystal's power for predicting future events on Volarn. Rhamus' thoughts turned to the future. So far, the elders had refused messengers sent by him for readings on Volarn's future. The vassi would not be drawn into predictions of such magnitude, knowing as wise men that such things often changed the chosen path of the receiver.

Rhamus stared off into the darkness surrounding the bed. He had hoped for only a sign, some indicator that Volarn's infertility problem was not going to lead to extinction. He had at first been angry when his messengers returned from their quest of the vassi, then simply irritated at the group of old men who held such sway over the populace. He'd figuratively turned his back on the elders, since they offered no help, and determined to bring the fertility problem under control, no matter the method.

This led his thoughts back to his wife, and he tightened his arms around her without being aware of it. He was so very glad his search had led to a blue and green world peopled with such exciting women.

His eyes blinking slowly now, Rhamus tried to keep Serena in focus. Rolan' said humans like expressions of love, since they do not have the reassurance of the choosing like we do. *I must remember to tell her that I love her.*

Chapter Twelve

Serena felt entirely too sluggish to move from amongst the covers. She watched in open admiration as Rhamus dressed in the faint morning light, feeling safe from his attentions, noting his haste. Sitting up and clasping her arms around her knees she inquired, "Will you be gone all day?"

Striding over quickly, he gave Serena a brotherly kiss on the top of her tousled hair. "Pretty much, but I hope to take you on a tour in the afternoon."

Cocking her head, Serena said mischievously, "If you're too busy, Jarvic could take me again."

Pausing with his hand on the door handle, Rhamus simply shook his head sternly at her. Serena giggled, pleased with the certainty of his refusal.

She took a long, hot soak in the bubbling tub to ease the stiffness in her legs. She winced as one calf muscle knotted painfully when she stepped out of the tub. She'd forgotten just how sore one could get from riding.

True to his word, Rhamus showed up later and rescued her from Hartoos' teachings. They spent the afternoon on a tiring but extremely entertaining tour. He told her serious stories about weapons, stories full of drama and history that Serena found fascinating. And he told tales she suspected were mostly made up, about the history of the paintings of ancestral kings and relations.

Rhamus poked fun at an austere looking relative, then remarked on the angelic beauty of a child prince. Serena discovered that her husband had a delightful sense of humor. She didn't miss Jarvic's amusing banter one little bit.

When they returned to their bedroom, Rhamus seemed considerate of her obvious tiredness and did not attempt to make love to her. Instead, he continued with his stories about his childhood, including Kasha and Jarvic as central figures in many misadventures. Serena enjoyed their evening immensely and found herself shyly admiring this funny, handsome man who entertained her. He appeared to relish their evening as much as she.

"Rhamus, I've been thinking. I need a regular meeting time with the other women, to see how they're doing."

"Do whatever you feel is right." He reached over and smoothed a piece of hair behind her ear. Grasping her chin gently and turning her face toward him, he said, "Just promise me you won't start an insurrection."

Serena had to smile in response to the laughter that crinkled at the corner of Rhamus' eyes and the sad tone he tried to put into his statement.

A week passed quickly. Serena found herself enmeshed in the rhythms of castle life and the ongoing training. Facts Hartoos drilled in her head about everything from etiquette to laws of the land were beginning to stick and make sense. Serena found that much of Volarn's codes were based on equality and basic premises of morality that seemed to be universal in context.

She began to feel a sense of pride in the people of this planet and wonder at herself that she accepted the role of Queen so readily now. She no longer drew back from each new experience, but looked forward to discovering more about her adopted land.

Serena held her first meeting with some of the women. She had divided them into smaller groups to make the meetings manageable, and planned to meet with each group once a week. She felt extremely lucky to discover a counselor in her first group. Marie agreed to be a facilitator. Serena could help with matters such as Deborah's problem, but was glad to have Marie's expertise with emotional issues of the other women.

Each evening, after attending the dinner in the banquet hall, she and Rhamus came to know one another better. Many of their nights were filled with passionate lovemaking that left Serena breathless with wonder. But some nights he came in exhausted and dropped wearily onto his favorite chair. Those evenings would be spent in companionable sharing, full of stories from his childhood and accounts of past bravery of warrior friends and relatives.

Her husband did not brag about his own prowess as a warrior, but she sensed the bold leadership underlying his stories. And Rhamus never pried into her past, but gently asked questions that urged her to reveal more about herself to him. She began to feel selfish as he openly shared his past while she held hers in close guard. She wondered if this openness she was beginning to feel with her husband would ever be strong enough to dissolve her hesitation and reserve.

Serena only felt comfortable sharing little tidbits from her past, ones she considered safe. She laughed as she told Rhamus about her days as a wrestler and told of the eccentric behavior of her dear aunt Betty. He shared in her humorous exploits, laughing along with her at the telling, causing her to embellish certain aspects. Catching onto the fun, he would begin a tale of ridiculous proportions.

Every day that he could, he would take her on a tour of parts of the castle as yet unseen. After several days, they began exploring the outside, including the warriors' barracks, the yasmir corrals and the nests of the strange elag. Serena discovered that the huge eggs she'd been consuming were from these large creatures. Besides their delicious eggs, the elag's feathers were used for decorating clothing.

They rambled the countryside, stopping to visit the families who tended the large, bountiful gardens from whence came the delectable fruits and vegetables. Serena was charmed by the courtesy and friendliness of the people, and was sure they would have been just as gracious if she'd been the daughter of another farmer come to call. Rhamus and she were both accorded respect by all the Volarnians they met, yet there was a casual acceptance of them that she found endearing.

Serena looked with curiosity and longing toward the lovely township near the castle, as yet unexplored. "Are we going to see the little town over there?" She waved toward the pristine village.

"Yes." He grabbed her hand and squeezed it. "I've planned a whole afternoon, two days hence, to show you my village. I wanted plenty of time so you would see everything."

His reference to her love of exploring made her chuckle. "Race you back to the castle!" Serena slapped her yasmir lightly as it started a sprightly dash toward home. They'd ridden this afternoon due to the distance of the farmlands, and her equestrian skills were increasing each time they went for a ride. Again, she was pleased as she contemplated Rhamus' thoughtfulness in taking her for rides whenever he could.

He was already dismounted and standing nonchalantly with folded arms, trying to look bored as Serena and old Daras came pounding up. Laughing, she leaped off and landed with a thud in his arms. His surprised look was priceless. She didn't know if Rhamus was more surprised at her recklessness, or her willingness to jump into his arms.

"You've a warrior's taste for excitement, my wife." Rhamus looked stern, but a smile hovered at the corner of his lips, spoiling the effect. He lowered her slowly, sliding her full against his body, letting her feel the effect she had on his composure.

"Aye," she agreed as she pressed herself up against her husband, keeping her arms tight about his neck. Her open mouth and the tip of her tongue, which flicked her lips in an unconsciously sensual gesture, sealed her fate for the next few minutes. She surrendered totally to Rhamus' kiss and a maddening, swirling heat shot up her loins and seemed to connect with her sensitive breasts.

He withdrew his mouth for a few seconds and kissed her ear lobe, and as he drove her mad with that sensation, he casually breathed into her ear, "I love you, my jicha."

Serena could barely think with his hands on her aching breasts, pressing and rubbing, so that his remark went unprocessed in her mind until much later. Her groan was caught in the nexus of their kiss. Rhamus' body seemed to ignite with heat as he pressed more fervently on her breasts and explored her hips with his hard hands.

"Um-hum." A familiar throat clearing jarred through the two lover's sensual haze, sending them apart. Nicole's impish features were fairly split with the broad grin plastered there. "Isn't there a proper place for an old married couple to be carrying on like that, like maybe the bedroom?"

He glared at her. "Is this a new occupation for you, being an interrupter?"

Nicole giggled. "Come on," she smiled winsomely. "It was time for my visit." She shrugged delicately and looked off at a far point, a smile flirting upon her Cupid bow mouth. "Can I help it if you and Serena can't keep your hands off each other?"

Finding the humor of the situation, he returned her smile while Serena frowned. "Nicole!"

"What?" she remarked innocently.

"You don't have to voice every thought in that little head of yours."

Nicole grinned at her friend, not taking offense at the snide remark concerning her size. After all, she had caught them off guard and embarrassed Serena to boot.

She was in a good mood when she returned to the royal suite after her visit with Nicole. She found this was often the case, with friend's amusing stories of her continued pursuit of Dr. Melat, and the humorous observations about Volarn that could only come from her friend.

A tap sounded at the door and Lalme brought in an evening meal, setting it on the little table. Serena looked up in surprise. She'd thought they were going to the formal dinner, as usual. Rhamus waved his hand at her chair. "I thought we'd eat in tonight."

Even though she'd started enjoying the dinners now that she'd made friends among the nobility, she much preferred a quiet dinner in their quarters. They'd only eaten a few bites when he spooned up a candied fruit and held it up to her mouth.

"Try this, it's delicious. The cook's specialty."

Serena opened her mouth and took the confection into her mouth slowly. As it melted on her tongue, she closed her eyes and savored the wonderful new taste. It was indescribable. She could have selfishly eaten a huge bowl full instead of the small bowl set out for the both of them.

Feeling suddenly childish at the discovery of such a wonderful treat, she dipped her finger in the bowl and plopped it in her mouth quickly. Some of the sticky substance still managed to drip down her finger, running toward her palm. Serena licked up the few drops, stopping when she felt Rhamus' eyes on her, absorbed in her actions.

"Why not share?" His hot eyes lingered on her wet finger.

Giggling, she dipped again into the bowl. Halfway to her mouth, he grabbed her hand and brought her finger to his mouth. He sucked on her finger, making it even more moist. A shock wave ran through Serena's body, starting with the contact of Rhamus' warm, wet mouth surrounding her finger with its heat. It tickled, it was wild, sensual and erotic. The heat of his mouth felt as though it were connected to the hot, liquid pool that suddenly gathered in her belly.

Lowering her finger, but still holding it in his grasp, he dipped a finger into the dessert and held it in front of Serena's full lips. She couldn't resist the tug of sexual desire and pulled his finger into her mouth with a greedy sucking sound. His reaction, plus the surprisingly erotic feeling of his finger in her mouth, made the heat in her stomach thrill throughout her whole body.

Rhamus pulled his finger out of her mouth and grasped the back of her head, bringing them together across the space of the table. Several dishes clattered to the floor, unnoticed as he and Serena licked hungrily on each other's lips.

All thoughts of the meal vanished as they moved toward the bed, urgently tugging and discarding each other's clothes along the way. As she lay stretched on the bed and he was about to join her, Rhamus stopped abruptly and jumped up. She watched in puzzlement as he picked up the dessert bowl, then sauntered back toward her wearing nothing but a wicked grin. Serena gasped in surprise as he tipped the bowl, juice landing with large plops on her torso and between her breasts.

Her shock at his actions turned to giggles as he attacked the dessert drippings with vigor, licking his way up her body and latching onto her lips lustily. He tasted sweet, his tongue a candy offered for her pleasure.

In seconds her merriment had faded, replaced by a sharp pang of desire. She wanted Rhamus so badly it hurt. When he released her lips she spread her legs, expecting him to plunge inside her as she wished. Instead he kissed his way slowly down her body, licking and nibbling. When his head moved past her belly button, her stomach quivered.

Oral sex. She had often wondered about it. The thought of him seeing her most private parts was embarrassing. Serena tried to close her legs, but his body was between them.

"No, jicha, open wider for me."

When she didn't respond, Rhamus sighed loudly in an exaggerated fashion. But then he slipped one finger inside her and she ceased to think--just feel. Her legs trembled and flopped weakly to the side when he pushed them apart. She seemed to have no will left, other than being his puppet.

His warm, wet tongue slid along the edge of her folds and she flinched. But his hands steadied her as he held her flesh apart. As his tongue delved deeper, between her inner lips, her thighs quivered. Up and down his marvelous tongue stroked, sending flames racing through her blood.

Serena gripped the sheets with her hands, clutching the material for dear life. She wanted to scream and shove her pussy hard into his face. But she did neither. She had not lost complete control of her senses--yet. Somewhere inside she realized it might happen if he kept licking her sensitive flesh as he was doing.

Should she stop him? Dragging her head up, she glanced down. The sight of Rhamus' black hair spilling over her groin made her moan. Laying her head back down, she twisted beneath his erotic torment. There was no small part of her that wanted him to stop. And her body only demanded more of his exquisite tongue.

Rhamus' tongue lapped and swirled, teasing her unmercifully, before he finally rubbed it along her clit. She whimpered as the deep ache inside her became boiling hot. His tongue flicked her nub in swift strokes. Her whole body arched and a rush of excitement hit her. Rhamus lost purchase on her for seconds as she reared upward, but then his tongue returned to torture her anew.

Now she felt the need to scream ripping through her body as her clit beat erratically. Plunging her hands into Rhamus' hair she pushed his face into her flesh as she lunged upward. Her orgasm washed through her in waves and she screamed loudly and unashamedly.

Her hips relaxed and her husband swiped her lips a few more times, making tiny erotic shudders ripple through her pussy. He moved up her body, pulling her into his arms.

She was sated and her body infused with a pleasant glow. She enjoyed being held in Rhamus' arms and laid there for five minutes before her mind strayed to her first encounter with oral sex. It had been wondrous, more than she could have hoped for. But it hit her that he had not climaxed, only she had reached her pleasure.

Idly, her hands stroked his firm chest. A secret smile lit her face as she watched Rhamus' cock awaken. When it reached its full length, she couldn't help but sleek her hand down his abs and close it around his cock.

"Not satisfied?" He laughed, his hand stroking her arm.

"Very." She sat up and turned to gaze at him. "I just think you deserve *satisfaction* as well." With that statement she leaned down and licked the head with one long caress.

Rhamus' cock jerked and his hand stilled.

Tentatively, she stroked the tip several times with her tongue, gratified by his heavier breathing. His skin was warm and soft, and she found it to be an erotic sensation.

Opening her mouth wide, Serena placed her lips just over the head and tried different techniques--sucking and bobbing up and down. Rhamus groaned and his hand moved to her hair. She hadn't been sure if she would like sucking a man's cock, but the pool of wetness that quickly formed between her thighs, said she did.

Withdrawing, she glanced at his face. "I'm not sure … about going down on you." She couldn't stop the blush that heated her cheeks.

"Don't do anything you don't desire to do," he said huskily.

"It's not that … what if I bite you?"

Rhamus chuckled and ruffled her hair. "That can happen, jicha, but only experience will teach you the right way."

She nodded, took a deep breath and slipped her lips down his shaft. It was a tight fit, reminding her of how he filled her completely. Just that thought made her go weak. She slid up and down gently, surprised by her body's response. Her lower lips felt swollen again and her clit throbbed.

"Teeth." Rhamus' word jerked her from the sexual haze.

Readjusting her mouth, it took several more attempts, with his guidance, before she fumbled on the right position. Lips over the teeth. Now that she had it right, Serena concentrated on sucking her husband's cock. He groaned and pushed his hips upward.

"Wonderful," he hissed.

Several minutes later, Rhamus pulled her off.

"Why did you do that?" She felt slightly frustrated.

He got to his knees and pushed her gently to the bed. "Because I want to come inside you."

A rush of pleasure shot through her at his words. Without his urging, she spread her legs wider. She wanted him badly.

Her breath exhaled in one swift gush when he rammed inside her with one stroke. No tender foreplay for them. They wanted to fuck. Serena ached for his cock to ease the wet neediness that had been reawakened when she sucked him.

"Yes," she moaned, arching toward him. Needing more contact with his body, she pulled him down for a kiss. Their tongues sparred in quick thrusts and she moaned into his mouth as his cock plunged into her repeatedly.

Rhamus sucked her lower lip into his mouth and she whimpered, overcome with hot flashes of sensation coursing through her.

"Mmm, mmm," she groaned into his mouth, shoving her hips upward to meet his strokes. Her nails raked his back and she jerked her head away, thrashing it against the bed as an orgasm ripped through her pussy.

"Serena," he bellowed, ramming forcefully into her sensitive channel. Shudders quivered through her lower body as his climax pulled more pleasure from her aching flesh.

Her breathing took long seconds to calm down and she smoothed her hands down Rhamus' back as her pulse returned to normal. She was completely wrung out. With a satisfied sigh, she cuddled against his chest after he rolled off. Serena believed she'd never felt anything so wonderful. The eroticism surrounding the new sexual acts that he taught her, involving full use of their lips and tongues upon each other's bodies, surpassed anything she could have imagined.

She snuggled under Rhamus' chin, sleep prodding her devilishly in spite of her best effort to stay awake. But, her drowsiness screeched to a halt when her thoughts flitted back over the day's events and she suddenly processed just what he'd spoken huskily into her ear. Now, she lay wide-awake, staring into the darkness as Rhamus' breathing deepened into sleep.

How can he love me? Part of her wanted to shove his words back into his mouth. She was too scared of her own fledgling feelings to be able to deal with his open ones. But there was another part of her that hugged those words to her as close as the pillow she clutched to her cheek.

Before he left the next morning, he ordered this to be her day of rest, to be spent as her heart desired. Serena secretly thought he was so pleased with their torrid lovemaking last night that he wanted to do something to please her. He even sent a messenger to Hartoos to cancel any classes. She smiled as she thought of the advisor's reaction to this news, for he seemed to thrive on his daily instructing of the Queen.

Serena was truly glad Rhamus had made this gesture today. Her period had arrived and she began feeling miserable soon after her morning bath. She was surprised that she'd forgotten it was "that" time, but then she'd been so busy. Normally her monthly period was a trivial thing, but now seemed to grip her guts with pain and announce its arrival loudly. She had heard stress could alter hormones-she'd certainly had her measure of stressful situations lately.

She was glad one of the women had suggested they all be prepared before leaving the ship, giving the ship's replicator machine orders for feminine hygiene products. Once the spaceship was unavailable, she guessed there would be a new product line produced by some entrepreneur-minded Volarnian. Or did Volarnian women already have something available? She made a mental note to ask Rhamus.

She was feeling better by the time her husband came back in the evening. Serena stopped him quickly when he made overtures toward her. Her face blushing crimson, she told him why they couldn't have sex. Thankfully, he was understanding and informed her that Dr. Melat had told him what to expect.

"Don't Volarnian women have periods?"

Rhamus shook his head. At Serena's questioning look, he continued, "Our women have their fertile time once a year, at least those who are not sterile. And there is no fluid loss like Earth women." Seeing her flushed face, he cocked his head. "Why are Earth people so uncomfortable discussing a natural part of being a living being?"

"I don't know." Serena shrugged. "Once a year," she whispered. "How wonderful."

"Hmm, yes and no." He looked thoughtful. "Good for females I guess, not to have to deal with being locked up but once a year. But not good for a society with reproduction problems, to have a fertility period of only once a year."

"Locked up!"

"I didn't realize you hadn't learned about this part of our hormonal cycle, a very essential part." Rhamus settled more comfortably in the chair and began telling Serena about this strange custom. When a young girl came into her first ventyl, she had to be locked up by her relatives for the cycle of her fertility period, about a week. And every woman had this same treatment once a year until they became too old to come into their cycle.

During her ventyl, every female exuded a scent that any Volarnian male could smell and respond to. Any male, excluding relatives, would find the female irresistible and sex would ensue. The women did not seem to have control over their urges anymore than the hapless male who might find himself within her range.

The Volarnians strongly respected a woman's right to choose, to select a mate through the Tarthra or to pick a lover. So, family members protected their women once a year from inappropriate matings and the resulting children that might be produced from a fertile union.

"Women can choose to take a lover and not go through with the Tarthra?" Serena was surprised by this revelation.

"Yes. But normally, a female waits until she finds a mate through the Tarthra."

"What if she doesn't find a partner?"

"Then once she reaches full age of maturity, eighteen in our years, she may choose to take a lover if she has not found a heart mate yet."

"What about these children that may result from an 'inappropriate union'? Are they acceptable to your society?"

"Of course they are." Rhamus seemed astounded at her question. "It's just that every male wants to raise their own child. Children on Volarn have always been highly prized, but especially now. If a child is born from a union that is not from a Tarthra choosing, then the real father cannot raise his child as he would wish to do. Fathers take great pride in their children and helping them attain warrior status. Jarvic is a child of such a union and it has caused his father great anguish, being unable to help raise his son fully."

"You mean the father cannot visit or anything?"

"Yes, they can visit. But the child stays with the mother and the clan of her chosen partner. The mother's partner and his clan relatives are responsible for helping raise the child and providing anything he may need, including training. This keeps the clan lines stable and strong."

Serena wanted to hear more of Volarn's interesting clan system. She asked Rhamus about the different symbols she'd seen on warriors' armbands and headbands, like the basami depicted in some fashion on all of Rhamus' pieces. As she suspected, he told her that the dragon represented his clan, and all his relatives wore one somewhere incorporated into a piece of their jewelry. Even distant relations who had never met certain members of their clan would know them by their dragon markings when crossing paths the first time.

Jarvic was a member of the basami clan even though his real

father came from the alati clan. Serena kept up a steady stream of questions. She thought it quaint that the clans were named for native animals, that Volarnians had no concept of a last name. A child was given their first name and a clan name for distinction.

"What about the west Volarnians?"

"We were having a nice little conversation." Rhamus frowned. "We could have gone all night without mentioning them."

Serena couldn't help the little smile that tugged at her lips. "Come on, Rhamus, do they have clans too?"

Staring across the room irritably, he replied, "Yes, they have clans, with names like our own."

"Then how can you tell one another apart?" His stare made her wish she could take that question back. She'd forgotten that Rhamus' enemies had red hair.

Trying to change the subject to ease his mood, Serena ran her thumb over the dragon design on her marriage bracelet and the two jewels, one clutched in each of the dragon's claws. "What's the significance of these two stones?"

He took her wrist in his hand and rubbed a finger lightly on one stone. "The blue crystal represents your acceptance into the royal house." Touching the lovely aquamarine crystal, he said, "This one represents Earth."

"Earth?"

"Yes," Rhamus laughed. "You don't know the problems it caused selecting the right color to represent our new women and their homeland. I met with the council to discuss this issue. Blue couldn't be selected because all shades of blue are already used by present clans and green also by the same reasoning."

"So someone recommended combining the blue and green into an aqua crystal," Serena reasoned out.

"Yes. It was actually Rolan' who made the suggestion, combining the blue waters of Earth with the green of the land. There is no crystal on Volarn of this shade, so it had not occurred to any of us.

"But Rolan' showed us a sample from a shipment he was taking elsewhere. Of course, the Moyds are pleased with the extra profits they'll be making from this deal." Rhamus examined the aqua crystal set next to the arj'ak's blue one. "It is a lovely addition to Volarn's crystals."

Looking at the aqua crystal made her think of Earth's blue and green splendor, and for a few seconds, Serena felt a stab of homesickness rip through her. When she spoke, her voice held an edge of fragility that was not in keeping with her question. "Let me get this straight. When a woman marries, she adds her colors to that of her husband's clan?"

"Yes, that way the bloodline of each clan is represented." Tapping the dragon, he said, "You are basami clan now, but also of the royal line."

"Then Jarvic is basami, but does he carry the arj'ak crystal, too?"

"No, he carries a slightly deeper blue crystal, which represents his bloodlines to the throne and of his adopted father. Only a direct descendant of the throne or their mate may wear the arj'ak."

"So Jarvic is basami and wears the dragon, but he does not wear the arj'ak blue, but Kasha wears the dragon and the arj'ak crystal."

"That's right," Rhamus confirmed. "But ... each warrior wears a bracelet with a blue arj'ak on their left wrist--the same as mine," he extended his arm and tapped the arj'ak crystal with his right forefinger. "Herein lies the power source for our battles when needed."

Serena nodded in understanding. "But, if Jarvic is adopted, how can he look so much like you?"

He laughed. "That could be confusing, but simply answered--Jarvic's mother was a distant cousin. He just happened to inherit the appearance of my close relatives."

Creasing her brow in concentration, she said, "Several days ago, you were telling me about Jarvic, and you mentioned all males are trained as warriors? You mean every male is trained or only those who wish to become warriors?"

"All male children leave their families when they reach puberty to begin training."

"They have no choice? What if they wanted to become ... an artist?"

Rhamus shook his head. "I can understand your concern and confusion. But it has been this way for as long as the very old can remember and no one protests this tradition. And as far as wanting to become an artist, musician, or whatever, males voluntarily serve four years as soldiers and then they can choose to stay on as warriors, or they may retire and do something else."

"The farmers that you met and many of the artists who created these paintings," Rhamus waved toward the wonderful paintings that filled much space in their room, "were painted by retired warriors. In spite of our warrior heritage, Volarnians prize artistic individuals. It is a highly respected occupation."

"Yes, I did wonder about all the lovely paintings and tapestries that I've seen here in the castle," Serena mused. "So, the women are not expected to become warriors like Kasha. They decide on their own if that's what they want?"

"Remember earlier, I explained that only infertile women could choose to go into the Getra?"

A distressed look flitted across Serena's features. "Then, Kasha is sterile?"

Rhamus shrugged noncommittally, and she wished she could pull that remark back into nonexistence.

Sterility. Kidnapping. Babies. Now was the time. There were questions she wanted answered about the abduction. Taking a deep breath, steeling herself against her growing feelings for him, she asked, "Rhamus, why kidnap women from another planet? Why couldn't Dr. Melat use his medical knowledge to help with the sterility problem instead?"

He sighed, and then took her hand gently. "Dr. Melat has spent years in research, testing, and looking at alternatives. Nothing worked."

"What about fertilizing eggs outside the uterus and implanting into the women? Even we have that medical advancement?"

He shook his head slowly, a frown creasing his brow. "My people consider such techniques against their religious beliefs, and won't allow tampering with the natural order either. Even the threat of extinction has not swayed the vassi to lead the people toward medical science which could be their salvation."

Serena simply stared at him.

"Do you think for one minute I've enjoyed my role as a pirate?" Rhamus' eyes were sad, his grip tightened on her hand.

"No," she replied hesitantly, not sure how she felt at this point either.

"If I had not ordered Earth women to be brought here, I never would have found you." His eyes now had a haunted, faraway look.

This was it, her opportunity to plead their case, ask for the women to be taken back to Earth. Yet, she couldn't do it, couldn't get the words to form. How could she push them past her lips, when the mere whisper of such thoughts seared her breast with pain?

Seeking to lighten his mood, Serena commented, "Well, then, I guess all the pressure is on you and I, to continue the royal line." He smiled slightly but still seemed lost in thought.

Chapter Thirteen

When Lalme brought their dinner a short time later, Serena looked at Rhamus in surprise. "I thought you would prefer eating here tonight; just a quiet dinner with maybe some pleasant talk."

She smiled and nodded her head, pleased with his thoughtfulness. They did indeed spend a very nice evening talking and getting acquainted further. He pulled out an odd shaped game later and taught her moves across a painted board. Of course he beat her horribly, but she enjoyed the simple pleasure of his company.

Later, they sat in relaxed companionship as Rhamus told her Volarnian tales. One concerned the basami.

"Are there any living close to the castle?" Serena asked, as she looked out towards the dark balcony, as if searching for signs of the beast.

He shook his head. "Unfortunately, we think they're extinct. None have been seen since my great grandfather's time."

"It's sad when animals become extinct. Maybe it was better in this case. Weren't the basami dangerous?"

"No," Rhamus replied. "They were fierce when hunted or when their young were threatened but, if left alone, they didn't bother anyone. At least, that's what my great grandfather reportedly said," he shrugged. "Who can say for sure, it was so long ago. Then, there are those among us who believe the stories about the dragons swallowing men whole for a snack."

"Hmm, well, I'm glad I don't have to meet any."

"Yes, there are other fierce beasts beautiful women have to be wary of."

Rhamus' silly grin made her giggle. His teasing continued until they snuggled in bed later, and she had to tickle him and threaten more if he didn't stop his verbal assault on her funny bone.

Serena felt her old self again the next day and two days passed quickly, filled with Hartoos' teachings. She understood more now as she adopted Rhamus' perspective and listened closer to the advisor. Serena was surprised when she realized that suddenly Hartoos' tedious presentations were no longer boring. He was very pleased with her changed attitude.

Rhamus surprised her once again when he informed her that she was to have another "day off" since her last one was virtually spoiled. Serena was very disappointed when he disclosed he would be tied up all day with troop inspections so they would be unable to share a morning ride. She even felt a momentary disappointment that she would miss lessons today.

Try as she might, Serena found she couldn't sleep late, as she had first thought to do. She had adapted to waking early with her husband. Taking a long, leisurely bath was relaxing and the sumptuous breakfast, brought by Lalme, welcome. But soon she was restless and decided to pay an early visit to Nicole.

The youthful guard outside her door readily agreed to drive her to the space ship in one of the carriages that had brought her to the castle. At first, she'd been very irritated by the guard's constant trailing of her, but sometimes, like today, his presence was helpful. Serena didn't feel like getting dusty from a ride and return smelling like a yasmir to boot. She could still pick up the scent of roses rising off her sun-warmed flesh from the crespassno oil she'd used during her bath.

Serena felt somewhat awkward approaching the entrance to the ship. It was now a symbol of her capture and of her unfortunate bid for escape. The reminder of her recent failure prodded wounds still fresh and painful.

This unlikely vessel had stolen her freedom, yet had made possible a freedom within herself that she'd never attained back on Earth. She was free to enjoy her life, make new friends, and enjoy the luxury accorded only to the rich. And maybe to, at last, have the freedom to allow love to enter her life. No, her mind whispered. The imp of pessimism rode heavily upon her shoulder still. *I cannot allow myself to fall in love, for to risk love, is to risk losing that loved one.*

Hesitating at the opening, Serena looked to the guard. He'd already taken up a stiff pose near the outer hull and stared straight ahead. Serena sensed that the unfamiliar ship made him nervous. He would stand guard while he waited for her return, but she didn't think he'd agree to enter the ship with her.

Apparently he was not worried about her trying to escape by herself. Shrugging her shoulders, she stepped quietly into the ship, but it made her feel jumpy when she heard the hollow echo of her footfalls.

Chewing on her lip, she wondered if this had been such a great idea. After all, Nicole loved making the short trip every day to the castle.

"May I be of assistance?" A feminine voice burst through Serena's thoughts from a speaker in the wall. Jumping, even as she recognized the computer-aided voice, she felt silly at her forgetfulness. You'd think it'd been a million years since I traveled on this thing, she thought.

She responded to the question by asking for directions to the lab. She followed the accommodating red light that appeared and led her again into the bowels of the ship.

Not sure whether she should knock or simply enter, Serena felt like a kid caught with her hand in the cookie jar when the door suddenly slid open with a hiss. Or maybe the room's occupants feel more like the kids, she thought, gazing at the situation in amusement. Nicole and the doctor were locked in a passionate kiss. At the sound, they looked up in dazed surprise. Nicole sat on the examining table while Dr. Melat stood in the circle of her clasped arms.

"I guess 'uh-hum' would be pointless now." Serena couldn't help the grin, which stretched her mouth wide and the twinkling that entered her eyes.

"I think you're right," Nicole answered pertly as she jumped down from the table. Doc had already backed away and turned to fiddle with some instruments nearby.

Not ready to give up her teasing, especially with the tables turned for once, she said, "I could return at a ... more convenient time." Nicole laughed and shook her head.

Serena enjoyed her visit and her friend's tour of the lab and explanation of various medical devices. But noticing her friend's wistful glances at the doctor and feeling as though she needed to escape the claustrophobic atmosphere of the ship, Serena brought her visit to a close.

Suppressing a laugh behind her hand, Serena made a stomping noise at the entrance, waking the dozing guard to immediate alertness. On the way back to the castle, she almost wished she'd taken a yasmir instead of the slow carriage. At least it would have been an outlet for the restless energy she felt. Once they regained the castle's grounds, she surprised the guard by opting to walk. He had no choice but to follow in the coach. She had walked a long way, nearly reaching the back gardens, when she heard shouts.

She sprinted around the garden wall, coming out on an open field. The source of the clamor caused her to duck back behind the wall as she assessed the situation. About twenty warriors stood in a circle beyond the wall while two of their number faced each other in the center. If Serena remembered right, twenty was about the size of a patrol group. She had learned that these groups not only went on patrol together, but practiced and fought together, sharing the same barracks, unless they were Getra or married.

She noted that there were only two Getra in the group including one of the central warriors. Peering closely, she saw that Kasha was the woman warrior within the circle. The princess faced a huge warrior, even taller than Rhamus, with a bigger, bulkier body build. They appeared to be practicing some sort of hand-to-hand combat. Both the giant and Kasha were dusty and sweaty, and seemed to be enjoying themselves thoroughly.

The two oddly matched combatants circled one another, looking for an opening. Taking the big man by surprise, the princess hooked one leg around his calf and pulled. Dust erupted all around the fallen giant, as he crashed to the ground. Serena worried her lower lip with her teeth, wondering if the male warrior would demolish Kasha in reprisal. The giant stood up, and, slapping his knees with his huge palms, let loose a great booming laugh. The onlookers chuckled as they and the big warrior commented on Kasha's tactic.

Kasha noticed Serena and frowned in irritation. She again took up her defensive stance, but this time her opponent got the best of her. The princess landed on her backside but it was her dignity that felt the blow. She hit at the dirt clinging to her skirt in agitation, glancing across the yard in her direction. Serena tried hard to wipe the look of amusement off her face.

With a steely glint in her eye Kasha strode purposefully across to the wall. "Maybe you can do better?" Her sarcastic tone left no doubt that she expected her challenge to go unanswered. "But, then again, you wouldn't want to get your hands dirty. Or, your pretty dress." The eyes of the other warriors had followed Kasha's progress and now, her challenge.

Curious and cautious, they watched Serena's reaction.

Aware of their scrutiny, she looked down at the delicate pink dress she wore. It wasn't the best choice for sparring, but was very close to the design of the wrestling outfit she'd worn on Earth. If the Volarnian females could be so casual about showing their upper thighs and glimpses of their undergarment, she could go along with it. When in Rome, Serena thought. Besides, she could use the exercise. She certainly had not had the opportunity to practice wrestling since her capture.

Shrugging, she undid the jeweled belt and earrings and laid them to the side. When she turned back to the group of warriors, she noted with satisfaction, surprise written on each face, but especially Kasha's.

The next instant her sister-in-law assumed an aggressive stance and an expressionless face. The two very attractive young women circled each other. Serena began looking for an opening and tried to gage the direction of Kasha's attack. The crowd moved back as each got in several minor blows to arms and lower legs.

The warrior princess suddenly swung her leg to try and catch her off guard. Her tactics were too closely allied to Olga's sneaky blows and were easily thrown off. Serena merely jumped high in the air and landed as Kasha completed her swing to empty space, which swung the princess around and down into an undignified heap. Serena could have given Kasha a good blow at this point but allowed her to rise again.

Sensing this fair play on her opponent's part, her face became flushed a dark-beige in a true Volarnian display of temper. Tossing strategy aside, Kasha ground her teeth and rushed at her.

Serena knocked the princess down onto her butt with an effortless reflex reaction. Jumping to her feet, Kasha put her head down and ran at her again with a low growl of frustration.

Using Kasha's momentum, and a little arm play, Serena helped the warrior princess flip over into a grand somersault that landed her flat on her back. Staring angrily about and wiping grit from her eyes, Kasha sat up. "Here, let me help you up, princess." One of the warriors extended his hand and pulled the downed princess to her feet.

"I don't think she's new to this." Serena heard him murmur to the princess.

"How nice that he's come to your aid. Perhaps your giant warrior would be willing to take over for you." Serena's voice was just as sarcastic as Kasha's had been earlier. Between the sparring, and verbal barbs from Kasha, her blood was boiling. She had to admit, she wanted to goad her sister-in-law into a good rousing match.

Kasha eyed her sourly. "Maybe he should." Her voice dripped with sarcasm, plainly indicating Serena was not up to that challenge.

Looking the big man up and down, like a farmer examining a good stock animal, she said, "He may just give me a little more sport."

The big man looked very uncomfortable to be in the middle of a cat-fight and fidgeted as he awaited his princess's reply.

"Be my guest." Kasha waved a hand in their direction as a witchy smile spread across her face.

Facing her with arms hanging loosely and looking extremely embarrassed to be pitted against the Queen, the giant stood uncertainly. "By the way, it's nice to meet you," Serena started slowly toward the man with one arm outstretched. "What is your name?"

"Yissell," the big man replied, stretching his arm to meet the Queen's. As he released her firm grip, he felt a blur of movement and the earth slam him hard.

"Did you see that?" Whispers of excitement came from the assembled warriors.

"Not clearly, it was too fast."

"She grabbed his arm and tossed him over her shoulder! Yissell must weigh 450 stones."

Kasha stood in open-mouthed shock. She closed it quickly as Serena swung around in her direction.

The big man looked stunned but determined as he towered over the much smaller woman circling him. He tried to grab Serena as she bounced around him, but she always moved just out of reach.

She waited for the opportunity to use her favorite and most impressive move. As Yissell rushed toward her, she jumped up high and kicked out with her muscled thighs. Both feet making contact with her opponent's hard, muscular stomach made quite an explosion of transferred energy. Yissell's body landed more than several feet from his original stance, crashing with an earth-shaking thud.

A hush descended on the warriors as Serena casually slapped at the dirt that had collected on the silky fabric of her dress and Yissell lay in stunned silence. Walking over slowly to the big sprawled figure, Serena asked nonchalantly, "Ready to call it quits?"

Yissell put both hands up in a surrendering gesture then sat up shaking his head at the warrior Queen. All eyes turned nervously toward Kasha. She stood a few feet away looking down at her fallen comrade, then turned and looked at Serena with a mixture of confusion and admiration.

"Can you teach me your fighting techniques?" Kasha asked with a serious face and respectful tone. At Serena's quick nod to the positive, the princess seemed to relax the tension in her shoulders and allowed a small, hesitant smile to tug at her mouth.

Seeing Kasha's changed demeanor, she inquired. "When do you want to start?"

"How about right now?" She asked hopefully and was pleased with Serena's accepting nod. "I'd really like to learn that kicking trick you used." She turned toward the fallen Yissell, who stood up and regarded them both in complete bewilderment.

* * * *

Jarvic and Rhamus stood in the distance, unnoticed by the gathered warriors. He hadn't been too worried when his wife and sister faced each other. He figured Kasha would knock Serena down and that would be the end of it. At first, he was surprised by his wife's victory over Kasha, but realized that women wrestlers of Earth must have greater fighting skills than he had first surmised.

When Serena faced Yissell, Jarvic had to hold him to keep him from rushing to interfere. His cousin reminded him of Yissell's gentle nature, and the fact that he'd have to be an idiot to do anything to injure Serena. Rhamus stood rigid and carefully watched the proceedings. He was stunned by Serena's fighting abilities against a male warrior, but relaxed slightly after she threw her huge opponent so easily.

And after she downed him with the kick, an almost physical sense of pride swelled his chest. He grinned at Yissell's reaction, one he was sure he would have felt in the warrior's place. He tensed a second time as Serena and Kasha faced one another and started wrestling again. This time he was concerned for his hard-headed sister.

It didn't take but a few minutes for the two men standing on the far hill to recognize that the match being played out between Kasha and Serena now was merely a teaching session. As his wife knocked his sister down several times, the princess jumped up each time, questioning Serena and listening closely to her answers. Rhamus watched this for a while, then saw Kasha succeed at throwing Serena. He wasn't sure, but he suspected his wife of letting Kasha win that hand. The proud princess bowed to her cheering audience, then turned to Serena and shook her hand.

Sprinting down the hill with Jarvic at his heels, Rhamus stopped abruptly near the sparring area as the warriors parted to let him through. As both his wife and sister turned to him in surprise, he slowly clapped his hands. "Well done, warriors."

* * * *

Serena didn't know if her husband's compliment was aimed at the fighting ability displayed by the both of them or the fact that she and Kasha had finally started to mend things between them. But she was pleased nonetheless. "Maybe I'll teach you how to wrestle one of these days," she teased.

Rhamus rubbed his lower lip and lowered his voice for her ears only. "I don't think so, I get enough wrestling in our bedroom."

Her pink face made him smile, but the quick laugh that erupted from Kasha told him that his voice had carried farther than he had intended. He frowned at his sister, who grinned back at him.

"Maybe you'd like to see the sword-fighting skills our warriors are famous for?" Kasha directed this at Serena.

She was curious about this hand-to-hand style of fighting used by

Volarn's soldiers. At the princess' nod, the grouped warriors quickly and efficiently reformed their circle and two warriors paired off for a display of swordsmanship. After they finished, Kasha asked Serena if she'd like to try her hand at sword fighting. Shaking her head vigorously and laughing, she stood next to Rhamus as Kasha took up a position across from a slim young warrior.

She was truly impressed with the fluid motions exhibited by the pair. Physical strength was certainly a key factor. Serena had already tried the hefty weight of the swords and knew that she wouldn't have the strength in her own wrists to wield the large weapons for long. She was amazed at the steely strength displayed by Kasha as she struck again and again at her opponent's defenses.

The princess paused and looked at her brother. "Should we show her the full scope of the crystal's power?"

A simple nod from Rhamus and the two again took up defensive stances. They both stared intently at their swords until a blue light radiated from their fists, arcing to the hilt. As the blue light maintained its contact with the fencer's fists, each appeared to suddenly be renewed with vigor and strength. She had seen their heaving sides and the sheen of sweat on their body's just moments before.

She was amazed at the extra power that surged through them from the blue crystal on their wristbands. Again they struck at each other, sometimes with amazing finesse and at other times with strong, hacking swings that clanged loudly as the swords connected.

"Is this the power from the crystal that you spoke of?" Serena turned to Rhamus.

Nodding, he replied, "One of the ways the arj'ak can be used, besides for the Tarthra."

His warm gaze and his last remark caused her to feel a glimmer of happy agreement within herself. *Yes, the crystal does have some wondrous powers.*

"If your people and the west Volarnians both know how to use the crystal's power, doesn't that cancel out any advantage to either side? Why use it at all?"

Rhamus shrugged. "Why does anyone use something like the arj'ak? Because it's there, and to keep the use of power equal for both sides."

A puzzled expression creasing her brow, Serena said, "But I still don't understand. If two warriors facing each other are equal because of the crystal's power, it seems pointless to use it."

"A good observation, my jicha. But each warrior brings with him or her their individual skill as a swordsman and their ability to control and sustain the power."

"I think I understand." She looked at her husband's heavily muscled arms and remembered the power that surrounded them during the Tarthra. "Are you very good at both?"

Rhamus smiled confidently. "Sometimes actions speak more loudly for a warrior than pretty words."

With that, he left her side and, drawing the sword from his scabbard, nodded at his sister and her fencing partner as he approached them. Kasha and the young male left the center area and joined the group of onlookers. Rhamus grinned at Jarvic. Serena saw in the next few minutes why he'd chosen Jarvic as his fencing partner, for even with her untrained eyes, she could tell they were both skilled swordsmen.

But Jarvic's arm seemed to flash a bit faster than her husband's and he moved slightly quicker. She thought Rhamus outmatched until she saw what happened when they began to tire, and paused to use the crystal's power. Now she noticed the ability her husband showed in using and controlling the blue power running from his fist through the sword. His sword arm seemed to grow stronger and he literally began hacking at Jarvic, wearing his opponent down with sheer strength.

Finally, his forehead beaded with sweat, Jarvic let his sword drop wearily. Serena guessed this was a signal, for Rhamus also lowered his sword and then re-sheathed it. He slapped Jarvic on the back, then they both rejoined her, grinning like little boys who were happy they had beaten each other in a race. Serena smiled. Rhamus had not only been demonstrating the crystal's power but had been showing off for her. She laughed as they approached.

"Let us in on the joke." Jarvic tried to sound teasing, but his statement came out in a huffed fashion.

"A woman must have a few secret thoughts."

"Goreth protect us from women and their secret thoughts," Jarvic laughed as he drew level with her.

"Sounds like you know a lot about women and secrets," Serena smiled wickedly.

He denied everything, even though Rhamus regaled her with several outrageous stories of Jarvic's exploits with the opposite sex. Kasha joined their little group and teased him about a girl who followed him relentlessly, and tried to convince him to use the Tarthra at each choosing that arose.

"Did Rhamus ever tell you how Kasha used to trail him everywhere, like a young konkol, when they were growing up?" Jarvic asked and looked to see the princess' reaction.

"Not everywhere," she said in an offended voice.

"Ho!" He laughed. "What about the time Rhamus was taken on his first patrol, when you stuffed yourself into the yasmirs' feed bag on the pack animal?" Jarvic laughed again and turned to Serena. "By the time we discovered her, Kasha almost smothered." Jarvic shook his head. "Poor Zares. He nearly had a heart attack upon finding the young princess along on a dangerous patrol."

"Yes," Kasha answered agreeably, "but he appreciated me being there later."

"What do you mean?" Serena asked.

"While the rest of the patrol were out scouting the area, Zares stayed with me at the camp. He was worried about protecting me." Her eyes twinkled. "But as fate would have it, two western warriors were out scouting themselves and happened upon us." Kasha was gratified by Jarvic's annoyed look and Serena's attention, which was glued to her every word.

"Did Zares kill them?"

"No. Remember, we don't kill unless it's necessary. Sending a warrior home with cuts and bruises brings more honor. Anyway, both warriors had Zares tied up in a fierce sword battle. Zares is a wonderful swordsman, but both of these warriors were very good. He was having a terrible time trying to defend himself."

"What happened?"

She chuckled. Jarvic chose that moment to interrupt, "Kasha does love to drag her stories out, but everyone has places to go and business to attend to." She made an ugly face at her cousin. "So I will finish this story."

"Kasha was this big." Jarvic held his hand at knee level. "So nobody noticed her. She picked up a large rock and bashed one of the soldiers on the toes. He fell to the ground because she'd broken several of them, and that gave Zares time to finish off the other fellow."

"You were so brave for such a little child," Serena said with admiration.

"It was nothing." Kasha shrugged. "That's what made me first begin to think of joining the Getra."

"And Rhamus agreed to let you become a Getra, even though you are a princess?" She looked puzzled.

Jarvic grabbed her by the elbow and spoke in a low voice, "That's a story we don't want to open up. Kasha and Rhamus had terrible fights about her becoming Getra, until she finally wore him down."

Serena got the distinct feeling from both Rhamus and Kasha that it was a subject neither cared to have discussed. What is the real story is here, she wondered. Sensing she'd get no further with that topic, she inquired, "What happened to the two soldiers?"

Her husband seemed relieved she'd changed the subject. He smiled and answered, "Zares wounded the fellow he was fighting and all the 'fight' had been taken out of the one Kasha defeated." He paused and grinned at the way his sister smiled happily at his praise. "We escorted them to the border and directed them toward their home. On foot, of course."

"I think I understand," Serena mused. "Your fighting is actually more like the American Indians' 'counting coup', there's more honor if the enemy is not killed." As they approached the castle, she had to explain her statement to them. She suddenly realized she was enjoying their new intimacy very much.

When they started to part near the castle's entrance, Kasha turned to Serena. "Would you like to come back tomorrow and show me some more of those wonderful fighting techniques?"

"No way," Rhamus interrupted before she could answer. "I promised to show her our village tomorrow."

Chapter Fourteen

Kasha frowned at her brother. Jarvic volunteered to be her fighting partner in Serena's place, to which the princess replied, "There'd be no sport in fighting you." They both walked off together, still quarreling in a good-natured fashion, as Rhamus raised his eyes upward.

"One can never rest as the royal guardian of the kingdom. Some hot-blooded Volarnian is always fighting about something."

Serena smiled gently at his affected humor, knowing that a real stream of truth ran through those words.

She spent the remainder of the day with Surad, taking bundles of flowers and trays of nutritious food to people in the castle who were ill. Everyone's good spirits picked up again at dinner when they regrouped. Jarvic dragged a laughing, protesting Kasha to where Serena and Rhamus sat, pulling his chair up next to hers and seating the princess on his other side. Surad and Nuad joined them, completing the small group of people that Serena was beginning to consider friends. Their laughter was contagious. Hence the whole length of the banquet table was affected. The nobles engaged in much joking banter and lively conversation.

Later, after they closed out the world behind their chamber walls, Serena and Rhamus discussed some of the morning's experiences. Simply sitting across from this gorgeous man and conversing in such a soothing, relaxed manner made her feel more contented than Serena could ever recall.

Much later, she had a hard time getting to sleep even though she was tired. She couldn't stop thinking of the tour Rhamus was to take her on the next day. Unfortunately, Zares pounded on the door the next morning with bad news--the enemy had burned a village's crops. Reluctantly, he kissed her and renewed his promise for the tour upon his return.

It was six days before her husband returned and Serena spent several of these training with Kasha.

If not friends yet, she and the princess at least developed a hearty respect for each other's fighting skills. She also met with another one of her women's groups, which were going well.

True to his word, when Rhamus came back from his patrol they started out the next morning for the nearby village, riding in one of the carriages. Serena noticed this carriage was more elaborately embellished then the others had been. The color scheme was no surprise, being the arj'ak blue. A mixture of gold and lais metal were used for ornamentation with, of course, the basami dragon being the central depiction.

When the royal carriage entered the main street, the villagers began to appear and line the street's edge. They were quiet with suppressed excitement, smiling and greeting the King and Queen in respectful tones. They were not subservient in their manner, treating Rhamus more like a commander. Serena remembered being treated in a like manner by the farm folk they'd met recently. She enjoyed their reception. A large spraying fountain sat in the center of a large circular crossroads. Quaint little shops lined the circle and Serena could see streets projecting out in all directions like the spokes of a wheel. The people moved closer, calling out good wishes. Several people seemed more pushy than the others and Serena understood their enthusiasm when they tried to entice them into their shops. Grabbing her hand, Rhamus entered the nearest one.

She was enchanted with the interior, which held true to the quaintness of the shop's exterior. It was a bakery featuring loaves of the most curious designs. She stared down at a display full of scrumptious smelling pastries. One large cake that looked like a miniature dragon took up much of the shelf.

Seeing the direction of her gaze, the excited merchant immediately cut off two slices for them to try. Serena tried to refuse but Rhamus said the shopkeeper's feelings would be hurt if she did not taste his creation.

After they finished the fluffy confection, he whispered in her ear. "Besides, just think of his business when he spreads the word that the King and Queen loved his baking."

Smiling conspiratorially, Serena turned to the anxious merchant, complimenting him on his culinary skills. The tall, lanky Volarnian was overjoyed with their approval. They couldn't leave his shop without taking the rest of the cake and several other goodies. She waved goodbye to the pleasant man as Rhamus led her into the next shop.

This one was full of gorgeous fabrics of every description. Serena learned that this was the favorite place for picking out dress fabric for the ladies of the nobility. Less wealthy patrons choose luxurious materials for special occasions, and there was a wide assortment of fabrics for everyday wear. Remembering the incident with the baker, she tried not to look too long at any one piece. But she couldn't seem to keep from touching several gossamer swatches that draped from a high shelf. They were the softest fabric she'd ever felt and the colors were extraordinary.

"Like them?" He inquired.

"Sure," she whispered urgently before the shopkeeper could hear them and rush over. The lady was hovering at a respectful distance, but was ready to spring forward in a second. "But I know these fabrics would be too expensive for that shop keeper to just give me a bolt."

"True," Rhamus whispered in her ear, being far closer than was really necessary. His breath stirred the short hair in front of her ear and sent a shiver down her neck. "But I am the King and can get anything my Queen desires."

Serena looked up into his face and knew he hinted at another subject entirely, and he also knew the effect his warm breath wafting over her ear and neck was having on her. "Well then, quick, tell the lady you wish to *purchase* my desires," she whispered in irritation, "for here she comes."

Sighing exaggeratedly, Rhamus said, "You give up too quickly, my sweet." He turned to speak to the shopkeeper before she could form a snappy response.

His purchase of a large piece from each of the wonderful fabrics cooled her aggravation. He loved teasing her, but would she ever stop rising to his bait?

Although the shopkeeper was thrilled that the King had made such large purchases, she pressed several matching long thin pieces of ribbon into Serena's hand. She was puzzled for a second, then remembered that many Volarnian women loved to tie matching ribbons in their hair for coordination. Her genuine thanks caused the woman to flutter her hands with excitement. As they left, she heard the owner regaling the people gathered outside her shop with the news of the royal couple's visit.

"I'll bet she sells the rest of the fabric on those bolts before the end of the day." At her questioning look, he said, "She'll have it known all over town that the Queen went nuts over those particular pieces."

Serena screwed up her face at him, making Rhamus laugh loudly. The people near them smiled and nodded to one another, feeling happy that their rulers seemed so in love. Serena lost count of the little shops they visited. She only remembered some of the interesting items displayed in each one. There was a dry goods shop, a dressmaker, a boot-maker, and a crafter for the needs of yasmir owners. Thank goodness they stopped for a drink at a pleasant place. She was parched and the cool drinks were refreshing and delicious.

Her favorite shop, she decided, belonged to an artist. The shop was full of wonderful paintings of the countryside and every corner and shelf was crammed with sculptures. Serena discovered the place was owned by two artists, a husband and wife team. He painted while she created the figurines of clay. They were a gregarious young couple, both active and interesting.

After they had entered and examined every shop in the circular market place, Rhamus led her back to the carriage. They spent some time going up and down beautifully landscaped streets, viewing the lovely homes and gardens. Serena saw no evidence of a section for the poor populace as in any town or city back on Earth. Some homes were large, others were small, but all were well-kept and made from the same golden colored stones as the castle.

She had not seen many children. A few were running between the onlookers' legs and followed up and down the streets as they traversed the town by carriage. "I noticed that the children run around so freely and I can't tell who their mother or father is." She was confused by the way the children seemed to pass from one individual to another, first being held by one, and then another in the crowd.

"Because there are so few children, they are allowed to run freely in order that all grownups may enjoy them."

"Aren't the parents afraid someone might steal their child?"

The King shook his head sternly. "No, this would be the highest crime and punishable by exile to the wastelands--which is considered worse than death to a Volarnian. Besides, everyone knows someone or has a relative in every clan. Therefore, such an act would be impossible to cover up. And each child's first year is marked by a large celebration wherein that child is officially recognized by the state and welcomed by every single clan member."

"Why wait until the baby's first year?" Serena asked curiously.

"These birth celebrations used to be held more often, but with the lowered birth rate, we've stretched it out to only once a year."

"Oh." Once again she felt as though she'd blundered into a sensitive area.

"On a more cheerful note," Rhamus stopped the carriage and turned to her, "next week we hold our annual birth celebration. You will get to meet all the infants born within the last year."

As they exited the carriage to enter another quaint shop, an exotic woman Serena had not met blocked their pathway. The thin white streak that flowed from one temple and stood out starkly against her midnight locks betrayed her middle-age years but did not detract from her beauty. "This is Zara," his respectful tone spoke volumes.

She stuck out her hand when the woman extended hers, although this was not a common greeting among the women of Volarn. Serena was surprised when the woman did not shake her hand, but grasped it in a strong grip and simply looked at her.

As if sensing her discomfort and confusion, Rhamus interjected, "Don't be alarmed, Serena. Zara is a highly respected 'seer' amongst our people. She is paying you a great honor by reading your emanations."

Serena stared back at the woman in consternation. Zara's eyes seemed to be focused on some far point, as if she stared right through her. The next instant, the woman blinked and let her hand drop. She smiled kindly, making her feel immediately comfortable with the woman.

"The Tarthra has made a good match," Zara congratulated the King, who beamed at her words. Patting her hand, she continued, "This young woman will be a great Queen for our people." Dropping her eyes to Serena's flat stomach, "And, already the future heir grows within her body."

Serena and Rhamus both looked shocked. Somehow, she believed Zara. A strange connection seemed to still be alive between her and the seer, initiated by the woman's grasping of her hand.

After exchanging everyday pleasantries and a special invitation for Zara to attend the ceremony next week, Rhamus escorted his bemused wife to the carriage. Once seated, Serena turned to her husband. "I don't understand why you looked so shocked by Zara's prediction. I would think you'd be used to such things by now."

He eyed her thoughtfully. "I am used to such readings, but usually it is much further along."

"Further along?"

"Yes, usually when the woman is at least a month pregnant." His eyes seemed to come back in focus and he grinned hugely, then grabbed Serena up in a hard bear hug. Looking down tenderly at her confused expression, he said, "By the way, thank you, my Queen."

"But Rhamus," she protested as she pushed against his solid arms, "I can't be pregnant. I just had my period last week!"

He continued his comforting hold on her and gave her a gentle smile as he replied, "I don't understand her early prediction either, but I can assure you that Zara is always right."

Serena's face went through several emotional upheavals and finally settled on joy. "You mean I'm really going to have a baby?"

"You can count on it." Rhamus' confidence was hard to shake.

"But if it will make you feel any better, we can have Dr. Melat test you tomorrow."

"After one week?" His positive nod confirmed the miracle of a science vastly overshadowing that of Earth. "It would make me feel more sure, Rhamus. I do come from a society that puts more merit in science, and where only the outer fringes believe in psychic powers."

"Then we'll pay a visit to the good doctor tomorrow." He kept one arm around her as he skillfully guided the horse through the winding streets back toward the castle. Serena couldn't keep her hand from touching her stomach briefly and the soft smile that lit her face at the thought that she really could be carrying the future ruler. No, not the ruler, not yet. Just our baby.

The next day, she was still in shock. Dr. Melat confirmed Zara's prediction. As the week sped by and Rhamus was caught up in the preparations for the annual birth celebration, her excitement didn't lessen. Not only was she carrying the future heir to the throne, but proof that a Volarnian and Earth coupling worked.

The night before the birth celebration, clans began arriving at the castle. Escorts had been arranged for their safe passage across the great distances. Serena was pleased that all were to be put up within the castle walls. No Volarnian was turned away, no matter their rank or lack of noble heritage. The nobility who lived year round in the castle shared their quarters with others of their ranking, or moved in temporarily with family and gave up their rooms for use.

It was a mad melee of people coming and going, yet there was an underlying sense of organization through-out. Serena found herself shepherding stray children who had wandered from distracted parents who'd been busy directing servants in the placement of their baggage. Several times she had to direct lost adults as well. The rooms were filled with bodies, lots of talk and laughter. Serena was hugged by so many excited strangers, her ribs ached.

Finally, during the wee hours of the morning, the guests were settled in. Serena snuggled wearily next to her husband. He had already dropped off to sleep, but not before he had kissed her soundly, thanking her for her help today, and again for their child. She could not remember a happier day.

The next day was filled with just as much chaos and good spirits as more guests arrived. Clan reunions took place with each new arrival. Serena met so many people she knew she'd never remember names and only a few faces. Yet she always felt welcomed, as if she were a part of a hugely extended family.

Olga and Zares strolled hand in hand, kissing and acting as in love as any couple she'd ever seen. She concluded that Olga, like herself, had decided to make the best of it, especially since they both carried feelings toward their husbands. She also saw other women from the ship that appeared to be trying to make their forced marriage into a real one. Even the unhappy Deborah appeared to be trying to have a good time.

Lunch was a fun affair. Large tables were scattered across a meadow situated beside the castle. Servants and guests alike helped carry trays heavily laden with an endless assortment of food to fill the whole of the expansive tables.

After filling their plates with delicious selections, Serena and Rhamus followed the lead of the hungrier guests who were already eating. They sat upon a soft blanket laid down by an observant warrior, and picnicked along with all the others.

She looked up from her plate as she felt a presence near her face. Rhamus held a flaky pastry for her to try. Remembering the last time they'd played this game, Serena giggled and nibbled at the treat. The hot look on his face made her realize that he too, was thinking of their last encounter.

Picking up a piece of chocolate with a nut center, she held it up in front of her husband's mouth. He took the candy carefully between his strong white teeth then sent a shiver up her spine when his tongue flicked out quickly to lick a dollop of chocolate that clung to her finger.

She leaned unconsciously closer to Rhamus, and then licked her lower lip to dislodge a tiny crumb of pastry. Taking her by surprise with his sudden movement, he closed the short gap between them and began a heated assault on her lips.

The sound of quickly stifled giggles and chuckles broke through their passion-filled haze. Glancing around, she was mortified to find her and her husband to be the center of attention. The Volarnians who encircled them on all sides either smiled knowingly or looked politely away. *Just when I felt like we were an ordinary couple,* she thought.

"It's good for the people to know that the King and Queen care for each other," he said softly.

Serena flushed warm with the joy his words gave her. She well remembered his whispered words of love. Were these feelings of pleasure in his presence the awakening of her love? She seemed to turn to putty every time he touched her, as he was doing now. Was that what love felt like? The next instant, she tried to shrug off the warm feelings she was experiencing, placing the blame on the excitement in the air. *Maybe we can be good friends, but I can't afford to fall in love with this man.*

The rest of the afternoon sped quickly by, Surad and Rhamus had organized a whole evening of entertainment. Serena watched as warriors competed good-naturedly in hand-to-hand combat, fencing matches, and even horse races.

Excitement filled the air as clans shouted for their own competing members. She crossed her fingers when Kasha raced pell-mell across a field against five other warriors, her hair whipping around her head, eyes bright with fierce joy. Serena held her breath at the seemingly precarious perch Kasha maintained on the racing steed. She shouted with the crowd when Kasha did indeed win the race.

The ecstatic princess joined them to watch the next event. Serena couldn't help giving her sister-in-law a quick hug of joy. Kasha's face lit with pleasure as she quickly returned the gesture. She thought the exchange was unnoticed since Rhamus' attention was riveted on Jarvic, coming into the cleared area ahead as the next sword challenger. The sound kiss he laid on her temple and pleased smile told her otherwise.

She returned her husband's smile and remembered something Hartoos had said. A King has to have the wisdom of all his people, and the eyes and ears of a thousand to help him maintain that wisdom. Truly, Rhamus seemed to miss very little that went on in his kingdom or in his family.

At first Serena was shocked when Jarvic's opponent appeared. He was as big in stature and build as Yissell. Remembering her own success with her bigger opponent, and Jarvic's skill, she relaxed and enjoyed the intense battle, which ensued. Jarvic's skill nearly won the day, but his opponent was a skilled swordsman as well, and his larger size took its toll on the King's cousin. Finally, Jarvic threw his sword down as perspiration dripped from his arms and face.

The combatants shook hands as the larger man slapped Jarvic heartily on the back. He nearly fell from the man's blow, but regained his posture as they both strode off together for drinks. "There are not too many warriors who can beat Jarvic," Rhamus said.

"Except you?"

He shook his head. "I could not beat Jarvic's skills with swordsmanship alone. Only with the crystal's power can I defeat him."

"Who is that man?"

"The best swordsman in all of Volarn." He gazed after the pair. "Too bad he's retired from service now. He was a powerful deterrent against our enemies."

"What do you mean?"

"Just knowing that Ulecki was on patrol kept the west Volarnians from raiding as much. He could cut a wide swath through their ranks, with many injured. And, he has more kills under his sword belt than any warrior in history."

"You mean he intentionally killed other warriors?"

"No," Rhamus shook his head. "Although most warriors wished to stay out of his way, there was always some hot-headed young one who was ready to challenge his status."

At Serena's uncomprehending look, he added, "Although we try not to kill unless it is necessary, Xarath has a different view. He encourages killings whenever possible. He has effectively destroyed an age-old code of honor during his short reign. The feat of killing Ulecki would bring a warrior instant fame and favor with their king."

Rhamus pointed out it was time for the hand-to-hand combat contestants to pit their skills against one another.

"Are you going to participate?" She asked Kasha.

"Of course," the princess waved a hand of dismissal. Giving Serena a friendly look, she inquired, "The question is, are you going to show off your fighting abilities? The people need to know that the royal family has solid warrior stock."

Rhamus and Serena both looked askance at Kasha. She was readily admitting Serena's abilities and accepting her into the family. Not only that, she wanted Serena to show off her prowess.

He quickly said, "Not this time."

"Why not?"

Smiling happily, he put his arm around Serena and let one of his hands rest on her stomach. "Because she carries the future heir to the kingdom, and I will not allow her to take the chance of harming him, or her."

Kasha's astounded face was worth the awkwardness she felt at his abrupt announcement.

"How do you know?"

"Zara felt it when we toured the village."

Turning to Serena, she said, "Then truly you are carrying the heir!" Her face took on a joyful expression and she launched herself at Serena, catching her up in a big hug. "I am so happy, now I will finally have a nephew to play with."

"Or niece." She disentangled herself from the princess.

"Hmm, you're right. It doesn't matter." Turning to her brother, she inquired, "Have you told anyone else?"

"No, you are the first. I will announce it at the ceremony tonight."

Jarvic appeared and told Kasha it was her turn in the contest. Grabbing Serena's hands in a tight grip, she exclaimed, "This one's for you and the next King or Queen."

Serena and Rhamus stood arm in arm as Kasha bashed her opponent with more enthusiasm than usual. Jarvic was very suspicious when he noticed that Kasha couldn't be torn from the royal couple's side for more than a few minutes at a time the rest of the evening. She followed behind them as they moved from event to event, often carrying on an excited conversation for Serena's ears only. He was very irritated with her mysterious behavior. Since when had Kasha and Serena become the best of friends?

Chapter Fifteen

Serena was very glad when a rest period was announced before
the night's festivities and she could slip away to take a short nap.
Rhamus left her at the door, but she was so tired she didn't even
question his leaving. Lalme showed up later and assisted her in a
quick bath and then dressed her hair. She directed her talented maid
to put her hair up in a large cluster of curls at her crown, with one
long, thick strand left to dangle over one shoulder.

Lalme reached into the wardrobe and reverently produced her
dress. The exquisite gown she and Jidroon had created was even
more beautiful than she'd imagined. She couldn't wait to put it on.
The pale blue silky sheath of a dress slithered into place and molded
to her figure. The side slit showed off one thigh in a subtle, yet very
sexy fashion whenever she took a step. The strapless top dipped low
enough to show her plentiful breasts. The blue made a lovely
contrast against the creamy coloring of her smooth skin. Her eyes
looked like they were cut from the same cloth as the arj'ak blue
dress, so closely did the colors mirror each other.

Serena had to admit, as she ran one hand down the soft material
that it was a heavenly creation, and Jidroon's suggestion of the
basami dragon did not detract from its impact. It was made of
sparkling crystals with the head of the creature at her right thigh and
its tail slanting diagonally upward.

The dragon's jaws clamped a large red jewel located at the top of
the slit, its smallish wings spread out to hug each hip, and its tail
curled partially around her left breast. It was composed of deep
purple crystals on its underbelly and dark blue ones on the top part
of the body, supposedly the true color of the legendary basami
dragon. Its large eyes were golden orbs with round pupils.

Lalme clapped her hands in glee. "You look beautiful, Your
Highness."

Gazing at her reflection in the mirror, she felt like royalty tonight.

Placing a gossamer wrap of matching blue around her shoulders,
Serena waited nervously for Nuad, who was to be her escort. The
old man was thunder-struck when he first spied her standing in the
middle of the room. "You are very beautiful, my dear. Rhamus will
be very pleased." Holding out his elbow gallantly, he walked with
just enough of a slow pace to accommodate the dress's confining

striding distance.

Serena's nervousness turned to sickening butterflies as Nuad paused for effect at the room's entrance before guiding her to Rhamus' side on the dais. Surprise was splashed on many faces at the stark difference of her dress to those worn by the other ladies. Many of the males wore admiring looks while some of the women looked thoughtful. Serena also noticed a few envious looks from some of the more attractive women.

Even with her thoughts concentrated on how Rhamus would respond to her appearance, Serena couldn't help staring with wonder at the huge dragon skull hanging on the wall behind her husband. It had been hung for this special ceremony, just as he'd said. The beige colored skull was about three feet wide with large eye sockets overlooking the room sightlessly. The skull length was much longer, with a long snout, and a widely gaping mouth full of impressive teeth. For a second, Serena thought it odd that the yellowish teeth were flattened in shape. She shrugged off this observation, really knowing very little about Volarn's animal population, and even less about its legendary ones.

Her eyes swung back to her husband. She was gratified by the flash of heat that washed over her from Rhamus' eyes. He jumped up as Nuad approached and escorted Serena to her chair. As she sat down, her wrap slipped and Serena felt her husband's eyes dip to her bosom.

"Need I tell you how beautiful you are, my jicha?" He whispered throatily.

She shook her head, while a flush of pleasure flooded through her cheeks.

Picking up her hand, Rhamus kissed it lingeringly. "Nonetheless, you have been told. Zara was right--you do make a wonderful Queen."

"You're making a scene," Serena leaned forward and whispered.

"By the sacred crystal, you are enough to make a man lose all reason." His eyes seemed drawn of their own accord back to where her creamy mounds pushed up above the silky bodice. "Cover yourself my Queen, else I will make a scene worthy of a warrior King."

She arched her eyebrows at him, but closed her wrap around her shoulders. Rhamus seated himself on his throne and stared straight ahead for a minute, jaw clenched, as if trying to compose himself. She'd never seen him look so splendid.

"I didn't know you had such a barbaric nature," Serena teased.

Turning back to her with hooded eyes, he remarked, "And I never

realized I was such a barbarian, until I got a woman such as you."
Examining the dress closely for the first time, he asked, "Where did
you get such a dress?"

"Jidroon and I created it together. It was my idea and he made it a
reality."

"Remind me to reward him later," Rhamus' statement was
ambiguous.

"I hope that means you like the dress. Jidroon and I have many
more ceremonial dresses ready for those special occasions you
Volarnians seem to love."

He groaned and put his forehead in his hand. "I can see I am in for
further tests of my strength."

"What do you mean?" Serena was very confused by his manner.

Looking at her directly and seeing her confusion, he finally
grinned. "You just don't know what you do to my royal composure,
do you?"

Comprehending the ardor that she had stirred in Rhamus, she
smiled, unaware of the seductive look that overcame her features.
"And you don't know what you do to my composure either."

"Your Majesty," Hartoos interrupted any further play between the
couple. "Everyone's waiting for you to open the ceremony."

Giving Serena a lopsided grin and a wink, he sprang up. "Bring in
the children," he commanded. A line of Volarnian women began to
make their way through the crowd, who parted to let them through.

Taking her hand, Rhamus led her to the edge of the dais. Each
woman held an infant of differing ages. They were all little cherubs
and Serena couldn't stop the "ah" that slipped from her lips. The
mothers smiled appreciatively back at her.

Gesturing to the babies, he simply said, "This, our future, is why
we are here." Glancing at her, he added, "It's why we are *all* here."

As the head of each clan came forward, the children were
presented in quick succession. After each mother told their child's
name and clan, Rhamus held up a large arj'ak crystal. It was on a
necklace, held within a lacy ball. The children were curious and,
those old enough, reached for the pretty plaything, taking it within
their tiny hands. The crowd would shout as each child accepted
their gift from the King, as if no child before had done such a thing.

The clan leader would hold up a necklace similar to the one the
King had given to the child, but within would be the crystal
representing the individual clan colors. Colors from every spectrum
were represented--blues, reds, gold, greens, and so on.

At first Serena was surprised by the number of children, surely
several hundred were shown to them. But then she remembered

they represented all the births in the last year on Volarn. She made this remark to Rhamus and was shocked by his response.

"I'm glad you enjoyed the presentation so much. We have several thousand children to welcome."

"Several thousand! How long does this ceremony go on?"

"With the number of children, I'd guess about two weeks."

Serena's shock dissolved when she thought the matter through, remembering Hartoos' lessons. Volarn's population for both east and west, equaled that of a large city on Earth. Most of south Volarn's population was adults. Another thirty percent was composed of the elderly with their long life expectancy.

She didn't know how to figure it out mathematically, but Volarnians were only reproducing an average of one child for every two parents. Thus, they were at a negative growth rate, not even replacing both parents. Serena looked around the room. There were a lot of infants, overwhelming when one multiplied several hundred times two weeks, but still too low a count.

After about two hours, when the presentation of the infants was through, Rhamus clanged his sword against the throne for attention. He held their clasped hands up, reminding Serena of the winner being announced after a fight. He's going to announce our baby, she realized nervously.

"We have joyous news!" He paused dramatically and silence reigned supreme in the huge room. Even the babies were relatively quiet. "There is an heir to the throne!"

The response from the crowd was deafening. Women's screams mingled with the men's shouts. The metallic sound of sword clanging rang through the room as male and female warriors struck them on the floor repeatedly. And now the infants screamed, making a new volume of noise arise from several hundred little throats. It took quite a while for the sound to decrease. The people talked excitedly, their individual voices raised so they could be heard by their neighbors in the crowd.

Servants appeared to take the tired babies and put them to bed, allowing their mothers to continue to enjoy the celebration. Serena and Rhamus were bombarded with people congratulating them. She began to hear a ringing in her ears before things quieted somewhat and her shoulder felt sore from all the thumps of well-wishers.

Entertainers appeared. Song and dance was the basis of any good Volarnian ceremony, along with lots of food. Mountains of food on tables against the walls had gone unnoticed by Serena. The gathered people began talking, eating and watching enthusiastically as dancers, musicians and singers performed.

Now that the people's attention was diverted, Serena turned to Rhamus. "Explain the crystal necklaces to me, please?"

"The arj'ak crystal is a gift from south Volarn to every child during the birth celebration. When he or she grows up, they may use the crystal in their warrior wristband, the one worn on the left. Or, if a girl is fertile and cannot become Getra, she may use the crystal to help her get started in her married life."

"A dowry." Serena looked thoughtful. "Then the other crystal must be the one that is placed in each child's wristband to designate their clan? And it's worn on the right arm?"

At Rhamus' nod of approval at her correct surmise, she asked, "What is the significance of the necklaces?"

"Nothing," he shrugged his shoulders. "Someone, I believe it was my mother, decided it would be handier to keep the crystal on a necklace until the child reached maturity."

"And it looks prettier besides." Serena's eyes twinkled with ill-concealed mirth. Rhamus and she had spent several evenings discussing his relatives, and she knew that his mother had a fondness for anything glittery.

A brief break in the entertainment ensued while servants scurried back and forth across the room delivering more refreshments to the tables. The guests took this opportunity to mingle and become reacquainted with those clansmen they'd not seen in some time.

"I'll be right back," Rhamus pointed to a banquet table nearest them. "I spotted my uncle Narak who I haven't seen in a year."

"Why doesn't he come to you?" Serena caught him with the question before he descended the dais.

"He's been trying to make his way over here." Rhamus grinned. "But my cousin Perris has had him cornered for the last hour." At her curious expression, he continued, "Perris is the biggest gossip in all of east Volarn. I am sure he's pumping uncle Narak for information on all our relatives and anyone else who might be of interest to him."

"Including us." Serena frowned.

"Afraid so, my jicha." Bowing, he entreated, "Now, if you don't mind, I'll go rescue my uncle."

As Rhamus approached them, Serena could see the family resemblance between the King and his uncle, but none with his cousin. Narak was tall and muscular, even though his hair was shot with gray. His face showed the same noble, aristocratic features as Rhamus', but a large hawk nose kept him from being as handsome as his nephew.

Her eyes swung to Perris, a Volarnian who was very short by their standards. He could have been no more than her own six feet two and no muscles bulged on his exposed arms. Perris was fat, something Serena had seen very little of on this world. All the Volarnians she'd met so far led very active lives, even when retired from the military. And mothers also stayed active through sports and hobbies.

Nicole finally showed up, giving Serena a welcome break from the stream of people who wandered by to meet her and ask questions.

"Where's the big guy?" Nicole asked impertinently.

"Over there," she waved her hand toward her husband and his uncle. Her friend giggled when Serena told her what Rhamus had shared about Perris.

"He's right." Her eyes shot heavenward dramatically. "Perris was introduced to me about two hours ago. He spent an hour drilling me for information on you and all the other 'important' Earthlings. That's what took me so long to get here."

"That accounts for one hour. What happened to the last one?" At Nicole's attempted innocent look, Serena said, "I happen to know Perris has been bugging Narak for the last hour."

Nicole threw her hands in the air. "OK, you caught me. Let's just say Doc and I have been a little busy the last hour."

"I'm shocked." Her laughing demeanor belied her statement.

"What?" Nicole defended. "Can't a hard working gal take a little recreational time out, every once in a while?"

"I'm just surprised you 'talked' Dr. Melat into a recreational break."

Nicole wrapped her hands around her knees and rocked gently. "You'd be surprised what I can talk Doc into these days."

The girlish giggles that erupted from them both were interrupted by a whining voice. "What are you two lovely creatures doing all alone, and whatever is so funny?"

Serena stared at the rude interruption of cousin Perris. Up close, his chubby cheeks and bright eyes lent him the look of a grown-up cherub. He appeared charming and innocent, until one looked deeper and saw the troublemaker brewing just beneath the surface.

"Permit me to introduce myself." Perris' feigned horror at his social blunder was almost comical. But Serena found him to be irritating and his ingratiating behavior distasteful. For the next few minutes she had to endure invasive questions from Rhamus' cousin and try to fend him off with neutral answers. In desperation she searched the room with her eyes, trying to locate Rhamus so he could rescue her, as he'd done for his uncle.

Her search skidded to a halt as her eyes reached her husband and a gorgeous female. They stood near the center of the vast room, giving Serena only occasional glimpses when the throng of people parted. By her behavior, she guessed that this was one woman who enjoyed being the center of attention. She was willowy slim, her features delicate. Her black mane fell in a straight inky curtain to her knees, shimmering with blue highlights when she moved slightly. I bet she knows the impression her hair makes when she moves like that, Serena thought.

A flush of heat rose in her cheeks as the woman softly touched her husband's hard biceps, as if for added emphasis. He leaned down and listened attentively to the woman, shaking his head at something she said. The silvery laughter that tinkled from her swan neck caused several men to turn and give her a second look.

"She's quite a beauty." Perris sounded smug as his bright eyes watched her with eagle-eyed attentiveness.

Nicole saved Serena from having to think of an immediate response. "She certainly is a beauty. But, Rhamus thinks Serena is the most gorgeous woman this side of the galaxy. That includes Earth and Volarn."

She tried to keep her eyes from soaring upward at Nicole's outrageous statement, but silently thanked her anyway.

"Who is she?" Serena could have bitten her tongue, but her jealous heart far outweighed her thinking mind. She'd fallen right into Perris' trap by the gleeful expression on his face.

"Why, she was the King's lover." At her carefully controlled look, Perris elaborated. "Her name is Szafra, which means 'fragrant flower'. They were a pretty hot item, before you came." Perris stopped and tapped one pudgy cheek thoughtfully. "Let me see, they must have been lovers for about three years."

"Looks like now that Serena is the Queen, things have cooled off," Nicole said sarcastically.

"Oh, I don't know, they seem to be pretty friendly to me." Perris stared worriedly at the couple and glanced sidelong at her. She didn't like the closeness of Rhamus and Szafra's heads as they spoke, but said, "Rhamus is not one to forget old friends, and I am sure they are just catching up on old times."

Again, she couldn't believe she'd stuck her foot in her mouth so horribly. *Did jealously make one into an idiot?*

Perris practically glowed with malicious enjoyment.

Thank goodness her husband chose that moment to look her way. Spying Perris, he excused himself and strode with a fast pace over to them. Serena felt some lessening of her tension at Rhamus' quick response, and the pouty look that came over Szafra's face as he left her side made her feel better somehow.

It didn't take long for Perris to excuse himself after Rhamus reached their side. The King's growled responses to his cousin's nosy questions convinced Perris that he'd get no more juicy information to add to his collection. Perris' watchful eyes were scanning the crowd for possible quarry and, noticing a merry widow with a taste for fast living, he left for livelier game.

Rhamus eased into his chair with a sigh. "Can you believe he used to be one of my favorite playmates before he grew into this terrible busybody?" At Nicole and Serena's incredulous looks, he explained. "Perris was very entertaining when we were children. He used to make up the most incredible stories." He shrugged. "I guess that talent turned from a magical gift to a nasty irritant."

"You seemed to be on pretty friendly terms with Szafra."

He eyed her tightly controlled features. "I am sure Perris has informed you that we were once lovers."

"Boy, you don't pull any punches, do you?" Nicole snipped.

Serena laid a restraining hand on her tiny friend's arm. "He's just stating facts. Haven't you learned yet that on Volarn it is not considered 'bad' for one to take a lover?"

"Yeah, I did forget." Nicole considered Rhamus. "But you could have been a little more diplomatic about it," she stared straight at him.

"Serena, I would rein in your friend's tongue if I were you. I'm in no mood for aggravating questions and remarks." His lowering brows caused Nicole to still her next remark and Serena to sit up tensely.

"She's only acting on my behalf. You did seem awfully cozy with that woman." Serena couldn't keep the accusatory tone from her voice.

He stared at her, speechless for a few seconds, then a wide grin split his face. "I do believe you are jealous, my Queen."

"Jealous! Why I just don't think it's a good idea for the King to be seen being so friendly toward his former lover." Her face flushed with emotion.

"Whatever you say, my jicha." Rhamus took her hand in his and rubbed her palm with his thumb.

Serena tried to jerk her hand back, but he held on with rock hard determination and she finally let it lay limp in his hold. Catching her chin with his other hand, he turned her to face him. "Truly, it is over between us. Besides, how can there be room in my heart for another woman when you take up so much of it already?"

His overstated romantic remark made her smile, and the kernel of truth in that statement caused a ray of happiness to shoot through her whole being.

Not one to be stalled for long, Nicole wedged a question between the intimate couple. "If you and Szafra were such a hot item, why didn't you marry her?"

Sending her a quelling glare, which had halted lesser mortals, but apparently not Serena's female friend, Rhamus had to calm his temper when he saw that Nicole wouldn't be budged or frightened from getting the answer she sought. "I really should rename you sooeul."

Noting her determined look, he said, "There are two reasons. The Tarthra did not choose her, and Szafra is sterile." Seeing the perturbed look that came over his wife's fine features, he added gratingly to Nicole, "You know, you really should learn to guard that mouth of yours. Otherwise, you may end up being a female Perris."

Serena grasped Nicole's upper arm to keep her viper's tongue under control. Her friend had a fierce temper when aroused and she didn't know how much back talk the King would allow. Feeling queasy, she asked, "So you loved Szafra?"

"Yes, but as I already told you, I no longer harbor any feelings but friendship toward her."

Searching her husband's eyes, Serena didn't know if she totally believed him or not, but she would take his word for now. She turned, glad to be distracted from their heated discussion, when a blaring instrument announced the resumption of the entertainment.

As the small group of singers regaled them with Volarnian love songs, she couldn't help but wonder if Rhamus would have discarded her as he'd done Szafra, if she'd not proved capable of conceiving. A momentary glimmer of sadness for the cast off mistress who apparently loved the King flushed through her. This lapse into empathy vanished as if it'd never been when the next entertainer was announced.

Serena sat up straighter and gripped the arms of the chair. Szafra was posed in the center of the crowd, which had made a wide half circle to accommodate her. She was dressed very scantily even for a Volarnian--her silvery bikini was overlaid by strands of dark blue crystals falling from a necklace. The beads hung down from her slim neck to the top of her thighs. Szafra had put her hair up into a high bun, which made her look even more fragile, and kept her abundant hair from covering the revealing costume.

The musicians started a slow, oddly rhythmic tune. The graceful dancer swayed and moved in time to the beat, sometimes slow and sensuous, sometimes faster, with sharp movements. The dance was different from anything that had been presented by the Volarnians tonight, and Serena had not seen anything exactly like it on Earth either. Each sway of her slim hips caused the beads to part in different areas, giving only slight glimpses of her long, slender waist or small, shapely bottom. Serena realized the hidden sensuality of the costume.

In spite of the green bug, which seemed to have bitten her hard, she admired the woman's technique and the fine quality of the dance's movements. It was a dance she wouldn't have minded learning, except that her husband's former lover was demonstrating it.

She noticed the avid attention of the males in the audience and the rapt looks they gave Szafra as her hips swayed in time to the music. Serena glanced at Rhamus and saw his attention was glued to the titillating performance. She could swear she saw the heat shooting from his eyes--hot glances that should have been hers!

The jealousy Serena felt turned from green to red-hot anger as she noted his interest. She bit her lip to keep herself from uttering a word. *Let him stare at her, see if I care.*

Chapter Sixteen

Szafra finished her dance with a flourish and knelt gracefully on the bottom step of the dais. Rhamus clapped as loudly as any of the other males. Serena locked eyes with Szafra and returned her challenging stare. A triumphant smile lit Szafra's face when his eyes followed her body closely as she approached.

"Well done, Szafra."

His sincere compliment caused her anger to go up another notch, to the boiling point. She worried her lower lip.

"Did I please you as well, Your Majesty?" Szafra addressed Serena but her smug tone told whom she thought she had pleased.

"You're a good dancer." She spoke stiffly.

Szafra looked surprised. "You seem able to recognize talent when you see it. Do you dance?" She spoke with a haughty manner.

"Perhaps I will dance, for Rhamus one day," Serena said thoughtfully. Her shoulders relaxed and she smiled pleasantly to all around her.

The dancer seemed confused by the Queen's acknowledgment of her skills and the easy consideration of her challenge. She shot Serena a look of annoyance, and left the next minute with a handsome young warrior in tow. Rhamus rubbed his chin and contemplated Serena's face closely.

"So, you may dance for me one day." He leaned close to her. "Maybe tonight?" His ardent look devoured her face before slipping down to flick her whole body with his lustful gaze.

She gave him a sullen look, still angry about Szafra and his reaction to her. Serena's stiff manner and coldly turned shoulder didn't deter him a bit from his attention to her. Rhamus continued to eye her roguishly. He grabbed her hand and idly stroked it in spite of her attempts to pull it out of his grasp, completely ignoring her pouty mood. Instead, he appeared to thoroughly enjoy the rest of the entertainment.

"Will you dance for me?" He asked again, humor edging his voice.

They had retired for the night, Serena walking quickly ahead to reach their bedroom first. He guessed she had other thoughts on her mind when she slammed the door in his face.

"Maybe on your grave," she mumbled between gritted teeth as

she began to jerk pins out of her perfectly coifed hair.

"I knew you were angry about something," he paused at her loud "hmph", "But I didn't think it warranted such *grave* lengths."

Turning quickly to stare at him, Serena was embarrassed that Rhamus had overheard her low-pitched remark. Seeing his grinning countenance, she snatched the earrings from her lobes, and quickly swallowed her chagrin. She decided it was good he had heard her. He took her feelings far too lightly, which made her furious.

By the time she had undone all the twists in her hair and removed her jewelry, Serena saw in the mirror that Rhamus had already disrobed. She felt his approach behind her without needing to see him in the glass.

He placed a hand on the buttons at the back of the dress. "Need some help?"

Jerking from his grasp, she turned abruptly to face her husband. "No, I do not need your assistance." Her eyes flashed. "Maybe you should go offer your help to Szafra."

"Maybe it's not Szafra I wish to make love to." He placed his iron-hard arms about her waist and leaned to kiss her.

Serena pushed free of his arms. "Well, maybe you'd better reconsider, because you will be getting no 'loving' from me…." She purposely left her sentence hanging, conveying clearly to her mate that she meant tonight and maybe more to come.

If she'd known Rhamus long enough to read the signs, she would have seen that he was becoming angry. He stood calmly, his eyes almost frosty in their perusal of her.

"I do not wish to have sex with Szafra or any other woman, but with my wife."

He started toward her, a steely look on his face that finally warned her, but to no avail; her temper was fanned too hot to control at this point. "Woman! You make it sound as if a wife were not a woman," Serena sneered.

At any other time Rhamus would have found Serena's remark silly and amusing. Now it only irritated him. He followed her across the expanse of the room as she backed away from him, picking up his stride as he saw her intention to lock herself in the bathroom. Catching her shoulders, he slammed her lightly into the wall near the bathroom door and held her there.

She was steaming now. *How dare he hold her like that!* The cold wall ground into her soft back with his forceful pressure. Serena forgot all about her skills as a fighter. She slapped at Rhamus, fighting for the first time in her life like a woman. Too late, she realized her mistake as her weak blows went unnoticed. He clamped both his arms around her and squeezed until she quit struggling.

"Are you going to let me help you off with that gown, or do I have to take it off the hard way?" His face filled her vision, his eyes flashing strangely. One minute his eyes looked cool as the ice of a glacier, the next, hot as the flames that seemed to leap from them and lick her body with their heat.

"You wouldn't dare!" Serena's mouth was set rigid with disapproval.

Not taking his eyes from hers for a second, he freed one of his hands and, placing it at her bodice, pulled in one swift tug. Before she could react, the silky material ripped at the back as buttons popped loose. Rhamus' eyes were glued to her breasts as they bounced free of their confinement. He deliberately brought his gaze slowly up her neck, reaching her eyes. He let her see the heat of desire that burned within them.

Serena didn't let a flicker of emotion flare in her eyes as she abruptly brought her fist up and gave Rhamus a jab to the chin. Not as effective as she'd like, considering the short space between them. Expecting him to get angry, as she wanted, she was taken aback when his countenance didn't change expression one bit.

He grabbed her free hand and brought it to lie flat against the wall. Pressing into her, he made her feel the pressure of being caught between the hard stone and his rock hard body. She didn't know which felt harder.

"Didn't you know, my jicha, that a little tussling before sex just gets a warrior's blood hotter?" His deep voice washed over her, making his male roughness seem as if it were embodied in his voice as well as his body.

Feeling breathless from the pressure he was exerting on her, Serena could only shake her head. Closing her eyes for a second, vast relief flooded her senses when Rhamus released her from the wall. That relief was short lived, when he again held her in a steely embrace, holding her wrists behind her back with one hand.

Opening her eyes with renewed anger, now that she could catch her breath, she started to open her mouth to protest his treatment of her. Instead she found his mouth attacking hers in a rough fashion, truly acting out the part of a barbarian now.

Against her will, she began to feel a weakening resistance to his force. Her body wanted nothing more than to give in and respond with every fiber of her being, while her mind rebelled and wanted to hold onto its hurt a little longer. Frantically trying to regroup within herself, Serena was glad when Rhamus lifted her and gently laid her on the bed. He had softened his approach when he felt her resistance fading. In the short time it had taken her husband to carry her to the bed, she had taken hold of her anger again, remembering afresh its reason for being.

He was stretched out on top of her, his arms on either side of her body, but allowing hers to be free. Serena waited until Rhamus drew back from a kiss then quickly flipped him off her. He landed with complete surprise, giving her just enough time to position herself. As he moved to encase her in his arms again, Serena drew her legs up and pushed hard. Rhamus went sailing across the bed and past the end of it, to land with a loud thump.

As soon as she kicked him, Serena was up and running for the bathroom. She paused for just a second and glanced to see him sitting up, rubbing one hip gingerly. Flying to the bathroom on hurried footsteps, she thought it a good idea to be in a safe area from Rhamus' anger. Locking the door securely behind her, Serena leaned against the heavy door with a sigh of relief. Sometimes she didn't think ahead--like how her husband would react after being stomach-kicked off the bed. Better to stay locked up until he had a chance to cool down.

Serena jumped in shock when the door shook violently. Not a word came from the other side of the door, but she backed up nervously. Again the door was struck from the other side, shaking even more on its frame.

She worried her bottom lip. Would the large door hold against her enraged husband? She couldn't stop the complete surprise that flickered across her features as Rhamus burst through the door on the third try. The door hung by one hinge.

She couldn't move, not even if she had wanted to. Something in the quiet calmness of his face told her to keep perfectly still, that she'd gone too far this time. A thrill of fear curled around the flame of anger in her belly, making her even more nervous. Rhamus approached her slowly and then before she could say a word, he dipped down and threw her over his shoulder. Striding quickly now, he dumped her hard on the bed.

He eased down slowly over her, letting her feel the full length and weight of his body. He was heavy and she found it hard to breath, but still she didn't protest openly. When Rhamus grasped a large handful of her hair and brought her lips to his in a violently controlled kiss, she tried to resist in the only way she could, by holding back her response from him. His hands grasped her breasts in hard kneading strokes that hurt. As his hands rubbed down her thighs, she knew her limbs would be marred by bruises tomorrow.

Suddenly, Serena discovered that the nervousness had disappeared and in its place was a thrill of sensation running throughout her whole body. She began kissing Rhamus back just as fiercely, and her hands came up of their own accord and began to caress him in a strong fashion as well.

She raked his back as her excitement built up to an almost unbearable level. Sensing her true response, his touch became more constrained, not hurtful, yet still savage. Somewhere along the way, Serena's anger had melted into lust, strangely making it more intense.

Serena's mind ceased to reason and her body seemed to be a wild creature bent on its own pleasure. She and Rhamus were nonexistent for a space of time. In their place were two primordial animals, grunting and mating in splendid savagery. Love was not a consideration, only lips, tongues, breasts, and satiation.

When she reached her peak, it felt as though her heart were going to leap out of her chest. Little shock waves of sensation ran throughout her whole body and caused her to tremble. Her toes curled in reaction.

Was this what her mother meant by toe tingling? As her breathing began to slow, Serena glanced up. Tears seeped from the corners of her eyes and she wiped at them, then looked in wonder at Rhamus. She was glad that her husband looked just as thunderstruck as she felt. Had any other people had such an earth shattering experience, she wondered. She was so tired, yet content. It didn't take long for a deep sleep to overcome her.

The activities picked up again the next morning. The clans would stay for another day of visiting and celebration, then leave so other clans could be accommodated. Serena enjoyed everything, from making new friends, to the lavish banquets and entertainment that continued at night. But as the last day of the celebration appeared, she was glad the huge castle, her home now, would be emptied of all but the normal flow of people who came and went within its walls. She was exhausted, but strangely content.

Serena floated through the last several days, a haze of wonder surrounding her and Rhamus every time they were together. She felt keenly the spark of desire that flared between. The memory of their last encounter was too fresh, too raw, its lingering traces pounding through her sensitive nerve endings.

Their nights together were not as savage. Lovemaking was as varied as she and her husband's mood that particular night. Serena dreamily thought of last night's encounter. He'd been tender and gentle in his approach, bringing her ever so slowly to the pinnacle.

That experience was as different from their primitive one as night and day. Yet she cherished each for its own unique quality.

"Daydreaming about me?" He sat next to her on the bed. The day had given up its golden glow of warmth and the sounds of the night's creatures filtered in through the open balcony door. "As a matter of fact, I was." Serena received Rhamus' kiss placidly.

Looking at her drawn features, he knew her mood. "You're tired. All these days of constant celebrating were probably too much on you, being in your early stage of pregnancy."

Shaking her head and yawning in agreement, she was glad when Rhamus assisted her as efficiently as a servant to get undressed. He even tucked her into bed and kissed her forehead. Only then did he prepare for bed himself.

Yawning again, Serena asked sleepily. "Since all the guests are gone now, can we rest tomorrow?"

"You may rest all day if you like. Many of the staff will be taking off. Unfortunately, my jicha, I will be taking a patrol out."

"Not tomorrow," she groaned and snuggled next to him, burying her nose in his neck.

"I'm afraid I don't have a choice. Xarath's warriors have been harassing the eastern borders since so many clans have been away."

Serena wanted to complain. Couldn't the clans look after their own borders? But she knew what Rhamus' answer would be, that as the people's leader, he must ever be ready to lead his warriors against Xarath's forces.

The next day, she didn't awaken when he left early, and she slept past her usual time. Lalme had been alerted by the King and checked in quietly on her several times. Feeling heavy-eyed, as if she'd consumed gallons of wine the night before, Serena took a long shower. She felt much better by the time she dressed and Lalme brought in a tray of food.

She looked with surprise at the familiar lunch choices offered to her and glanced toward the window. Bright sunlight filtered through every crack. "It's noon," Serena said under her breath, after reading the wall clock.

"Don't worry, almost everyone's taking the day off." Her maid's pert voice irritated her somehow. "You'll feel better after you get something to eat. You and the babe must be starving by now." She continued to hover over Serena, offering her different delicacies and filling her glass.

Serena's irritation disappeared at the mention of the baby. Lalme was just as excited as her mistress. She spent the remainder of the day visiting with Nicole and Surad, then nibbling and resting. Her quiet evening, empty without Rhamus, was spent in the bedroom trying to think of baby names. She looked down at the short list she held in her hand. Her job was doubly hard. Would the baby have a Volarnian name, an Earth name, a combination, or one from each?

The next day, Serena woke up feeling refreshed and longing for exercise. She went for a long stroll in the gardens and then out to the meadowlands. Many warriors were gathered in small groups, practicing fencing or hand-to-hand combat. She stopped to watch for a short while. A warm pleasure flushed through her when the tough soldiers greeted her in friendly fashion and then congratulated her and Rhamus.

Without even realizing it, she was keeping an eye out for Kasha. She found the princess near the stables, saddling her yasmir. Kasha greeted her with genuine affection. Serena was still amazed at how much the presence, or soon-to-be presence, of a baby could change some people. Out of the corner of her eye, she noticed Kasha's konkol scamper under a nearby bush, as if it sensed her dislike. She was glad the princess had made an effort to keep her pet unobtrusive.

"I was going for a ride in the forests. Would you like to come?" Kasha asked cheerfully.

Serena was glad Volarnians did not consider women weak little things. They would not think twice about a pregnant woman riding, as long as she was healthy and not too far along. The guard who was always at her disposal, appeared to gear up her yasmir. *I guess maybe they do think twice about pregnant women.* She really hadn't been looking forward to lifting the heavy saddle and was glad for the young warrior's assistance.

While the princess waited patiently for the guard to finish saddling the mount, she extracted an extra pair of pants and handed them to Serena. She slipped them on, wondering at Kasha's preparedness.

"You know that Rhamus ordered that you were not to be allowed to lift anything heavier than a goblet."

"Oh." Serena felt an odd rush of pleasure at her husband's thoughtfulness. But her independent nature reared up and pushed hard against such antiquated behavior. She glanced back at Kasha and realized that her sister-in-law read every conflicting emotion crossing her features.

Giving her a charming smile, Kasha remarked, "It's OK for a Volarnian male to pamper his wife, pregnant or not. The women give their men plenty of attention too, so neither feels left out, or demeaned."

"I think Nuad was very wrong about you."

"How?"

"You know much more about Earthlings than he would ever guess."

"Never let your old tutor figure out just how much you do know, or are willing to learn." Kasha winked.

Serena smiled back at her playful countenance. But she wondered what it would be like to really be the princess's enemy. Kasha was good at playing the errant, unthinking sister or bored former student, whichever suited her mood, but she was very clever.

As they left the castle and started across a meadow, Serena noticed a slim woman slipping into the shadows of the forest's edge. She wondered briefly why a lone woman would be acting so furtively, then smiling to herself, realized the woman must be secretly meeting someone. Maybe a lover. Her mind took a romantic meandering as she and Kasha rode slowly down a pathway through the thick overhanging trees.

She loved the cool, mysterious depths of the woods and the strange bird calls she heard even through the heavy foliage. Not really bird songs, Serena though humorously to herself. It had to be either wild konkols or sooeuls. Two of the guards accompanying them kept a slow pace behind so as not to intrude on their privacy, while the other two scouted ahead. They'd ridden several hours, when they suddenly came upon an enchanting hidden pool in the midst of towering forest giants.

"Oh, Kasha, this is so delightful."

"I thought you'd like it."

"I do, but how did you guess?" Serena cocked her head at her sister-in-law.

"I listen and pay attention." At her continued look of puzzlement, Kasha laughed in a self-conscious manner. "All right, I asked Rhamus what kind of scenery you like to see when you go riding." She dismounted and Serena followed suit.

"You planned this whole thing," she burst out. "The accidental meeting at the stable, stumbling across this wonderful little place."

"I waited a whole hour for you to come across me at the stables," she confessed, then paled in embarrassment.

"But, why?"

Kasha looked like an errant child. Staring down at the ground, she kicked a pebble. "Because I did a rotten thing, bringing my konkol to dinner that night. I wanted to make it up to you."

"Kasha." She stepped close and gently placed her hand on the princess' shoulder. "It's the nicest apology anyone ever made to me, except your brother." Serena smiled at the fond memory of their garden encounter.

She placed her hand on Kasha's shoulder, a gesture she'd seen Volarnians do, when exchanging greetings with close warrior friends.

"What did my brother do, to beat me in his cleverness?" Kasha's eyes lit with interest.

She never got a chance to answer. A deafening yell erupted suddenly and seemed to vibrate all around them. Even though Kasha whipped around and drew her sword with the speed of an alati, she was not prepared for the ring of western warriors who sprang from the concealment of the bushes.

For a heart-stopping few seconds, Serena wondered if Kasha had sold her out to the enemy. That thought was shoved completely out of her mind when the warrior princess ferociously attacked those nearest her. She was frightened for the princess. There were too many even for her skillful swordsmanship. The two guards who had followed behind them, lay deadly still on the ground behind the wall of warriors. She could only hope that the other two had escaped and gone for help.

Catching a warrior near her by surprise, Serena joined in the fray by knocking the unwary soldier unconscious with a quick punch to his chin. Seeming to realize the two women were not to be taken lightly, the warriors' expressions changed from leering and derisive, to cold and considering. Serena stood back to back with Kasha. The warriors facing her threw their weapons to the side when they saw she was swordless, holding out their brawny arms as if to grab her.

The princess tried to keep the soldiers to her front and sides at bay, but her arm fell with weariness from the repeated blows of several swordsmen attacking at the same time. Kasha realized there was no time to take the few seconds she would need to draw from the energy of the crystal--the enemy gave her no reprieve. Besides, this was not a fight of honor, but a brutal ambush.

They were both surprised when the warriors suddenly paused. The swordsmen placed the point of their weapons to the ground, as if awaiting further orders. *Why had they not taken advantage of Kasha's faltering arm?* Both women turned with a feeling of uneasiness as they heard a yasmir approaching.

Serena heard Kasha's in-drawn breath and felt the sudden rigid stance of her body. Coming toward them was a Volarnian male--a noble, she guessed by his rich clothing. Now that she and Kasha were no longer fighting, and while they awaited the slow approach of the man, she'd had time to examine the warriors and their trappings.

The west Volarnians looked exactly the same as their southern enemies, except their hair was black with red highlights instead of blue. Serena touched a lock of bright hair that fell over her shoulder. Now she better understood Rhamus' initial hatred of her auburn tresses.

The "redheaded" warrior's hair grew longer, to their shoulder blades, and the ends were shaggy. They didn't pull their hair back as was the custom of the southern natives, but let it fall wild and free. *Wild.* Serena realized that even though she'd called Rhamus a barbarian, here was true barbarism represented in its most raw form. These warriors looked outwardly the same, yet something about them exuded a fierceness and savagery one didn't see in her people. A jolt of surprise shot through her--she considered the warriors facing them as her enemy, too.

The nobleman stopped his yasmir and examined them thoroughly, as if they were strange animals on display. "So princess, I caught you out on a pleasure ride. I thought iron maidens such as yourself only participated in warring campaigns." The man's tone dripped with sarcasm.

Serena grabbed Kasha's arm to restrain her from lunging at him.

"The question is not what am I doing out here," Kasha retorted. "But what are you doing so far into our territory, Xarath?" The princess spat out his name as if using a dirty swear word.

Worrying her lip as she realized that this was her husband's worst enemy, she looked the man over. He was of average height for a Volarnian but extremely slim. His gaunt cheekbones gave his face a satanic appearance. Xarath dressed in the rich trappings of the nobility but with somber tastes. His shirt and rezel pants were a dark purple, almost black.

Serena felt a shiver run up her arm as his eyes turned to her. They were large, deep-set eyes. Rhamus' enemy fell just shy of being handsome, with his brooding, sharp-angled features giving him a sinister look.

"What have we here?" Xarath examined her, his eyes hiding their thoughts under hooded lids. "With that lovely red hair, you could almost be a--"

Kasha stepped in front of Serena. "She's pure southern Volarnian through and through."

"I tire of your insulting manners." He waved a hand at several soldiers standing tensely near him. "Get the princess out of the way and bring the Queen with us." He turned his mount swiftly, not bothering to see if his orders were carried out.

Chapter Seventeen

The warriors engaged the princess with their swords while from behind several more snuck up and threw a heavy net over her, knocking the angry princess to the ground. Serena was busy trying to keep several of the hulking warriors from grabbing her and could only watch helplessly as the soldiers tied Kasha up.

Two warriors lay on the ground where she'd thrown them, one unconscious from hitting his head on a rock. The other warrior got to his feet gingerly, limping on one leg. As she stood shakily, her sides heaving as she tried to catch her breath, two more warriors attacked her from the front and then too late, she felt iron-hewed arms wrap around her from the back.

Serena saw one soldier who appeared to be in charge nod his head at the soldier holding her. Those bulky arms gradually tightened around her until she became faint and weak. She barely held onto consciousness as she was dumped on the back of a yasmir, head hanging down.

She tried to kick out as ropes were tied securely to her hands and feet beneath the beast's belly. Her stomach lurched sickeningly as the yasmir jumped nervously at her unfamiliar smell. His movement caused Serena to get her last view of Kasha, bound and struggling mightily to release herself. The princess' eyes burned with hatred and sorrow as she bellowed a stream of dark curses at the warriors' departing backs.

The yasmir continued with his mulish behavior, bucking a few times to try and throw her off, then lurched toward the side of the pathway the soldiers were following. Serena saw a large tree branch rushing toward her just before it connected with her head.

She awoke to the dark night. Feeling as though needles were stabbing through the back of her eyes, she gingerly turned her head toward the only source of light. The soldiers were eating and drinking around a small fire, talking in quiet tones. She guessed they were not overly concerned about discovery, but cautious nonetheless.

A figure dressed in a dark cloak emerged from the shadows. Serena felt a chill run down her arms and couldn't discern if it were the cool night air or Xarath's approach that caused such a reaction.

"So, you are finally awake."

Xarath stood over her, his body throwing a deep shadow. The meager warmth of the fire was blocked by his presence, yet there seemed to be a chilliness seeping from him that came not from the surrounding coolness of the night. She wondered if her fanciful thoughts stemmed from the blow to her head.

"Not very talkative, huh? I like that in a woman."

"Where are you taking me?" Serena's mouth felt full of wool, but she managed to get out a sensible question.

Sighing dramatically, he answered, "Now you've ruined one of your lovely assets." Stirring no further comment from her, he continued, "You are going with me back to my castle. It is a six day journey, so tomorrow you will spend the night with me at a fortress near our border."

"Are you crazy? What do you hope to gain?"

Moving quickly, Xarath knelt over her and placed one hand above her waist, his fingers spreading upward and touching the underside of one breast. Her heart thudded hard against the invasion of those icy fingers. She would give anything to be able to throw the King to the ground and punch his lights out--if only her hands and feet were not tied securely with rope. Now she understood his reference to "spending the night with him".

Feeling her pulling against the ropes, Xarath rubbed his hand up and down her waist, letting his hand come to rest lightly upon her breast.

"You cannot escape me. I decided soon after hearing Rhamus took a bride to kidnap his new Queen. Imagine his agony at having his love stolen away, and imagine my joy when I heard reports that the Queen loved her consort as well."

Noting her sharply in-drawn breath, he chuckled. "Now, I have even further reason to rejoice." Xarath ran his hand up her body. Reaching her face, he rubbed one finger across her bottom lip. "You are everything I desire physically in a woman."

Serena moved quickly, grabbing his finger with her teeth, biting down hard, and catching him by surprise. She was satisfied as blood oozed over her lips.

He hissed and pinched her jaws with his other hand until she released his finger. He continued his painful grip as he spoke, "You will regret that tomorrow."

Too late, Serena felt Xarath's body move closer, and she smelled his heavy musk essence before his lips ground against hers. No finesse was evident in the kiss, it was meant to be one of possession and dominance. Serena tasted his blood on her tongue as he forced her lips open with his hand. He paused and seemed to reconsider.

He drew away slightly. "You would bite my tongue, wouldn't you?" He stated in a humorless, flat voice.

"Off, I would hope." She spit the taste of him from her mouth.

Xarath stood. As he turned to leave, he remarked, "You will be begging for my kisses tomorrow."

Tiredness overcame Serena as she let her head sink back down into the mossy earth. *What did he mean by that remark?* Before sleep drew its inky blanket over her consciousness, she thought of the arj'ak's power and how affected she'd been by the Tarthra. A flash of alarm shot through her system, but not enough to keep her from being pulled into a deep, dreamless sleep.

The next day went by in painful flashes as she drifted in and out of consciousness. She wondered if she had a concussion. Luckily, she was seated in front of a warrior who held her body when it sagged. Even the warrior's free play of his hands as he readjusted her meant nothing to Serena at this point. Anything was preferable to hanging head down over the back of a yasmir. She placed a hand softly over her stomach for a moment. Such a ride could have been dangerous for her unborn child.

Xarath rode back only once and paced his yasmir alongside them for a minute. She had wondered why he'd not made her ride in front of him, if nothing else to torment her with his presence. But the cold, calculating grin he turned on her as she slapped the warrior's hands from her thighs, even as Xarath watched, made her realize his game. He wanted her to know that if she didn't give in to him, she could be given to the warriors as a plaything.

The furious pace he set for the group didn't help the pounding in her head and pushed her into periods of unconsciousness. At sunset they finally arrived at their destination. Serena had an impression of a small fortress, ancient and crumbling in places.

She noted the algae and wild vines creeping up the stones as they passed through the entrance. It didn't look well maintained. In a haze, she was pulled through dark musty hallways, lit only by makeshift torches stuck in holes where stones had fallen loose.

She was shoved unceremoniously into a large, freezing room. Surprisingly, it was well kept and furnished with good pieces of furniture. Serena stumbled to the bed and barely wrapped a thick blanket around her before plunging into a dead tired sleep.

Feeling as though she were swimming upstream against a black current, Serena awakened slowly. She batted at the hand clasping her arm, shaking her into wakefulness. Her swim had turned into a boat ride and someone was very determined to tip over the precarious perch she maintained inside the watery vessel. Blinking her eyes in astonishment, she felt wetness running down her cheeks. She put a shaky hand up to her face, then took a deep breath of short-lived relief when she looked up and saw the glass of water Xarath held in one hand.

Half of the water was gone. *He poured it in my face!* Serena struggled against the other hand that restrained her arm, but felt too weak to gather any real anger at his action. Xarath set down the glass and clasped the back of her neck with his free hand. Serena could barely keep her enemy's features in focus and stared at him as if down a long tunnel. She wondered if he'd take advantage of her in her weakened state.

A look of disgust overcame his face as he plopped Serena's lolling head back onto the bed. "You certainly won't be any fun tonight."

Staring off into the distance, Xarath seemed to be mulling over his options. "Fine. You win this time. Or, at least, you might think of it that way. It's a five days ride to my castle ... and I don't want to wait that long to have you, *my* Queen.

Serena struggled to awaken, but could only lay and listen as Xarath continued his evil ranting.

"With your husband safely off to the far east, I suppose I have time to tarry an extra day." Dropping his scorching gaze to her cleavage, he leered. "I'm sure you'll be worth the extra time. Perhaps after a good night's rest, you'll even be grateful."

He moved closer, catching her eyes in a paralyzing look. "I dare say you'll be worth the price I paid for your betrayal." He chuckled. "Who would have believed she would seek me out? Ah, closeness to the King is no guarantee of fealty." He grinned at Serena's confused expression. "She's on my payroll, now."

She struggled to piece together Xarath's words. What is he talking about? Who betrayed me? Someone close to Rhamus? Surely not Kasha. Oh, please, don't let it be Kasha, she thought as she felt consciousness slipping away.

Serena dozed until she was again shaken awake, but gently this time. A haggard looking young Volarnian stood over her, light from the fireplace picking up the reddish glints in her hair. She sat up slowly, sliding the blanket down as the welcome warmth of the fire washed over her. The girl held a goblet, which had seen better days, its sides dented and nicked with much use.

"I brought you a healing potion from our vassi." The girl held out the drink tentatively, trembling slightly as if she thought Serena would strike her.

"Thank you," she pushed the goblet gently back toward the girl, "but I don't think so."

"Truly it's nothing more than a healing drink which will help with the bump you took to your head."

The young girl seemed emboldened by Serena's quiet manner. Taking a big gulp of the fluid, the girl again held it in front of her reluctant face.

Remembering the vast repertoire of ailments the vassi were capable of healing, she reached hesitantly for the goblet. Hartoos said the sorcerers only worked for the people, whether they be from west or south Volarn, and they had a strict code of ethics. Serena eyed the girl again. She had taken a large drink of the stuff. Pausing, Serena requested, "Take another drink."

Shrugging her shoulders, the girl took another gulping mouthful of the dark liquid. "Lucky for me, its bedtime." At Serena's raised eyebrows, she added, "This potion will give you a good night's sleep, even if you're not sick."

Taking the goblet from the girl, she drank down the rest in a few swallows. If it was poison, the girl just did herself in, as well as Serena. Besides, Xarath had good reasons to keep her alive and healthy. The girl left and she started yawning and feeling suddenly very relaxed. She hoped it was a good healer who concocted the drink.

Pale sunlight seeped past the heavy curtains as she finally awoke. Getting up gingerly, she stood and stretched cautiously, glad she had no nausea or headache. Serena ran her hands around her head and gingerly touched the large bump on the side. It was sore, but otherwise she felt fine again. Walking slowly to the window, she was surprised to see the sunset when she pulled the curtains back. That was some powerful drink, she thought.

The window looked down on the practice area. She could see targets set up for swordsmen to hack at, but only a few soldiers were in sight. A few warriors sat or lounged around the area's perimeter, seemingly more interested in the drink they swilled than practicing. These warriors yelled encouragement to two men half-heartedly swinging at each other; watching closer, Serena saw the two were not disinterested, they were drunk. One warrior struck the other on the arm, opening a gash along the man's forearm.

Neither warrior seemed to notice as blood oozed from the man's wound until it dripped onto his pommel. Stopping suddenly, he staggered, then righted himself and shook his hand in puzzlement. The watching soldiers laughed uproariously. Apparently the drink had dulled their senses to the point of silliness. The sparring warriors laughed with the others and tottered to the side to join their comrades in serious drinking.

She recognized a few of the drunk warriors from the group who brought her here, but none of the more alert soldiers guarding the parapet looked familiar. Even they occasionally took long pulls from bladder bags, like those commonly used by soldiers while on patrol. They must not be worried about discovery or else Xarath is a slovenly leader. And he didn't impress her as such. Her spirits went down another notch when she realized just how confident the warriors were of not being bothered in their fortress.

"Glad to see you up and about." Xarath's gleeful voice came from behind her.

Serena spun around quickly, facing her enemy cautiously. "What do you hope to gain from this kidnapping?" she asked angrily.

The ruler of west Volarn approached her slowly. "I already told you my plans yesterday. What else is there to explain?" He spread his hands as if puzzled by her attitude.

"You will most certainly cause an escalation in the warring. But you cannot keep me a prisoner."

He shook his head slowly. "It's true, I hope to push Rhamus into a final confrontation so I can win back Volarn under one ruler. But, as I said before, you will now become my Queen. I will rule Volarn and have Rhamus' woman. Just rewards I believe for all the years of waiting."

"You are crazy! You may end up with this confrontation you desire, but I would never consent to become your Queen."

"You will." His eyes burned with fanatic enthusiasm as he approached closer.

Serena didn't understand what he spoke of, but she backed away slowly from his approach. She was uneasy, like an animal that senses the nearness of the hunter. Finally, positioning herself in the center of the room, where she would have more room to maneuver, she stopped and awaited Xarath.

He paused just out of arm's reach and simply stared at her. She didn't know what game he sought to use on her, but she was ready whenever he made a move toward her. She looked forward to grinding his face into the floorboards.

Suddenly, her nervous feelings turned to trembly ones of longing. Her body flushed with sexual urgings, her breathing became faster. She stared at Xarath in alarm. He was standing stone rigid, nothing looking alive but his eyes. Her own eyes opened in dawning panic as a blue light emitted from the area surrounding his evil orbs. He was using the crystal's power on her!

She tried to move her body, to struggle against the encroaching thread of throbbing sexual desire that didn't stem from within herself. It did no good--Xarath's power overtook her feeble efforts. He came closer, to within touching distance, but just stood staring at her. Serena tried to pull her gaze from his, but felt lethargic and couldn't gather the energy it would take to accomplish such a feat.

Her eyes half-closed with the aching that overtook her limbs. Her heart set up an erratic fast pace all its own and her breathing became labored. The rivulets of dark power coursed through her veins, making her a creature that ached for Xarath's touch. When he finally reached out and stroked slowly down one arm, she groaned aloud at the feeling it evoked.

His eyes glittered with triumph as he began to touch her body wherever he desired, causing her to tremble. Serena desperately tried to fight the feelings washing over her. Evil satisfaction flashed in her enemy's eyes as a voice deep within her cried out in anguish. She pictured Rhamus' face and that voice within cried out for her beloved to help her. Her body jerked abruptly, as if a puppeteer had pulled invisible strings, and Serena realized that for a second she'd broken Xarath's control.

The disgusting beast was too intent on plundering beneath her dress to notice her momentary break. As he pulled her dress down off one shoulder and his breathing became more labored with his pawings, she concentrated with all her will on Rhamus' face and the love she held for him. She didn't have time to stop and consider the fact that she finally acknowledged the love she felt for her husband, but gathered it to herself as a source of power and comfort.

Suddenly, Serena felt Xarath's control snap from her completely. She was in control again as she looked down with hatred at his head, which rutted at her breasts. Just like the pig that he is, she thought. Serena brought her knee up sharply between his thighs and was gratified by the pained, stunned expression Xarath gave her before he collapsed on the ground.

She straightened her clothing as she sprinted toward the door. The king had more strength then she gave him credit for, because he managed to alert the guards waiting outside the door with a high-pitched scream. Serena spent the next few minutes waging the hardest battle of her life. She wanted to escape Xarath's clutches more than she'd ever wanted anything else.

She managed to knock down both the guards waiting outside but, as she started to run down the dark hall, she found her escape route blocked by the huge men who appeared at its end. Any warrior within hearing distance must have come running when they heard Xarath's scream, she thought. Serena ran back the way she'd come and found the two warriors back on their feet and angrily awaiting her. Xarath stood behind them, a furious expression on his face.

A flushed feeling overcame her at the thought of being put back in the evil King's hands again. She fought the warriors who jumped her like a she-demon, to no avail, but still managed to leave several of them groaning upon the cold floor before her arms were pulled roughly behind her back. Her arms were jerked with force and her wrists tied as she once again stood before her enemy.

Xarath poured himself a drink and calmly downed it while he waited for the warriors to leave. The two guards remained. Serena had the feeling he didn't like to let his feelings get out of control. She had angered him more by forcing him to display emotion, than by any actual injury she may have caused. When he came to stand in front of her, his expression was inhumanely cold.

"So you have chosen the hard way of becoming my lover." His voice was flat and emotionless, making the contrast with his features more chilling.

His demeanor and tone scared her more than what he'd done to her before. Serena knew instinctively that whatever Xarath had in mind for her now would be far worse. *Maybe he's going to kill me.* Serena waited for his pronouncement.

"Guards," he spoke to the warriors standing on either side of her, "escort our guest to the dungeon. I wish to introduce her to the *quamus.*"

The guards grinned and grabbed her arms roughly, pulling her out the door and down the hall. Serena could hear Xarath walking briskly behind them.

The warriors pulled her through a large door and then down steep narrow steps. The stairs went down a long way; Serena could see drips of condensation as they went deeper into the rock walls. The stairs ended at another gigantic door, which the warriors unlocked with a key. Pushing the heavy door open took both warriors. It creaked in protest, as if it were unused to such treatment.

She'd thought the dank hallways and stairs smelled bad, but the odor that hit them once the door was open was even more offensive. It smelled of filth, rotting wood, and mustiness. Serena shivered. A chilly draft blew past them, laden with all the odorous smells of the ancient dungeon and its dark secrets.

The guards pulled the struggling Serena past gaping holes in the rock face, which once served as cells. No glimmer of light fell within their dark interiors, and neither she nor the guards peered inside as they passed.

They halted in front of a cell with a heavy door still attached to its facings. Metal bars set in a small square allowed the jailer to peer at the prisoner inside, and a cumbersome rusty lock kept the inmate from escaping. I guess I get to sit in a damp, smelly cell, Serena thought. She shuddered, but considered it a more preferable choice to Xarath's earlier attack on her mind.

Once inside, the guards cut her ropes but kept a firm grip on each wrist as they pulled her over to a post set in the center of the cell, then drew her wrists up and clamped them within cold metal wristbands. Serena was surprised by the size of the cell, about fifteen feet square. No cot, chair, or even straw was provided to rest upon, and she guessed that, for the duration of her stay, she would be hanging from the pole.

"How do you like your new quarters?" Xarath asked with a dark humor edging his voice.

"You know, it's pretty smelly in here," she said slowly, "but it's preferable to your foul presence."

"I see I'm wasting my time talking to you," he hissed. He stood in front of her and held her face in a vise-like grip. "As I told you earlier, you will regret fighting me." He walked away a few feet and then drew what looked like a whip from his belt.

"So, you're going to beat me," Serena tried to keep her voice nonchalant, as if she could care less what he did with her.

Xarath laughed, a wicked sound that cut through her and grated on her nerves. "No. I am pulling my *zimit* in case I need it for self-defense. It's time for you to meet your cell mate, the quamus."

Serena's gut churned. What would Xarath need to defend himself against with a weapon? The two guards stood at the far end of the cell, swords drawn. She heard a heavy grating sound and noticed a large metal door at the far end of the cell begin to move slowly upward. A fluttery sensation gripped her stomach when the smell hit her full force, as the door groaned to a stop. The King stepped backward until the cell's rock wall was at his back.

A fetid, foul odor arose from the dark that lay hidden behind the open doorway. All the hairs on her arms stood up, as if pulled by an electrical charge, even before she heard the sounds from the black hole. A rasping, sucking sound slithered past the doorway and set the cell's occupants into nervous alertness.

Chapter Eighteen

Her eyes strained toward the doorway, trying to see past the darkness. A tentacle limb scrabbling for a hold within the cell was the first glimmer Serena had of the creature that approached. She no longer wished to see what lay behind the doorway. The animal that emerged from the shadows was more frightening than any monster she could have dreamed up on her own. Her tongue clicked against her dry mouth and the hairs on her head rose up.

The creature slithered into the room with a sideways motion. A large, glistening, bulbous body sat atop six dark green legs. It stood about three feet tall. The tentacle-shaped limbs must contain bones, for it stood in a spider posture, as if ready to pounce on its next victim. Its body was a sickly grayish-green color and gleamed, as if mucous oozed from its pores, and a sparse growth of short stiff hairs only added to its horrific appearance.

A swiveling head rested on top, with large eyes that zoomed in on Serena with unblinking intensity. When the quamus opened its wide mouth and flicked its long tongue out, she thought she would faint. Its mouth was full of sharp teeth--teeth that could rend and tear soft flesh easily.

The monster started to move toward her, but Xarath flicked his whip, holding it at bay temporarily. The whip crackled against the beast's skin, giving out an electric jolt, which halted it, but not without protest. The creature let out an ear-shattering screech, which echoed resoundingly in the small space.

"This is the quamus." He said in a pleasant voice, as if he were introducing her to an old friend. "He's a very nasty looking fellow, isn't he?"

When he received no answer, Xarath continued, "I'm afraid his eating habits are just as nasty as his appearance. Do you wish me to elaborate?" He waited for a reply and sighed as if disappointed. He edged closer to her cautiously, keeping a watchful eye on the hideous animal.

"The quamus is really a cowardly beast, preferring to pounce on its victim in the dark, catching it unaware. But their favorite method of finding prey is to choose those who have suffered an injury and can't put up a fight."

"Sounds like you're cousins," Serena managed to keep her voice from trembling, but her legs wouldn't stop quavering.

"Tsk, tsk." Xarath shook his head at her. "We really are going to have to do something about your manners." He cracked the whip at the creature, which had begun to inch closer. It hissed and backed up a scrabbling step.

Maybe he's just trying to scare me, she thought.

"As I was saying, the quamus catches its victim and then he has to prepare his prey before he can consume it." Waiting for a response from his captive, Xarath continued, "Preparation consists of the quamus covering his victim with a mucous fluid excreted from his forelegs, which makes the victim digestible."

"The quamus is a creature of habit or instinct, he always follows the same procedure. He starts at his prey's feet, covering them with his predigesting matter, works his way up to the prey's head, and then he starts to take bites from them."

Getting no response, he continued. "Don't you think it's interesting that the beast leaves his prey's head uncovered, so they can survive longer? Keeps his meal fresher, I guess." Xarath grinned at her wide-eyed stare of horror, "Oh don't worry, in all the times I've seen it ingest a meal, I've never seen it change its routine."

"What do you mean?" Serena's voice came out weak. She wondered how many others he'd tortured this way.

"Remember I told you that you'd regret not submitting to me." Xarath waved a hand to indicate the cell's interior. "You've been brought down here to be taught a lesson in obedience." He ran the whip down her side and paused at the pants covering her thighs. "I don't intend for the quamus to have you as his next meal, but you will wish you'd never fought me." He withdrew a dagger from his belt and began cutting the leather pants from her.

Serena struggled against the metal cuffs in alarm. "What are you doing?" The frigid air of the dungeon hit her legs like a blast of wintry air.

He finished cutting and stripping the pants, until her long legs were totally exposed. Her only defense against the cold and the men's lustful eyes was the thin dress that covered her upper body. Xarath stepped back from his handiwork, keeping an eye on the quamus as he noted the beauty of his captive. Her arms were stretched above her head, causing the dress to pull up and brush the top of her thighs. She was very frightened, her lovely eyes wide pools of blue terror, but still she tried to maintain a semblance of defiance.

He began walking slowly backwards, stopping when the wall was at his back. "In answer to your question, Serena, I think you need the full benefit of the quamus' preparation for you to be properly submissive. You wouldn't be able to feel much through those thick pants you were wearing."

As if responding to its name and recognizing that Xarath had left the area clear for it, the quamus began its slow, scratching, approach.

Serena's fear rose past terror as the creature reached her feet and wrapped a tentacle around one of her calves. It was frigid, feeling as though it came from the icy depths of a bottomless ocean. Her body went rigid in reaction, as if it were afraid to breathe or her heart to beat. A scream welled up inside her, but she couldn't get it past her lips, which were frozen shut with horror.

The quamus oozed more of the mucous, which covered its body and began rubbing its tentacles around her legs. Her breathing was shallow and rapid and she was light-headed. The alien, nightmarish creature worked its way up her limbs. Numbness invaded her body, though whether from the mucous or fright, Serena couldn't tell.

Its hot breath fanned her waist and she smelled its rotting-corpse odor. Fearing to look, yet seemingly compelled, Serena glanced down. The eyes which examined her were black, the flat death orbs of a shark. She shuddered, setting up a rippling effect throughout her whole body as it went into spasms. The scream she'd felt locked inside finally broke free from the paralysis gripping her.

Her scream echoed loudly within the small space, bouncing off the walls. She relaxed into the arms of a safe blackness, as if the scream released her hold on reality and sanity. Serena's last impression was hearing the creature echo her scream as Xarath's whip sizzled across its wet skin.

She awoke feeling groggy and confused. She looked around slowly and saw that she was back in Xarath's bedroom. *What am I doing in the bed?* She threw the cover back, wanting to get as far away as possible from his bed, and looked with shock at her naked body. Throwing the blanket around her as a makeshift dress, Serena got up shakily and looked around the room for her clothes. It was odd that the last thing she remembered was going to sleep fully clothed.

"You've awakened just in time to greet me properly."

Xarath's darkly humorous tone cut through Serena's fog like a well-honed knife. She gasped and paled with shock as her living nightmare experience in the dungeon came rushing back to her in an overwhelming moment. She watched nervously as he began to slowly disrobe. His nude body was skinny, yet still rigidly muscled. He strolled casually toward her and stopped a few paces away.

"Drop the blanket and get into bed." His expression and voice left no doubt that he expected to be obeyed this time.

"Wait." She put up a hand, trying to come up quickly with a way out of her situation while distracting her enemy. "How did I get all cleaned up?"

"Simple. My servant washed you." Xarath's expression became darker, more sinister. "Now quit stalling and get into bed right now, or do you wish to pay another visit to the quamus? My patience is at an end. If I send you to the dungeon this time, you won't be returning."

A glance into his malicious eyes told her he meant what he said. She couldn't face the dungeon's denizen again, even if Xarath didn't mean what he said about letting the beast devour her. Feeling sick to her stomach, Serena dropped the blanket and turned slowly.

"Wait." His voice stopped her.

He approached from her back and a shiver ran up her spine at his nearness. He stood in front of her and examined every detail of her body, then walked slowly around her. A blessed feeling of numbness washed over her, canceling even her revulsion. Serena followed Xarath's instructions to get in bed. She lay quietly as he stretched out alongside her and began kissing her slowly. He seemed frustrated with her lack of response and attacked her lips savagely, bruising them with his force.

She couldn't stop a slight quiver that rippled under her skin when Xarath's hands began grabbing the soft flesh of her stomach and breasts. He grinned, seemingly satisfied that she did react to his invasive hands. She knew that much of Xarath's pleasure would come from her revulsion to his touch and the horror that she would feel at having to endure a rape at his hands. She vowed not to bare those emotions to his pleasure. It was all a mental power game to him, one in which he held the whole deck against her.

Serena endured his mouth upon her breasts and his hands invading in her body's private territory, where only Rhamus had been allowed previously. But she didn't know if she could endure the final insult to her mind and body. Yet she knew she had to, for she surely wouldn't survive her other choice. Her mind felt fragile, on the breaking point beneath the horrific reality of having to stay unresisting while Xarath's hands and mouth played freely with her body, and his crude comments and wicked eyes played havoc with her mind.

He moved her legs apart and posed on his elbows, as if wanting her to be aware of the exact moment when he thrust himself into her. One forlorn tear escaped down her cheek and ran unnoticed into her hair. She closed her eyes, not wishing to see the triumphant look in Xarath's eyes. Her mind turned to Rhamus' beloved face and her soul called out for him. Serena was unaware that she'd cried his name aloud desperately, as a talisman against evil.

He nudged his staff against her upper thigh to gain her attention. "It won't do you any good to call for your husband. You belong to me now."

A loud explosion of sound erupted into the room, startling the two people on the bed. They looked up just as the door burst in with another explosive impact. Rhamus stood in the threshold, breathing heavily, covered in splotches of blood. Xarath jumped to his feet and rushed for his sword, but not before a dumb-struck Serena saw the hard glare her husband threw their direction as they lay locked in an apparent embrace.

"Pick up your sword and prepare to die." Rhamus' raw voice urged a hesitant Xarath to grab his sword off a chair.

Still feeling numb from her earlier experience and the closeness of her rape, Serena sat up and watched her husband and their enemy engage in battle. She already knew Rhamus was an excellent swordsman and could see the two enemies were evenly matched in skills. But her husband had the advantage of his rage, if he didn't allow it to hinder his abilities.

Xarath must have been thinking along the same line, for he began to taunt Rhamus. "I will enjoy the pleasures of your wife's body immensely once I've dispatched you to *jahum*."

Her husband appeared distracted by his enemy's remarks and Xarath got in a quick thrust past his guard. A long cut bled along his left forearm where Xarath sliced it open.

"Maybe I'll dump your body on the bed after I've killed you and take her next to your corpse." His features wore a fiendish expression.

Instead of becoming upset by Xarath's newest comment, Rhamus seemed to become calmer as they continued to hack at one another. Serena recognized that Rhamus was violently angry by the frigid look that came over his face. She was glad to note that his anger did not seem to affect his fencing skills, perhaps even enhancing them now that he had his emotions under a stony control. She was surprised neither warrior used the crystal's power, fighting man against man, strength against strength.

He pounded at Xarath, seeming to forgo all thought of skill and finesse, driving the smaller man back, back, until his body hit the stone wall. Xarath realized too late he'd been expertly checkmated into a corner, and like a cornered rat began fighting desperately.

Regardless, Rhamus rammed past his enemy's defenses and stabbed his sword through his heart. Blood spurted as the sword jutted out of Xarath's back and rang against the solid walls behind him.

Feeling queasy as she saw the amount of blood that shot out of the body, Serena turned her face away slightly. She sensed Rhamus' approach without having to hear his heavy tread, as one feels an electrical charge in the air at the approach of a storm. Tears slid down her face in relief and she looked up slowly, raising her arms to receive Rhamus' comfort. The look on his face made her drop her arms instantly.

"Are you unhurt?" His voice was flat and emotionless. At her nod, he said, "Get dressed. I don't wish to stay any longer in this stinking fortress than is necessary."

"I don't know where my clothes are." She hadn't been able to find them before, and looked around the room doubtfully.

Rhamus gave her a suspicious stare and walked over to a closet. Quickly jerking out a pair of pants and shirt, he thrust them at her. "Put these on, maybe it will comfort you to wear the clothes of your dead lover."

She finally became aware of how it must have looked when Rhamus burst through the door. Her heart seemed to sink into her stomach and lay there like a large rock, hard and rigid. It didn't help that she couldn't locate her clothes either. But, the last thing she wanted to do was wear *his* clothes.

When Rhamus thrust them at her, Serena's sweating hands grasped the fabric as if it were a bundle of snakes. Neither did she want to stand naked and defenseless against his scathing glare. She dropped the sheet and dressed quickly, not able to stop the shiver that overcame her whole body at the thought of slipping into his trappings. Xarath's clothes hung on her.

Her feet crunched up, her flesh shrinking from contact with the stone's icy flooring. The cold seeped into them, chilling her whole body. Xarath's boots were large and would probably fall off if she attempted to wear them; besides, the thought of sliding her feet into his boots made her toes curl in reaction.

"You will have to go barefooted."

Rhamus' remark cut through her chill with the blandness of his tone, as if he could care less if her feet were freezing and unprotected from the rough ground.

Serena tried not to look at the blood pooling around Xarath's body, as Rhamus turned and started out the door and she followed behind him. She barely glanced at the body of an enemy guard lying outside the door. They moved quickly down the dark hall and Serena became even more numb as the dank stones sent new chills up through her sensitive feet.

When Rhamus stopped abruptly at the end of the hall, she peered past his shoulder and saw that they were at the entrance of a central living area. A huge ruggedly built fireplace took up much of the far wall. Looking down, she saw a sprawled body just past Rhamus' feet, an enemy warrior, cut to pieces with many hacking wounds. She stared at her husband's back, no longer interested in seeing the room's contents, sure that it held many more gruesome reminders of the battle just waged.

"Rhamus! Are you OK? Did you find Serena?" Kasha's voice called across the room.

She never thought she'd be so glad to hear another person's voice. "I'm right here," Serena replied, stepping around Rhamus. She put a hand up to mouth as the nausea almost overwhelmed her. Several bodies lay strewn around the room, like bloody discarded dolls.

"Take her to the yasmirs," he ordered his sister, in a no-nonsense voice that made Kasha raise her eyebrows in puzzlement.

She was glad Kasha dismissed her brother's stiff manner with a shrug and turned to help her. The princess threw her cloak over Serena's head and guided her carefully away from any corpses and out into the fresh air.

"Thank you." She handed Kasha's cloak back to her.

"You keep it," she pushed it back into her hands. "It looks like it could drizzle again, and we wouldn't want you to get sick."

"Are you all right?" Serena placed one hand on her sister-in-law's forearm. Kasha squeezed her hand quickly.

With a wicked grin, she said, "I'm fine. Do you think a confrontation with Xarath would keep me down for long?"

"No," she smiled slightly in response. "I'm beginning to think any man would have a hard time getting to you."

"Anyway," she waved away Serena's remark modestly, "are you sure you're fine? You look kind of pale. Xarath didn't hurt you, did he?" Her suddenly stricken look and the whiteness of her face alarmed Kasha. She hugged the weak-kneed Queen next to her body, supporting her until Serena straightened.

"Where is he? I am going to kill him!" Her violent tone left no doubts that she'd make good her threat.

"He's already dead," she said wearily. "Rhamus killed him."

"You'll feel better in a minute." The princess tried to soothe her. "Rhamus will be back when he gets through checking the fortress for any more of our enemies. I'm sure having his arms around you

instead of mine will make things better." Serena trembled in her
arms, then jerked away.

"I think I'm going to be sick." She held her hand over her mouth
and managed to walk a few steps before she heaved up what little
liquid sat in the pit of her stomach. She'd had very little to eat and
drink lately. She heard Kasha near the yasmirs, then felt her arm
clasped firmly. The princess wiped her brow and then her mouth
with a wet cloth. She was too weak to protest and push Kasha away
as she wished. Instead she stood up and took the cloth, then bathed
her whole face. Kasha led her to a log and they sat side by side.

"Don't be embarrassed," she said, noting Serena looking down
and off to the side. "You've just been through a very traumatic
experience, and you're pregnant, too. I'm not too sure I wouldn't be
throwing up if I were in your shoes."

"I am glad you came along." She placed her hand on Kasha's,
leaving it there.

She looked down at Serena's hand and placed hers gently over it.
"Look, there's Rhamus." Kasha pointed toward the castle, trying to
distract her sister-in-law; she was alarmed as Serena's features once
again paled and she looked faint.

"What's the matter Serena? Did Rhamus say something to upset
you?"

Her eyes misted and, even though she turned her head away, she
couldn't stop the few tears that straggled slowly down her cheeks.
She knew the princess had spied her tears when she heard Kasha's
in drawn breath. She jumped to her feet so quickly, Serena had to
move fast to place a restraining hand on the princess' arm, to keep
her from rushing toward Rhamus.

"Let go. I just want to talk to him." Kasha still felt the
protectiveness that had suddenly overtaken her when she first saw
Serena's tears. She knew her relative was not a crier, and even
though her pregnancy might account for it, she didn't think so.

"No, please don't," she said quietly.

"If that's what you want. But Serena, I could knock some sense
into that hard head of his. Why one time when we were little I...."

They both quieted as Rhamus suddenly appeared around a clump
of bushes, Jarvic and Ulecki trailing behind him.

"Are these all the warriors you brought with you?" Serena asked.

"That's all that were needed," Rhamus answered sharply, causing
the three other people with them to look questioningly at him.

"What he really means," Kasha gave her brother a stern look. "is,
that we," she waved a hand to encompass their little group, "were all
that was available."

"I thank each of you very much." Tears trembled in her eyes and voice. "You saved my life." Serena looked at each one in turn, saving Rhamus for last. He stared back at her briefly then turned toward the yasmirs.

She stayed close to Kasha, not sure where to go and with whom. No tame mounts were available for her to ride. Everyone mounted and her husband waited impatiently on his great steed. Finally he turned and stuck his hand out towards her. She thought Rhamus was too rough in pulling her onto the saddle in front of him, but it felt wonderful to have his arms about her, even though she could tell by his rigid stance that he wished she were anywhere else but resting therein.

She fell into an exhausted sleep, waking only once when the group stopped for a quick rest and food. Feeling too drained of energy, Serena couldn't stir up enough interest to ask one question during their stop. Rhamus still acted cool and distant, but urged her to eat from their sparse supplies. She ate mechanically, for the baby, even though every item touching her tongue was tasteless and flat.

When they remounted, Serena groggily resettled herself in his arms, going to sleep almost immediately. It was dark, the air heavy with moisture. In her sleep, awareness of her environment seeped into Serena's slumbering world, making sense of her surroundings in a crazy, surreal fashion. She was back in the damp dungeon, Xarath cackled insanely in the corner, whispering horrible things that she could barely make out. Something slithered into her view and she screamed as if the demons of hell were upon her heels.

All four yasmirs reared and snorted as Serena's terrifying scream tore abruptly through the gathering dusk. It took all the warriors' skills to get their mounts under control, especially Rhamus, who carried the source of the yasmirs' terror. Even after they calmed down, the mounts stood nervously, their ears cocked forward as if awaiting the approach of something from the dark trees.

"What in Goreth's name?" He shook her gently and then harder when she didn't respond. She whimpered like a child caught in the horror of her nightmare. Just before she roused fully, she groaned a low phrase that was heard by them all. Words so full of pain and terror that the psychically attuned Volarnians felt shivers run over their skin, as if baby konkols had skittered across it.

"Dungeon, the dungeon. It's coming!" Serena groaned, then sat up in Rhamus' arms and shrilled, "Quamus!" She finally shook herself free of the clinging dregs of her nightmare and looked around, seeing that she had an intense audience watching her. They looked at her like she'd gone quite mad.

"I'm OK," she mumbled, pushing at his arms, which were squeezing her so tight, she could barely breathe.

"We better stop for the night." Rhamus ordered and Jarvic scouted ahead for a good spot. He tried questioning Serena but she was withdrawn and evaded his questions like the best of ambassadors.

They stopped in a small, moonlit clearing, surrounded by the immense trees and low growing bushes. It gave good cover in case their enemy was pursuing them, but the three moons overhead wouldn't be deterred from shooting their rays through the leafy canopy. An enemy could spot them easily if they made it through the outer protection of bushes. Rhamus posted Ulecki to guard the perimeter. They could see him circling the camp at a distance, his tread silent.

The three warriors went quietly about their business, briefly wiping down the mounts and feeding them. Only when they finished did they prepare bedrolls and fished rations from their packs. Seeing Serena's bare feet without the cloak covering them, Jarvic rummaged in his pack and came up with an extra pair of boots.

She accepted them gratefully and was surprised when they fit rather well, only being a little loose on her feet. "How convenient that you had an extra pair," she said curiously.

Jarvic shrugged. "You never know when your feet might get wet, and I hate for my feet to be cold."

"Me too," she couldn't help sliding her eyes sideways in Rhamus' direction. When he didn't react, she poked a utensil at the tasteless food Kasha had handed her.

Chapter Nineteen

Rhamus watched worriedly as Serena again picked at her food. He was glad Kasha encouraged her to eat, and that his wife seemed to respond to his sister. He didn't know which he felt more of-- anger, worry, or happiness. His conflicting emotions were eating at his gut, making it hard for him to eat decently, too. Instead, he stared at one of the moons overhead.

He hadn't been this angry since Xarath had killed his father. The pain of his father's death could easily be dredged up by other painful incidents, such as the death of a warrior friend. And now Xarath was again at the center of something extremely painful to him.

Had he really seen what he thought he saw, when he burst through his enemy's chamber door? Perhaps his enemy had been on the verge of raping Serena, but she had lain so quiet and unresisting, it appeared otherwise. Rape or consensual sex, he was glad he had interrupted something, which would have been hard to dismiss from his mind and their marriage.

His eyes went back to his lovely wife's attempt at eating. He was worried about their child and how it fared through this ordeal. He couldn't wait to get Dr. Melat to check Serena out. Now, he was doubly worried. Rhamus had guessed she would have some trauma once he rescued her, but he had no idea it would be this bad for her. What had Xarath done to her? He never had any doubts that he would get her back from her captor. He couldn't take two such great loses in his life--his father, then his wife.

He ran his eyes over his wife's lovely figure, visible plainly in the moonlight. His eyes were drawn back to her exquisite face and the real reason he loved her. The King shifted on the log. It made him more confused to feel so angry with her, but at the same time, his love strove to dominate his negative feelings.

He loved her gentle nature even though she tried to hide it beneath a warrior's facade. The way she adored children, her joy in taking yasmir rides with him, and her interest in his people and their fine arts. He loved the way her eyes lit up whenever he approached her, the fact that she could match him in passion, and the way she became easily embarrassed by his teasing. A shyness was evident in her flamboyant body and bold nature that he found endearing.

He had been ecstatic when he knew he was close to getting her

back in his arms. That feeling had been squashed as completely as a
baby auk underfoot when he broke down the door and saw Serena
wrapped in Xarath's arms. He didn't know what to think anymore,
or what to feel. He felt everything, but most of all he was confused.
Did Serena have a deceitful heart like Szafra?

He dragged his thoughts from their dark arena to Serena's
emotional frailty. What had Xarath done to her to cause such terror
as her nightmare indicated? She refused to talk about it now, but she
would have to tell him, soon.

The idea of what might have occurred in a dungeon pounded at
his brain. It probably was not as bad as his imagination was
conjuring up. He was glad when Kasha leant over and began to
engage his wife in conversation.

They were too silent a group, like mourners at a gravesite.

"Serena, you wanted to hear about my famous escape from
Xarath's trap, didn't you?"

Kasha's overly enthusiastic tone, plainly meant to drag her from
her doldrums, made her smile slightly in return. If nothing else, she
smiled to make her sister-in-law feel better. She certainly felt no
reason for joy. Her happiness at the thought of her reunion with
Rhamus had been spoiled by his continued coldness and suspicion.

Didn't he realize she'd been at the mercy of her captor? He had no
idea what she'd been through. Even though she knew the telling
would be difficult, she would share it all with Rhamus as soon as
they could be alone. He'd be very sorry after she told him, then he'd
take her in his arms and offer her the comfort she sorely needed.
Serena smiled briefly to herself and looked to her husband. He sat,
silent and unfeeling as the log he sat upon.

She turned back to Kasha, now feeling a real interest in finding out
how the princess had escaped her bindings and found her brother.
"How did you manage everything?"

"It wasn't easy." The princess sat cross-legged and elegant, even as
she told a tale any warrior would be proud of owning. "I called for
the guards who had been with us, but all I heard was one groaning
every once in a while. I started wiggling along the ground toward
that warrior and finally managed to get to his side. Luckily, he was
just past the first bush I encountered."

"Was he hurt badly?"

Shaking her head sadly, Kasha said, "He was dying from a gut
wound, there was nothing I could do. But, I spotted the dagger he
had dropped near the bush. Our enemy had taken all the other
weapons they could find, including my dagger. I managed to cut
my ropes. Since I could do nothing to save him, I held the guard

while he died.

Serena saw the painful memory reflected in her face. "What did you do after he died?"

"Covered him with his cloak. We'll have to send back a patrol to bury him--and the others." She said grimly.

"All of them were killed?" She whispered. At Kasha's nod, she asked, "What did you do then?"

"I started jogging for home, and I couldn't believe it when I saw Rhamus and Jarvic riding toward me."

"I thought they were with a whole patrol group and that they were going on a long trip?" Serena addressed her question to Jarvic.

"Maybe I ought to take over from here," he interjected. "We were with the other warriors, but we'd only gone one day out when we ran across an unusual occurrence."

"What was it?" She asked curiously.

"We found a dead mare and the colt she'd just delivered. Even though it's rare to come across a wild colt, we wouldn't have stopped to consider keeping it, except." Jarvic paused dramatically.

"Except what?"

"The colt had lavender fur." At her confused look, he explained, "The color is very rare, you might see such a yasmir once in your lifetime."

"Like a white buffalo," Serena said to herself. "What happened to the foal?"

"Rhamus decided you must have the colt as a gift and sent the rest of the patrol ahead, and kept me. We were headed back to the castle, when we saw a striking female running across a meadow."

She wondered where Ulecki came into the picture, but waited for Jarvic to explain. She couldn't stop the sudden feeling of joy that coursed through her when Jarvic explained Rhamus' thoughtfulness. Her husband sat through the story, saying nothing, simply staring at the ground in front of him. She couldn't help smiling at the princess and Jarvic as they crossed verbal swords briefly, Kasha taking offense at being called a "running female". She didn't seem to mind being called "striking" though.

She coughed to get their attention. "Where's the colt?" Jarvic cleared his throat and looked at Rhamus. Serena turned to her husband in alarm. "You didn't leave a new born foal all by itself, did you?"

"No. But we would have, if Jarvic hadn't remembered a farm nearby where we could leave it. Finding you was more important." For the first time tonight, she felt her husband's full attention was on her. He seemed to consider her for a moment then his veil of uncertainty once again slipped into place.

"By the way, that's how Ulecki joined us. He lives on the next farm, and we stopped and asked for the assistance of his wondrous sword arm." Jarvic's eyes twinkled, as if he guessed she'd been wondering about that very subject.

Serena didn't want to ask if they were going to stop and pick the colt up on the way back, suddenly she felt too weary to even care. She settled herself as comfortably as she could against the hard ground and listened as the princess and Jarvic's sparring continued. This time Kasha teased him about knowing the whereabouts of the farm, because of a farmer's daughter that he visited.

After Jarvic and Kasha seemed to run out of anything to say, they settled down for sleep. Rhamus peered in her direction, then reluctantly got up and placed his sleeping blanket next to hers. Serena turned away from him and remained stiff, hoping he would not try to make her sleep within the cocoon of his arms. Then she felt angry when he did not even offer to hold her. She started to nod off to sleep, but thought she heard something slithering in the trees at the edge of the thicket. Her eyes were suddenly wide and straining through the dark and she knew she'd get no sleep tonight.

A few hours before dawn approached, Jarvic relieved Rhamus from guard duty, as he had relieved Ulecki earlier. But Kasha had insisted on taking the first watch. He was glad when dawn finally lit the thicket with welcome warmth. Now they could be on their way home, and a much safer place for Serena and the future heir.

"Did she ever go to sleep?" Rhamus asked Jarvic as he joined him near the yasmirs. They saddled the mounts as they talked.

"No, never shut her eyes during my watch."

"Nor mine." Ulecki said as he joined them.

"I'm worried about the baby's health. Serena needs to get adequate rest." His eyebrows drew together thickly.

"And Serena's health as well," Jarvic added, looking to see his cousin's response.

"Of course," his voice became irritated. "Go scout the area before we leave," he ordered.

Jarvic gave the King an inscrutable look before disappearing into the bushes.

"My, my, big brother, I'd forgotten just how grouchy you could be in the morning." Kasha sauntered over to adjust a strap on her yasmir's bridle.

Frowning at his sister, he said, "I don't recall you being a cheerful soul early in the morning either." He pounded a bedroll down firmly on the yasmirs rump.

"Is Serena ready to go?"

"Humm, as soon as she finishes visiting mother-nature." They both turned as Serena came out from behind some trees. She looked wan and sad. Kasha walked back to where she stood as if indecisive, staring at the ground. The princess began to briskly gather the last of their supplies, Serena pitched in, and they soon made short work of that task.

They all regrouped as they had the day before, Serena riding in front of Rhamus, sagging in his arms again from her sleepless night. It didn't seem very long before they approached a charming cottage and Jarvic left to get the colt. He paid the kindly old couple a small bag of coins, while a lovely young girl peered around the barn door at the handsome warrior carrying the frisky young yasmir. Ulecki said goodbye and headed for a cottage in the distance.

Serena could feel Rhamus' impatience to get home, so she didn't request that Jarvic bring the colt over to get a better look at the wondrous little animal. Jarvic struggled with the furry baby yasmir, seeking to secure it in front of him. He finally had to tie its front feet together, then its back ones to each other, and hang it over the steed's broad back. The colt seemed to finally realize it couldn't move and that it rested on a relatively comfortable place. It settled down and nosed the fur of Jarvic's stallion, probably gaining comfort from the familiar smell.

She kept nodding off, repeating yesterday's behavior. She glanced around in surprise when an increased volume of noise entered into her light cat-nap. They were back at the castle and a huge crowd of people were running to meet them. The two suns were barely visible above the tree line, making her realize it'd taken much longer than she'd first guessed to reach home.

Serena fell gratefully into Jarvic's arms as he helped her off the yasmir. She was transferred to Rhamus' arms and sank into a deep sleep immediately, as if reaching their safe haven had released the last of her strength.

She awoke to see Surad and Lalme hovering nearby. She smiled to reassure them. It was really good to see familiar faces.

"We've been so worried about you, my dear." Surad smoothed a hair near her cheek.

"You've been out for hours, Your Majesty," Lalme held out a tray with choice selections of flaky pastries stuffed with ground auk, mixed with tender vegetables. It was one of her favorite quick lunch treats. "I bet you're famished too."

The older woman helped prop her up against many pillows. "I'm not an invalid. I could get up and sit over there." She pointed to her chair.

"No. Rhamus ordered that you aren't to get out of this bed until Dr. Melat has a chance to check you out thoroughly," Surad said with a firm tone.

"Where's Doc then?"

Lalme giggled and Surad gave her a look before she answered.

"He's waiting right outside the door."

"Chomping at the bit, you might say." Lalme grinned.

"Clean up these dishes while I help Serena get freshened up."

"Yes, grandmama," the girl responded sweetly.

"Lalme's your great granddaughter?" She knew that the term "grandmama" was used to indicate the mother of a Volarnian's grandmother.

"I thought you knew." Surad brought a pan of warm water and crespassno soap and sat next to the bed. She handed Serena a cloth. "Only those who are connected directly with the royal line may serve the King and his family."

She scrubbed the dirt from her face, and then asked, "Where is everybody?"

"Kasha has taken out a patrol to retrieve the guard's bodies. Rhamus sent out messengers to our border patrols, to see if any other soldiers were ambushed and killed. And he's probably trying to figure out who else was involved in this kidnapping." While she talked, Surad selected a pale blue dress for Serena to slip on after she finished her pan bath.

"What do you mean?"

"It's pretty obvious that Xarath knew Kasha's plans for a ride and that you went with her."

"I can't imagine Kasha telling anyone her plans. She tried to make it all look like an accidental thing, anyway."

Surad shook her head understandingly. "That's how Kasha makes her apologies, something that looks spontaneous, but was really thought out before hand."

"Then how would someone be able to find out, unless they hung around the stables keeping an eye on Kasha," Serena said, then shook her head. "That doesn't make sense. They'd have to watch her all the time and how would they know she planned on asking me to ride with her?"

"I don't know, unless whoever was spying for Xarath just happened to get lucky and noticed you two going out."

"But how would this *spy* contact Xarath so quickly?"

They both looked stumped then Lalme wandered over. "Maybe the spy was already planning a meeting with our enemy, and an opportunity just presented itself when the traitor saw you two leaving."

"It seems too coincidental to be real." Serena looked thoughtful. "But, you know, I did see someone slipping into the woods when we were leaving." Suddenly, her expression hardened in concentration. "Xarath said a woman betrayed me. Unfortunately he didn't name her."

"You must tell Rhamus," Surad said.

A loud rapping interrupted them and they all turned as the door opened cautiously. Lalme giggled as Dr. Melat's worried face appeared around the door frame.

Surad and Lalme left only after the doctor ordered them out. Dr. Melat began at her ears and then carefully worked his way down. He checked all her vital signs with small, unfamiliar instruments and even listened to her stomach with a round disc held to his ear. Although he fussed at her for not eating enough and commented on other aspects of her behavior that should be improved for the baby's health, he had a warm bedside manner that soon put her at ease.

"You're in pretty good shape for someone who has just been through a kidnapping. Now tell me, what caused these acid-type burns all over your legs?"

"Thanks, doctor. The baby's fine too?"

"I can see you don't wish to discuss the burns right now. But, you must promise to tell me tomorrow when you feel better." He waited until she shook her head in agreement. "Here's some salve for the burns." He handed her a small jar.

"As far as the baby, it's fine. No signs of stress, although I think you ought to take it easy for a few days, Your Majesty."

Neither saw Rhamus enter the room but turned upon hearing his footsteps. "How is she, doctor?"

"She seems fine but--"

Serena quickly interrupted, "The baby's fine, too and that's the most important thing, isn't it doctor?"

With a questioning look at Serena, Dr. Melat said thoughtfully, "Remember, both of you, that an ordeal such as this asks an emotional price, as well. I have a feeling your symptoms have not all been revealed."

"I'll see that she stays in bed a few days," he said.

"No need for such drastic measures." Dr. Melat chuckled. "Just as long as she doesn't go galloping about the countryside the next few days, and gets some rest."

After they both thanked the doctor again, there was an uncomfortable silence that filled the room. Rhamus walked slowly to the foot of the bed. "I will be out a lot the next couple of days checking on matters. I wanted to see for myself that you and the baby are fine."

He looked her over in a quick unreadable fashion and turned to leave. "Wait! Are we going to talk tonight?"

Rhamus turned slightly and spoke over his shoulder. "I will be sleeping in the barracks tonight. We'll talk after you've rested."

He strode briskly out the door before she could say a word. Serena sat in stunned silence. She felt abandoned. *He was going to sleep in the barracks!* For a few moments she sat and wept in self-pity. After this emotion swept through her, she wiped her tears away quickly, replacing pity with anger.

Let him go. She got up cautiously and felt a little weak, but otherwise normal. After going to the bathroom, she curled up in her favorite chair and thought about her situation. She remembered Kasha's description of the barracks. A large room lined with small, hard beds and austere surroundings. Go ahead and cool your heels amongst your fellow warriors, she thought. Eyeing the large, comfortable bed, Serena thought Rhamus would be the first to want the comforts of their bed, and maybe even her arms.

She spent an uneventful and quiet evening with Surad and Nuad who came to visit. Doc was limiting her visitors strictly. He wouldn't allow Nicole to visit her until the next day, saying when she asked earlier that Nicole would be too excitable a presence for her right now. Serena found soon after sleep gripped her in its dark arms, that she'd been wrong. It was she who needed the comfort of Rhamus' arms around her.

She woke screaming in the middle of the night, not remembering her dream, but making a good guess what it entailed. Surad was summoned by the guard, and although Serena argued with the elderly lady that she was OK, she refused to leave. She spent the night on a single bed brought in by a servant. After she awoke two more times in a cold sweat, her heart pounding furiously, she was glad for Surad's comforting presence.

Nicole's visit brightened the next day considerably. Of course, her inquisitive friend wanted to know all the details of her capture, but Serena was not up to that yet. She managed to generalize the events and turn the topic of conversation to Nicole and Doc. The two had finally become lovers and Dr. Melat was becoming more enchanted with Nicole.

* * * *

After her friend left, Serena felt cooped up in the bedroom and was happy when Kasha stopped for a visit. When she questioned her, the princess gave her a sketchy summary of her duties in retrieving the guard's bodies, probably not wanting to upset her.

"What's up with my hard headed brother?" Serena turned to look out the window, but Kasha plunged ahead anyway. "I heard he spent the night in the barracks."

"It's true," she turned back to face her visitor, wondering how to fend off the sharp mind hiding behind those lovely violet eyes. "Rhamus said he had a lot of things to take care of, in regard to the kidnapping."

"Hmm, that's true. But, there's no reason why my dear brother had to sleep in the barracks, other than him cooling off that terrible temper of his."

"Maybe it's for the best then," she shrugged noncommittally.

"You aren't going to tell me a thing are you?" Kasha grinned and patted Serena's hand lying on her lap. "That's understandable. All of the basami clan are a closed mouth group. But I can see that you and Rhamus need to talk. I'll speak to him."

"Kasha!"

"No, no, I insist." At her stubborn look, the princess crossed her arms and said, "I know about your nightmares. It's not good for you to be by yourself right now. And aunt Surad is too old to be sleeping on a child's bed. Rhamus should be here."

"I have a feeling you're as stubborn as my husband," Serena said in exasperation.

"More," she smiled. "Well, there's still lots of work to do. I'd better be going."

"Kasha."

"Yes?" She paused by the door.

"Don't be too hard on him." Her grin didn't make Serena feel any assurance. If Rhamus "came around" in his thinking she didn't want it to be due to having it knocked through his thick skull.

She frittered the rest of the afternoon away catnapping in her chair and snacking. She had just come from freshening herself in the bathroom when Rhamus walked in.

"How are you feeling?"

"Good." Serena again sat in her chair, feeling comfort in its solid lines.

"I heard you've been having nightmares."

She shrugged. "Is that all you came here for, to ask how I've been sleeping?"

Rhamus strode within a few paces from her, his lips a flat line held within a stiffened jaw-line. "I think you know Kasha and several other relatives have been by to hound me for neglecting my

Queen."

"I only knew about Kasha, and I asked her not to interfere."

"That's like asking the wind to stop blowing," Rhamus said unconsciously rubbing his head. "Kasha has a way of getting one's attention, even if she has to knock you in the head to get it."

"She hit you!" Serena tried to sound contrite, but couldn't help a slight giggle from escaping.

Rhamus frowned. "Besides whacking me on my head with a stick, I think she and Jarvic conspired with my warriors last night." At her questioning look, he said, "I've never heard so many loud snores as last night, and most of them came from Jarvic and his friends."

Now Serena laughed freely and Rhamus grinned back. They both stopped in the middle of their mirth and stared at one another. He sat in his chair across from her.

"Tell me what happened from the time you and Kasha left the stable. I've heard her version already."

"OK." She didn't get far into her story before Rhamus stopped her and asked questions about the woman she'd seen near the woods.

"It's probably as you guessed, a woman on the way to meet a lover. But we'll check it out to be safe."

But her next words concerning what Xarath had said to her caused him to curse profusely. He finally waved her to finish the story, staring with a hard look at the stones in front of him.

He stopped her again when she told him about being knocked unconscious by a branch. "Did Dr. Melat check out your head?"

"Yes, Rhamus. I told Doc about my head and he said everything was fine. I guess we're both hard-headed." Serena's attempt at humor fell flat. Rhamus simply asked her to continue with her story.

From this point on, her telling became harder, partly because her memory was so fuzzy up until Xarath's first attempt at seduction. Then, it was difficult to actually say aloud what Xarath had done to her. She didn't really understand it, and besides it was embarrassing. When Rhamus didn't say a word, simply sat and stared at her, Serena plunged ahead, wanting to get through with it as best she could. She verbally stumbled over some parts concerning the dungeon and the quamus, but managed to convey the whole story in spite of the fear that was reawakened.

"When you tell a story, you really tell a story."

"What do you mean?"

He jumped to his feet, showing the first signs of life since she'd started the difficult part of her story. "You expect me to believe such an obvious lie?"

Chapter Twenty

"I'm not lying." Serena's voice rose shrilly in anger and she jumped up too.

"Then tell me this," he stood rigid, hands clasped behind his back. "How could Xarath use the dark power of the crystal, a thing which hasn't been done since my great great grandfather's time, and then only by a powerful vassi?"

His voice rose as he stepped nearer, causing her to unconsciously take a defensive step backward.

"And what is this 'quamus', a creature from your own planet? *We* have no such monster on Volarn. Besides, we checked the dungeon when we were there and saw nothing but empty cells." Rhamus emphasized his words even as his voice boomed between the stone walls.

"Did you look into every one?"

"We made a quick check, there was *nothing*."

"Then you didn't search thoroughly," Serena's body was stiff in defiance. "And we don't have monsters like that on Earth either," she shouted back.

"Then you must have imagined it."

"Imagined these burns on my legs?" She pointed to the dark red splotches splattered along both limbs. "Instead of disbelieving everything I try to tell you, why don't you use that brilliant brain of yours to try and figure out where the quamus came from?" Her voice trembled with anger.

"I didn't know about your injuries," Rhamus took a step forward, but her angry look stopped him. "Maybe Xarath caused those," he waved to her burns, "and you don't remember because of your head injury."

"No!"

"Well your 'quamus' is impossible. I told you, there's no such creature on Volarn. And, it is forbidden for any animal to be imported. We don't want to disturb the delicate balance of animal and plant life here."

"Well, maybe you'd better start checking more closely on recent shipments? And how do you know what Xarath gets shipped in? That man was *evil*! I saw it. I felt it."

"I know just how evil he was." A nerve jumped in Rhamus' jaw.

"As far as shipments, that's one of the duties of the ambassadors and his aides, to check on shipments being received by the enemy."

"How can you be sure Xarath didn't slip illegal shipments past your ambassador? Or that your ambassador wasn't bought off?"

"I think you're grasping at straws," he said smoothly. "And how I am supposed to explain away Xarath's abilities with the dark power?"

"Why don't you think up an explanation? Why does it have to be me? It's your planet."

"Suppose I could come up with an explanation for both of these unbelievable events."

"So you're willing to concede there might be an explanation."

"I'm not willing to concede any point. But if either could be explained away, how do you explain you having sex with Xarath?"

"How dare you!" Her whole body trembled. "I told you what happened, how ... how I was forced to be in that situation. And I ... he did not have sex with me, he was starting to when you entered the room."

"That explains everything perfectly." Rhamus' voice dripped sarcasm.

"Shut up!" Serena screamed. Tears shimmered in her eyes as she visibly tried to get control of herself. "I think the best thing is for you to leave right now. You're upsetting me far too much with your insensitive stubbornness."

"Insensitive? I think I've been very understanding, considering the circumstances."

She walked a few paces away and turned back to face him. "It's true, you didn't walk into the best of 'circumstances', and you had a right to be angry at first. But, you should listen to what I'm telling you and try to understand what I've been through."

She lost the ability to hold her tears back as pain lanced through her. "Stupid me! I thought you would understand, would welcome me with open arms and hold me." Serena had to stop when the hurt overcame her and she was on the point of bawling like a baby.

"Don't cry. I know you've been through a lot. I just don't understand how you could have been on the point of letting Xarath--"

Serena cut off his remark, her disgust slicing through her hurt. "He was a worse monster than the quamus." She looked at Rhamus' face, seeing the anger and confusion reflected there only refueled her own anger. "I can see that you'll never understand how I was forced into my situation, because you don't even believe it was possible."

"Xarath was not the man you are. He had a twisted set of rules. He could think of no better way to destroy you than to destroy me. I see he is the victor, even in death." She turned her back on him. "I think it's time for you to go back to your buddies in the barracks."

* * * *

Rhamus surprised his warriors when he made his appearance in the barracks for a second night. He said not a word to anyone, simply made his bed efficiently and fell into it exhausted. He was too angry to speak to anyone and lay on the hard bed for hours rethinking what Serena had told him. Try as he might, every explanation he came up with fell short of reason and was rejected by his logical side.

Take this creature, this "quamus". How could this be? They searched the castle and saw no sign. Still, there was that putrid smell in the dungeon. Perhaps there was a secret chamber. And Xarath's power. By Serena's description, it sounded like he used the dark power, but how? Yet, Serena would have no way of knowing how to describe such a use. Still, she had.

He couldn't totally ignore his emotional self, the one that whispered to take Serena's word as fact and worry about explanations later. Finally, he realized one part of the reason for his intense jealousy. He was not totally sure of her love. She'd never said the words, words he knew were important to humans. He'd taken her actions as proof. Now, this incident with Xarath had pushed his small uncertainty into a huge festering fear.

This turmoil caused him hours of tossing and turning on the small bed, and the resulting creaking of the springs caused much grumbling from warriors trying to sleep around him.

Finally, disgusted at his inability to sleep or stop thinking about Serena, Rhamus got up and left the barracks. He stopped outside his bedroom door, ignoring the guard who eyed him curiously. He wasn't sure what he wanted to say to his wife, only that he wanted to understand. His quest for understanding only seemed to lead to more questions.

He was on the point of tapping softly on the door to alert aunt Surad to his presence when he heard a shrill scream through the thick door.

"That's the third one tonight," the guard said impertinently.

Rhamus gave the young warrior a stern look before opening the door. Everyone in this castle seemed intent on making him feel like a culprit. He found Surad sitting on the edge of his bed holding Serena gently in her arms. "I'll take over, aunt. You go back to your own bed. And thanks for your help."

"Are you sure?" Surad examined her great nephew's features. "She needs an understanding, caring touch."

"I may not be as 'understanding' as everyone wishes me to be, but I do care about Serena." He kissed his aunt on the forehead and urged her to leave. He replaced Surad's arms with his own, and felt strangely touched when Serena's arms went about his waist. She laid her head on his chest as if trying to hide from something, but he had a feeling it wasn't from him.

"Did you mean it?"

Her softly spoken words were almost lost against his shirt. The feel of her warm breath through the silk made his heart beat a little faster in response. Trying to fight the rising heat that their entwined bodies created, Rhamus almost blurted out a hurtful retraction. But this was not the time for vindictiveness and neither was it a part of his nature to be so. "I meant it," he whispered into her hair. Placing his hand on her head and stroking softly, he said, "Go to sleep."

It didn't take long before Rhamus heard Serena's deep breathing, signaling she'd fallen asleep. He laid her gently on the bed and covered her. He eyed the bed set up next to theirs as he disrobed. Grimacing at the thought of another small sleeping space, He got cautiously into bed beside Serena. He had not moved her from the middle of the bed where she rested, not wanting to chance awakening her again.

So, he lay on the far side of the bed. As the comfort of the bed began to make him feel drowsy, Serena rolled over and snuggled up against his side. Sighing, he placed one arm around her, pulling her closer. His eyes became heavy as he fought sleep a few moments longer, trying to think what it was he would say to her the morrow. A warm contented feeling pulled rational thought from him as his body succumbed to a dreamless state of rest.

A scream seemed to erupt in his head as Rhamus aroused himself swiftly, and he realized it was his wife screaming in his ear. As had happened while on the yasmirs traveling home, she seemed to be caught in the middle of a nightmare and it took him a minute to shake her awake. Her mumbling about a dungeon and quamus sent a shaft of unrest into his heart.

This time Serena didn't awaken fully but quieted quickly and nestled back into his arms. It took him longer to fall asleep this time, his mind full of questions at the horror his wife kept reliving. As if sensing his protective presence, she slept the rest of the night peacefully.

Rhamus awakened before Serena and looked down at her face. He was shocked at the dark circles beneath her eyes. Those lovely blue eyes opened and, before she seemed completely aware of her surroundings, held a haunting look of fright. The next instant, she blinked and stared back at him with a questioning gaze. That fleeting look in her eyes made his decision for him.

Untangling himself from her arms, he arose to get dressed. "How are you feeling this morning?"

"Tired." Serena sat up with the sheet tucked modestly around her.

Even with her drawn face and wildly tousled hair, her beauty couldn't hide from his observant look. "I will be going on a short trip, perhaps two to three days. I need to check on the patrols close to the borders."

"You don't have to explain your actions to me." She turned to look out the window at a sooeul, which perched on the balcony and serenaded them with morning chirping.

"No, as the King I don't have to--but as your husband I think it only *sensitive*." He couldn't seem to stop himself from making that last remark and could have kicked himself when a tear trickled down Serena's face.

Rhamus walked around the bed and stood in front of her. "I'm sorry."

"For what?" She straightened the sheet lying over her legs, trying to act as if nothing had happened.

"For being an insensitive brute." He sat on the bed next to her. "Are you going to be all right while I'm gone?"

"Sure. I think I will get out of this room today and do some visiting."

"I agree. You've been cooped up inside this room for two days. I think even that will satisfy the good doctor." He looked at her downcast head and was afraid to kiss her. She might not be receptive to him.

"Rhamus, what will happen now that Xarath's dead? Will his people retaliate?"

"We can't be certain, that's one reason I'm going to check on my troops. But in reality, Xarath was not well liked by his people. He was a hard king and changed some ancient yet popular traditions. He won much disfavor for this."

"Like pushing his warriors to kill instead of honor fighting?"

"Exactly."

Serena looked at him, her eyes large with worry. "What about the killings that were done during my rescue?"

"That couldn't be helped. Xarath's personal guard would call no quarter." He looked down a moment in thought. "And, I was not ready to give them that opportunity."

"It's my fault," her voice sounded teary.

"No, it's not your fault you were kidnapped." He reached out one hand as if to touch her, but withdrew it. "If not this time, Xarath would have thought up some other scheme to push things."

"What about the bloodshed?"

Rhamus shrugged. "If the roles were reversed, I'm sure they would have done the same."

Serena didn't feel very convinced, but decided to pursue another thought. "How will the western people choose a new king? I didn't get the impression Xarath was married."

"You're right, he wasn't married, nor had any children. But, he does have two brothers whom I'm worried about." At Serena's prompting look, he continued.

"There's not a lot of information on them because Xarath kept one overseeing a fortress on his northern border near the wastelands, and the other with a fortress on his far southern border. Some reports have been passed that the older brother who would be next in line to inherit the throne is crazy."

"And the younger brother?"

"He is still very young, but it is said he's already a barbarian."

They both seemed at a loss for words and Rhamus got up to leave. He paused at the door, not sure what to say, then inanely said. "Take care of yourself." His last look took in her mixed expression of puzzlement and pleasure at his remark.

He'd awakened even earlier than his usual time, feeling anxious to be gone once he'd made up his mind. It gave him no small satisfaction to catch his warriors still abed. He stood next to Jarvic's peacefully sleeping boyish face and clanged his sword several times hard against the metal headboard.

"What the--" Jarvic sat up quickly and looked up at his cousin towering over him.

"Pick three of your best men and meet me at the stables in ten minutes."

"It's about time you came around," he grinned.

Placing his booted foot on his cousin's chest, Rhamus asked, "Does everyone in this whole castle know my business?"

Jarvic chuckled. "You should know the answer to that cousin. Our servants have the best grapevine in the kingdom. Word's out that you're being a pig-headed--" Seeing the king's lowering brows, he said, "But everyone doesn't know the whole story. In fact, I don't even know the whole story and I was there. Care to share the details?"

He removed his foot and replaced it with Jarvic's discarded pants, which lay nearby. "Get dressed and shut that pretty mouth of yours."

Chuckles arose around them at the king's reference to Jarvic's looks. He'd often teased Jarvic that his looks were too pretty for a man. The two had gotten into many scuffles while growing up, and picking on his cousin's looks was one way Rhamus knew to get him upset.

"I'm not looking for a fight today," Jarvic grumbled.

"You may get one anyway, but not with me."

Jarvic jumped to his feet and brushed at his pants and shirt. "Would you do me a favor? Next time you want to hold me down with your boot, watch where you put your foot first." His nose curled as he sniffed his clothes. "I have to get clean clothes now. I can't go anywhere smelling like yasmir droppings."

Laughter erupted around Jarvic and he yelled for his men to get ready. Rhamus grinned. "Where we're going, I don't think you'll need to worry about smelling good."

Jarvic exchanged a silent look with his cousin, one of understanding and agreement.

They rode at a steady pace all day, stopping to refresh their yasmirs when needed. The small group of warriors ate handfuls of rations while their steeds took a break. They had no time for a good meal until nightfall.

They followed the same trail they'd come down when returning from Xarath's fortress. Rhamus wasn't too worried about an ambush. He'd received reports that Xarath's people were confused and his nobility quarreling amongst themselves. He doubted they would post sentries along this trail, and he wouldn't be surprised if the old fortress hadn't been abandoned completely. He certainly hoped so.

Xarath had been the only one who had shown interest in the ancient ruins because of its proximity to his lands, but no one else had any interest in its crumbling walls.

After nightfall, they pressed ahead at a slower pace using lanterns to light the trail. This was a dangerous, reckless way to proceed and Jarvic tried to persuade Rhamus to stop several times. He only listened with half an ear to his cousin's reasoning, his concentration centered ahead of his yasmir so as not to lose the faint path in the dark. After many hours, he called a halt and ordered the three warriors to rotate watch. Jarvic looked surprised, but then seemed to realize he was saving their strength for something more important.

Daylight crept into the small glade where they slept after only a few hours rest. Rhamus once again pressed them forward, but at a harder pace. It was but another few hours before they reached the edge of the woods and spied the ruined fortress in the distance. The three warriors scouted ahead, but returned with reports of seeing no movement of any kind around the walls. They approached cautiously anyway and found the gate gaping open as if someone had left in a hurry and didn't bother closing it.

After they'd returned home with Serena, he'd sent a message to another outlying post nearby, letting his enemy know where to find the body of their king. A patrol would have already removed Xarath and the other warrior's bodies, and taken them back to the town of their birth for the ritual burning.

As they quietly entered through the gate and found no one, Rhamus again reacted with a shiver to the psychic vibrations that emitted from the very air around them. Out of the corner of his eye, he saw Jarvic look uncomfortable. The strong psychic abilities of many of the Volarnian people would cause most trained warriors to avoid walking into such a charged environment.

The feeling in the atmosphere and from the stones themselves, were of dark things better left undisturbed. A feeling persisted as though ghosts walked those dank hallways, or evil had been let loose and soaked the damp walls with its dark force. Rhamus knew from his spies that, in the past, Xarath sent soldiers to this fortress for punishment. He'd also been known to frequent the ancient place for his own secret purposes.

The small group of warriors had traversed the courtyard and stood inside the great hall. It was empty of furniture or any signs that anyone had ever occupied its premises. Their footsteps echoed hollowly, as if imaginary ghosts were treading softly behind them.

Rhamus split the soldiers up, keeping Jarvic with him. He didn't pause to peer inside any doors, walking swiftly down the dark halls looking for a particular door, the peculiarly thick door of the dungeon. He wished now that he'd checked this area more thoroughly on their first visit. Their enemies had free access to the fortress in the days since Xarath's death. What could they still hope to find?

He paused in front of the overly large, heavy door. The light from the lantern Jarvic held showed a steep spiral stair leading down. Taking the lantern from Jarvic and holding it up high to light the darkness, it felt as though he was stepping into a bottomless pit. Rhamus trod carefully down the narrow flight of long stairs and Jarvic followed a few steps behind, each watching where they set their feet on the slippery stones.

At the end of the stairs was another huge door, set with an old rusty lock. Strangely, it was still locked shut, as if their enemy had wanted to keep something secure inside. Rhamus felt a flash of foreboding. He took a mental grip on the psychic vibrations that had not let go of him since entering this ruined place.

This was the very reason the people of Volarn still could not retake the wastelands for their own. Not because the dark power had left the countryside in complete ruination, but because the people's psychic abilities would not allow them into the ancient destroyed cities. They would feel and hear the ghosts that haunted the old places.

Jarvic seemed to sense his dilemma. He nudged in front of Rhamus and hacked at the lock with a small hand ax he pulled from his belt.

"Not the usual weapon for a warrior," he observed with wry humor.

Grinning as the lock gave, Jarvic said, "No, but I remember the dungeon you threw me into that time you got mad at me when we were youngsters. These old locks are nearly impossible to pick open."

"I remember," he chuckled. Rhamus' father had caught his son in the act and had thrown him in the cell with Jarvic, so both hot heads could cool their tempers in the cold dungeon for an hour. After arguing and shivering for a few minutes, they had both tried their luck at picking the lock with the short daggers in their belts with no result.

They walked together into the pitch black hole that looked and smelled like the gateway of jahum. Proceeding cautiously, they stopped to shine the lantern in every cell, every space, every gaping hole in the rock wall. A few doors had to be hacked open for them to look inside, but luckily most had metal bars, which they could peer through.

"Exactly what is it we're looking for?" Jarvic's voice echoed eerily.

"You'll know if we find it."

Rhamus stopped in front of a solid, strong door from whence a terribly foul odor arose. He pushed the lantern through the metal bars and lit the interior to dull gray shadows dancing from the reflected light. When he started to retract his hand, Jarvic stopped him.

"Shine it over in that far corner." Jarvic pointed.

They both saw another door when he redirected the lantern. Sighing, Jarvic again hefted his ax. It took them a little more work to get past the heavy lock. Rhamus almost wished they hadn't succeeded when the door creaked open and the fetid air hit them full force.

"Pugh! What did they do, dump all their refuse down here?" Jarvic withdrew a perfumed handkerchief and placed it on his nose. Seeing Rhamus' look, he said archly, "A souvenir from one of my lady friends."

"That's a relief."

Digging under his shirt, he said, "I think I may have another one if you want to borrow it."

"No!" Rhamus held up a hand and grimaced. "I can take this smell better than the strong perfume some of your 'friends' wear."

"Suit yourself," he shrugged.

Rhamus paused in the center of the cell, feeling his heart beat heavier when he noted a post just as Serena had described, with manacles attached. He jerked the ax from Jarvic and attacked the other door with fury. Jarvic's handkerchief went flashing back to his nose after they manhandled the metal door open. Rhamus noticed a chain system and following it with his eyes, saw the wheel at the other side of the room which would have easily opened the door.

Seeing the same thing, Jarvic said. "You always did like to do things the hard way."

"And you never know when to shut up."

Directing the light past the doorway, they saw a roughly hewn tunnel carved from solid rock, which lined the back of the cell.

"I've never seen anything like this before," Jarvic said. "What do you suppose they kept down there?" He inclined his head toward the blackness beyond the lantern light.

"Come on and we'll find out."

"I was afraid you were going to say that."

After taking a few steps, Rhamus paused when his foot crunched on something. Looking down, he saw a *nysk* skeleton, completely denuded of flesh and fur. Holding the light a little higher, he was able to see a scattered profusion of small white skeletons a few feet ahead.

"Look at that bone."

He swung the light toward where Jarvic pointed. It picked up the white outlines of what looked like a Volarnian thigh bone. A high-pitched shrilling scream suddenly sprang from the darkness further down the tunnel. Rhamus' hair on the back of his neck rose up and Jarvic dropped his handkerchief. It floated gracefully down and landed on a nysk skeleton, covering it like a shroud.

"You still don't want to go down there, do you?" Jarvic couldn't keep the sarcasm from his voice.

"No, the quarters are too close here. Start backing up slowly."

Whatever screamed from the tunnel's other end apparently heard their retreat or had very acute sight because, as they slowly stepped backwards, a slithering, scratchy sound approached from the yawning pit of darkness.

Quickly now, they backed up and took positions side by side in the center of the cell. Rhamus felt an acrid sickness well up in his stomach, not because of the fear of an unknown adversary, but because he knew what was coming up that tunnel toward them. And the pain of that realization almost overwhelmed him with feelings of remorse and guilt.

The beast holed up down the black tunnel had been subsisting on the small nysks, which infested the dungeon since its keepers had left the premises. It must be ravenous. As the quamus made its appearance into the room, fouling the very air with its loathsome odor and presence, a red-hot anger overtook Rhamus.

This was what his beloved wife faced all alone and defenseless. He felt no fear, only a need to hack the disgusting creature into a million pieces. Blue light glowed eerily in the dark cell as both he and Jarvic tapped into the crystal's power. A warrior's yell rose from his throat as he sprang forward, sword raised, Jarvic right beside him.

Chapter Twenty One

Serena spent day after day being welcomed by, it seemed, everyone in the castle. From servants to warriors and nobles, they all appeared joyous at her safe return. She found herself sneaking more than once to the bathroom to wipe the away tears that her people's enthusiasm evoked. Serena put the blame on her pregnancy moods and tried not to think how sad it was that Rhamus was the only one who had not reacted so to her.

Well, Rhamus and Szafra. Of course, Serena wouldn't expect her husband's former lover to welcome her with open arms, but neither did she expect the angry looks the dancer threw her when they accidentally passed in the hall.

The other women from Earth were very excited by her safe return. Even Olga gave her a firm pat on the shoulder. Shy Heather said, "We're so glad you're back with us. I don't know about everyone else, but I really missed our meeting, and your support." Several other women standing around them joined in agreement.

"Thanks," she put an arm around the girl's shoulders.

"They finally let you out!" Nicole joined the group.

Serena laughed. "I wasn't exactly in jail, but it does feel good to be out of that bedroom."

Kasha came strolling up and the other women soon left, feeling uncomfortable with the looks the princess cast them. "I don't know how you can stand those cackling elags."

"Just because other women aren't warriors, doesn't mean they're useless gossips."

"That's right," Nicole said, challenging Kasha with her gaze.

The princess grinned at the little woman. "I didn't mean you. You fulfill a needed occupation, and besides you have the spirit of the sooeul."

"I still don't know if I like being called a little lizard."

A warrior ran up and whispered in Kasha's ear, then left running again. "Rhamus and the others are on their way in. I'm going to meet him." She left at a jog, heading for the stables.

"What are you going to do?" Nicole asked, aware that Serena was very hurt by Rhamus, although still not sure of the details.

"I'm not going to meet him, nor be waiting like an obedient wife when he comes home." She glanced toward the woods and then turned back toward the castle. "I'm simply going to go about my everyday duties. Let him be the one to make the first move."

Later, Serena was enjoying a few moments of peaceful solitude as she picked some flowers to take to Surad, who wasn't feeling well. A flurry of activity moved from the stables to the back entrance of the castle. The King's in his castle, Serena thought with a touch of humor.

She had placed Surad's flowers in a lovely crystal vase next to her bed and sat talking quietly with the older woman. Surad looked tired but was happy to tell Serena little tidbits about motherhood. As she was leaving Surad's room later, a warrior ran up to her.

"The King asks that you join him in the royal suite in about fifteen minutes."

"Why fifteen minutes?"

"His majesty wants to make himself presentable first."

As she turned to go about another errand, Serena wondered why Rhamus even bothered getting cleaned up for her. Their last few days together he certainly had not tried to please her in any manner.

Thirty minutes later, Serena entered their bedroom and found her husband standing with hands clasped behind his back, staring out the window. He turned and walked toward her. He looked exhausted.

"Have you been well?"

"Yes," she answered almost cautiously, surprised by the gentle tone of his voice and sad look in his eyes. "Was your trip successful?"

Rhamus took a few seconds before answering, as if weighing his response. "Very." He looked at her strangely and then said, "Serena, I am not an unforgiving man, except when it comes to my own actions. I think ... hope ... that you are as forgiving in nature as you've shown me so far."

"What are you trying to say?"

He walked within arms length from her. "I'm asking you to forgive me for not believing you."

She was totally confused. He went on a three-day patrol and came back all contrite, as if he believed everything she'd been trying to tell him? She looked past her husband, not wanting to see the pleading look in his eyes. *How had he come to that decision?* Her eyes were drawn to a lumpy heap near the bathroom-Rhamus' discarded clothes lay in a pile on the floor. He never left his clothes lying around, not even dirty ones.

She walked quickly around Rhamus. Before she even reached the clothes, she could smell the stench coming from them. Serena stopped and looked down at the foul greenish mucous, which covered much of the material. A wave of nausea and dizziness passed over her. She spun around, almost bumping into her husband, who had come up behind her.

"You know," she gasped, fighting for control. She backed away a few steps, anger making her eyes flash blue fire. She pointed to the heap of clothes. "That's why you're ready to apologize. You found the quamus!"

"Found it and killed it."

"So, you couldn't take my word but had to have proof."

Rhamus took one step toward her and held out one hand as if to touch her, but dropped it when she flinched back. "I know, now, that I should have believed you. But by the sacred crystal, Serena, you must also consider how hard it was for me to believe such a story."

"And I guess you found 'proof' concerning Xarath's use of this dark power too?" She asked sarcastically.

"No," he shook his head. "The monster was there just as you described, therefore I must accept the truth of Xarath's use of the dark power too." He didn't want to tell her of the psychic vibrations leaking from the fortress, those of dark forces and the evil Xarath would have had to perpetrate in order to saturate the stones with such dark presence. He'd been too angry the first time to notice any vibrations.

"Now, you are ready to concede that I had no choice?"

Stepping closer, Rhamus grasped Serena's arms, ignoring her attempt to jerk away. "I wish to Goreth I could go back in time and throw Xarath in with his beast, and let him get a taste of what he did to you. It sickens me when I think of that ... thing touching you." His face did look flushed and ill.

She didn't know if Rhamus meant the quamus or Xarath. Maybe the thought of either of them touching her made him sick. "So, it will probably make you sick every time you touch me from now on."

"I am touching you now," he placed slight pressure where he gripped her arms. Suddenly he went down on one knee and slid his hands down her arms until he held a hand in either of his. "I am the King of my lands, proud and stubborn. And I'm on my knees to you, my Queen, to ask your forgiveness."

"There've been a lot of hurtful things said between us."

Placing his cheek against her hands, he said, "I cannot live like this, thinking that you hate me now."

"I don't hate you, Rhamus."

He looked up with regret in his eyes. "Then love me, Serena. Love me enough to forgive me." He looked down and his voice cracked, "When I think of what was done to you, that I was not there to protect you, and that I could have lost you--I hate myself."

"No," she said as she withdrew one hand and pulled his chin up. "There've been enough bad feelings. Somehow, we must put this behind us. You are a King and must see to your people, and I have my obligations also."

"You were a queen before I ever chose you, my jicha."

His face was so beautiful, filled with the love that he openly showed her now. Serena couldn't resist the pull she felt between them. She clasped his head against her waist and then slid gracefully to her knees. Rhamus arms went about her waist, pulling her next to him. She had a hard time keeping her tears from falling, so great had been her need to be held by him.

His kiss was light, gentle and she found herself leaning towards him. He picked her up, holding her close so they could continue their kiss. They stretched out on the bed, their lips deepening their pressure now, causing him to groan. Serena felt breathless as fire ran through her veins.

Then Rhamus' hand slipped inside her dress, pressing her breasts hard in his excitement. At that contact, Serena felt a great fear well up inside and queasiness in her stomach. Suddenly, her breath became shallow as feelings of fright overcame her. He loomed over her, she knew this within her mind, yet it was Xarath's leering features she saw. Serena screamed and threw him from her.

"What is it, did I hurt you?"

"No," she choked back tears. "It's not you. I don't know what happened ... I ... suddenly I saw Xarath instead of you."

Rhamus brushed her hair from her face with his hand. "You've been through a lot. I guess it's natural that it will take some time to get over your fears."

She sniffed like a little child. "Can you just hold me?" And he did, continuing his soothing touch by petting her hair. After a while, Serena found herself drifting off to sleep and felt very contented and safe.

Rhamus was gone when she awoke, but he reappeared as she dressed for dinner. He escorted her to the dining hall where she was greeted warmly by everybody. They had a very pleasant time, but she was tired by the evening's end and was glad to retire to the royal suite.

He did not attempt to make love to her again, simply holding her in his arms until she fell asleep. As had been happening every night since her return, Serena awoke several times during the night screaming or moaning. It felt comforting to have her husband there to hold her. Although Nicole had stayed with her while Rhamus was gone and provided great support, nothing could compare to the safe feeling of being in her husband's arms.

The next day, they got back to their regular routines, except that Rhamus was still trying to discover who had aided Xarath in the kidnapping. He was checking among his ambassadors and their aides for possible traitors. Every night Serena's nightmares continued, worrying him and exhausting her. He approached her once more sexually, with the same results. The days flowed into one another, each one much the same as the one before.

One morning, Rhamus got ready more slowly than usual, watching Serena eat her breakfast. "I thought you might enjoy getting some fresh air."

"I would! Where did you have in mind?"

He held out his hand. "Come on, it's a surprise."

She sprang to her feet, feeling bubbly in response to his playful manner, reminding her of happier days past. She recognized the stables as they approached and wondered if Rhamus had a new yasmir to show her.

Going to lean over a corral, he turned and indicated for her to come and look over the fence.

"Remember this little fellow?"

"Oh, Rhamus," Serena gasped. "I forgot all about him." She watched as the frisky little colt ran around the corral, bouncing and frolicking on his long legs. His fur was still a fuzz ball coat of pale lavender. He was a beautiful little animal and seemed to be showing off especially for his audience.

"I intended him to be yours, but I'm afraid too many days have passed and he has already bonded with the stable boy who cares for him."

"What do you mean?"

"Remember I explained how a yasmir must be taken and raised by a Volarnian immediately, or else they are too wild?"

"Oh, I'd forgotten."

"Thank you for trying." She reached up spontaneously and gave him a soft kiss on the mouth.

Eventually the frisky colt became tired and seemed to notice them standing there. Fearlessly, he approached the fence, sniffing the air near them. Then came right up to Serena's hand resting on the rail and sniffed it as well.

"That's strange," Rhamus mused.

"Really?"

"Yes, he seems to like you."

She stretched her hand through the fence, not noticing his worried look. She heard his in-drawn breath as he grasped her arm to stop her, but the baby yasmir had already licked her hand.

"Goreth! What goes on here? Normally, he would have bitten anyone but the one he bonded with."

"Maybe he likes humans," she laughed.

Serena dared more, trailing her hand down the silky nose of the colt. He nuzzled her hand, then ran off and began a spirited run around the corral.

"Can I go in there with him?"

He shook his head in puzzlement. "Under normal circumstances I wouldn't allow it, but, perhaps you should try."

She entered slowly, Rhamus behind her a few steps. Serena crouched down, and within a few minutes the tiny yasmir was again rubbing against her hand. The stable boy who'd been watching bemusedly, brought a bottle over and handed it to Rhamus. Serena took the bottle from him and was very pleased when the colt drank thirstily.

"It seems it is not too late after all, for you and the yasmir to bond." He watched them carefully.

"Maybe there's something different in our blood or hormones," she spoke softly.

"It seems so, at least with you."

"I'm so happy, he's precious."

For the first time in days, Serena felt a lift in her spirits and laughed more than once with joy at the antics of the colt.

"If you are to be his exclusive mistress one day, you must be the main one to hand raise the wild colt."

"It'll be a pleasure."

It gave him hope that she seemed so happy with the little yasmir, maybe she would be back to her old self soon.

"You must name him."

"Hmm, let me see." She looked thoughtful, then giggled. "I think I will name him Rocky."

"Rocky? It is a strange name."

"He's a strange 'horse'."

Rhamus grinned back at Serena's enjoyment.

"Hey! I didn't know you were out here," Kasha yelled from a short distance away and started toward them. She'd reached the corral and started to go through the gate when an unearthly scream pierced the air.

Serena was standing next to Rhamus, screaming, a look of paralyzing fear replacing her joy.

Looking confused, because Serena seemed to be staring at Kasha, it took him a few seconds to realize the cause. Blast his sister's stupidity. Her konkol sat comfortably on its favorite perch--her shoulder. Kasha directed Lor to take off when she noticed Serena's frozen stare.

Holding her body next to his, Rhamus got her swiftly through the gate and started for the castle. Jarvic, who had been right behind the princess, came up to them. "Can you take Serena back to our chambers? I need to talk to Kasha."

"Sure," Jarvic patted Serena's shoulder.

"Aren't you coming?" Her teeth chattered slightly as she spoke.

"I'll be there shortly. Jarvic can stay with you until I get back." He watched a moment as Serena hurried away quickly on shaky legs, making Jarvic sprint to catch up with her.

"Before you yell at me," Kasha held up a hand as her brother approached, "I'm really sorry for upsetting Serena again. I just forgot Lor was still with me."

"That's good to know." His features did not look angry, but worried.

She gazed toward Serena's distant figure in puzzlement. "I thought she'd gotten a little used to our konkols by now."

"I must tell you more about what happened in the fortress. You'll understand then why Serena became so upset." Rhamus told his sister only the details concerning the quamus.

"Curse Xarath's evil soul." Kasha spit on the ground. "I wish I could dig him up and kill him myself."

"I said something to the same effect to Serena." He leaned wearily on the corral. "You must keep this to yourself. I don't want our people to start imagining monsters around every corner."

"Or lose faith in our government's ability to oversee such matters," she added dryly.

Rhamus nodded in agreement and filled her in on what had been done to ferret out traitors in the kingdom. He watched the baby yasmir run around its boundaries. "I hope the colt will give Serena something to get her mind off these fears."

"She's still having nightmares?"

"Yes, every night. And, there are other complications I can't discuss."

Kasha merely raised her eyebrows at her brother's statement. "I've noticed how tired she looks all the time since we returned. Has Dr. Melat checked her out lately?"

"He came at my request several days ago. She and the baby are fine, but he's worried about her nervous state and lack of sleep."

"Have you thought of asking a vassi to help her overcome these nightmares?"

Rhamus stared at her and then ran one hand through his hair. "Truthfully, I've been so busy with these other matters, and I've been depending on Dr. Melat to help with this."

"That you haven't even considered our people's healers," she interrupted then patted him on the shoulder. "Don't worry big brother, you've had a lot on your mind. Why don't you let me take care of contacting vassi?"

He nodded wearily.

"I heard of a skilled one in the Bivoet village, not more than a day's ride from here. I'll send a messenger immediately." Kasha gave his arm an affectionate squeeze.

After another two days had passed Rhamus was ready to try anything to help Serena. He was almost as tired as his wife from being awakened several times every single night, and he was worried about her state of mind. It continued to send chills up his spine every time she screamed or moaned in the grip of her nightmares.

The colt helped take her mind off matters during the daytime, but the pleasure she derived from Rocky didn't carry over into nighttime. Kasha escorted an elderly vassi male to their bedroom at the end of the two days. The healer requested to be left alone with Serena. He was only with her an hour before he re-entered the hallway where Rhamus waited.

"Can you help her?" The King asked anxiously.

The old man shook his head regretfully. "Her fear is too deep for my abilities."

"Do you know someone with those skills?"

"Yes. Only three possess such powers. You must take her to the elders."

"Are you sure they are the only ones who can help. It's a long, dangerous trip. I don't wish to endanger Serena or the baby."

"Your Majesty, I felt enough from my encounter with the Queen that I think it is imperative for her health to take her to the elders."

Rhamus spent the next day getting everything prepared for the trip. He checked with Dr. Melat about Serena's condition, and reluctantly the doctor agreed that she could ride a mount at a slow pace, with frequent breaks. His personal patrol was to ride with them. Jarvic also insisted on going along.

Kasha wanted to go too, but he convinced her to stay and run the

kingdom's affairs. Someone was needed to direct activities if
Xarath's people decided to attack. And, Rhamus didn't say that
which his sister already knew--that someone from the royal family
needed to be left alive in case something happened to them.

Serena knew Rhamus was up to something. He spent the whole
day away, stopping only to have a quick dinner with her in their
suite. His whole countenance had changed. He had a more cheerful
air about him. She wondered if he was getting ready for another
border patrol. He was a restless, active man and seemed happier
when he was involved in such activities.

When Rhamus reappeared at bedtime, he finally told her that they
were starting for the Zanzai Mountains the next day. She was
surprised, but when he explained his reasons, Serena had to agree
with him, even if she wasn't sure if the elders could help her. She
was becoming mentally and physically exhausted from the
nightmares.

If it'd been just her problem, she would stoically bear it, hoping
that eventually she would overcome the memories. But there was
the baby to consider. She was worried how her nervous state was
affecting the fetus. And then there was Rhamus. He had been the
epitome of kindness and consideration, showing his love in many
little ways. But no matter, she couldn't bring herself to make love to
her husband. Every time, Xarath's wicked ghost seemed to rear its
ugly head.

Nicole ran up to her excitedly as they headed for the stables,
giving her a quick hug and some important news. Doc had
proposed and the ship was scheduled to leave within a week. But
when the happy couple had informed Rhamus of their decision
earlier, he had requested that they delay the take off until they
returned from the mountains. Dr. Melat was well respected, and he
and Nicole were well liked by the Volarnians. The people would
want to send them off with a proper marriage ceremony. Also, her
thoughtful husband said Serena would be very sad if Nicole was not
there when she returned.

She eyed Rhamus as they walked. He knew her so well at times.
When they reached the stables, warriors were mounted and ready to
go. Jarvic and Kasha stood nearby. Jarvic's equipment indicated that
he was going too, the princess' mode of dress and her unhappy
expression indicated she was not.

Serena hugged Kasha and whispered, "I wish you could go."

"I know. But my brother insists someone stay and run the
kingdom."

Jarvic brought old Daras and Rhamus helped her mount up. She turned around in the saddle and took a last look. Kasha looked a lonesome figure against the huge castle in the background. She was to think with longing of the castle and her comfortable bedroom in the days ahead.

She lost count of the days, measuring time by how many stops they'd made for the day. She found herself aching for the next break after they rode for a little while. Because of her condition and Daras' lack of stamina, they went at a leisurely gait. Rhamus remarked that, at this rate, it would take them approximately one week to reach the elders.

Several times they had to hide from the west Volarnians patrols. One time, she even saw their yasmirs' hooves when they rode by the heavy brush cover in which they hid. Serena had a feeling that if she had not been with them, Rhamus and his warriors would have engaged in battle with the enemy.

Then there was the treacherousness of the lovely landscape. They passed carefully around one area that could only be described as a huge swamp. Mossy plants hung down for several feet from disfigured, waterlogged trees. Stout golden vines twined from trunk to trunk and branch to branch, creating an intricate, lacy network.

There were many lizards of different sizes crawling through the mud and among the tree limbs. She even saw a ripple in the muddy, violet water that could only be caused by something large swimming underneath. Serena shivered and was glad they did not walk their yasmirs through the smelly water.

The warrior on the lead mount held a long stick, which he poked at the ground in front of his yasmir. Serena nervously wondered what he probed for, then suddenly the stick sunk halfway into the mire.

"*Sessma*," Jarvic said as he rode beside her. Translated, the word meant sink mud. "There've been whole yasmirs and men lost to that." He pointed to the area as they passed cautiously.

She grimaced, "We have something similar on Earth, called quicksand."

They traveled the rest of the day through the swamp land. The next day, she felt like she'd been transported to another country, so different was the landscape. They rode their yasmirs through endless fields of crespassno flowers of every imaginable color. It was a very pleasant part of the arduous journey.

The third day was spent traveling through a forest of immense trees, whose foliage was so thick, they rode in a dusky shadow land. Moss and ferns cloaked the shadows beneath the forest giants. At first, she was enchanted, but as they continued through dark woods with its wet, musty odor, she was eager to see sunlight again.

The warriors were constantly alert and examining the foliage around them. "What are they looking for?" Serena found herself whispering to Rhamus.

"This is alati country and the felines hunt in packs. Very dangerous animals to fight in this dense cover."

She made no more complaints when they reached the mountain range of Zanzai and had to carefully watch where their yasmirs stepped. One slip of a misplaced hoof and the rider could plunge hundreds of feet to their death.

Stretching, Serena put one fist in the small of her back and rubbed hard to get the kinks out. Thank goodness they'd finally stopped for the night. Someone approached from behind, then strong hands took over the massage of her back. She leaned her head back against Rhamus' chest. He'd given her a back rub every night. It was the only thing that relieved the intense knots.

"We'll reach the pass into the elder's territory tomorrow," he spoke softly into her ear, causing a shiver to run down her arms.

She sighed, "I am so happy to hear that." She turned and found herself in the circle of his arms. "I thought you said no one knew the way to the elder's cave?"

"That's right. To find the elders, you proceed up the pass. The way is shown."

Serena held a finger up and pressed it gently against his lips. "Please don't try to explain that to me, I'm too tired to be able to understand. You can just show me tomorrow."

Rhamus kissed her finger and smiled. "Let's get settled for the night, I have a feeling tomorrow will be a big day for the both of us."

Shifting her weight on the bedroll, she was very glad he'd had the foresight to include a small mattress stuffed with soft downy feathers from the elag. It fit perfectly under the bedroll and made sleeping on the hard ground bearable. She took the mild tranquilizer as she had every night to prevent her nightmares. She had refused any medication previously, but her screams could alert their enemies to their presence.

The next morning, they continued traveling upward. The scenery was breathtaking, but Serena was so nervous watching the steep cliffs and narrow trails that she could only enjoy it during breaks. Finally, they came to the pass, which looked like a cave or tunnel, but was open to the sky. It took them several hours to traverse the pass, filing down the stony trail, one by one.

The end of the pass flowed into a meadow that stretched as far as they could see. The bright sunlight was a welcome change from the cool interior of the rocky passage. The warriors, including Jarvic, began to dismount.

Rhamus rode up to her. "We go the rest of the way alone."

"By ourselves? Why?"

"It is the elder's rules. Only those who petition for help from them must travel the unknown pathway."

"Great. How do you propose we do that?"

"I suggest we start by crossing the meadow."

"Which way?" Serena looked at the vast landscape in confusion.

He walked his yasmir a few paces and then stopped and closed his eyes. Serena watched as he got an intense look of concentration on his face.

"We go that way." He pointed toward the right.

She prodded old Daras to follow Rhamus, wondering if they were on a wild goose chase--no signs, no trail, just "psychic feelings" to guide them.

It took them several hours before they came to the end of the meadowland. Every once in a while, he stopped and concentrated, then led them on. The meadow stopped at a large rocky outcrop, another mountain range standing starkly behind it. He dismounted and came to help her off.

"What now?"

"We wait."

Serena didn't argue. She was glad for any excuse to take a needed rest. Rhamus spread her bedroll and she took a nap, her head lying in his lap. It felt as though she'd just closed her eyes when he shook her awake.

"We've got visitors."

Rhamus didn't need to add that it was the elders who came toward them. Three very old men on yasmirs made their way slowly toward them. She was surprised to see that the old man riding in the center rode a yasmir the same lavender shade as Rocky.

"We have been awaiting your arrival." One of the elders spoke to them.

Serena couldn't help feeling shocked and a glance sideways at Rhamus told her he was also surprised. She couldn't begin to guess their ages, so old did they appear. The elders wise faces were filled with wrinkles, and their hair flowed white as goose down. The one who spoke appeared to be the oldest, his face as deeply furrowed as the mountains behind him.

His accent was another surprise. Serena had noticed that the west Volarnians had an accent different from Rhamus' people. Did that mean the oldest elder was from the west?

"Yes, I was once from the western lands." He smiled at them kindly, as if answering questions from children. "The sacred crystal does not discriminate when choosing its guardians."

"You can read our minds?" She asked in stunned wonder. All three elders simply smiled and gave a slight nod.

He cleared his throat and said, "Elders, we have come--"

"My son, we know why you have come," the elder on the right answered. "Please follow us, Rhamus and Serena."

"Do they know we're the king and queen?" She whispered to her husband. "They didn't address us so."

"The elders are considered to be on equal terms with any king or queen," he answered softly back.

The old men wound their way around the large rock and took one of many trails leading off into the wilderness of the mountains. They took so many different routes along the way Serena didn't know how anyone could remember their way back.

Finally, they came out of the forest into a small meadow. At the far edge rose a cliff, in the center of which was a large cave opening, the dwelling place of the elders and the sacred crystal. She and Rhamus followed the old men inside. They both paused inside the entrance, overwhelmed with the beauty of the interior.

The cave opened into a vast area, with formations of stalagmites and other crystalline rock configurations. The shapes were fantastic. Light pierced the cave from above, shooting through natural holes in the ceiling. The sunlight brightened the area and picked out brilliant hues on the dripping formations created by Mother Nature.

The elders had paused, letting them take in the majesty of their surroundings. Then they headed across the expanse of the cave toward an opening across from the entrance. Rhamus and Serena followed, craning their necks upward in wonder as they went.

They followed the vassi down a tunnel and came out in another much smaller cavern. She was shocked by the homeliness of this new space. It was decorated with comfortable furniture, thick rugs covered the cold stone floor, and there was a pleasant warmth to the air which indicated a heating system. A multitude of lighting fixtures emitted a blue glow. The light source was a crystal.

The eldest vassi spoke, "Have a seat and we will serve refreshments."

One of the other elders retrieved wine and biscuits from a shelf in the corner. At their pleased expressions as to the tastiness of the offered food, the elder who had served them said, "Besides being a healer, I like to cook."

When they finished, the eldest vassi again spoke, "Serena, are you ready to begin?"

"Don't you want me to tell you about what caused my problem?"

The three elders smiled gently. "We have no need for you to go through the pain of telling us. We have already 'read' the story from your mind."

At her uncomfortable look, he said, "You have nothing to fear from us. Anyone who travels to us for help must expect their thoughts to be read. This helps us in understanding the cure."

"What are you going to do?"

Taking her hand and clasping it between both of his, the elder explained. "We must make a deep connection with your mind, with the help of the sacred crystal. It will be as if we are a part of you. This will be the only way to see if we can help take away your pain and fear."

If the old man had not been holding her hand, she would have jumped up and run away. He was talking about an invasion into her very soul! It was not his firm, confident grip that held her in place, but the peace that radiated from the contact with his withered hand. As she had learned earlier with Zara, physical contact with a psychic sorcerer enabled them to "read" something about that person. Serena sensed she could trust the elders with the secrets of her heart.

The eldest healer nodded at one of the others who left the room briefly and returned with a heavily carved box. It was encrusted with arj'ak crystals, and he placed it carefully on a table. The old man reached into the box, withdrawing an arj'ak crystal the size of a grapefruit. She heard Rhamus' sharp intake of breath and turned to see his rapt gaze.

The elder bore the crystal to where they were assembled, cradling it in his hands as he carefully took his place to one side of the oldest vassi. The other elder had already taken up a position on his other side. The eldest one quietly held Serena's hands. All three men closed their eyes. After a few seconds she felt a thrumming in the air, reminding her of the Tarthra.

She gasped slightly when the sacred crystal left the elders' hands and floated gently over toward her. It stopped at eye level just above their clasped hands. She held her breath as she sensed a voice speaking to her, but knew it had not been heard by the others. She closed her eyes as the voice instructed.

A sense of extreme well being flowed through her and she relaxed in the chair. It was as if she were floating, just like the sacred crystal. Suddenly, she felt a presence within her mind--a place, until now,

singular in its entity. For a second, she was very confused. She
knew that the eldest vassi was supposed to make contact with her,
yet the presence she sensed seemed vast, boundless--a pool of
knowledge, caring and reassurance.

Don't worry. The disembodied voice floated gently to her inner
self. *We are three separate beings with one mind, brought together
by the crystal's power.*

Serena realized that the elders' minds had joined and were being
directed by the vassi who held her hands. She let go of her last
qualm and listened to the silent, powerful voice within. The voice
pulled her back in time to the fateful day when she had awakened in
Xarath's chambers. She resisted momentarily, the fear rising up,
making her moan.

A hideous dungeon-dwelling beast swirled around and round
through her thoughts. Spiders, konkols, and the quamus mingled,
became a small whirlwind, their colors and limbs merging together,
then were sucked upward, out of sight.

The elders quickly calmed her fears. She felt soothed, as if cool
water had been poured over a scorching burn. A numbness filled
her mind, making it easy to relive the painful events. The elders
whispered in her mind, telling her to let the fear die and with it, the
pain that Xarath had caused.

She was able to view the events as an outsider and realize that she
had actually made the best she could of a hopeless situation. She felt
as a little child, held by a loving grandparent, and protected in their
arms from a roiling tempest outside. Her fear was replaced by pride
and confidence. She was strong again.

She sensed their gradual withdrawal from her, and then suddenly
they stopped. It was as if she heard them whispering amongst
themselves. *Serena,* the voice called to her again. *There is more that
can be done to help you. You have pain buried so deep, we almost
missed it.*

No! She screamed in her mind, trying to throw them from herself.
She was powerless against them. Unwillingly this time, she sank
under their hypnotic influence again as they led her deeper into her
past. Her body jerked on the chair as she mentally struggled.
Feeling helpless all over again, she was towed down the dark paths
of her inner self.

Chapter Twenty Two

Serena felt dizzy with a physical sense of spiraling faster and faster downward. Flickers of events from her past flashed by, some so precious, she wanted to scream for them to stop so she could take a good look. Suddenly, she was floating again, and it was as if she were a ghost observing herself at a younger age.

Teenage Serena lay on her bed, music blasting in her room, disgruntled at her parents because they'd grounded her for smoking. The ghostly apparition that was herself moved through the walls of a house, which no longer stood. She saw her parents asleep, her mom's lovely face peaceful after a full day of running around after children. Her dad's face was tired and he snored loudly.

She floated through another wall and recognized the twin's room. Her two young sisters were sprawled across their beds, three-year-old cherub angels fast asleep after running mom ragged. She wanted to reach out and touch their soft cheeks once more, but they were only memories from the past. Serena felt tears spring to her eyes, unaware that real tears poured down her cheeks as she lay moaning in the chair.

She tried to protest. She didn't want to see anymore but she was led, an unwilling spirit, to the next room in the large, rambling house. In this room rested her three younger brothers. Two slept on bunk beds while the third had a single bed to himself. Tom, the eldest of the boys had been so proud when he earned a bed all his own.

She screamed for the elders to stop. She knew her brothers. They weren't really asleep. Soon, one would throw a sock from the top bunk down on his younger brother below. Screams would erupt as Bob imagined a giant bug had jumped down on him. Gales of laughter would follow and all three would start throwing smelly socks and hitting each other with pillows. Any minute now, mom or dad would burst through the door, aggravated by the boy's nighttime shenanigans.

Please, she pleaded with the elders silently. I can't bear anymore.

You must go on. You have been suppressing the memory since your youth. Let us help you uncover the truth. You will see that the reality is far better than the mistaken beliefs you buried within yourself, along with your family.

Serena hated them at that moment--hated their intrusion and their insistence on digging up a pain so deep, she only wished for it to stay locked up in her subconscious. She fought them mentally as long as she could, then their combined strength knocked down the last layers of her mind's defense.

Suddenly, she was again floating over her old room, watching as young Serena lit a cigarette hidden away in a coat, in defiance of her parents. She tried to shut her ghostly eyes from what came next, but couldn't. The girl fell asleep, cigarette smoldering near the bed sheets.

She watched in despair as the girl on the bed awakened in fright. Smoke filled the room and fire raced up one bedroom wall. The girl tried to get out of the door to warn her family. But the fire was too close to the door, and she escaped the only other way out. Serena climbed out the window as the smoke almost overcame her. She lay gasping on the ground for a minute, then sprang up, intending to run back through the house.

The girl stood in the front doorway in shock. The stairs were aflame, leaving no way for her to run upstairs and warn anyone. Smoke filled the living room and fire ran along the ceiling greedily. She knew she had to get out and call for help. But first she screamed and screamed, trying to get a response from upstairs.

Finally, she ran to a neighbor's house and the fire station was called. Young Serena stood outside with a neighbor and watched the frantic efforts of the firemen. When the fire was finally extinguished, the house was but a smoldering ruin.

Days later, she stood as the report was read to her, tears streaming down her face. They said all had died from smoke inhalation. Fortunate, they said, because the family didn't suffer. Fortunate? Her mind could only connect two facts--she'd been smoking in bed --and the house had caught fire, killing her entire family. Although the investigative officers said the fire was caused by faulty electric wires, Serena's mind refused to accept the truth. She knew the truth--she was a murderer.

The Serena of the present, the one who now floated over the black ruins of a once happy home, had never felt so miserable in her whole life. Suddenly she was whisked away again, and she went unresisting, feeling too hopeless to care.

She was once again in her bedroom, floating over the girl as she started to fall asleep. Were the elders simply going to make her relive this over and over? Was this their idea of a cure? Did they hope, perhaps, that repeated exposure would bring acceptance?

Serena watched with dull eyes as the girl slept, her cigarette dangerously near the bed linens. This time, the elders didn't pull her away; she continued to observe the action below. The cigarette fell from her hand and landed on a small mound of bedding, charring it as it rolled to the side of the bed. Bumping over the edge, it hit the oak flooring where it scattered a fine spray of sparks and then, simply went out.

She stared from above and continued to do so. The elders let her remain, watching the girl sleep on, the cigarette now cold and completely harmless. She was stunned. Then there was a gentle tugging and she found herself in the hallway outside her door. She watched as sparks ignited from an electrical outlet and fire leapt up the wall at astounding speed. All these years she'd been blaming herself because she was the only one to survive.

Feeling at first as though she were moving underwater, Serena felt herself traveling in an upward direction. A feeling of lightness spread through her whole body and welcomed the company of the elders as they helped her ascend from deep in her psyche to her conscious mind. She heard them say, *They are at peace. Now, let peace flow into yourself.*

She obeyed the eldest vassi's command and opened her eyes. She looked at his kind face and those of the others. She thought she'd never loved anyone as much at that moment, except her family and Rhamus. It was as if were opening her eyes for the first time in many, many years. The world looked brighter, happier.

Serena spent the next few minutes telling Rhamus about her experience while the elders looked on patiently. They both turned to the old men, not sure how to thank them for such a wondrous gift. She didn't know if she should kiss their hands or give them something in appreciation.

"We are in your debt," his simple phrase held a world of meaning for anyone who knew how to interpret it.

"My son," the eldest of the three spoke, "you do not owe a debt to us, but to the sacred crystal." He indicated the crystal, which once again rested in the palms of one of the elders.

The one holding the crystal said, "Only the sacred crystal can request repayment of such a debt." He looked deeply into the blue lights shining within the depths of the crystal. "It may never require anything from you, but then again, one day it may require all."

"What does he mean?" She whispered to her husband as they arose and headed back to the cave's entrance.

"Don't worry about it. The vassi love to spout prophecies and riddles for us simple folk to try and figure out."

As they started to mount their yasmirs, Serena said, "Please, wait a minute. I don't feel as though I've properly thanked you." She walked quickly to the three and, reaching up to each of their weathered cheeks, gave them a kiss. They didn't respond verbally, but their pleased expressions told her they didn't mind a peck on the cheek from a young woman.

The trip down the mountain was a quiet one, with each seemingly lost in their individual thoughts. At the rock outcropping, the elders paused. "Head back the way you came, Rhamus. We will guide you mentally so you will find the way back to your companions."

"Frankly, I'm concerned," he said. "I have knowledge of the location of the sacred crystal." He tapped a forefinger to his head. "And, even though you led us a roundabout way up to the cave, I'm sure I could relocate if I needed to. And if I could do that, an enemy with great powers may be able to read this information from me."

"My son, there's no need for concern. As soon as you rejoin your warriors, any knowledge you had of the way here will be wiped from your memory."

"That's a relief."

"Now, Serena," The eldest vassi walked his yasmir up to hers, "join hands with me once again. We wish to bestow a gift on you that will help during your long journey back home."

Without hesitation, she let the elder take her hands. She trusted them with her very life now. She had just a momentary sensation of the elder's presence and then she opened her eyes. The elder patted her hands into place on her lap.

"Do you understand?"

"Yes." She looked at each of them in turn, tears sparkling in her eyes. "Thank you so much," she whispered and turned her yasmir quickly to follow her husband.

As they rode back over the meadow, Rhamus pausing every few miles as if listening to an inner voice, he asked, "What did the vassi do?"

"They have given me a painless journey." At his confused expression, she giggled. "The elders ... have made it so that I will feel no soreness or pain from riding long hours on the yasmir."

"What a wonderful gift. If it could be bottled and sold, you could be rich enough to buy--"

"What, your love?" She interrupted teasingly.

"There aren't enough crystals in the kingdom to purchase my love away from you." He grabbed her hand and kissed it loudly.

Their banter and play went on until they heard a noise and, and looking up, saw the warriors camped out, patiently awaiting their return. It was nightfall and Serena was very hungry. The warriors teased her about her appetite, but each kept coming by to offer her some tidbit from their own rations. It was a wonderful time of fellowship for her, sitting around the campfire, joking and telling stories with her people.

The journey back home was a magical time for her. The elders had made it possible for her to enjoy the ride, spending many hours admiring the passing scenery. She felt so carefree, almost as if she'd been returned to herself--before the tragedy with her family. Rhamus picked up on her good spirits and spent most of the trip riding by her side, talking about their future or flirting outrageously.

At one point, they passed a large web, probably twenty feet across. Serena saw the huge wild konkol, which made its home in the sticky trap. It was twice as big as the tame pets kept by her people. The group passed by respectfully and Serena, watching the creature carefully, did not even shudder in reaction. The elders had truly worked some magic for her benefit.

The nighttime was full of discovery for her as well. Her first night was so restful she threw away the pills Dr. Melat had given her. They were surrounded by the protective, watchful eyes of the warriors. But that didn't keep her from cuddling up next to Rhamus every night. A great longing to arrive home hit her, so she could pursue the physical side of their relationship.

She did not fully realize the extent of her interest until several nights into the trip when she leaned over her husband, who lay stretched out on his bedroll. She couldn't help but smile in the darkness. Firelight played on her husband's features enough to see that his eyes were closed. At least that's what he wanted her to think. Serena had learned many weeks ago this little trick of his. He liked to pretend to be asleep or exhausted and close his eyes, but all the time he observed her through slitted eyelids. She caught onto his trick tonight because the faint flicker of the campfire picked up the shine of his eyes beneath his lowered lids.

She looked her fill of her handsome husband, playing along with his game, as if she were unaware of being observed. She had felt her love blossoming for Rhamus over the last few days. She thought she was already in love with him, in spite of her earlier hesitancy, but she'd truly not let herself feel the deeper side of her emotion, covering it beneath layers of pain and denial.

What she felt now went deep within herself, touching her mind and soul, reaching levels only the elders had been able to touch before. And her body reacted with a physical craving that matched her emotions. Serena reached out and caressed his face gently and Rhamus gave up his pretense as he smiled happily up at her.

She loved this man so very much, more than she would have ever thought possible. He was very masculine, intelligent and a wonderful lover. He had a sensitive nature, which many men never came close to, but that most women desired in a partner. He was a King, yet she suddenly realized he was her prince, the soul love of her heart.

She leaned down and kissed him gently and lovingly. He reached up slowly and drew her upper body on top of him and into his arms. He'd been very considerate since her ordeal, but especially so since visiting the elders. He was waiting for her to make the first move. This was the first time she'd made a physical overture and Rhamus reacted carefully.

But Serena could see by the look in his eyes that it took much restraint on his part, this patient wait for her to act. She kissed him again, letting her lips press deeper and linger. Drawing back briefly, Serena looked into his eyes, seeing them clearly in the firelight. She caught her breath at the depth of love reflected in them.

He reached up with one hand and gently stroked the hair over one temple. "Do you know how much I love you, my jicha?" he whispered.

A glimmer of tears rose in her eyes, a spilling over in joy from hearing and seeing the evidence of his love. She shook her head in answer to his question, unable to answer with the lump that arose in her throat. Finally, she managed to say, "Do *you* know how much I love you?" The happiness that lit his face was priceless to her.

She again dipped her head for another kiss and this time Rhamus put his hand behind her head and met her halfway. Their kiss changed from one of emotional love to a deeper one of physical passion. He reacted with a jerk of his arms when Serena plunged her tongue into his mouth with bold intent.

Serena was mindless for a few minutes as an aching sprang up in her body, one that only could be fulfilled when they reached home. She groaned as Rhamus lips played havoc with hers then moved to her neck. His heavy breathing and moan fanned the sensitive hollow of her neck.

"Ahem," Jarvic cleared his throat near their feet. "If you wish, I could take the men on a night hunt ... oh, I don't know ... perhaps for an hour or so?"

A slight heat flamed her cheeks, but she didn't feel as embarrassed as she would have previously. She glanced over at the campfire and saw that all the warriors were looking at each other or examining the dark forest, glancing anywhere but in their direction. She grinned in the night and the wicked side of her nature hoped that

Rhamus would take Jarvic up on his offer.

"Are you a fool?" He pushed Serena gently to his side. "Serena doesn't need the discomfort of the forest floor."

"Just trying to be helpful." Jarvic shrugged and strolled back over to the others.

"What do you think Serena, could Nicole and Jarvic possibly be related?"

"What do you mean?"

"They both seem to be experts at interrupting us at the most inopportune times."

She giggled and snuggled up against his warm body. She listened to Rhamus' strong heartbeat and found herself blinking to stay awake. She was surprised to feel so sleepy.

The rest of the trip passed with ease. They didn't run across an enemy patrol, and neither the swamp nor alati-filled forest seemed as threatening.

An air of excitement filled everyone as they rounded the last bend in the road and saw the castle in the distance. They'd already been spotted and Kasha led a group of warriors to greet them.

The princess stopped her yasmir so quickly when she reached them that a small cloud of dust swirled up around the mount's legs.

"Ho, sister! How do things stand in the kingdom?"

Jarvic interrupted by saying, "Did you cut off any heads while we were gone, or perhaps start a war with our enemies?"

Frowning in annoyance, she ignored him. "We had no problems here, Rhamus. But, in west Volarn things have been disturbing."

"What happened? Have they chosen a new king?"

"Chosen is not the right word. The eldest brother from Xarath's line, Jouko, has taken over. He apparently raised a lot of warriors who followed him and overthrew the temporary government."

"I thought it was automatic that the older brother would take over?" Serena asked in confusion.

"That's pretty well true," he answered thoughtfully. "But the next in line for the throne, whether they be from west or south Volarn, must be approved by each country's council. It usually is just a formality, but in this case the council may have been seeking to select someone more suitable."

"That's what I heard," Kasha confirmed. She frowned again. "I think we may be in for trouble with Jouko."

Rhamus shook his head in agreement. "Now, sister, we're all elated to be home, and have much information to exchange, but I think Serena could use a good hot soak and a nap."

She did feel much better after a hot bath and good sleep. Nicole came in to check on her and fill her in on the gossip.

"Surad and some of the other noble ladies want to host a celebration in your honor."

"Really? What for?"

"Well, they think there should be a celebration to congratulate you and Rhamus on the heir. And they wanted to do something to welcome you back, when you returned from the fortress. But you were feeling bad, so they decided to put it off until you were feeling better."

"I hope they're not planning this tomorrow?" She sighed.

"No. They've got it planned for next week. And guess what?" She raised her eyebrows and shrugged. "Doc and I will be married during the celebration."

Serena hugged her. "That's wonderful, I'm so happy for you! What are you going to do when Dr. Melat leaves with the Moyds?"

"Go with him. I thought having an Earth woman on board will help ease the captives' misery. And, maybe I can help them understand things better."

"Hmm. You don't mind being involved in this kidnapping business?"

"Of course I mind!" She looked frustrated. "Just as much as you do." She shrugged, "But, they're going to keep on doing it in spite of what we think. I figure why not go along so I can be with my husband and try to assist the women in any way I can."

"I admire your spunk. I'm not sure I could do it, though. Tell me, do you know if Surad is planning entertainment for this affair?"

"Sure. Along the line of what they did during the birth ceremony, but on a much smaller scale. And I think it will only last a few hours." Nicole giggled and she smiled, both thinking of the two-week celebration that had left them exhausted.

After her friend left, Serena sent one of the guards posted outside on a mission. It annoyed her that after her kidnapping, Rhamus had two guards at her disposal at all times. One had been bad enough, but she understood his concern. The guard returned shortly with Jidroon.

"Your Majesty," Jidroon greeted her with enthusiasm. "We're so glad that you've returned, and that you are feeling better. How can I be of service? Do you wish a new gown for the celebration?"

"No." She smiled with fondness at the tailor. "I have a dress you made that I haven't even worn yet. What I want is…." Jidroon was mystified as to what kind of costume she was planning to make. Serena only wanted him to acquire the materials for her, stating that it was a surprise for the king and she would make it. The tailor left with a broad smile lighting his features, as if he were enjoying the mystery as much as she.

She spent many hours that week working on her costume, telling Rhamus she was tired. She stayed cloistered in her bedroom, hiding her materials whenever he entered.

One day, Rhamus convinced her to go outside for fresh air. Taking the yasmirs and a picnic basket, they rode through the forests, stopping at one of their favorite spots. The stream gurgled merrily and they spread the blanket on the bank. Their food was quickly eaten, and they relaxed afterwards on the blanket. Rhamus teased her about eating so much, and then their talk turned to the baby. They both found the subject endlessly fascinating.

Later, Serena excused herself and went to the bathroom behind a nearby bush. Just as she got finished, Rhamus stepped around the bush and said in a loud voice, "Do you know what happens to beautiful women who are alone in the woods?"

His voice was deep and sent a shiver through her. She couldn't hold back a giggle. "No, tell me." She walked closer and stood with her arms folded.

"They get eaten up by big, bad alatis." He took several exaggerated pounding steps toward her.

She grinned. Serena had never seen her husband act so silly, but found it charming. Turning, she started to jog down a trail, calling over her shoulder, "Not if she's not caught."

Rhamus' heavy footsteps were right behind her. She put on a burst of speed, not quite ready to stop this childish game. She felt carefree and loved how boyish the King was acting.

Breaking through two thick bushes, she stepped out into an immense meadow. No time to appreciate its beauty. Laughing, she turned and walked quickly backwards, keeping her eyes on her fast approaching husband. His lumbering steps had turned into a purposeful stride.

"Serena, watch out."

Too late. She backed into something and was held fast. Ignoring Rhamus, Serena glanced to one side. Webbing. She was caught in one of those huge webs that wild konkols spun.

"Oh my God, get me loose!" Serena tugged. Her arms were held firmly by the strong, sticky threads. Trying to step forward, her legs refused to budge, and she realized her whole backside was stuck. She could move slightly, but bounced back at each effort.

"Quit standing there laughing and get me out of this." She shook the web and raised her voice, just shy of a scream. Rhamus was clutching his middle and laughing hard.

Pulling at the steely threads in frustration, she remembered the konkol. Nervously, she glanced around. Because her hair was stuck, she couldn't stretch her neck to peer above her.

"Rhamus, is the konkol on the web?"

"No." He swiped at his eyes. "Remember, you have no reason to fear them."

Regardless of their sweet nature and her resolved fear of them, Serena didn't like being in one of their webs. It was an unpleasant feeling. The thought of one of those huge, spidery creatures crouching nearby and staring at the strange human caught in its web, was unnerving.

"The konkol might not appreciate having a human messing up its web," she fumed, more irritated now by his behavior than her predicament.

"Oh, it won't be back." He pointed to an *azdor* tree fifteen feet away. "You've terrified it."

Serena frowned irritably and stared at the tree. The konkol was in plain sight on a lower limb, several of its legs moving erratically. She had learned enough konkol body language to know it was upset. She sighed. Great. Now Rhamus made her feel guilty.

"Don't worry, my jicha, it will only take it a day to spin a new web."

Her husband walked to within touching distance.

"Wonderful." She saw the konkol scamper down the tree and run for a tall *inlo* tree in the distance. Frowning, she fixed him with an "I'm going to kill you" look. "Now that I've destroyed its web, will you cut me down," she screeched, shaking the strands with her entwined hands.

Rhamus stared at her and thumped his chin. "This kind of opportunity doesn't come about every day."

"What are you talking about?" She blew a strand of hair from her eye and pierced him with a hard glare.

"Having you tied up and helpless." He grinned, running his eyes over her figure.

"Why you…." She paused, at a loss for words. She did feel helpless. And he was going to make this into some sexual game?

He stepped in close, holding her face between his large hands.

"You better get me out, if you know what's good for you."

"But I do." Rhamus swept down, capturing her mouth in a searing kiss.

She kept her mouth closed, but didn't know how long she could maintain her coldness. Her body was flushed. Why did she always have to be so responsive to his touch? Damn!

His tongue managed to slip between her lips and her mouth went lax as his hands played with the ties of her dress. She trembled, wanting him to caress her skin. The strings slipped down as he undid them, and then he shoved the material down.

Her breasts were in his palms, being kneaded by his experienced touch. Serena clutched at the webbing near her hands, uncaring that they too were now stuck. She felt as helpless as a baby, like putty in his hands. She watched his head in a daze as he moved downward.

A deep moan escaped her mouth as he tongued one nipple. In a few strokes of his hot tongue, she was panting.

"Rhamus, this isn't right," she managed to gasp.

Releasing her pebbled flesh, he answered, "Isn't it? Tell me if it doesn't feel good and I'll stop." Watching her face, he pushed her breast up and then flicked at the tight nub.

Her clit was throbbing like mad and her nipple ached to be sucked. Another strong lick and she whimpered. She was incapable of further speech. Instead, she groaned and pushed her nipple toward his tongue.

Serena's head flopped back onto the web while her hands clutched at the strands. Oh God, what was he doing to her? Her body was on fire. Electric sparks shot from her nipples and clit, along her limbs, making her tremble.

He pulled on the nipple, sucking deeply while he played with the other one. She moaned and thrashed her head. Ecstasy. Speech returned to her. "Harder," she moaned again, shoving her breasts into his mouth and hand. Complying, Rhamus drew on her nub more fiercely while rolling and tweaking her other nipple harder.

"Yes," she screamed.

An orgasm flushed through her lower lips. After the pleasure receded, she moaned anew as Rhamus' licks to her aching nipple stirred her already heated flesh to new heights. Cool air hit her beaded skin and she opened her eyes. Rhamus drew back and rubbed his jaw.

"Too much clothing." Touching his belt, he withdrew his dagger and began cutting at her rezel pants.

"What are you doing?" She screeched.

"Cutting off your pants." Humor etched his words.

"Stop. I won't have anything to ride back in."

"Don't worry, I have an extra pair in my pack." He efficiently cut the material to shreds and then pulled the pants off. The back part stuck to the web, leaving her front parts exposed. Serena suddenly realized her legs were free since only the suede fabric was stuck. She tugged hard, but blew out her breathe in frustration. Her feet and upper body were still caught firmly. There was no getting loose.

"Rhamus, cut me loose," she demanded, shaking the strands.

"Now, why would I do that when we're having so much fun?" His eyes were burning lavender flames. Turning his gaze downward, his hands followed their track, picking up the end of her dress. Bringing it up on each side, he pressed the silky material into the webbing.

"What?" She stared down. Rhamus had completely exposed her. The tunic was stuck to the web on either side of her waist, while the rezel pants were cut away. Well, not completely exposed. The one piece undergarment covered her below the waist. Rhamus had shoved the garment down earlier, along with her tunic. Being a strapless piece the bra's front had offered no resistance.

She was so angry at his exposing her this way, making her feel vulnerable in a way she hadn't since Xarath kidnapped her. But it also turned her on so much her pussy was throbbing and swollen, and her clit galloped with wild pulses.

Smiling at her, Rhamus gave her nipple a few licks then suckled it deeply. He seemed determined to again ignite the heat he'd started but moments before. Try as she might, Serena couldn't hold onto her anger, not against the stabbing thrills coursing through her blood. Running his hands around her breasts, he knelt.

When his hands smoothed across the satiny undergarment, she trembled. His fingers slid to the fastening and it snapped open with ease. Staring into her face, he rolled the fabric up, until it hung across her hip bones. Serena closed her eyes, awaiting his next move.

Her breath hitched as she felt his silky hair brush her mons. She moaned and flopped her head backward. Her body was boneless as well and needed the webbing for support. She would have crumpled at his feet otherwise.

His tongue slipped inside her inner lips, smoothing them with long strokes. Groaning loudly, she panted as shards of pleasure shot through her.

When his tongue touched her clit she whimpered, "Yes." Her body twisted beneath his administrations. His tongue picked up the tempo, flicking her acing nub with rapid strokes.

Serena screamed so loud a flock of *sooeul* erupted from the tree overhead, screeching even louder than her. The orgasm ripped through her, shattering her senses until she felt light-headed. Rhamus gently lapped at her flesh and she rocked her hips, whimpering as sensation after sensation flowed through her.

Finally, it was too much and she begged him to stop. Getting to his feet, Rhamus began to undress. She'd forgotten he was still clothed. It made her feel vulnerable all over again.

As his cock sprang from his *tanla* she took a deep breath. Her lower lips were throbbing again, longing for his length. She was astonished at the depth of her response after receiving several very satisfying orgasms. But she had no time to question her body's reaction--Rhamus had stepped between her thighs.

The large head of his staff nudged her entrance and she became wet just from the slight touch. Easing slowly inside, he dipped in and out. He asked, "Want to stop?"

"You bastard, you know I don't." Serena managed to move down slightly, sheathing her slick channel half way upon his cock.

"Guess not." His quirky smile contradicted the hot lust in his eyes. He thrust upward, his engorged flesh firmly lodged inside her.

"Yes," her breath exhaled in relief and satisfaction. She was stretched and filled, temporarily relieving the ache deep inside. But then he started moving in and out, and the burning need returned sharply, as if it'd never been assuaged.

Placing his hands on her hips, Rhamus pushed downward and then released. She bounced up a few inches, courtesy of the springy webbing.

"Oh." The exclamation was ripped from her. It was a surprisingly unique and fiery sensation.

Rhamus repeated the action again and again, while plunging into her at the same time. By the savage look on his face, it must be as hot to him as well.

Shards of pleasure rippled through her while electric tingles raced along her nerves. Every cell in her body seemed to zing with feeling. Her hands tightened around the webbing, her fingers moved restlessly. Serena's body went taut as her inner muscles clamped down on his penetrating cock. Swiping her head against the web, she screamed, making the *sooeul* take flight once again.

A low moan escaped her lips as Rhamus' staff swelled and his seed filled her in short bursts. Tiny shudders flushed through her pussy as she climaxed again in time with his release.

After a few deep breaths, she felt his withdrawal. Weary, she stared at him. Rhamus picked up his dagger and began cutting the sticky webbing. She collapsed into his arms, not protesting when he directed her to lie on her stomach. It took some time for him to pick the threads from her body.

"Finished."

She rolled over, then ran one hand through her hair. Bringing a lock around to her face, she frowned.

"It will come out when you shower." Cocking one eyebrow at her, he asked, "Ready to head home?"

"No." She stretched out on the soft grass. "Strangely, I have no energy." She had to bite her lip to keep from smiling. Rhamus had no such qualms and chuckled softly. She heard him settle next to her. She really should give him a piece of her mind, but she was too tired. Serena drifted off to sleep with ease.

A tickling beneath her nose awoke her. Her husband was using the ends of her hair to tickle her.

"Time to go sleepy-head." He gazed toward the skyline.

It was twilight and they would have to hurry or else be blundering about in the woods, trying to find their way back. Darkness did close in around them on the last stretch, but Rhamus' yasmir knew the way and trod the path with confidence.

Later, in bed, Serena knew she should say something to Rhamus. Fuss at him for being a cad and leaving her bound in the webbing. But each time the thought came to mind, she blushed with remembered pleasure. She would be a hypocrite if she berated him for the wild sex, for she loved each minute of her helpless bondage situation. Never, had she thought she would enjoy such a sexual adventure and found it rather surprising.

Rhamus was nice and didn't tease her about the hot session. But a few times he held her hands above her head while they made love, his strong hands firm around her wrists. His eyes would flame with heat so hot it seemed to burn her skin. He well remembered the experience, as did she. Whenever he held her thus, her body would fill with a liquid, burning weakness, and their lovemaking would be savage and very satisfying. Each time they made love since her recovery, she felt like she was experiencing it for the first time all over again, her feelings of love were so intense. Rhamus was thrilled that Serena showed her love openly for him, now that she had unburied her hidden emotions. The week passed quickly. Serena enjoyed visiting her friends and spending the evenings with her husband.

She dressed for the celebration carefully, wanting to look her best for him. The deep purple color of her dress set off her red hair beautifully. It was another creation she and Jidroon had worked on. It was simply made, another form-fitting sheath, its hem sweeping the floor until she put on small-heeled slippers.

Her breasts pressed together boldly above the bodice with its low-cut straight line. Tiny straps covered with amethyst crystals kept the top from slipping down. Serena smoothed the silky material over her thighs. This dress had no slit to show off her legs but still looked sensual.

She had given Jidroon fits again when she came up with an item
of clothing he was unfamiliar with, a pair of elbow length gloves.
She slipped on matching amethyst crystal jewelry, including a
bejeweled bracelet placed over the glove on her left wrist. The
elegant earrings fell in five strands of the purple gems. A necklace
made from tiny pieces of crystal, stretched from her neck to dip into
her bosom, ending in a large teardrop amethyst, which nestled in
her cleavage.

Lalme came in time to do her hair. Serena had her leave most of it
falling in shiny curls, pulling the temples and front up into a high
ponytail. The girl added the finishing touch by wrapping an
amethyst-encrusted ribbon several times around the band, creating a
pony tail which stood up so the purple wrapping showed to
advantage, and curls cascaded from the top of her crown.

Rhamus entered a few minutes after she was done and hurriedly
donned his royal vestments. He was stunned by her appearance, his
eyes opening wide appreciatively. "I don't know if you were more
beautiful last time or now, but I can see I'm more in debt to Jidroon
than ever." He grinned and walked around her to examine the
costume from every side.

"You truly like it?" She asked, pleased with his interest.

He picked up one of her gloved hands and kissed it with a courtly
bow. "My dear, if you were not the Queen, you could make
yourself rich by designing dresses for the nobility."

Laughing, Serena said, "There is one disadvantage to gloves I
hadn't thought of." At Rhamus' raised eyebrows, she smiled. "I
couldn't feel your lips through the material."

"We can remedy that," he said, tugging at the gloved hand he still
held.

"Don't you dare," She squealed and pulled the hand out of his
reach. She readjusted the glove. "You wouldn't believe how hard it
is to struggle into a pair of gloves this long." At his sour look she
added, "Besides, isn't it time to go?"

Once Rhamus had escorted her into the throne room, Serena saw
that he was right in his evaluation of her designing abilities. Many
of the noble ladies had floor-length dresses on, in imitation of her
"new" style of dress. Their imitation was the highest form of
compliment and acceptance, and Serena smiled at them with joy,
feeling more welcome in their midst than ever before. They
examined her new dress with avid interest and she heard many
whispers with Jidroon's name mentioned.

The dinner was sumptuous and rich, but Serena only picked at hers lightly. He was concerned, but she answered that she was too excited to keep much down, and he seemed satisfied with this response. The meal took more than an hour to consume, with servants constantly running back and forth with platters.

This time, the room was set with small tables, creating a more intimate setting. It was one of Serena's suggestions and the people seemed to enjoy the uniqueness of this eating style for a large affair. Rhamus and she shared an elegant table set before them.

Once the food and table set-ups had been moved, different singers regaled them with songs, from bawdy ones to sweet love sonnets. Rhamus and she both reached toward each other at the same time during the first love song, holding hands like young lovers.

After the last love song drifted away, Dr. Melat came forward, holding Nicole formally by one elbow. Tears formed in her eyes at the happiness shining from the bride's eyes and the petite beauty of her form. Nicole had chosen to follow Earth's tradition, wearing a simple floor length dress that shimmered with its delicate eggshell color.

She held a bouquet of delicate flowers, representing every color in a rainbow, and wearing a matching wreathed band around her head. Dr. Melat looked elegant in his native costume. The coat was long, reaching to his knees, opening all the way to his waist. He had chosen to wear the same pale color as his bride.

Hartoos came forward to perform the ceremony, much as he had done for Serena previously, only this bride was more than willing and her smile lit up her face with an enchanting beauty. Rhamus and Serena hugged and congratulated them afterwards, and seats were set up next to them, indicating their close friendship to the royal couple.

The singers returned and sang syrupy sweet songs to the newlyweds, causing the doctor to groan and Nicole to giggle. Serena saw, out of the corner of her eye, that the dancers were getting ready to perform. And there was Szafra, bedecked out in another revealing costume and capturing the attention of all the males around her. She excused herself, telling Rhamus that Mother Nature called. He nodded his head absently at her, being caught up in the entertainment and Dr. Melat's comical reactions.

Serena walked briskly to their bedroom and retrieved the costume she'd been secretly working on from the back of the closet. She quickly slipped out of her formal wear and put on her dance costume.

Rhamus still did not know everything about her. He did not know that she had studied jazz when her aunt Betty sent her for lessons, or that she'd also become enthralled with Dance Oriental, more commonly known as belly dancing, when she saw a troupe practicing in the same dance studio. Or, that she'd paid for lessons to learn its ancient art form.

It had taken a lot of hard work and many years for Serena to gain the level of dancing ability that she desired. She smiled wickedly to herself. She thought this was as good a time as any to let Rhamus in on her little secret, and remove Szafra as a source of competition at the same time.

She examined herself objectively in the mirror. She was almost three months pregnant now, but only a slight thickening of her waist was noticeable. Since her figure was normally very hourglass-shaped, the extra inch hardly detracted from the sensuousness of her figure. She was glad she'd eaten lightly in order to move fluidly.

The gleaming bronze material she'd requested from Jidroon had been made into a bra, French cut panties, and belt for the hips. She had to enlist the tailor and his assistants to help her with the coins that she'd added to the costume. She selected native coins slightly smaller than a penny that were bronze colored. The coins had to have one hole made in the top and a thin strong chain attached. Then each one was sewn to the different pieces of the costume.

Serena chose an opaque lavender silk for the skirt, to be worn under the belt. It was not transparent, but would still show the outline of her long limbs. The other scarves, which completed her outfit were shimmering, yet sheer.

She shook her head in self-wonderment. She'd always worn costumes with more coverage when performing with her dance troupe. Now the scanty one, which would be revealed when she removed the scarves bothered her not a bit. How many times had she cringed at her short skirts or low-cut dresses? It was as if the vassi had helped her accept her body as well as given her inner peace.

She touched the gorgeous necklace and decided to leave the jewelry on. Rhamus might recognize the pieces as a clue to her identity, but she hoped not. Serena let down her hair and added a coin headpiece that draped across her forehead, drawing attention to her brilliant eyes. She added a thick liner to her eyelids, drawn out at the corners in the Egyptian style, and brightened her lips and cheeks.

Serena examined her image in the mirror. The coins swung at each gentle movement ... together, they hung down to cover the entire area of material underneath. Long strands of coins were sewn to the bottom of the bra and dangled down to her belly button. The belt was also covered by jingling coins, with long coin-filled chains hanging to mid-thigh. Although modest in nature, Serena knew she looked good. Would she mesmerize Rhamus, she wondered.

She picked up an arj'ak crystal lying amongst the scarves and, with a dab of easily removable glue obtained from Rolan', Serena put the crystal in her belly button until it held firmly. She rotated her hips experimentally and found the blue jewel held fast. Next, she picked up one of the gossamer thin scarves and draped it over the skirt, tucking it artfully. The bright yellow looked brilliant against the lavender.

Draping the rest of the scarves on various parts of her body in a graceful manner only took a few minutes more. She knew she didn't have much time left. Rhamus would become concerned that she'd gotten ill and come looking for her.

Serena moved quickly down the hall and approached the open doors to the throne room with as much nervousness as the first time she'd seen them. She always felt butterflies when she performed, but now she had to make the right impression on her adopted people, but most importantly on her husband.

One thing made her feel more confident. No one in that room had ever seen such a dance, and if she were not at her peak in performance, they wouldn't know. Of course, she'd practiced all she could during the week while Rhamus was not around and, if not one hundred percent happy with her moves, she was at least satisfied.

She just hoped Rolan' had brought everything as she'd instructed. She had to enlist his help. She had to go with Rolan' to the ship and search through the vast library in the computer's memory banks for Arabic music with the appropriate rhythms to fit the repertoire of dances she wished to perform.

Serena waited outside the room, out of sight, until a dancer finished her performance. A flash of anger shot through her at the way the woman danced flirtatiously in front of her husband. It was Szafra! The dancer accepted accolades for her performance, throwing sultry glances toward the throne as she went to stand at the front edge of the crowd. She stepped into view and Rolan', alerted to her presence, nodded in her direction. He had brought the portable player for the music and she took a deep breath of relief. Watch and learn. She directed her thought toward Szafra. *You are about to be upstaged by a real performance artist.*

Chapter Twenty Three

Rhamus was glad to see that Szafra was acting cheerful. She was putting on quite a show for the people. He hoped her attitude meant she'd begun to finally accept his marriage. She'd staged quite a few emotional scenes before the Earth women were brought to the planet. Szafra knew some alien beauty was to take her place, one she had considered to be hers. She chose to ignore the facts--a Tarthra match had never been made between them, for he would never be capable of the deep, true love that a life-union demanded. And she could never bear him an heir.

As usual, Rhamus enjoyed her dance, but halfway through her steps, he began to wonder if Serena were all right. He looked several times toward the door. His inattention seemed to affect Szafra, because she came closer to the throne, trying to gain his eye. He could hardly take his gaze from her when she practically danced in between his legs and made several sweeps of her arms close to his face.

Rhamus smiled at his ex-lover, but with a coolness that seemed to drive her determination to gain his flagging attention. Once, she even passed her hand gracefully across his chest as if it were a part of the dance. Several ladies in the audience gasped, offended by the dancer's familiarity with the King.

He frowned. Had he been wrong about her? He glanced to the doorway, but saw nothing but a shrouded figure standing in the shadows. He hoped Serena would not make her entrance until after the dancer got through, otherwise she would probably cause another jealous scene. And he wouldn't blame her. Szafra was acting brazenly.

When she finally finished her dance, Rhamus gave a sigh of relief. An interlude between dancers provided him with the opportunity he sought. Rhamus stepped from the throne a few paces and was met by his cousin.

"Where are you headed? The entertainment's not over yet!" Jarvic said gaily.

"I'm going to look for Serena. She's been gone a long time."

His cousin yawned and glanced toward the crowd. "Serena told me on the way out she might be a few minutes. Go sit down," Jarvic pushed him toward the dais. "You're turning into aunt Surad with your worrying."

Rhamus shrugged and returned to his throne. His attention was grabbed by the activity in front of the dais. Rolan' had taken center stage, holding one of the devices from his ship which played music.

"Your Majesty, ladies and gentlemen," Rolan announced with a self-important tone. "I have the honor of introducing a special dancer for your entertainment tonight. She is one of your lovely wives from Earth and will present an ancient dance from her native world. The lady will do two different dances. The first is called *The Dance of the Seven Veils.*"

Rolan punched the button on his machine and strange music rose from the box, an odd mixture of instruments. The crowd parted as the dancer walked gracefully through them to the center area. He noticed she'd been moving in a gentle rhythm as she walked and then danced with fluid grace around the circumference of the cleared area.

He was intrigued by the veiled woman. Only her eyes were visible, and he couldn't tell their color with the material casting shadows on them. She continued to move gracefully in time to the beat of the music, then removed the gold veil from her shoulders and swirled it above her head. Rhamus watched as the dancer was suddenly encased between two folds of the material. As she continued to move in small circles, her hands flickered inside the enveloping veil and then reappeared with the material again held in her hands.

He didn't see when the woman released the pale blue veil, which covered her breasts. She seemed as one with the two veils floating about her. Her fluid grace and flashing scarves concealed the release of the veil draped across her upper waist. Dancing around the cleared area with the three veils, she swirled them in graceful arches, flitting among them. Rhamus watched with growing astonishment at the skill needed for such "tricks".

His eyes opened slightly wider. Goreth! *What did the rest of her costume look like under all those gauzy veils*? The dancer's round, tantalizing breasts were covered by scant triangles of material. The area above her waist was bare and temptingly revealed in the partings of the curtain of coins, which dangled below those generous mounds. She removed the bright pink veil, which covered her waist and, through the sheer veil draped below, a shimmering belt was revealed, riding low on her hips.

The coins, which dangled from the top and belt were in constant motion, their jingling sound seemed to keep rhythm with the music. He'd been in error when he thought the metallic tinkling sounds were a part of the music. Swirling and dancing with the veils, the woman made them appear as creatures alive with their own movement. It was the most graceful, elegant dance Rhamus had ever seen.

When the deep purple hued veil that clung to the belt was removed, he at last got a clear view of the costume's seduction. A nerve ticked in his cheek as he watched the dancer's gently rolling hips. The coins responded with sways all their own that caused his eyes to become glued to those curvaceous hips.

He glanced to the see the audience's reaction, and noting the hot expressions on many of the male's faces, tried to keep his features unaffected, for Serena would return at any moment. But it was hard not to feel an attraction to the sensual grace of the dancer. He wondered idly which of the Earth women danced for them.

His eyes swung back to the woman's light stepping dance around the floor. She removed the thin black veil tucked in her belt and brought it to play with the other veils. Rhamus quickly counted the scarves, there were only two left, one covering her legs and another her face. When the bright yellow one was removed, a skirt was visible beneath the swinging belt.

His breathing became heavier as he got a full view of the uncovered costume. The lavender skirt was not transparent, but he could still see the outline of the dancer's elegant legs beneath. Her supple shape drove him mad with its siren's call. Who was this lovely woman? A feeling of familiarity itched at the back of his mind. Serena was the only woman he'd seen with such gorgeous legs. He shook himself mentally at his flight of fancy. Now the dancer's true skill with the floating veils came into play. She danced in and out of the pattern she created with all six.

Finally, she began dropping one veil after another onto the floor as she continued with the slow, fluid steps of her performance. As she danced with the last veil, except for the one covering her face and hair, she moved up the dais. The tempo of the music slowed down, then the temptress moved her hips in smaller circles and at the same time reached up and slowly drew the gossamer silver scarf from around her head and into her hands.

Several surprised gasps erupted as his wife's very recognizable red hair and lovely face was uncovered. As the veil floated and draped across his lap, he looked up with eyes burning into the wickedly teasing ones of his wife.

He sat in rigid shock, his hands gripping the chair arms. She stood posed as she ended the dance, then her hips seemed to come alive and moved separately from her body as the next song started.

This music was fast, the beat making one feel like clapping your hands or tapping your feet. As if prearranged, Jarvic and Rolan' indeed did start clapping in time to the music and the crowd picked up the tempo enthusiastically. Serena spun in small circles, sometimes only her hips rotating within a tight circle. Her arms moved like snakes to the front and then to the sides. She glided sideways across the floor, her arms moving up and down fluidly.

The music became more frenzied and Serena moved up the steps again, causing him much discomfort by her closeness. Now her hips shimmied from side to side at a frantic pace, causing the coins to swing madly. With her closeness, he saw the arj'ak crystal, which somehow held within her belly button. He had a sudden urge to reach out and pluck it out with his teeth. His cini was hard as a rock and he wanted to ram it inside her soft flesh. He looked into her eyes again and was struck with the responding heat he read in them, heat he knew was reflected in his own eyes.

Now his wife moved in an amazing fashion. Serena's stomach began undulating, up and down, rolling in waves from under her rib cage to below the belt. It was the most sensual act he'd ever seen and his cini reacted with a will of its own. He again thanked the sacred crystal silently, this time that he was the only one who could get a good view of this part of her dance. Sweat broke out on his forehead. Serena finished by posing beautifully just an arm's length away. His eyes never left hers as the crowd responded with an uproarious clapping. Some of the warriors clanged their swords against nearby objects to add to the deafening noise.

* * * *

She breathed heavily near the end of her performance and sweat glistened on her bare skin. Being pregnant and a little out of shape had taken a heavier toll than she expected. Nonetheless, she was proud of her dance routines and the people's enthusiastic praise. Rhamus had reacted with a lustful response that she found gratifying. As she threw her body into the pose of her final dance, she felt almost burned by his hot eyes. She couldn't help but steal a glance toward Szafra. The dancer looked more than angry to be upstaged--Szafra looked ready to slap her.

Rhamus stood abruptly and took one of her hands. Never taking his eyes from her face, he said, "I'm afraid the Queen has overexerted herself with her fine performance." Then he turned to face the crowd of Volarnians and Earthlings. "So, I wish you a good night. Please, go on without us. Enjoy the entertainment."

After that statement, he bent swiftly and picked her up in his arms, making Serena clutch at his neck with surprise. He strode through the crowd quickly, nodding at his people's final congratulations on the coming heir, as well as further praises of his wife's dancing skills. He ignored the shocked looks from some of the noble ladies, and knowing ones of the males at his uncouth behavior.

Serena sighed at Rhamus' barbaric act and laid her head wearily on his shoulder as he carried her easily all the way to their bedroom. A smile flitted around her mouth. She was secretly pleased at his public display of attraction to her. Rhamus slid her slowly down his body when he came near the bed. Almost casually he leaned down and kissed her deeply, the heat from their contact feeling much hotter than even his gaze previously.

"Serena, do me one favor," he said as he pulled her body into a tight squeeze.

"What?" She wiggled against the hardness below his belly.

"Don't ever dance for anyone else but me, from now on." He pressed his hands into the small of her back. "And if you don't stop that, I shall take you right here on the floor."

"Threats! Don't you know that threats just make a woman's blood run hotter?" Serena mimicked an earlier statement he'd made to her.

He groaned as Serena again pressed against him, then gripped his buttocks and forced him into an even closer contact.

"You are a she-devil. And you didn't give me your answer yet."

"OK, OK." She scrunched her nose up at him. "I won't dance for anybody but you." Her face felt very hot, her body still overheated from the exercise, not just their physical closeness. "Can you do me a favor before we make love?"

"Anything, my jicha."

"Can you get me a drink of fruit juice? I'm parched."

Rhamus turned to the decanter near him and frowned. He poured the meager portion left into a glass. "That Lalme is falling down on her duties." He shook the bottle which was usually kept full of the healthy fruit drink Serena loved. He handed her the glass and Serena downed the drink in one big swallow.

"Don't blame her. There's been a lot of excitement today and I guess she just forgot to check the bottle."

He kissed her quickly. "You're too kind as well as being too beautiful and sexy." Letting her go, he lifted the decanter again from its cooling plate. "I'll just run down to aunt Surad's room. She always has your favorite drink."

Grabbing her by the elbow, Rhamus pushed Serena gently toward her chair. "Sit down and rest while I'm gone." He pointed toward the balcony. "Listen, your favorite little sooeul has come to sing to you."

She laughed at his attempt to charm her into relaxing. She did indeed feel boneless after she flopped down in the stuffed chair. She closed her eyes, a contented smile on her face as he left.

Hearing the door creak open a few seconds later, she smiled again to herself. He must have forgotten something, or perhaps he came to steal a last kiss from her. She heard a light tread and thought that she'd been mistaken. It sounded more like Lalme's footsteps. But then, Lalme never entered without knocking first.

Serena turned in curiosity to see the intruder. A blur of movement shot toward her, she instinctively shoved her arm up in a blocking motion. A searing pain shot through her arm as she recognized Szafra. She didn't have time to think as the wild-eyed woman attacked her again with a long, sharp dagger. She tried to wrestle the dagger from the frenzied woman, but she was at a disadvantage. The soft chair hindered her movements, making it difficult to try and get up to better defend herself.

And as she struggled with the strong figure trying repeatedly to stab her in the chest, Serena had a few seconds to come face to face with her attacker. Szafra's eyes seemed quite mad. She realized she had a strong disadvantage. The insane are able to tap into an inhuman source of power unattainable by rational people. The dancer managed to nick her just below her collarbone and the crazed woman screamed in triumph as she redoubled her efforts to end Serena's life.

Feeling her strength flag, she wondered for a second if the battle was already lost. Realizing the danger this woman put not only herself but also her unborn child in, gave her the extra surge she needed. Serena managed to push Szafra several feet away and leapt to her feet. She didn't know who the winner would have been, for at that moment Rhamus stood in the doorway.

"What's going on here?" he demanded, his eyes widening in alarm as blood dripped down Serena's arm and from the cut on her chest. The juice bottle he'd been holding shattered on the floor. Rhamus lunged across the room and grabbed Szafra who had turned at his entrance.

"Rhamus," Szafra held out one bloody hand pathetically, "I did it for us." She sounded very reasonable, then her face took on a wild, feral expression. "Why don't you leave and let me finish her, then we can be together, my jicha."

Anger suffused his face but then he saw the madness in his ex-lover's features. "Come, Szafra, give me the dagger," he held out his hand. Seeing the hesitation in her face, he said, "You've done enough, my jicha. Let me take care of things."

"Yes," her eyes became soft and loving at the tender tone in his voice. She handed the narrow, dangerous weapon over, smiling happily up at him.

Rhamus took the bloody dagger with a grimace and threw it into a far corner. He yelled loudly for the guards and they appeared immediately. He waved a hand in the dancer's direction. "Put Szafra in her room and guard her carefully." The guards looked at the trio before them, but did as instructed and gripped the dancer's arms, one on each side.

"Wait!" She screamed and jerked between the two warriors. "You tricked me!" she screamed again, spittle flying from her mouth as she spoke.

By some great will, the dancer calmed herself and tried to sound reasonable again. "Rhamus, we can still be together." She flounced her head in Serena's direction. "She's only a brood mare. You can't really love her as you love me."

He sighed sadly. "I do love Serena. I'm afraid our love ended a long time ago."

"No," the words came in a barely heard whisper. Szafra drew herself up, a strange calm smoothed her features. She continued with her love-crazed perception, ignoring what he'd had just told her.

"You see, Rhamus? I showed you how much our love meant to me when I tried to get rid of her." The dancer's lips drew up in a pout of disappointment. "Xarath was supposed to dispose of her, but he lusted after her."

"It was you!" Serena took a step toward the traitor.

"Serena, keep back," Rhamus commanded and she halted. "Szafra, if you were not mad, a just enough punishment in itself, I would kill you myself for what you did to my jicha."

"You are the traitor!" She screamed loudly, "You do love her." She stared at Rhamus, as if waiting for him to refute her statement. Suddenly, she seemed to lose all fight as her body sagged and the guards' grip went slack for a second. Szafra twisted free of the two holding her, catching the warriors off-guard. She fled quickly across the room toward the balcony. By the time Rhamus and the guards started after her, she stood on top of the balcony rail, her dancer's body elegantly balanced on the narrow ledge.

"Remember you loved me once," she said, then made an arching leap, her hair flying wildly as she plunged down over the edge and into the night.

"Oh my God!" Serena cried as she followed the men to the balcony.

Rhamus held his arm out, not letting her close to the edge. "Serena, you don't need to see this." He turned and, holding her arm gently led her back inside.

Turning to the guards, he said, "See that her body is returned to her birth village." He gave them both a firm look as they started to follow his orders.

"And no word about anything you heard within this room. Szafra is dead. There's no reason to dishonor her name any further. And send immediately for Dr. Melat."

"You truly loved her once, didn't you?" She asked softly.

"Yes, she was a great comfort to me after my father's death." He went into the bathroom and returned with a small box. "Now, let me cleanse and dress those wounds."

He was an efficient nurse and she barely felt any pain as he cleaned the wounds carefully.

"Feel better now?" he asked considerately.

Before she could answer, Doc came running in, still wearing his wedding apparel, an anxious Nicole right behind him. He cleansed the wounds and sealed the cut on her arm with a laser-stitching instrument and then dressed both injuries.

"This medication will kill any naci germs," Doc said. "Perhaps I should also give you something for shock."

"I'll be fine," Serena assured him. "I just need some rest."

"I'll check on her in the morning." Dr. Melat eyed Nicole meaningfully. He finally took a firm grip on one elbow as he told her they needed to leave the couple to a quiet evening. As Rhamus walked them to the door, they both agreed to keep the evening's ending a secret.

He sighed, "Alone at last." He turned to Serena and said, "I'll keep a close watch on you tonight, in case you have a reaction to the medication or the shock."

"That's good to know." She sounded drained. "You wouldn't want a perfectly good brood mare to become sick." He laughed and she said in sudden anger, "You laugh at me?"

"I laugh at anyone who talks foolishness."

"Is it foolish for me to acknowledge that I *am* nothing more than an incubator for your heir?" Her voice came out teary.

"My jicha." Rhamus ran his hands down her upper arms, ignoring her attempt to pull away. "Look at me," he commanded.

She did, so authoritative was his tone. Feeling flustered by the need to cry and the stress she'd just experienced, Serena looked into her husband's eyes and saw only love shining within them.

"If I wanted a brood mare, I could have chosen from dozens of beautiful Earthlings, as well as Volarnian women." He caressed her arms gently. "But I wanted--no needed--more than just a womb to carry my heirs. I needed a love, someone to rule by my side, someone worthy of the title 'Queen'. You have fulfilled this need more than I could have dreamed." He lowered his head until their eyes were straight in line. "I am a very contented man, because *you* came into my life."

"I have become so silly since I've been pregnant." She laid her head against his chest.

"My jicha," he petted her hair. "One is allowed a certain amount of silliness, and tears, when pregnant."

"Rhamus," she spoke from within the confines of his shirt. "What if I hadn't been able to conceive, or our union didn't work because of the gene differences?"

"Then I would have had to rethink some matters."

"Such as?" She raised her head to stare uncertainly into his eyes.

"Whether to adopt, or maybe just let Jarvic take over the throne when the time came."

"Oh, Rhamus," Serena laughed. "Now who's being silly?"

He grinned and said, "I don't think Jarvic would like that solution." He patted her stomach. "But luckily for us and him, we don't have to worry about such matters." He pulled her closer and rubbed his nose against hers, making her giggle. "Now, weren't we about to engage in a more pleasant activity, before--"

Rhamus intentionally stopped his sentence, not wanting to mention the unpleasantness that had happened in the sanctity of their room, or dare hope that she would welcome the advance.

"Hmm, I think my memory has been affected by my pregnancy as well," Serena playfully said. "Why don't you refresh it?"

"Gladly," he latched onto her lips like a man needing sustenance after a long famish.

Chapter Twenty Four

Nine Months Later

Serena stood looking down in the cribs, as she'd done many times since the twin's birth three months ago. They were so precious and she just knew they were the most beautiful babies to ever be born. So much had changed in her life and those around her since first coming here to Volarn. She thought about those changes as she continued to watch the twins sleeping peacefully, and waited for Rhamus.

Rolan' and Pulack had made two more trips, returning with more women each time. Nicole had gone both times with Doc, but now the next trip was curtailed until Nicole delivered her child, which was due any day now. Those two made such an odd looking couple, being so very different in physical appearance, and Serena couldn't wait to see what their child looked like. Even pregnant, Nicole continued to be her giggly, irrepressible self and Dr. Melat doted on her every wish. If ever a man had been enslaved by love, Doc was.

The first group of women had all acclimated to their new home, and all had either delivered babies or were pregnant. This group of women had formed a buddy system for welcoming the next group of women to be brought to Volarn, and this had helped the new captives settle in easier. Serena smiled to herself. The Volarnians considered the Moyds almost heroic figures for their uncanny ability to select the right women needed "to get the job done"

Deborah had been allowed to return to Earth since she still wanted to be reunited with her betrothed. She had cried as she bid goodbye to the friends she had made, knowing that once she arrived back home, Pulack would use the memory-erasing device and her new friends would be forgotten.

Together with the Moyds, she'd concocted a story to be implanted in her mind to cover the months she was missing. It sounded like something from a soap opera, but should work. When the Moyds had taken her, Deborah's car had been left by the side of the road. They were going to say she'd bumped her head after running her car off the road, resulting in amnesia. The rest was an elaborate fabrication of her stumbling around for months, not knowing who she was, and getting by the best she could.

Olga had delivered a son one-month after Serena, and she and Zares were a very happy couple. But, sometimes Serena noticed her former rival looking at her twins and a great sadness would come over her face. She knew Olga's thoughts were on her brother, Eric.

Jarvic participated in the second Tarthra but still did not find any woman to suit him. He had declined to take part in the third. Secretly, Serena thought he was not ready to give up his playboy ways or make a commitment. But she could not fault his enthusiasm as an "uncle", a name he called himself in relation to the twins.

Kasha was also wonderful with the two babies, wanting to rock and sing to them whenever she could. The princess was already planning on a trip to secure the twins proper yasmirs, once they were able to walk. One time Serena strolled into the nursery and found the nanny flustered because Kasha and Jarvic were arguing over who could hold the babies. She resolved this easily by giving them a twin apiece.

Just yesterday, Serena had come up quietly behind the princess, who was talking so softly to one of the twins in her lap, that she'd not noticed her. She was struck with the tenderness in the princess' face and voice and wondered if Kasha was thinking of babies of her own. Then with a feeling of sadness, she remembered that Kasha was Getra and couldn't have children. Maybe that's why she doted on her two so much. Rhamus entered, breaking into her musings.

"Are you ready to go, my jicha?" He spoke softly so as not to wake the babies.

"Yes, just let me give them a kiss." Serena bent down and gave a gentle kiss to Sasha, her little girl with fire-red fuzzy hair already sprouting on her head. The infant's eyes were the lovely pale lavender of her aunt Kasha's. They'd decided to name her after Kasha, taking the "S" from Serena's name. The warrior princess had been thrilled, to say the least.

Then, Serena kissed her little boy, Vork, softly on his curly black head. Named after Rhamus' father as he had asked, Vork had also inherited his father's thick black hair, but his eyes were a true arj'akian crystal blue. The people were awed by the first Volarnian with the sacred color and predictions were made that he would grow up to be a great leader.

Sasha awoke and began fussing. Her brother woke also at her incessant cries. Serena handed the demanding baby girl to the nanny and then turned to cuddle Vork. From their first days, the twins seemed to have personalities all their own. She should have gotten a hint from the way the twins were born. Sasha came first, crying lustily from the time her head appeared, while Vork was born quietly into the world. In fact, the more calm-natured Vork had "hidden" in the womb behind his energetic sister. This was why Zara had sensed her pregnancy so early.

Everyone had been surprised by the twins' birth, even the doctor. Apparently, Sasha's heartbeat had also muffled her smaller brother's beat. The Volarnian people were truly astounded, because they were unable to produce multiple babies. They considered it a good omen that the first birth was from the royal couple and that two possible heirs were born. As the first born, Sasha was first in line for the throne, with Vork next in line.

Serena smoothed the silk of her evening dress. Rhamus and she were to open the ceremonies of the annual birth celebration, one in which the twins would take part later tonight. She still had a little weight to lose from the "baby fat" accumulated around her waist and hips, but a look into her husband's eyes told her that she looked beautiful to him.

"Ready?" He held out his hand toward her.

"Yes," she answered as she curled her fingers within the larger ones of her husband. As they walked out hand in hand, she thought to herself, yes, ready to go with you anywhere, my love. I have gained so much from your world--friends, a home, my darling babies.

And then there is love. Serena's last musing was whimsical. *I came to you as a captive, and truly a captive have I become, as you have also. For surely there can be no stronger captor than love.*

THE END